The Vengeance of the Dearg Due

By

Kathleen Carlson

ISBN:

Paperback: 978-1-964963-86-0

Hardback: 978-1-964963-87-7

Dedication

This book is dedicated to my mom, Donna Sue Shaffer. She knew how much I love to read and supported my love for anything Dark and the Supernatural. May she rest in peace.

Prologue

To the forgotten whispers that linger in the shadowed corners of ancient castles, to the folklore that bleeds into the moonlight, and to those who find beauty in the melancholic grandeur of decay. May this tale resonate with the part of you that understands the night, not as an absence of light, but as a realm of profound, transformative power. It is for the souls who have known betrayal deep enough to curdle the heart, who have endured suffering that reshaped them into something other.

For those who understand that the most potent revenge is often born from the deepest wounds, and that sometimes, from the cold earth of despair, something terrible and magnificent can rise. This is for the dreamers who can still hear the echo of a mournful howl on the wind, and who recognize in its sorrow a kindred spirit, forever bound to the shadows, yet forever seeking a final, brutal absolution. For the resilience found in the darkest of nights, and the eternal hunger that fuels the most chilling of legends. May you find a reflection of your own enduring spirit within these shadowed pages.

Table of Contents

Chapter 1:
The Whispering Village

The village of Oakhaven was a place that time seemed to have forgotten, nestled in a valley cradled by ancient, brooding hills. Here, life unfolded with the slow, predictable rhythm of the seasons, a gentle cadence that lulled its inhabitants into a comfortable, if sometimes stifling, routine. For Iris, a wisp of a girl with eyes the colour of a summer sky and hair the shade of ripe wheat, Oakhaven was the entirety of her known world. It was a world of thatched roofs that sagged with age, of smoke that curled lazily from stone chimneys, and of the perpetual, earthy scent of damp soil and woodsmoke. Her days were a tapestry woven with simple threads: helping her mother with the mending, gathering herbs in the sun-dappled woods that skirted the village, and the endless, quiet chores that defined the life of a peasant girl.

Her dreams, however, were not confined by the valley's embrace. They stretched beyond the mist-shrouded peaks, as vast and boundless as the celestial expanse she often gazed upon at night. These dreams were painted in hues of a life yet unlived, a future in which the claustrophobia of Oakhaven receded, giving way to a sense of freedom and possibility. It was a life imagined, a whisper of a yearning that even she, in her youthful innocence, could not fully articulate. The village, with its tight-knit community and shared burdens, offered a sense of belonging a comforting familiarity. Yet beneath this contentment, a subtle current of hardship flowed. The harvests were often meager, the winters long and unforgiving, and the constant specter of scarcity loomed like a persistent shadow. It was this quiet desperation, this undercurrent of struggle, that lent a potent allure to the idea of escape, to the tantalizing prospect of a life where such anxieties did not hold sway.

Iris's world was intimately connected to the land. She knew the whisper of the wind through the ancient oaks that gave the village its name, the gurgle of the brook that meandered through its heart, and the subtle shift in the air's scent that signaled an approaching rain. The sun, when it broke through the often-overcast skies, cast a golden benediction upon the humble dwellings, illuminating the dust motes dancing in the marketplace air and warming the rough-hewn timbers of the communal hall. Evenings brought a different kind of magic, a softening of the day's harsh edges. As twilight deepened, the village sounds shifted the lowing of cattle being herded in for the night, the distant bark of a dog, the murmur of voices from open windows. It was during these hushed hours that Iris's dreams felt most vibrant, most within reach.

Her small cottage, shared with her parents, was a place of worn but sturdy furnishings. The hearth was the heart of their home, its warmth a constant, comforting presence, especially during the colder months. The air within was thick with the mingled scents of drying herbs, woodsmoke, and the subtle, pervasive aroma of boiled roots and stale bread that characterized peasant fare. Her mother, a woman whose hands bore the indelible marks of toil, moved with a quiet diligence, her face etched with the lines of worry and enduring labor. Her father, Bernard, was a man of fewer words, his presence often a silent, weighty one, his gaze frequently fixed on some distant point, as if calculating the odds of survival in a world that offered little in the way of surplus.

Yet, it was not the hardships of Oakhaven that occupied Iris's thoughts most frequently, but the bright, nascent hope that bloomed within her heart. This hope was inextricably tied to the village itself, to the familiar faces and the shared history, but most of all, to the boy who had become the sun around which her young world revolved. Julius. His name was a melody on her lips, a whisper of joy that lifted the weight of her everyday existence.

Their shared laughter echoed in the village square, their stolen glances in the communal market spoke volumes, and the simple walks along the dusty paths that led away from the clustered cottages were the highlight of her days.

She remembered the day the traveling merchant had passed through, his cart laden with trinkets and fabrics from lands far beyond their valley. Iris, her eyes wide with wonder, had gazed at a small, painted wooden bird, its wings spread as if in flight. It was, she felt, a symbol of the freedom her dreams yearned for. Julius, seeing the longing in her eyes, had bartered a portion of his meager earnings for it, presenting it to her with a shy smile that made her heart flutter like the wings of that very bird. It was a small gift, insignificant in the grand scheme of their lives, but to Iris it was a treasure a tangible representation of their shared hopes and his affection. She had kept it tucked away, a secret talisman, a reminder that beauty and dreams existed beyond the confines of Oakhaven.

The simple celebrations of the church calendar punctuated the rhythm of village life. Harvest festivals, where the bounty, however meager, was shared and acknowledged with gratitude. The solemn observance of midwinter, when families huddled closer to the hearth, sharing stories and meager rations. The fleeting warmth of spring is celebrated with simple dances and offerings at the ancient standing stones on the hill overlooking the valley. Iris participated in these rituals with a natural grace, her youth a bright counterpoint to the elders' weathered faces. She was, in essence, a product of this place, her innocence reflecting the simple beauty of its pastoral landscape, the quiet dignity of its hardworking people, and the earnest hopes of a young girl on the cusp of womanhood.

But even in its most idyllic moments, the village held a certain claustrophobia. The hills that enclosed the valley, while providing shelter, also served as a constant reminder of the world beyond, a world that felt both distant and alluring. The narrow, winding paths, the closely packed cottages, the ever-present eyes of neighbors who knew each other's business all too well, contributed to a sense of being perpetually observed, perpetually constrained. It was a comfortable prison, perhaps, but a prison nonetheless. And for a spirit like Iris, with dreams that soared higher than the village church steeple, the bars of that prison, however gilded by familiarity and affection, were beginning to chafe.

She would often find herself standing at the edge of the village, gazing out at the shadowed slopes of the hills, a wistful ache in her chest. The air there was cleaner, sharper, carrying the scent of pine and damp earth from the deeper woods. It was a place where the village sounds faded, replaced by the rustling of leaves and the distant call of a hawk. Here, her dreams felt less like fanciful illusions and more like potential realities, whispers of a destiny that lay just beyond the familiar horizon. The hardships were real, the routines were binding, but it was the yearning for something more, something *other*, that truly defined the nascent spirit of the peasant girl named Iris. It was a yearning for a life where her dreams could unfurl, unhindered by the small, yet persistent, weight of Oakhaven.

The quiet rhythms of Oakhaven were not merely a backdrop; they were an integral part of Iris's existence, shaping her perceptions and her aspirations. The communal well, where women gathered to draw water and exchange gossip, was a nexus of village life. Iris, often accompanying her mother, would listen to the hushed conversations, learning the subtle currents of village politics and the quiet dramas that unfolded beneath the veneer of placid existence. The blacksmith's hammer, a steady, percussive beat against the anvil, was a constant reminder of the manual labor that sustained them. The distant chime of the church bell marked the passage of time, a solemn, resonant sound that punctuated their days with reminders of faith and mortality.

Her connection to the land was more than just aesthetic; it was practical. She knew which berries were safe to eat, which roots could be used for medicinal poultices, and how to read the subtle signs of the changing weather. This knowledge, passed down through generations of peasant women, was a vital part of her inheritance, a silent testament to her lineage. She understood the interconnectedness of all things in their small world how the rain nourished the crops, how the crops fed the livestock, and how the livestock, in turn, sustained their lives. This fundamental understanding of natural cycles fostered a deep respect for the earth, a sense of belonging that was both profound and, at times, binding.

However, beneath the surface of this pastoral existence, the ever-present shadow of poverty was a constant reminder of their precarious lives. The meager harvests meant careful rationing, the long winters necessitated vigilant preparation, and the threat of illness, without access to proper remedies, was a grim reality. Iris had witnessed firsthand the toll that hardship could take the gaunt faces of neighbors during a particularly lean year, the quiet despair of a mother unable to feed her children, the somber procession to the small village graveyard after a harsh winter claimed its toll. These experiences, though etched into her young consciousness, had not yet extinguished her spirit. Instead, they had perhaps fanned the flames of her longing for a life where such anxieties were not the dominant force.

Her dreams, then, were not merely flights of fancy, but a nascent form of rebellion, a yearning for a life beyond the limitations imposed by circumstance. The vastness of the sky, the distant, hazy outlines of the encircling hills these became symbols of a world brimming with possibility. In this world, her innate kindness and gentle spirit could perhaps flourish without the constant threat of want. This is not to say that Iris harbored any ill will towards her village or its inhabitants. There was a genuine warmth and affection for the familiar, a sense of rootedness that provided a fundamental sense of security. But the very completeness of her world its undeniable charm and palpable limitations created a tension within her, a quiet dissonance between the life she lived and the life she dared to dream of.

The allure of the unknown was a potent force, a subtle siren song that whispered of a different existence. The tales brought by occasional travelers of bustling cities, grand castles, and lives lived with a freedom and abundance unimaginable in Oakhaven stoked this yearning. These stories, often embellished and fantastical, painted vivid pictures of a world beyond the valley a world where the soil and seasons did not solely dictate one's fate. They offered a tantalizing glimpse of a life less constrained, a life where dreams even those as vast as the sky might actually take flight. And so, the pastoral beauty of Oakhaven, while cherished, also served as a constant reminder of what lay just beyond reach, a perfect canvas for the unfolding tragedy that was soon to shatter Iris's world and redefine her very existence.

The ephemeral bloom of love, so often fragile and fleeting, found a tender blossoming in the heart of Oakhaven, nurtured in the quiet corners of everyday life and under the benevolent gaze of a benevolent moon. For Iris, the world, once a tapestry of mundane chores and shadowed by the specter of scarcity, now shimmered with an ethereal glow, all thanks to Julius. He was the hearth fire of her dreams, the melody that silenced the anxieties of their humble existence. Grand gestures or opulent gifts did not mark their courtship, but by the quiet currency of shared glances, hushed conversations, and the gentle brush of hands that spoke volumes more than any spoken word.

Their stolen moments were the true treasures of Iris's days. Under the vast, star-dusted canvas of the Oakhaven night, they would seek refuge from the prying eyes of the village, their whispered confessions carried on the cool, night air. Beneath the gnarled branches of the ancient oak that stood sentinel at the village edge, their figures would meld into the shadows, two souls finding solace and burgeoning hope in each other's presence. It was here, amidst the rustling leaves and the distant hoot of an owl, that Julius would trace the curve of Iris's cheek with a calloused finger, his touch sending a tremor of exquisite delight through her. "Iris," he would murmur, his voice a low rumble, thick with an emotion that mirrored the burgeoning tenderness in her own heart, "when I look at you, I see a light that Oakhaven has never known." And Iris, her breath catching in her throat, would lean into his touch, her sky-blue eyes reflecting the silver glow of the moon, "And when I am with you, Julius, the valley walls seem to melt away, and I can almost see the world you speak of, the one beyond the hills."

Their conversations, even in their youthful simplicity, held a profound depth. They spoke of the future, of a life where the earth yielded its bounty more generously, where the winters did not bite so deeply, and where their love, untainted by worry and want, could unfurl in the warmth of shared prosperity. "I will build us a cottage, Iris," Julius vowed, his gaze earnest, his young face alight with a fierce determination. "A cottage with a sturdy roof and a garden that blooms with more than just survival. We will have a fire that burns bright, and enough food to fill our bellies, and we will watch the stars from our own doorstep, just as we do now, but without the chill of the night biting at our bones." Iris would listen, her heart swelling with a hope so potent it felt almost tangible. She saw it too, this future he painted with such vibrant strokes a future where their laughter would be unburdened, their smiles genuine, and their days filled with a quiet joy.

In the bustling, if somewhat modest, heart of the village square, their shared affection was a silent current, understood by those who cared to look. A shared smile as they passed the baker's stall, a lingering touch as their hands brushed while reaching for the same loaf of bread, a moment of shared laughter over a clumsy stumble these were the quiet declarations of their love, as potent as any grand pronouncement. The other villagers, accustomed to the slow, predictable rhythms of Oakhaven, saw their budding romance with a mixture of amusement and perhaps a touch of nostalgia for their own lost youth. They saw two good souls, two hardworking youngsters, finding comfort in each other's company, a natural progression in the tapestry of village life.

One crisp autumn afternoon, as the leaves painted the valley in hues of amber and crimson, Julius presented Iris with a gift. It was not the elaborately carved trinket of a traveling merchant, but a small, intricately woven basket, fashioned from reeds gathered from the riverbank. Within it lay a single, perfect wild rose, its petals a deep, velvety red, still clinging to the morning dew. "I found it near the old mill," he explained, his voice soft with a boyish shyness. "It reminded me of you, Iris. Strong, and beautiful, even in the wild places." Iris accepted the gift with trembling hands, her heart aching with a sweetness so profound it brought tears to her eyes. She carefully placed the rose in her hair, its fragrance a delicate perfume that mingled with the crisp autumn air. "It is the most beautiful thing I have ever seen, Julius," she whispered, her voice thick with emotion. "And it will be my most cherished treasure." In that simple exchange, a silent promise was made, a reaffirmation of the purity and earnestness of their affection.

Their shared vision for the future was a fragile shield against the encroaching shadows of their reality. They spoke of children, of little ones with eyes that held the sparkle of both their parents, their laughter echoing through the fields of Oakhaven. They dreamt of quiet evenings by the fire, of hands clasped tightly, of a life built on a foundation of unwavering love and mutual respect.

"We will teach them to read the stars, just as we do," Julius would say, his arm encircling Iris's shoulders as they sat on the hillside, overlooking the slumbering village. "And we will tell them stories, not of hardship, but of courage, and kindness, and the beauty that can be found even in the most unlikely of places." Iris, nestled against his side, would nod, her gaze fixed on the distant, hazy outlines of the hills, her heart overflowing with a love so pure and so potent it felt capable of defying the very fate that Oakhaven seemed to dictate.

The simplicity of their love was its greatest strength, its purest expression. It was a love unburdened by the complexities of the world beyond their valley, rooted in the shared hardships and quiet joys of their village existence. They found beauty in the ordinary in the warmth of the sun on their faces, in the taste of freshly baked bread, in the comforting rhythm of the blacksmith's hammer. These were the building blocks of their shared dream a life lived simply yet with an abundance of love.

Yet, even in the midst of their tender courtship, a subtle melancholy would sometimes cast its shadow over their moments. It was the unspoken awareness of the precariousness of their situation, the knowledge that their idyllic world was a fragile bubble, easily burst by the harsh winds of reality. "Sometimes," Iris confessed one evening, her voice barely a whisper, "I fear this dream is too beautiful to be true. That Oakhaven will hold us here forever, and that our love, like a wildflower, will eventually wither under the weight of its demands." Julius would pull her closer, his embrace a silent reassurance. "Never, Iris," he would vow, his voice firm. "Our love is stronger than Oakhaven. It will be our wings, carrying us beyond these hills, to a place where dreams are not just whispered, but lived."

The innocence of their affection was a stark contrast to the brewing storm that lay just beyond the horizon. Their earnest promises, exchanged under the watchful eyes of the moon and stars, were uttered with a sincerity that belied the tragic irony of their unfolding lives. They were two young souls, caught in the gentle eddy of burgeoning love, utterly unaware of the tempest that would soon sweep them apart, shattering their tender dreams and leaving behind only the echoing whispers of what might have been. Their love, so pure and so precious, was a flickering candle in the encroaching darkness, its warm glow a poignant testament to the beauty of hope, and a somber prelude to the sorrow that was to come. The simplicity of their courtship, the earnestness of their promises, the shared vision of a life filled with love and quiet prosperity all these elements wove a narrative of profound tenderness, a stark and heartbreaking counterpoint to the grim realities that awaited them. Each stolen glance, each hushed confession, each shared dream, was a thread in a tapestry of love that would ultimately be torn asunder by forces beyond their control, rendering their fleeting romance a poignant symbol of lost innocence and shattered aspirations. The quiet beauty of their connection, forged in the crucible of their humble lives, served as a beacon of hope, a testament to the enduring power of love, even as the shadows of a more sinister fate began to lengthen over the tranquil village of Oakhaven.

The air in Iris's small cottage always seemed to hold its breath when Bernard was near. He was not a man of boisterous laughter or warm embraces. His presence was a heavy blanket, woven from the threads of ceaseless worry and a grim, unyielding pragmatism that had calcified his heart. Even the scent of his pipe tobacco, usually a comforting aroma in the village, seemed to carry a bitter undertone in his presence, a smoky exhalation of discontent. He moved through their meager dwelling with a purposeful stride, his gaze sharp and assessing, cataloging the worn furnishings, the patched clothes, and the ever-present scarcity that clung to them like damp earth.

His hands, calloused and strong from years of toiling in the unforgiving soil of Oakhaven, were rarely still. When not engaged in some practical tasks   mending a tool, sharpening a blade, or counting their dwindling coin   they would clench and unclench at his sides, a restless energy that spoke of a mind perpetually at odds with itself. His face, etched with the hard lines of labor and unspoken anxieties, was a landscape of perpetual seriousness. Smiles were rare, fleeting things, quickly suppressed as if acknowledging joy was a weakness, a luxury they could ill afford. His eyes, a pale, washed-out blue, seemed to hold a perpetual storm, a tempest of responsibility and a deep-seated fear that Oakhaven's unforgiving nature would one day claim them all.

Iris, accustomed to this atmosphere since childhood, had learned to navigate its treacherous currents. She understood the unspoken language of his silences, the subtle shifts in his posture that indicated displeasure, the way his jaw would tighten when his worries weighed most heavily upon him. Her own youthful exuberance, so easily ignited by the simple beauty of a blooming wildflower or the comforting presence of Julius, often found itself muted in her father's vicinity. It was not a conscious suppression but an instinctual adaptation a learned behavior that ensured a fragile peace within their small home.

One evening, as the last rays of the setting sun bled through the single, grimy windowpane, Bernard sat at the head of their rough-hewn table, his supper untouched. Iris watched him, a familiar knot of apprehension tightening in her stomach. Julius had spoken of their future that afternoon, of a life beyond the confines of Oakhaven, and the memory of his hopeful words, so vibrant and full of light, felt like a fragile bloom amid her father's deepening gloom. Bernard's gaze was fixed on the meager contents of his bowl, his brow furrowed in thought. The silence stretched, taut and expectant, broken only by the distant bleating of sheep and the gentle sigh of the wind through the eaves.

Finally, he cleared his throat, the sound a dry rasp that cut through the quiet. "The harvest was poor again, Iris," he stated, his voice devoid of inflection. It was not a question, but a pronouncement, a grim confirmation of a truth they all knew. He did not need to elaborate; the shriveled stalks of grain in the barn, the half-empty larder, the persistent ache in their bellies these were eloquent testaments to their predicament.

Iris nodded; her own voice small. "I know, Father." She tried to infuse her tone with a quiet resilience, a hope that Julius's unwavering belief had nurtured. "But the winter may not be as harsh as the last. And perhaps," she ventured, her gaze flickering towards the window as if seeking an omen in the twilight sky, "perhaps things will improve."

Bernard's lips thinned into a grim line. "Improve?" he scoffed; the sound devoid of humor. "Improvement is a luxury for those with fertile lands and strong backs, child. We have neither. We have Oakhaven. And Oakhaven takes, it does not give." He finally looked up, his pale eyes fixing on Iris with an intensity that made her flinch inwardly. There was something in his gaze beyond the usual paternal concern; a flicker of desperation, a raw hunger that unnerved her. "This village," he continued, his voice dropping to a more conspiratorial, yet still unnervingly level, tone, "it has a way of settling accounts. And we are deep in its debt."

He picked up his spoon, stirring the watery stew as if searching for answers within its depths. "You are a young woman now, Iris. Of age to be thinking of more than just pretty words and moonlit promises. A good match can secure a family. It can lift us from this mire." His words, though seemingly practical, landed like stones in Iris's heart. She knew what he meant. He was speaking of the transactional nature of their community, of marriages that were not unions of hearts, but alliances of necessity, barters for survival in a world that offered little else.

The unspoken implication hung heavy in the air: Julius, a good man, a hardworking man, but a man with no land, no substantial holdings, could offer no such security. His dreams of a cottage and a garden, while beautiful, were ephemeral against the harsh realities her father so acutely felt. Bernard's pragmatism, once a source of his quiet strength in navigating Oakhaven's challenges, now seemed to curdle into something colder, something that looked upon love as a mere inconvenience, a frivolous distraction from the grim business of survival.

"I… I have no interest in matches, Father," Iris said, her voice barely audible. "Not at this time." She dared not mention Julius by name, fearing the inevitable disapproval that would cloud her father's already shadowed countenance. She had seen the way he looked at Julius when they chanced to pass in the village square a brief, appraising glance, devoid of warmth, as if measuring the young man's worth solely by the coin he could not produce.

Bernard merely grunted, a noncommittal sound that offered no comfort. He pushed his bowl away; his appetite had seemingly vanished. "The world is a harsh place, Iris," he murmured, his gaze drifting towards the deepening twilight outside. "It does not care for young love or hopeful hearts. It cares for strength. For alliances. For security." He turned back to her, his eyes holding a glint that Iris could not decipher, a mixture of weariness and something akin to resolve. "And sometimes," he added, his voice barely above a whisper, a chilling undertone seeping into the words, "sometimes, one must make difficult choices to ensure that survival. For oneself, and for those one is responsible for."

A shiver traced its way down Iris's spine, unrelated to the evening chill. It was not just the pragmatism of her father's words, but the subtle shift in his demeanor that unsettled her. The usual anxieties were still present, the worries about the harvest and the coming winter, but beneath them, something else was stirring   a calculated desperation, a willingness to consider paths she had never imagined. The transactional nature of their community, a fact of life she had always accepted with a resigned sigh, now seemed to be taking on a more sinister hue under her father's gaze.

He stood abruptly, the chair scraping loudly against the wooden floor. "I have business to attend to," he announced, his voice regaining its usual clipped efficiency. "Important business." He did not elaborate, and Iris did not ask. She knew better than to probe too deeply into the shadowed corners of her father's concerns. He was a man who carried his burdens in silence, and when he chose to share them, it was usually with a pronouncement rather than a discussion.

As he pulled on his worn coat, his shadow stretched long and distorted across the small room, momentarily engulfing Iris. In that fleeting instant, she felt a premonition, a cold dread that settled deep within her bones. It was the unsettling feeling that the fragile peace of her world, so recently illuminated by Julius's love, was poised on the brink of a precipice. The stern pragmatism of her father, once a shield against the harsh realities of Oakhaven, now seemed to be transforming into something far more dangerous. This force might, in its desperate pursuit of security, shatter the very foundations of her happiness. The air in the cottage, usually merely heavy with her father's presence, now felt thick with an unspoken threat —a subtle foreshadowing of a darkness that was beginning to gather, not from the encroaching night but from within the very heart of her own home.

The night had swallowed Oakhaven whole, a velvety shroud punctuated only by the mournful hoot of an owl and the distant, restless murmur of the forest. Inside their small cottage, the air was thick with a tension that had been building for weeks, a palpable thing that pressed down on Iris's chest, stealing her breath. Her father, Bernard, sat not at their usual table, but on a stool by the hearth, the dying embers casting long, dancing shadows that contorted his familiar features into something gaunt and unfamiliar. He had been quiet for hours, a stillness that was more unnerving than his usual restless pronouncements. Iris, pretending to mend a torn seam on her only good shawl, watched him from the corner of her eye, her heart a frantic bird trapped within her ribs. The silence was not peaceful; it was the pregnant hush before a storm, a chilling premonition that clung to the very dust motes dancing in the meager firelight.

Suddenly, Bernard spoke, his voice a low rumble that seemed to emanate from the very earth beneath the cottage. "He came," he stated, his gaze fixed on the flickering flames, as if the answers to all their woes lay within their dying glow. Iris's needle froze mid-stitch. "Who, Father?" she asked, her voice barely a whisper, laced with an apprehension that made her throat tighten. She knew, with a dread that had been festering since his cryptic pronouncements about "important business," that this was no casual visitor.

"Chieftain Bjorn," Bernard replied, his tone devoid of emotion, as if discussing the weather or the price of grain. The name itself sent a tremor through Iris. Bjorn the Bear, the chieftain of the Northern Clans, a man whose reputation preceded him like a winter storm a figure of brute strength, territorial ambition, and a deep, unyielding grip on the old ways. His word was law, his will absolute, and his shadow loomed large over the fringes of their meager territories. He was a man who valued strength, power, and... what? Iris dared not complete the thought.

"He came to discuss... an arrangement," Bernard continued, his fingers absently tracing a pattern in the soot on the hearthstone. "An alliance, of sorts. For the good of the village. For our survival." The words were a carefully constructed facade, a flimsy veil thrown over a far more brutal reality. Iris could feel it, a cold certainty seeping into her bones. An alliance with Bjorn the Bear rarely involved simple trade agreements or shared patrols. It involved oaths, loyalty, and often, a price far steeper than coin.

Iris slowly laid down her mending. Her hands trembled, and she clasped them tightly in her lap. "An alliance?" she echoed, her voice thin and reedy. "What kind of alliance requires the Chieftain to visit you here, Father? And what does it have to do with… with us?" Her gaze, desperate for understanding, met her father's. His eyes, when they finally lifted from the fire, held a depth of weariness she had never seen before, but beneath it was a glint a hard, unyielding resolve that chilled her to the marrow.

"Bjorn is a practical man, Iris," Bernard said, his voice gaining a low, steady rhythm that was more persuasive than any argument. "He understands the harsh realities of these lands. He knows that survival is not a matter of sentiment, but of strength and strategic advantage. He sees the potential in Oakhaven, its resources, its… people." He paused, and the unspoken implication hung heavy in the air between them. He saw the people. He saw *her*.

"He offered… support," Bernard elaborated, his gaze returning to the fire. "Protection from the harsher elements, from the… incursions from the wilder territories. In return, he requires… a token of our loyalty. A demonstration of our commitment to this new accord." The word "token" felt like a cruel mockery, a euphemism for something far more profound and devastating.

Iris felt a wave of dizziness wash over her. She gripped the edge of the rough-hewn table, her knuckles white. "A token? Father, what are you saying?" Her voice cracked, betraying the terror that was beginning to bloom within her. The carefully cultivated hope she had held onto since Julius's words —the fragile dream of a life filled with warmth and simple joy —felt like it was shattering around her, piece by agonizing piece.

Bernard finally looked at her fully, his expression unreadable in the flickering shadows. "Bjorn is a man who values lineage, Iris," he said, his voice dropping to a near whisper. "He understands the importance of continuity, of securing his own future and the future of his clan. He seeks a… union. A consolidation of ties." He took a breath, a slow, deliberate inhalation that seemed to gather all the grimness of their existence into one agonizing exhale. "He has agreed to provide for us, Iris. To ensure our sustenance through the coming years, to see that this village does not wither and die under the weight of its misfortunes. In exchange…"

He let the sentence trail off, but the unspoken truth struck Iris with the force of a physical blow. Her father was not selling their land, nor their meager livestock, nor their future harvests. He was selling *her*. The realization was a jagged shard of ice piercing her heart. Her agency, her dreams, her very future, were being bartered away like a sack of grain, exchanged for promises of survival. The brutal pragmatism that had always defined her father had, in this moment, transmogrified into an act of utter, soul-crushing betrayal.

"No," she whispered, the word a broken plea. "Father, no. You cannot." Tears, hot and stinging, began to blur her vision. The image of Julius's earnest face, his kind eyes, his promises of a life built together, flashed before her. How could her father do this? How could he extinguish the only light that had dared to dawn in the oppressive gloom of Oakhaven?

Bernard's jaw tightened. He rose from the stool, his movements stiff, as if each step was an agonizing effort. He walked to the small, grimy window and stared out into the oppressive darkness. "You do not understand, Iris," he said, his voice strained. "You see only your own small world, your own fleeting happiness. You do not see the hunger that gnaws at our bellies, the cold that seeps into our bones, the creeping despair that threatens to consume us all. Oakhaven is dying, Iris. It has always been a struggle, but now… now it is a fight for our very existence."

He turned back to her, his face a mask of grim determination. "Bjorn's offer is not a luxury; it is a necessity. It is salvation. He has agreed to take you, to provide for you, and in doing so, he finds himself to us. His protection will extend to this village. His resources will see us through." He stepped closer, his eyes, usually so weary, now burning with a fierce, almost fanatical light. "He sees your worth, Iris. Your youth, your… potential. He recognizes what you can bring to his clan. And he is willing to invest in that future. A future that we will also benefit from."

"My worth?" Iris choked out; the words laced with a bitter irony. "My worth is to be a pawn in a chieftain's game? To be traded like chattel?" She stood, pushing her chair back with a scrape that echoed the tearing of her own heart. "You speak of survival, Father, but what kind of survival is this? A life where my own father sells me into… into what? To a man I do not know, a man whose reputation is that of a brute?"

"He is a chieftain, Iris," Bernard stated, his voice regaining its familiar authoritative edge, as if trying to impose order on the chaos of her grief. "He is a man of power. And in these times, power is the only true currency. He will treat you with the respect due to one who will bear his lineage. He will provide for you. More than I ever could." The words were meant to soothe, but they landed like molten lead. He could provide more. He could offer a future that Bernard, with all his toil and worry, never could. It was a stark admission of his own perceived failures, a cruel indictment of their impoverished existence.

"And Julius?" Iris asked, her voice trembling, daring to voice the name that had been a beacon of hope. "What of him? What of the life we spoke of?"

Bernard's expression hardened further. "Julius is a good man," he conceded, the words tasting like ash on his tongue. "But he is a poor man. He has nothing to offer you but dreams. Bjorn offers reality. Security. A future that is not precarious, not dependent on the whims of the weather or the scarcity of the harvest. Julius cannot protect you, Iris. He cannot feed you. He cannot ensure the survival of this village." He stepped even closer, his rough hand reaching out as if to grasp her arm, then stopping short, as if even his own touch was now fraught with the weight of his decision. "This is not about your desires, Iris. This is about survival. Mine. Yours. Oakhaven's."

He had struck a bargain. A cold, calculated transaction that stripped her of her voice, her dreams, her very self. The terms had been laid out, not in a joyous exchange, but in a somber negotiation between father and chieftain, shrouded in the dying embers of their hearth and the oppressive darkness of the night. The "arrangement" was a marriage —a sacrifice —a blood-binding oath made in the name of pragmatism. Bjorn, with his keen eye for opportunity and his insatiable need for alliances, had seen not just a village in need, but a young woman who could cement his influence, a lineage to be fostered.

Bernard had walked to Bjorn's temporary encampment, a collection of sturdy tents pitched on the outskirts of the village, a place that reeked of woodsmoke, animal hides, and the rough camaraderie of warriors. The Chieftain, a hulking figure with a beard as wild as a winter storm and eyes that missed nothing, had listened with a placid indifference that was more terrifying than any rage. He had not haggled over price, nor questioned Bernard's motives. He had seen what he wanted, and he had named his terms. A bride. A woman of good stock, young and fertile, who would bear him heirs and serve as a symbol of Oakhaven's fealty. In return, Bjorn would ensure a steady supply of grain, protection against raids, and a modicum of stability for the beleaguered village.

The negotiation had been brief, brutal, and utterly devoid of warmth. Bernard, his usual stoicism amplified by the gravity of his decision, had laid bare the village's desperate plight. He had spoken of the failing crops, the harsh winters, the dwindling numbers, and the ever-present threat of lawlessness encroaching from the untamed wilds. He had presented Iris not as his daughter but as a valuable asset —a strategic investment. Bjorn, in turn, had spoken of his own need for a strong alliance and for a wife who would bring honor and continuity to his clan. He had, in essence, appraised Iris like a prize stallion, noting her perceived qualities her youth, her presumed health, her Oakhaven lineage, which, though humble, was rooted in these lands.

"She has a certain fire," Bjorn had rumbled, his gaze, even from across the flickering firelight of his tent, seeming to penetrate Bernard's very soul. "A spirit. Good. It will be tempered. She will learn her place. She will be well provided for. She will be Chieftain Bjorn's mate." The pronouncement had been final, a decree rather than a proposal. There was no room for negotiation, no space for Iris's consent. Her future, her very life, had been decided in a conversation that lasted no longer than it took to consume a tankard of ale.

Bernard had returned to his cottage under the cloak of the pre-dawn sky, the weight of his bargain a crushing burden on his shoulders, yet tinged with a grim satisfaction. He had secured Oakhaven's future, and in doing so, he had secured his own. He had made the hard choice, the pragmatic choice, the one that would ensure the survival of his people, even at the cost of his daughter's happiness.

Now, facing Iris, the stark reality of his decision settled over him. He saw the raw pain etched on her young face, the dawning horror in her eyes, the silent accusation that screamed louder than any words. Her innocence, her dreams of love and a simple life, were about to be crushed under the heavy boot of necessity. He had traded her for the continued existence of their village, a transaction as old as time itself, yet one that felt impossibly cruel in the quiet intimacy of their small home.

"Father," Iris's voice, though trembling, held a newfound strength, a desperate resilience born of utter despair. "You have not saved Oakhaven. You have condemned me." She stepped back, her gaze sweeping over the meager furnishings of their cottage, the worn blankets, the chipped pottery. This was the life he had deemed insufficient, the life he had so readily traded away. "You chose this place," she said, her voice gaining a fierce edge, "you chose its survival. But at what cost to the one person who was supposed to be your most precious possession?"

The unspoken question hung between them, a chasm that could never be bridged. He had made his bargain. He had struck his deal. And in the silent, suffocating darkness of that night, Iris realized that the whispers of Oakhaven were not just the rustling of leaves or the creaking of timbers. They were the echoes of a soul being bartered, a future being sold, a life being surrendered to the insatiable hunger of survival. The cold, calculated reality of her father's bargain had descended upon her, leaving her stripped bare, helpless, and utterly alone in the face of a future she had never imagined, a future forged in the brutal crucible of necessity and the chilling indifference of a chieftain's decree. She was no longer Iris, daughter of Oakhaven. She was a token, a bride, a sacrifice upon the altar of her father's desperate pragmatism.

The air in the cottage, once thick with Bernard's palpable tension, now thrummed with a different kind of energy the frigid stillness of utter despair. Iris, her voice barely a thread, felt the words she had just uttered "You have not saved Oakhaven. You have condemned me "hang in the air like shards of ice. She watched her father's face, searching for a flicker of remorse, a hint of the father she had known, the man who had once held her hand and told her stories of ancient heroes. But all she saw was a reflection of the harsh, unforgiving landscape that had shaped him, a landscape that demanded brutal sacrifices in the name of endurance.

Bernard's shoulders slumped, not with defeat, but with a weariness that seemed to have settled into his very bones, a constant companion born of years of struggle. He did not offer apologies, nor did he attempt to reframe his actions with soothing lies. His silence was a confession, a testament to the grim calculus that had guided his decision. "There are burdens, Iris," he finally murmured, his voice raspy, as if the very act of speaking these truths tore at his throat, "that cannot be borne alone. A village is a fragile thing. It is like a sapling struggling to take root in stony ground. One strong gust of wind, one prolonged drought, and it is broken. We have faced too many winds, too many droughts."

He walked to the hearth, where the embers had finally surrendered to ash, leaving only a grey, lifeless residue. He ran a calloused finger over the cold stone. "Do you know what it is to see the faces of your neighbours, their eyes hollowed by hunger, their children thin and shivering, and know that there is nothing you can do? Nothing but watch them fade. We have rationed. We have prayed. We have worked until our hands bled. And still, the gnawing emptiness persists. The winter… the last winter was the worst. We lost more than half our livestock. The grain stores were meager, and by the time the thaw arrived, we were a hair's breadth from starvation."

Iris listened, a knot of cold dread tightening in her stomach. She understood the hardship; she lived it every day. But she had never imagined it could lead to this. She had believed in resilience, in the inherent strength of their community, in the quiet hope that things might one day improve. Her father's pragmatism, which she had always admired as a sign of his strength and leadership, now felt like a weapon turned against her.

"Bjorn's offer," Bernard continued, his gaze fixed on the empty hearth, "was not a gift. It was a lifeline. He is a powerful man, Iris. His word carries weight, and his resources are vast. He can ensure that our granaries are filled, that our homes are warm. He can protect us from the roving bands that have become bolder each year, from the very elements that threaten to break us. This is not about your happiness, child. It is about ensuring that Oakhaven *endures*. That your neighbours, that your father, that *you* have a tomorrow."

He turned to face her, his expression a mixture of defiance and a profound, unsettling sadness. "You speak of condemnation. I see it as salvation. For years, I have watched this village struggle. I have felt the weight of responsibility for every soul within it. Every lost harvest, every sick child, every life claimed by the harshness of this land… it has been a burden I carry. And I have failed. We have failed to truly prosper, to escape the cycle of want and despair. Bjorn's alliance offers an escape. A chance for a stable future. And the price… the price is a sacrifice I must make. For all of us."

The word "sacrifice" landed with a sickening thud. It was a word steeped in folklore, in tales of ancient Kami and vengeful spirits, of maidens offered to appease some unseen horror. But this was no mythical entity; this was a man, a chieftain, driven by ambition and the unyielding demands of his own clan. Her father, in his desperation, had reduced her to a pawn, an object to be traded for the collective good.

"But Father," Iris pleaded, her voice catching on a sob, "there are other ways. We could… we could try to petition the lords in the south. Or perhaps, if we worked even harder…"

Bernard let out a short, bitter laugh that held no humor. "Petition the lords? They care nothing for a forgotten village on the fringes of their dominion. We are too small, too insignificant. And harder work? We work until we drop, Iris. We have no more reserves. Our hands are already calloused raw, our backs perpetually aching. We are at the mercy of the seasons, of the whims of nature. Bjorn offers certainty. An end to the constant, gnawing fear of what tomorrow might bring."

He stepped closer; his gaze intense. "Think, Iris. Think of the children who will no longer cry from hunger. Think of the elders who will no longer shiver through the endless nights. Think of the men who will not have to fear for their lives when they venture beyond our borders. This is not a small thing, Iris. This is the difference between life and death for an entire community. I have chosen life. For Oakhaven."

His justification, however rationalized, did not lessen the sting of betrayal. She understood his desperation, the immense pressure he must have felt, the crippling weight of leadership in a dying world. But understanding did not erase the image of Julius's face, of the quiet promises exchanged under the moon. It did not erase the fundamental truth that he was trading her autonomy, her potential for happiness, her very personhood, for collective survival.

"And my future, Father?" she asked, her voice barely above a whisper, the question heavy with the unspoken sorrow of lost dreams. "What of the life I might have had? The love I might have found? Is that to be simply… erased?"

Bernard's jaw tightened, a muscle twitching beneath his weathered skin. "Love is a luxury, Iris, that many in this world cannot afford. Security is a necessity. Bjorn will provide for you. He will give you a position of respect within his clan. You will be safe. You will be provided for. More than I ever could. He is a man of power, and in these times, power is the only true currency. He will see you treated with the honor due to the mate of a chieftain. You will have a future. It is simply not the future you envisioned."

The words were a balm of poison, offering comfort even as they highlighted the irreparable damage done. He presented it as a betterment—a step up a gilded cage. But to Iris, it felt like an utter diminishment. To be the mate of a chieftain, a man renowned for his ruthlessness and his insatiable hunger for control, was not a prospect that sparked joy. It was a future steeped in obligation, in subservience, in a life dictated by the needs and desires of another.

"He sees potential in me, you said," Iris murmured, her gaze drifting to the window, where the inky blackness of night still held sway. "He sees my youth, my Oakhaven lineage. He sees a vessel for his heirs. Is that my true worth, Father? To be a fertile field for his ambition?" The question hung in the air, unanswered. Bernard offered no further words of comfort or justification. He had made his choice, and now he had to live with its consequences, just as she would have to live with its price.

The weight of his decision pressed down on Iris, a suffocating blanket that stole her breath. She saw now that survival in Oakhaven was not a matter of simple resilience or hard work. It was a brutal, unending negotiation with a world that offered no quarter, a world where the cost of staying alive could be the very essence of one's being. Her father, a man trapped by the desperate circumstances of their existence, had chosen the path of least resistance in terms of the village's physical survival. Still, in doing so, he had inflicted a wound upon his own daughter that might never heal. The whispering village had demanded its due, and the price, it seemed, was her very soul. The cold reality settled upon her like a shroud, and in the dim light of their humble cottage, Iris understood that her life, as she knew it, had ended. The future stretched before her, a dark and uncertain road, paved with the broken pieces of her own shattered dreams, a road she would now have to walk alone.

Chapter 2:
The Chieftain's Keep

The weight of her father's decision settled upon Iris like a shroud, muffling the familiar sounds of Oakhaven, distorting its comforting, albeit harsh, contours into something alien and threatening. The farewells were perfunctory, hushed affairs, laden with the unspoken sorrow of a community that had traded one of its own for a semblance of security. Her neighbours, their faces etched with a complex mixture of pity and relief, averted their gazes, unable to meet the silent accusation in her eyes. She was not departing as a bride, nor as a welcomed envoy, but as a tribute, a sacrifice laid upon the altar of communal survival. The familiar paths, worn smooth by generations of Oakhaven folk, now seemed to lead her away from everything she knew, towards an abyss that had no name.

The escort, a grim contingent of Bjorn's men, was not cruel in overt ways, but their very presence was a constant, suffocating reminder of her diminished status. They were iron-clad figures, their faces weathered and impassive, their speech gruff and infrequent. They moved with an unsettling efficiency, their horses' hooves striking the frozen earth with a sound that echoed the finality of her displacement. Iris rode a sturdy, unremarkable mare, its gait steady but devoid of spirit, much like her own. Beside her rode Kael, a hulking man with eyes the colour of a winter sky and a beard braided with crude metal rings, who seemed to be the appointed guardian of their grim cargo. He offered no words of solace, no platitudes, his silence a wall as impenetrable as his chainmail.

The journey began under a sky the colour of bruised plums, the weak dawn offering little warmth. The familiar rolling hills that cradled Oakhaven soon gave way to a landscape that grew progressively more severe. The trees, once robust and full-branched, became gnarled and skeletal, their limbs twisted like arthritic fingers against the pale sky. The ground, no longer merely uneven, transformed into a treacherous tapestry of jagged rocks and plunging ravines. Snow, which had been a gentle dusting in her village, now lay in thick, unforgiving drifts, swallowing the paths and making the ascent arduous even for the seasoned riders.

As they travelled deeper into Bjorn's territory, the very air seemed to change. It grew colder, sharper, carrying a scent of pine resin and something else – something wild and primal, a scent that spoke of untamed forests and ancient, brooding spirits. The cheerful babble of the stream that had always flowed near Oakhaven was replaced by the ominous rush of unseen waters carving through rock. This sound hinted at depths and currents far more powerful and dangerous than anything she had ever known. The sun, when it managed to pierce the perpetual grey, cast long, distorted shadows that danced like spectres, imbuing the already desolate landscape with an aura of foreboding.

Iris found herself gazing at the faces of her escorts, searching for any sign of empathy, any crack in their hardened exteriors. But there was none. They were men accustomed to hardship, to the brutal realities of a chieftain's dominion, where sentimentality was a weakness to be purged. Their eyes, when they met hers, were devoid of emotion, registering her presence as little more than a necessary conveyance. They spoke amongst themselves in low, guttural tones, their conversations punctuated by the jingle of their armour and the snort of their horses. Occasionally, one would cast a furtive glance in her direction, a look that held no curiosity, only the detached assessment of a beast of burden.

The hours stretched into an eternity, and each mile traversed was a deliberate step further from her former life. The memory of her father's words, his justifications for her sacrifice, played on repeat in her mind, each utterance hollower than the last. The spoke of salvation, of security, of a future for Oakhaven. But all Iris felt was the cold, gnawing certainty of her own immolation. Her youth, her hopes, the whispers of love that had begun to bloom in her heart all were being trampled under the relentless march of Bjorn's men towards his keep.

She recalled the stories her grandmother used to tell, tales of ancient pacts and appeasements, of maidens offered to mountain Kami or to placate vengeful river spirits. These were bedtime stories meant to instill a sense of awe and caution, not literal prophecies. Yet, here she was, a living embodiment of those chilling fables, her journey a descent into a realm where the folklore of old seemed to hold a grim, tangible power. The further they rode, the more the world around her seemed to shed the veneer of civilization, revealing the raw, untamed heart of a land that belonged to the strong and the brutal.

The landscape itself became a character in her unfolding tragedy. The wind, once a gentle caress in Oakhaven, now whipped around them with a fierce, biting intensity, tearing at her cloak and chilling her to the bone. It moaned through the skeletal branches of ancient pines; a mournful lament that seemed to mirror the silent screams trapped within her own chest. She saw no sign of other settlements, no smoke rising from distant hearths, only the vast, indifferent expanse of wilderness. It was a land carved out by force, ruled by the sword, and the very rocks and trees seemed to bear witness to its savage origins.

During a brief, uncomfortable halt for their horses to drink from a frigid, black pool, Iris noticed Kael observing her with an unnerving intensity. His gaze wasn't predatory, nor was it sympathetic. It was the gaze of a craftsman assessing a newly acquired tool, cataloging its potential uses and limitations. He said nothing, but the brief, silent appraisal sent a shiver down her spine that had nothing to do with the cold. She was not a person to him, nor even a bride-to-be, but a possession, an asset being transported to its new owner.

As the day wore on, the sky darkened further, not with the natural progression of evening, but with an oppressive gloom that seemed to emanate from the land itself. The rugged terrain gave way to a more imposing spectacle: the jagged peaks of the northern mountains loomed on the horizon, their summits shrouded in perpetual snow and mist. It was in the shadow of these formidable peaks that Bjorn's stronghold was said to lie, a fortress carved from the very stone of the mountains, a testament to his power and his dominion over this harsh, unforgiving realm

The realization of her irreversible fate began to crystallize with a clarity that was both terrifying and strangely liberating. There was no turning back. Oakhaven, with its familiar hardships and its fragile hope, was now a distant dream. Her father's pragmatism his desperate attempt to secure his village's survival had effectively severed her from her past. She was now a pawn in a much larger, more dangerous game, a game played by chieftains and warlords in a world where sentiment and compassion were liabilities.

The journey was a descent, not just in miles, but in spirit. Each rhythmic thud of the horses' hooves was a hammer blow against the walls of her former life, dismantling it piece by piece. The wild, untamed beauty of the rugged landscape was a stark contrast to the gentle, nurturing familiarity of Oakhaven. It was a beauty that was sharp and dangerous, a beauty that demanded respect and instilled fear. It was the beauty of a predator's domain, and she, Iris, was now a lamb being led to the slaughter, albeit a lamb adorned with the trappings of a bride. The realization dawned with the slow, chilling certainty of a frostbite she was not merely leaving home; she was entering captivity.

The escort halted not before the gates of wood, but before a colossal maw of hewn stone, impossibly dark and raw, as if the mountain itself had been gouged open to form an entrance. This was not a welcoming threshold; it was a scar. High above, banners of dark grey and blood-red snapped in the relentless wind, bearing the sigil of a snarling wolf's head a symbol that seemed to pulse with primal aggression. The air here was different, colder still, and laced with the metallic tang of ancient blood and the acrid scent of smoke from unseen hearths.

As Iris's mare was led forward, the rough-hewn stones of the keep's outer walls pressed in, towering and oppressive. They were not smoothed by plaster or adorned with carvings of any pleasantry, but left in their brutal, natural state, a testament to a strength that cared little for aesthetics beyond their intimidating presence. Stalwart warriors, clad in mail that gleamed dully even in the overcast light, stood at intervals, their faces obscured by visored helms, their stances rigid and watchful. They were statues of iron and vigilance, their mere presence radiating a silent, unwavering authority.

The cavernous entryway opened into a vast hall, echoing with the clang of metal and the low murmur of many voices. The sheer scale was breathtaking, but it was a brutal kind of grandeur. The ceiling soared into darkness, lost to sight, supported by massive granite pillars. Torches, burning with an unnaturally fierce, almost blue flame, were mounted in iron sconces, casting flickering shadows that danced across the uneven stone floor and the stark, utilitarian furnishings. No tapestries depicted heroic deeds or pastoral scenes; no inlaid wood or polished marble. Instead, the walls were adorned with weapons – racks of swords, polished axes, and shields bearing the same grim wolf sigil. The very air seemed to hum with a suppressed energy, a latent violence that clung to the stone like frost.

Iris dismounted, her legs stiff and trembling. Kael, the hulking man who had been her silent sentinel for days, offered no assistance, merely gesturing with a curt nod towards a figure emerging from the deeper shadows of the hall. This was not the jovial, booming Chieftain of her father's anxious descriptions, nor the romanticized lord of ballads. This was Bjorn.

He was a man forged from the same harsh landscape that surrounded his keep. Tall and broad-shouldered, his presence filled the space around him, a tangible force. His hair, the colour of raven's wings, was pulled back severely from a face that bore the marks of a life lived in conflict – a jagged scar bisected his left eyebrow, and his jawline was set in a perpetual, grim line. His eyes, the colour of chipped flint, swept over Iris with an unnerving intensity, not with curiosity or desire, but with the detached appraisal of a man assessing a newly acquired piece of property. He wore a tunic of dark, supple leather, cinched with a wide belt from which hung a formidable war-axe, its haft worn smooth from countless grips. Around his neck, a heavy silver torque, inlaid with dark, polished stones, spoke of wealth, but it was a stark, unadorned display, devoid of any warmth or ostentation.

"So," Bjorn's voice rumbled, a sound like stones grinding together, "the tribute has arrived."

There was no welcome, no nicety. The word hung in the air, heavy and chilling, confirming Iris's deepest fears. She was not a guest, not a bride, but a tribute, a bargaining chip laid at the feet of a mountain king. The stark reality of her situation, stripped bare of any pretense, was more terrifying than any imagined horror.

He turned, a silent signal for her to follow, and began to walk deeper into the keep. Iris, her heart a frantic drum against her ribs, had no choice but to comply. Kael fell back, his gaze still fixed upon her, a silent promise of constant surveillance. The hall was a thoroughfare, and as they moved, other figures emerged from its shadowed recesses. They were men and women, dressed in the practical, rough-spun clothing of servants and guards, their faces etched with the same hard resilience that marked the warriors at the entrance. They moved with a quiet efficiency, their eyes downcast, rarely meeting Bjorn's gaze, and never Iris's. There was no lingering curiosity, no whispered gossip, only a palpable sense of order and obedience. This was a well-oiled machine, and Iris was the new, foreign cog.

The contrast to the imagined warmth of a life with Julius was stark, almost painful. She had envisioned a simple cottage, perhaps, or a modest hall, filled with the comforting scent of baking bread and the murmur of everyday life. Julius, with his gentle smile and thoughtful eyes, had painted a picture of quiet domesticity, of shared laughter and stolen moments. This place, however, was the antithesis of all that. It was a testament to power, to dominion, built on a foundation of strength and, she suspected, ruthlessness.

Bjorn led her through a series of corridors, each one as stark and unadorned as the last. The stone was always rough, the light always dim, emanating from the same fierce, blue-flamed torches. There were no windows that offered a view of the outside world, only the solid, unyielding embrace of the mountain. The silence, broken only by the echo of their footsteps and the distant clang of metal, was more unnerving than any noise. It was a silence that spoke of secrets, of hidden depths, of a life lived behind impenetrable walls.

They reached a set of heavy, iron-bound doors. Bjorn pushed them open, revealing not a bedchamber, but a room that spoke of a grim sort of luxury. It was larger than any room in Oakhaven, the walls lined with what appeared to be wolf pelts, thick and dark, absorbing what little light there was. A large, unadorned wooden table dominated the centre of the room, scarred and gouged from years of use. Beside it, a sturdy bench. The only concession to comfort was a large hearth, at present banked with embers that cast a faint, ruddy glow.

"This is your chamber," Bjorn stated, his voice devoid of any softening.

Iris stepped inside, her eyes taking in the details. The furnishings were sparse: the table, the bench, and a simple, straw-filled mattress upon a wooden frame in the corner, draped with a coarse woollen blanket. There was no chest for her belongings, no washbasin, no mirror. It was a cell, albeit a large one, designed for function, not comfort. The air was thick with the scent of woodsmoke and something else, something animalistic and wild, perhaps from the pelts on the walls.

"There are servants," Bjorn continued, gesturing vaguely towards the door. "They will bring you food and attend to your needs. Do not mistake their service for familiarity. They obey me." His gaze fixed on her, sharp and unwavering. "And you will obey me."

It was a clear, unambiguous declaration of ownership. Iris felt a tremor run through her, a cold dread that had nothing to do with the stone's chill. She was property, a captive, her fate inextricably bound to the whims of this formidable Chieftain. The stories of his domain, whispered in hushed tones by the elders of Oakhaven, had painted him as a brutal, unyielding leader, a man who had carved his empire from the unforgiving wilderness through sheer force of will. Now, standing before him, she understood the terrifying truth of those tales.

"You will be brought to me when I require your presence," Bjorn concluded, his tone leaving no room for argument. "Until then, you will remain here. Do not wander. Do not speak to those you do not know unless you are spoken to first. Make no trouble." He turned, his heavy boots echoing on the stone floor as he strode back into the corridor, leaving Iris alone in the oppressive silence of her new confinement.

The heavy door swung shut with a decisive thud, plunging the chamber into a deeper twilight. Iris sank onto the rough-hewn bench, her legs buckling beneath her. The sheer, unyielding nature of this place, of this man, was overwhelming. It was a world built on stark power, where sentiment was a weakness and obedience were paramount. The wolf pelts on the walls seemed to watch her, their dark eyes glinting in the firelight, ancient predators in their natural habitat. The very stones of the keep seemed to exude a silent, brutal history, a chronicle of dominance and survival.

She thought again of Julius, of the life she had been promised, a life that now seemed impossibly distant, like a dream from another existence. The gentle warmth of his hand, the light in his eyes, the quiet promise of a shared future all of it felt like a cruel jest in this stark, unforgiving reality. This was Bjorn's domain, a place where the natural world's harshness was mirrored in the very fabric of its architecture and its ruler. There was no softness here, no tenderness, only the cold, unyielding strength of the mountain and the wolf.

A hesitant knock sounded at the door, followed by its opening. A young woman, no older than Iris herself, entered, carrying a wooden tray laden with a hunk of dark bread, a wedge of hard cheese, and a wooden goblet filled with a dark, unappetizing liquid. Her hair was pulled back tightly, her face pale and unsmiling. She placed the tray on the table with a quiet efficiency, her eyes never meeting Iris's.

"My lady," she murmured, her voice barely audible, "your meal."

Iris managed a weak nod. "Thank you."

The servant bowed her head slightly. "If you require anything else, you must ask Kael. Or one of the guards. They will inform the Chieftain." Her gaze flickered towards the door, a subtle hint of fear. "He is… particular."

With another brief bow, the servant retreated, closing the door softly behind her, leaving Iris once more with the silence and the heavy presence of the wolf pelts. The bread was dry, the cheese surprisingly flavourless, and the drink tasted faintly of fermented berries and something earthy, almost bitter. It was sustenance, nothing more.

As she ate, her gaze drifted around the room. The wolf pelts were indeed impressive, with their dark fur thick and lustrous, but the sheer brutality of their origins overshadowed the wealth they implied. Each pelt was a testament to a hunt, a kill, a victory in this savage land. They were trophies, displayed not for beauty, but for the assertion of power. The room itself was a reflection of Bjorn's character – imposing, functional, and utterly devoid of gentleness. It was a space designed to dominate, to remind its occupant of their place within the hierarchy of his domain.

She ran a hand over the rough wood of the table, feeling the deep gouges and scars. What arguments, what feasts, what plans had been made here? What decisions, forged in the heat of ambition or the chill of strategy, had been carved into its surface? This was not merely a room; it was a chamber that bore witness to the raw, unfiltered reality of a chieftain's life, a life lived on the edge of survival, where strength was the only currency.

The sheer isolation began to press in. The silence, once merely unnerving, now felt suffocating. There was no familiar sound of the wind rustling through oak leaves, no distant bleating of sheep, no children's laughter. Only the hollow echo within the stone and the faint, persistent whisper of the wind against the unyielding mountain. She was a prisoner in a fortress carved from the very heart of the wild. The rough wool of the blanket offered little comfort as she huddled on the bench, the meagre warmth of the banked embers doing little to dispel the gnawing chill that had settled deep within her bones. This was Bjorn's domain, and it was a domain of stone, of steel, and of the unblinking stare of the wolf. Her journey had ended not in a new home, but in a gilded cage, its bars forged from the unyielding will of a man who ruled a land as unforgiving as his own heart. The stark, utilitarian nature of the chamber was a constant, brutal reminder of her new reality – a reality in which she was not a woman but a tribute, a possession, and her future was entirely at the mercy of the Chieftain.

The days that followed blurred into a monotonous cycle of oppressive silence and gnawing dread. Iris's existence within the Chieftain's Keep had become a grim testament to Bjorn's burgeoning cruelty. He rarely summoned her, preferring to let her stew in the gnawing uncertainty of her confinement, a tactic that proved far more insidious than overt torment. When he did deign to grace her with his presence, his eyes, like shards of flint, would take over her, not with a flicker of warmth or even simple curiosity, but with a chilling possessiveness that spoke of ownership, of a prize acquired and to be kept, displayed, and perhaps, broken.

One evening, the heavy door to her chamber creaked open, its groan a familiar harbinger of his arrival. Bjorn stood silhouetted against the flickering torchlight of the corridor, his imposing frame filling the doorway. He did not enter fully, but leaned against the stone jamb, his gaze fixed on Iris as she sat on the edge of her straw-filled mattress, her hands clasped tightly in her lap. The wolf pelts on the walls seemed to absorb the faint light, their dark, matted fur appearing to writhe in the periphery of her vision.

"You are quiet," he stated, his voice a low rumble that seemed to vibrate through the very stones of the keep. It wasn't an observation, but an accusation, a subtle prod designed to elicit a reaction, any reaction, from the woman he had claimed.

Iris swallowed; her throat dry. "There is little to say, Chieftain."

A flicker of something – amusement, perhaps, or disdain – crossed his rugged features. "Little to say? You have been brought to my keep. You are to be my wife. A queen, in all but name. And yet, you sit there like a wilting flower, offering platitudes." He pushed off the doorframe and took a step into the room, his presence immediately amplifying the suffocating atmosphere. The scent of pine and something musky, like an untamed animal, clung to him.

He moved towards the table, his movements deliberate, predatory. He picked up a piece of the dark bread she had been given earlier, turning it over in his thick fingers. "This is not enough, is it? This meager offering for a woman plucked from her comfortable life. You expect silks, perhaps? Sweetmeats brought from distant lands? Music to lull you to sleep?"

He tossed the bread back onto the table with a clatter. "This is the life you are given now. You will eat what is provided. You will wear what is given. You will be grateful for the roof over your head, for the safety my walls provide." His voice hardened; the undertone of amusement replaced by a chilling authority. "You are a tribute, Iris. A symbol of your father's capitulation. Do not forget your place."

He walked around the table, his gaze never leaving her. She felt trapped, exposed beneath his scrutiny. It was as if he could see the fear coiling in her gut, the desperate hope for escape that flickered within her. He stopped directly in front of her, his shadow falling over her small frame.

"Your father sent you to appease me, to secure his own fragile peace. And you, my dear Iris, are the price. Do you understand that?"

Iris could only manage a stiff nod, her eyes fixed on the scarred wood of the table. She refused to meet his gaze, fearing what she might see there, what further degradation he might inflict if she showed any sign of defiance, however small.

Bjorn let out a low, rough chuckle, a sound devoid of mirth. "Good. Ignorance breeds foolishness. And foolishness is a weakness I cannot afford in my keep." He reached out, not to touch her, but to run a thick finger along the rough edge of her tunic. The movement was slow, deliberate, each inch of fabric seeming to sear beneath his touch. "You are soft," he observed, his voice almost a whisper now, sending a fresh wave of apprehension through her. "Untouched. Much like a lamb delivered to the slaughter."

He paused, letting the implication hang in the air, heavy and suffocating. Iris's breath hitched in her throat. She could feel the heat rising in her cheeks, a flush of shame and fear.

"But I do not slaughter lambs, Iris," he continued, his voice regaining its commanding tone. "I break them. I tame them. And you, my little songbird, will learn to sing my tune."

He turned abruptly, his wolf-pelt cloak swirling around him like a predatory shadow. "You will be brought to my hall tomorrow evening. Be ready. And do not disappoint me." The door closed behind him, leaving Iris alone once more with the oppressive silence, the scent of him lingering in the air like a venomous perfume. The weight of his words settled upon her, heavier than the stone walls that imprisoned her. She was not a bride; she was a captive, a plaything for a man whose cruelty seemed as boundless as the mountains that surrounded his fortress.

The following evening, two guards, their faces impassive and their movements silent, escorted her to Bjorn's Hall. The vast chamber, previously a place of imposing, if stark, grandeur, now felt like a den of predatory power. Torches burned with an unnervingly bright, almost spectral blue flame, casting long, dancing shadows that seemed to mimic the predatory instincts of the beasts whose pelts adorned the walls. Bjorn sat at the head of the long, scarred table, a goblet of dark ale in his hand, his eyes already fixed on her as she entered.

He gestured to a place beside him, a place of honour, yet one that felt more like a sentencing bench. As she sat, the rough wool of her simple dress prickling against her skin, Bjorn began to speak, his words weaving a tapestry of dominance and possession.

"Tonight," he began, his voice echoing in the cavernous space, "we celebrate your arrival. And your submission." He took a long draught of his ale, his gaze never leaving her face. "My people have grown restless. They have heard whispers of the tribute from Oakhaven. They expect to see their new Chieftain's prize. You will show them that she is worthy of my claim."

He pushed a wooden trencher towards her, laden with roasted meat, dark bread, and pungent cheese. "Eat," he commanded, his tone leaving no room for refusal. Iris picked at the food; her appetite extinguished by the knot of anxiety in her stomach. Bjorn watched her every move, his keen eyes dissecting her hesitation, her small portions.

"You have a delicate appetite," he observed, a dangerous glint in his flint-grey eyes. "Perhaps you are not accustomed to hearty fare. Or perhaps you are simply afraid to taste the bounty of my lands." He leaned forward, his voice dropping to a conspiratorial murmur that somehow amplified its menace. "Do you know what happens to those who refuse to partake in the hospitality of the wolf clan, Iris?"

He did not wait for an answer. "They are cast out. They starve in the wilderness. Or worse, they become the prey themselves." He picked up a thick slice of the roasted meat, its juices glistening in the torchlight. "This meat," he continued, holding it out towards her, "was once a proud stag, running free through the mountains. Now, it fuels my strength. It fuels the strength of my clan." He lowered the meat, his gaze piercing. "And you, too, will be fueled by what I provide. Or you will wither."

He watched as she hesitantly took a bite of the meat, her jaw working slowly. A subtle nod of approval, barely perceptible, passed over his features. It was a victory, a small one, but it felt like a surrender.

Later, as the feasting in the hall began to wind down, Bjorn turned his attention back to Iris, his expression shifting from that of a chieftain presiding over his clan to something far more personal, and far more sinister. He reached across the table, his hand closing not on her arm, but on her wrist. His grip was iron, inescapable, his thumb tracing a slow, possessive circle on her skin.

"You are mine now, Iris," he stated, his voice a low growl. "Every breath you take, every beat of your heart, belongs to me." He leaned closer, his breath warm against her cheek, carrying the faint, unsettling aroma of fermented berries and something wild. "And I do not share what is mine."

His words were a declaration of ownership, not of love, nor even of desire, but of raw, unadulterated dominion. He was not claiming a bride; he was asserting ownership over a conquest. A wave of cold dread washed over Iris. This was not the future she had envisioned, not the gentle affection she had longed for. This was subjugation, pure and unvarnished.

He tightened his grip slightly, and Iris flinched, a small gasp escaping her lips. Bjorn's eyes narrowed, a shadow of annoyance crossing his features. "You would do well to learn to endure," he said, his voice laced with a chilling warning. "Pain is a lesson. Fear is a teacher. And I am an excellent teacher."

He released her wrist as abruptly as he had seized it, leaving behind a faint redness and a lingering sense of violation. He rose from his seat, his imposing figure casting a long shadow across the hall. "To your chambers," he commanded, his voice resonating with an authority that brooked no argument. "And think on what I have said. Tomorrow, our true lessons will begin."

As the silent guards led her away, Iris felt a profound sense of despair settle over her. Bjorn's cruelty was not a sudden eruption, but a slow, insidious poison, seeping into every aspect of her new existence. His words were calculated, his actions designed to erode her spirit, to break her will, to make her utterly dependent on his capricious favour. She was a tribute, yes, but more than that, she was a captive being systematically dismantled, her resilience tested, and her hope slowly extinguished within the cold, unforgiving stone of his keep. The darkness that had seemed so absolute in the previous days now felt like a prelude to a far greater, more personal torment, orchestrated by the Chieftain himself.

The chill of the stone floor seeped through the thin soles of Iris's worn leather shoes, a constant, unwelcome reminder of her current station. The dawn, a hesitant smear of grey light against the narrow, barred window of her chamber, offered no solace. It merely heralded the commencement of another endless cycle of servitude. Bjorn had decreed it, his words from the previous night still echoing in the hollow chambers of her mind: "Tomorrow, our true lessons will begin." She had naively assumed these lessons would involve the intricacies of his clan, its customs, its lore. She had been a fool.

The summons came not with the clatter of armor or the heavy tread of guards, but with the quiet scraping of a bolt being drawn back. A woman, older and hard-faced, with eyes like chips of flint that mirrored Bjorn's own, stood in the doorway. Her name, Iris had learned, was Maeve, the Chieftain's house-mother, and her cruelty was a subtler, more insidious thing than Bjorn's brute force. It was a sharp, cutting instrument, wielded with practiced precision.

"Up," Maeve commanded, her voice devoid of warmth, like ice fracturing on a frozen river. "The Chieftain's keep does not sleep, and neither do its workers." She gestured with a calloused hand towards the meager pile of clothing laid out for Iris: a coarse wool tunic, patched and faded, and a roughspun skirt that promised only chafing and discomfort. "Dress. You have tasks to attend to."

Iris rose, her limbs stiff and protesting from the hard straw mattress. She dressed with a practiced, numb efficiency, the rough fabric scratching against her skin. Maeve watched her with an unnerving stillness, her gaze assessing, judgmental. It was a look that stripped away any vestige of Iris's former life, reducing her to a mere tool —an object to be used.

"Your first duty," Maeve announced as Iris stood before her, her hands clasped, awaiting instruction, "is the hearth of the Chieftain's hall. It has gone cold overnight. The fires must be rekindled, the ashes cleared. A warm hall is a happy hall, and a happy hall pleases the Chieftain."

The heart of the Chieftain's hall was a monstrous thing, a gaping maw of blackened stone that dominated one end of the vast chamber. It was as large as Iris's own former bedchamber, and the ashes accumulated within its belly were thick and heavy, mixed with the charred remnants of bone and unidentifiable debris from countless feasts. The task of clearing it was back-breaking. Iris was given a stout wooden shovel and a large basket. She dug into the cold, gritty mass, her muscles screaming in protest. The air was filled with a dry, acrid dust that caught in her throat and stung her eyes. Maeve sat on a nearby bench, her arms crossed, observing Iris's struggle with a detached air, offering no assistance, no word of encouragement.

Hours bled into one another. The grey light outside deepened into the harsh glare of midday, and still Iris toiled. Her hands, accustomed to the delicate work of embroidery and the gentle turning of pages, were raw and blistered. Her back ached with a bone-deep weariness, and her breath came in ragged gasps. She felt a constant, gnawing hunger, the meager portion of dark bread she had been given hours ago having long since vanished.

When the last of the ashes was finally cleared, and the soot-stained stones of the hearth gleamed dully in the torchlight, Iris slumped against the cold stone, her body trembling with exhaustion. Maeve approached; her expression unreadable.

"Adequate," she stated, a single word that was both damning and strangely devoid of praise. "Now, the floors. They are thick with the leavings of last night's revelry. Bones, spilled ale, scraps of meat. You will clean them. Every last morsel."

And so, Iris was set to scrubbing the flagstone floors of the Chieftain's Hall. She was given a rough cloth and a bucket of icy water. The task was as demeaning as it was physically demanding. She moved on her hands and knees, wiping away the filth, her knees protesting against the unforgiving stone. The stench of stale ale and congealed fat was overwhelming, and she fought back waves of nausea. She saw scraps of meat, still recognizable, and her stomach churned. It was a stark reminder of the opulent feast she had been forced to witness, a feast from which she had been allowed only the meagerest scraps herself.

As she worked, the warriors of the clan began to drift into the hall, their booming laughter and rough jests filling the space. They paid her little mind, or perhaps they did, their eyes lingering on her bent form with a casual, dismissive assessment. She was just part of the scenery, another piece of furniture in Bjorn's keeps, a servant to be ignored or, at best, to be ordered about. She saw the flicker of curiosity in some eyes, the predatory gleam in others, and a fresh wave of humiliation washed over her. She, Iris of Oakhaven, daughter of a chieftain, was being ogled like a common wench while scrubbing the floor.

"Mind you don't miss a spot, girl," one of the warriors sneered, his boot deliberately stamping down near her hand, smearing a fresh patch of grime. Iris flinched but said nothing, her gaze fixed on her task. To engage, to protest, would only invite further torment.

By the time the sun began its descent, painting the sky in hues of bruised purple and fiery orange, Iris's body felt like a collection of aching, protesting bones. Her fingers were numb, her back a constant throb, and her mind was a dull, weary fog. Maeve appeared again, this time with a rough, wooden bowl filled with a thin, watery stew.

"Your supper," she said, placing it on the floor a few feet away from Iris. "Eat. You will need your strength for the morrow. There are furs to be cleaned, arms to be polished, and the Chieftain's hounds to be fed and tended."

Iris's throat tightened. Furs. Hounds. These were the duties of the lowest servants, the ones who toiled in the shadows, rarely seen, their lives a constant cycle of grime and stench. She, who had once dreamed of weaving tapestries and composing songs, was now to be a cleaner of animal pelts and a feeder of beasts.

She ate the stew mechanically, its blandness a stark contrast to the richness of the food she had seen served in the hall. It was sustenance, nothing more. As she ate, she watched the flickering torchlight dance across the warriors' faces, their boisterous revelry a stark counterpoint to her own silent misery. Bjorn was not present in the hall, but his presence was everywhere, a palpable weight that settled upon her spirit. His possessiveness, his claim over her, was not confined to his private chambers; it permeated every corner of his keep, extending even to the menial tasks he forced upon her.

Later, when the hall had emptied and only the dying embers of the hearth offered a meager light, Iris was led back to her chamber. The guards who escorted her were the same silent, impassive figures who had brought her from the hall. They said nothing, their presence a constant reminder of her captivity.

Back within the confines of her small room, Iris sank onto the straw mattress, her body too exhausted to even weep. The rough wool of her tunic scratched at her skin, a constant, irritating reminder of her degradation. She looked at her hands, roughened and calloused, so different from the smooth, soft hands she remembered. Her spirit felt as battered and bruised as her flesh.

The loss of her autonomy was the most profound burden. She had no say in her tasks, no control over her time, no respite from the endless labor. The whim of Maeve and the unspoken demands of Bjorn dictated her days. Her identity, once rooted in her lineage, her education, her aspirations, was being systematically eroded, replaced by the stark reality of her servitude. She was no longer Iris, the Chieftain's daughter, the lady of Oakhaven. She was simply a servant, a drudge, a tool to be used and discarded as Bjorn saw fit.

She thought of the stories she had read as a child, tales of brave heroines and noble quests. Those were fairy tales, she now understood. The reality of her situation was far grimmer, a dark fantasy steeped in the harsh realities of power and subjugation. Bjorn's keep was not a place of adventure or romance, but a prison, and its walls were built not just of stone, but of drudgery, humiliation, and despair.

The wolf pelts on the walls seemed to mock her, their silent, predatory forms a constant reminder of the wildness that surrounded this place, and the wildness that resided within its Chieftain. She felt like a small, trapped creature, caught in the jaws of a much larger, much more dangerous predator.

As sleep finally claimed her, a fitful, exhausted oblivion, Iris could only cling to the faintest glimmer of hope: that somehow, someday, she would find a way to break free from this suffocating burden, to reclaim the person she once was, before the Chieftain's keep had claimed her soul. But as she drifted into unconsciousness, the image that lingered was not of freedom, but of the cold, hard stone of the keep, and the endless, grueling tasks that awaited her with the dawn. Her life had been reduced to a series of demeaning chores, a testament to Bjorn's cruelty and her own forced resilience. She was a servant now, and the burden of that role was heavier than any physical labor.

The coarse tunic chafed Iris's skin, a constant, low-grade torment that served as a perpetual reminder of her transformed existence. Each day was a grueling march through a landscape of menial labor and unspoken cruelty, and with each sunrise, her senses sharpened, a primal instinct for survival taking root. The Chieftain's keep, a sprawling edifice of dark stone and shadowed corners, was more than just a physical prison; it was a labyrinth of whispers and veiled threats, a place where power was wielded not just with brute force but with insidious suggestion and the chilling weight of unspoken consequences.

Her duties, though physically taxing, had inadvertently granted her a unique vantage point. As she scrubbed floors, polished weaponry, and hauled water, she became a silent observer, a shadow moving through the periphery of Bjorn's boisterous hall. The warriors, clad in furs and iron, moved with a swagger, their voices a cacophony of boasts and rough laughter. Yet, beneath the surface bravado, Iris began to detect a tremor of fear, an almost palpable deference that they directed not towards each other, but towards the absent Chieftain.

She learned to discern the subtle shifts in the atmosphere, the way conversations would abruptly cease when Bjorn's name was mentioned, the quick, sidelong glances that would dart towards the heavy oak doors of his private chambers. Even Maeve, the house-mother whose flinty gaze seemed to hold an entire universe of disdain, bore a grudging respect, laced with a distinct unease, for her Chieftain. Iris saw it in the way Maeve's back straightened ever so slightly when Bjorn entered the hall, in the measured cadence of her voice when she addressed him, a stark contrast to her usual clipped commands.

One evening, while clearing away the remnants of a feast, Iris found herself lingering near a group of Bjorn's most trusted warriors. They spoke in low, conspiratorial tones, their words a tapestry of strategy and suspicion. They spoke of border skirmishes, of rival clans encroaching upon their lands, but what truly caught Iris's attention was their hushed discussion of Bjorn's recent mood.

"He has been restless these past few nights," one warrior, a burly man named Torvin whose scarred face was a testament to countless battles, rumbled, his voice barely above a whisper. "His dreams are troubled. He speaks of shadows and ancient things stirring."

Another, younger warrior, with eyes that still held a spark of ambition, scoffed, though his bravado seemed forced. "Dreams are the folly of weak men, Torvin. Bjorn is no weakling. He will crush whatever shadows dare to dance in his sleep."

"It is not the waking world that concerns me," Torvin countered, his gaze fixed on the flickering torchlight. "It is the darkness that he carries within him. It is a hunger that cannot be sated, a power that grows with each passing moon." He lowered his voice further, leaning in. "Have you not noticed how the beasts of the forest grow wary when he passes? How the very air grows colder in his presence?"

Iris froze, her heart hammering against her ribs. She had felt it too, a subtle yet pervasive chill that seemed to emanate from Bjorn, a primal aura of danger that set her teeth on edge. She had attributed it to his sheer physical presence, his imposing stature, and the predatory gleam in his eyes. But the warriors spoke of something more, something ancient and unsettling.

As she continued her work, carefully gathering discarded platters and bone-laden trenchers, she overheard another exchange, this time between two women tasked with tending to the Chieftain's hounds. Their voices were hushed, filled with a mixture of fear and pity.

"Did you see her?" one whispered, her eyes wide. "The new captive. Bjorn keeps her in the east wing, away from the main hall. They say he… treats her poorly."

The other woman shivered, pulling her shawl tighter. "I heard the sounds last night. Screams, muffled by the stone. It is a mercy that Maeve keeps us from seeing such things. But her fate is sealed. Once Bjorn claims someone, there is no escape."

Iris's blood ran cold. She knew, with a certainty that chilled her to the bone, that they spoke of her. Though she had not yet experienced the full brunt of Bjorn's depravity, the implications of their hushed tones and the fear in their eyes painted a grim picture of what awaited her. The whispers in the halls were not just idle gossip; they were fragments of a truth too terrible to be spoken aloud, tales of Bjorn's cruelty that were passed down like dark folklore.

She became a creature of observation, her senses honed to a razor's edge. The scrape of a boot on stone, the rustle of fur, the low murmur of voices from behind closed doors – all were cataloged and analyzed. She learned to read the subtle cues: the tightening of a jaw that signaled displeasure, the averted gaze that betrayed guilt, the clench of a fist that hinted at suppressed rage. She saw how the warriors jockeyed for Bjorn's favor, their camaraderie a thin veneer over a deep-seated rivalry. She witnessed the quiet punishments meted out for perceived slights, the casual brutality that was woven into the fabric of daily life in the keep.

There was the incident with the blacksmith's apprentice, a young man named Finn who had dared to question Bjorn's command regarding the reinforcement of a gate. Bjorn had not raised his voice, had not even moved from his seat by the hearth. He had simply gestured with a flick of his wrist towards the corner of the hall, where a stout, muscular guard stood impassively. Within moments, Finn was being dragged, screaming, towards the dungeons, his pleas for mercy ignored. Iris, unseen behind a stack of furs, had watched the entire scene unfold, her stomach churning with a mixture of horror and helplessness. The other warriors had merely continued their card game, their faces impassive, as if the brutal spectacle was a common occurrence.

She began to understand that silence was her greatest shield. To speak out, to question, to even acknowledge the injustices she witnessed, was to invite the same fate upon herself. Her suffering had taught her to be invisible, to fade into the background, to observe without being seen. Her world had shrunk to the confines of her assigned tasks, but her awareness had expanded exponentially, encompassing the intricate, often brutal, power dynamics that governed Bjorn's keep.

One afternoon, while polishing a set of ceremonial axes, she overheard Bjorn himself in conversation with his most trusted advisor, a wizened man named Kael, whose eyes seemed to hold an unsettling knowledge. Bjorn's voice, usually a thunderous roar, was a low, guttural growl, laced with a cold fury.

"She is a pawn, Kael," Bjorn said, his words sharp as shards of ice. "A valuable one, perhaps, but a pawn nonetheless. Her lineage, her pride – these are simply tools I will use to bend her will. She will learn that obedience is the only currency she possesses here."

Kael's voice was a dry rustle, like leaves skittering across a barren field. "The old ways run deep, Chieftain. The spirits of this land are not easily appeased. She carries a spark of something wild within her. You must be careful not to extinguish it entirely, lest it turn against you."

Bjorn let out a harsh laugh, a sound devoid of mirth. "Let it turn. Let it rage. The fire within her will only serve to forge her into the woman I desire. She will break, Kael. They all break, eventually."

Iris's hands trembled, the polished axe slipping slightly in her grasp. The casual cruelty of Bjorn's words, the cold calculation in his voice, was more chilling than any physical threat. He saw her not as a person, but as an object to be molded, broken, and reshaped to his will. The "old ways," the "spirits of the land," the "spark within her" – Kael's words resonated with a deep, unsettling truth. There was a darkness in this keep, a primal force that seemed to seep from the very stones, and Bjorn was its embodiment.

She began to notice other things. The way the hearth fires in the great hall seemed to burn with an unnatural intensity when Bjorn was present, casting long, dancing shadows that seemed to writhe and twist like living things. The hushed prayers some servants would murmur before entering his chambers, their faces etched with a familiar dread. The unsettling stillness that would fall over the keep when a storm raged outside, a stillness that felt more like a held breath than a moment of peace.

The whispers in the halls of the Chieftain's keep were not merely sounds; they were the breath of a hidden world, a world of power, fear, and a darkness that permeated everything. And Iris, the former lady of Oakhaven, was slowly, painfully, learning to navigate its treacherous currents, her survival depending on her ability to remain silent, to observe, and to remember every hushed word, every veiled threat, every flicker of fear in the eyes of those who lived under Bjorn's shadow. Her education was not in weaving or song, but in the grim art of survival, a curriculum written in the language of fear and etched in the stone of the Chieftain's formidable keep. The lessons Bjorn had promised had indeed begun, but they were of a far more brutal and ancient nature than she could have ever imagined. They were lessons in understanding the true cost of power and the depths of human cruelty.

Chapter 3:
Nine Years of Night

The coarse tunic, a perpetual irritant against her skin, became a second hide over the years. Each day dawned with the same gray light, the same biting chill that seeped through the thick stone walls of the Chieftain's keep, and the same crushing weight of unending labor. Nine years. It had been nine years since the torchlight of Oakhaven had been extinguished, nine years since the scent of burning wood and dying hope had been the last memory of her former life. The relentless cycle of servitude had begun subtly, a slow seep of drudgery that promised merely hardship, but had, with the passage of each season, transformed into a soul-devouring chasm.

Her mornings were an assault on the senses, a cacophony of waking sounds that predated even the first hint of dawn. The clang of metal as the guards stirred, the low guttural calls of the dogs being let out into the frigid courtyard, the shuffling of feet as the other servants, gaunt and hollow-eyed, began their own weary preparations. Iris's place was in the kitchens first, the heart of the keep, a place perpetually shrouded in steam and the smell of roasting meats, of simmering broths, of the ever-present scent of woodsmoke and the fainter, more disturbing undertones of spilled blood and unwashed bodies. She learned to anticipate the needs of the cooks, the hulking, grim-faced women who wielded their knives with the same ferocity they reserved for the Chieftain's enemies. Her hands, once accustomed to the delicate touch of embroidery needles and the smooth polish of polished wood, were now raw and calloused, perpetually chapped from harsh lye soaps and the unforgiving scrape of metal on stone. Scrubbing floors until her knuckles bled, hauling buckets of water from the icy well until her shoulders screamed in protest, tending to the fires until her face felt permanently scorched these were the rhythms of her existence.

The tedium was not just physical; it was a corrosive agent that ate away at the edges of her mind. Days bled into weeks, weeks into months, and months into the unyielding expanse of years. The intricate patterns of the woven tapestries that once adorned her chambers at Oakhaven were replaced by the monotonous, repetitive strokes of her cleaning cloth against flagstone. The melodies of the bards that had once filled her father's hall were silenced, supplanted by the grunts of exertion, the sharp commands of overseers, and the ever-present murmur of the keep's dark undercurrents. She learned to exist in a state of perpetual weariness, her body a vessel for tasks, her mind a flickering ember struggling to survive the relentless wind of her circumstances.

There were no grand dramas, no sudden turning points in these years. Bjorn's cruelty was not always a thunderous roar; more often, it was a slow, suffocating embrace of neglect and demeaning labor. He rarely laid a hand on her directly, but his presence was a constant, oppressive force. His gaze, when it fell upon her, was a cold, appraising assessment, as if she were a piece of chattel to be judged for its utility. The other servants, too, offered little solace. They were a community forged in shared hardship and a pervasive fear, their interactions limited to gruff necessities and a shared understanding of the unspoken rules. To draw attention, whether positive or negative, was to invite scrutiny, and scrutiny in Bjorn's keep was a dangerous luxury.

Iris developed a keen sense of observation, not out of curiosity, but out of necessity. She learned to read the subtle shifts in the mood of the household, the way the guards' posture would stiffen when Bjorn was near, the almost imperceptible tremor in Maeve's voice when she relayed the Chieftain's directives. She saw the subtle hierarchies within the servant class, the unspoken pecking order that dictated who received the slightly less rancid scraps of food, who was tasked with the most back-breaking work. She became adept at blending into the background, a ghost in the halls, her presence marked only by the absence of any disturbance.

The relentless nature of her duties was designed to break not just the body, but the spirit. There was no room for contemplation, no quiet moments to nurture nascent hopes or to recall the vibrant tapestry of her past. If a moment of respite presented itself, it was fleeting, snatched between tasks, and often filled with the gnawing anxiety of what awaited her next. Sleep offered little true escape; her dreams were often a jumbled echo of her waking hours, filled with the endless scrubbing, the weight of impossible burdens, and the looming shadow of Bjorn's displeasure.

She remembered, with a pang that had long since dulled to a persistent ache, the feel of soft fabrics, the warmth of a fire that was not solely for cooking or heating, the taste of food that was not a mere sustenance. These memories, once sharp and vivid, had become blurred, like ancient tapestries faded by time and exposure. They were ghosts of a life she could no longer fully grasp, their edges softened by the sheer, grinding reality of her present. The hope that had once burned fiercely within her, the desperate conviction that she would one day escape, had slowly been leached away, replaced by a weary resignation. It was not a surrender, not yet, but a profound understanding of the monumental task that lay before her, a task that seemed to grow more impossible with each passing, monotonous day.

The cumulative effect of these years was a gradual erosion of her former self. The bright spark of defiance that had once flickered in her eyes was banked, hidden beneath layers of practiced impassivity. The quick wit and sharp intelligence that had once defined her were now employed solely for the purpose of anticipating the next demand, of fulfilling the task at hand with minimal fuss. Her world had shrunk to the immediate present, to the next chore, the next meal, the next sunrise that promised nothing new but more of the same.

There were moments, fleeting and sharp as shards of ice, when the sheer injustice of it all would threaten to overwhelm her. A glimpse of a bird soaring freely in the sky outside a high, barred window, the distant sound of laughter from a passing group of warriors – these would trigger a sudden, unbearable wave of longing, a raw ache for the life that had been stolen from her. But these moments were quickly suppressed. To indulge in such feelings was to invite weakness, and weakness was a luxury she could not afford. Instead, she would double her efforts, her movements becoming more frantic, her focus sharpening on the task, pushing the dangerous emotions down into the deepest recesses of her being.

The grinding routine served a specific purpose, she understood now, even if she lacked the energy to actively strategize against it. It was a method of slow attrition, designed to wear down her will, to make her forget who she was, to render her compliant, broken. It was a different kind of battle than the bloody skirmishes fought in the outer lands, but no less devastating. It was a war waged against the very essence of her being, fought with the relentless weapons of exhaustion and despair.

The years had not been marked by milestones of joy or achievement, but by the sheer, unyielding pressure of her servitude. Each sunrise was a reminder of another day to be endured, each sunset a brief respite before the cycle began anew. The once-vibrant colors of her memory had faded to muted grays and browns, reflecting the stark, unyielding landscape of her present. She was becoming a creature of the keep, her resilience forged in the crucible of endless, soul-crushing labor, her spirit a hardy, but weary, flame that flickered defiantly in the encroaching darkness. The grind was constant, unyielding, and in its sheer, monotonous persistence, it was the most potent form of her subjugation.

The thick, oppressive silence of the keep was a fragile veneer, easily shattered by the raucous laughter that often spilled from Bjorn's chambers. Iris, tasked with replenishing the embers in the hearth of the great hall, would often find herself frozen, her broom hovering over the cold ashes, as the sounds drifted down the stone corridors. It was the sound of revelry, of boisterous men and the shrill, often forced, laughter of women. These were not the women of the keep, the servants who toiled in anonymity. These were the others, brought in for Bjorn's pleasure, adorned in furs and silks that mocked the coarse wool of Iris's own attire. Each peal of laughter, each heavy thump of a goblet on wood, was a fresh stab, a reminder of her own stark isolation.

She learned to recognize the scent of them before their presence became known – a cloying mixture of expensive perfumes, wine, and the faint, musky odor of arousal. It would precede the flurry of activity, the increased demands on the kitchen staff, the hushed whispers that snaked through the servant quarters like poison ivy. Bjorn, in his grand pronouncements and his pronouncements of strength, was a man ruled by his baser instincts, and he made no effort to conceal it from those who served him. The women were paraded through the keep with a deliberate ostentation, their presence a public declaration of his virility, his power, and his utter disdain for anything resembling fidelity or respect.

There were times, when the snow lashed against the narrow windows and the wind howled like a banshee, that Iris would be summoned to serve them. Clutching a tray laden with steaming meats and overflowing goblets of mead, she would be forced to stand at the periphery of their drunken revels. Bjorn, sprawled on his furs, would often gesture to her with a careless flick of his wrist, not to offer her a drink, but to point her out, a specimen of his possession, to the women he was currently entertaining. Their eyes, often glazed with drink and a mixture of boredom and predatory curiosity, would flick over her, appraising her as they might a piece of livestock. Sometimes, a crude joke would be made, a lewd jest about her supposed subservience, her barrenness, her utter lack of any allure. And Bjorn, instead of rebuking them, would often chuckle, a harsh, grating sound that echoed the emptiness within him.

The opulent setting of the keep, with its heavy tapestries depicting scenes of brutal conquest and its carved oak furniture, served only to amplify the coldness that permeated her existence. The very stones seemed to absorb the laughter and the drunken pronouncements, trapping them in their depths, only to release them later as a suffocating reminder of her own exclusion. These women, her rivals in some abstract, torturous contest she never agreed to join, were often treated with a fleeting tenderness that Iris herself had not experienced since her capture. Bjorn would run a hand through their hair, murmur words that were undoubtedly lies, and offer them trinkets of silver and gold. These gestures, small as they were, were monumental in their contrast to the relentless, unfeeling drudgery that was Iris's daily bread.

The psychological toll was insidious. Each encounter, each forced witnessing of his indiscretions, chipped away at the remnants of her self-worth. It was not merely the act of infidelity that wounded her, but the deliberate, public nature of it. He wanted her to see. He wanted her to understand her place, to know that she was not even worthy of the pretense of affection, that her existence was merely that of a tool, a convenience, a slave whose emotional landscape was utterly irrelevant. The hollowness in her stomach was not always from hunger; it was often the gnawing emptiness left by these public humiliations.

She would retreat to the meager solitude of her sleeping alcove, the straw mattress a lumpy testament to her poverty, and try to scrub away the feeling of being soiled, not by any physical contact, but by the sheer proximity to his callousness. Her hands, rough and scarred, would clench and unclench, her jaw tight with a silent rage she dared not express. The women he brought were ephemeral, their smiles bought with coin and fleeting attention, yet their very presence was a testament to his power to command desire, a power he wielded with casual cruelty. Iris, on the other hand, was a permanent fixture, a symbol of his enduring conquest, and in that permanence, she felt a profound and crushing insignificance.

The other servants, bound by the same oppressive hierarchy, offered little comfort. They had learned to navigate Bjorn's whims by presenting a facade of utter indifference, their eyes downcast, their responses clipped and functional. To show emotion, to empathize with Iris's plight, would be to risk drawing Bjorn's ire upon themselves. They had their own small battles to fight, their own meager scraps of dignity to cling to. So, they averted their gazes, their silence a form of self-preservation that felt like a betrayal to Iris. She was alone in her torment, a solitary figure adrift in a sea of shared subjugation.

The concept of love, of affection, of partnership, had become a distant, almost mythical concept, something from the stories her mother used to tell, tales of heroes and their devoted consorts. In Bjorn's world, relationships were transactions, a display of dominance and possession. The women who shared his bed were mere acquisitions, their bodies a testament to his wealth and status. And Iris, bound by a contract of servitude that was far more binding than any wedding vow, was the ultimate possession, the one he could take for granted, the one whose feelings were of no consequence.

She would often find herself staring into the flickering flames of the hearth, the heat a welcome sensation against her chilled skin, and wonder what it was about her that rendered her so utterly invisible to him, so unworthy of even a flicker of genuine regard. Was it her silence? Her compliance? Or was it simply that he saw in her only the spoils of war, a symbol of his victory, and nothing more? The women he brought were fleeting distractions, their laughter and their perfume a temporary balm to his restless nature. But Iris was a constant, a reminder of his power, his dominance, and in that, he found a perverse satisfaction that superseded any need for tenderness or respect.

The cold, unyielding stone of the keep seemed to mirror the coldness in Bjorn's heart. It was a place of power, of conquest, of raw, brutal masculinity, and within its walls, sentimentality was a weakness to be exploited. Iris, in her quiet endurance, her silent suffering, was an unwitting testament to his strength. He would look at her, his gaze sweeping over her as she performed her duties, and see not a woman, but an object. An object that had been claimed, that served its purpose, and that was utterly, irrevocably his. The infidelity, the public displays, the casual cruelty – they were all facets of his dominion, designed to further subjugate her, to erase any lingering spark of her former self, and to leave her a hollowed-out vessel, fit only for the tasks he deemed her worthy of. Her worth, in his eyes, was measured only by her utility, her ability to serve, and her silence in the face of his transgressions. And in that bleak assessment, Iris found a new, profound layer of her despair. The infidelities were not just a betrayal of a phantom bond; they were a public decree of her worthlessness, a constant, grinding erosion of her spirit, leaving her feeling more alone and insignificant than ever before.

The chill of the stone seeped into Iris's very bones, a constant companion in the echoing halls of the keep. It was a cold that went deeper than the biting winds that swept down from the mountains, a cold that had settled within her soul, born of years spent under Bjorn's heavy hand. Her body was a tapestry woven with the threads of his cruelty, each mark a story of his dominance, a testament to the nine years of night she had endured.

Her hands, once nimble and soft, were now a roadmap of her suffering. The knuckles were perpetually raw, a testament to the times she had been struck, the impact of his fists against her skin leaving behind a throbbing ache that never truly subsided. Faint, silvery lines crisscrossed the backs of her hands, scars from where his dagger had grazed her in moments of unchecked fury, the sharp edge biting into flesh during his drunken rages. These were not the clean, surgical wounds of a skilled blade, but the ragged marks of a man who inflicted pain for the sheer, brutal pleasure of it. She would often trace them in the quiet solitude of her small sleeping alcove, the rough texture a constant, tangible reminder of his power over her. Each scar whispered a tale of a specific transgression, a moment of defiance met with swift, brutal retribution, or a perceived slight that ignited his volatile temper.

Her arms, usually covered by the rough spun wool of her tunic, bore a constellation of bruises, some faded to a sickly yellow, others still a deep, angry purple, a perpetual testament to the times he had seized her, his grip like iron bands, leaving his fingerprints etched onto her skin long after the physical pain had dulled. There were times he had dragged her, her feet scraping against the unforgiving stone floors, his impatience a tangible force that left abrasions and torn skin. These were not wounds that healed cleanly. In the harsh, unforgiving environment of the keep, with its meager provisions and lack of true cleanliness, even the simplest injury could fester, adding another layer of discomfort to her already burdened existence.

The ache in her shoulders was a dull throb that never truly ceased. Bjorn's preferred method of asserting his authority, particularly when she dared to meet his gaze for too long, was to grip her by the shoulders, his thumbs digging into her flesh with enough force to make her teeth clench and her breath hitch. He would hold her there, a prisoner in his embrace, until her muscles screamed in protest, until the fear of further violence forced her to avert her eyes, to surrender to his will. The pain was a constant, gnawing presence, a reminder that she was not her own, that her body was merely an instrument for his subjugation.

Even her legs, often unseen beneath the layers of her coarse clothing, were not spared. There were the numerous contusions, the result of kicks and shoves that sent her sprawling across the floor, her dignity as bruised as her flesh. Once, during a particularly violent episode, he had thrown a heavy goblet of mead at her, the ceramic shattering against her shin, leaving a deep gash that had taken weeks to heal and had left a permanent indentation, a tender spot that would ache with the changing weather. She learned to move with a practiced wariness, her body instinctively bracing for impact, a subtle tension that was etched into her very posture.

But the physical scars, as numerous and as painful as they were, were only a part of the torment. The true wounds, the ones that festered in the darkness of her soul, were far deeper. The constant degradation, the relentless erosion of her spirit, had begun to warp her perception of herself. She no longer recognized the woman who had once dreamed of a life beyond the village, the woman who had felt the warmth of her mother's hand, the woman who had believed in kindness. That woman felt like a phantom, a memory of a life lived by someone else.

Her spirit, once vibrant and full of a quiet resilience, had become a fragile thing, perpetually shrouded in a haze of fear and despair. The laughter of the other women, the forced gaiety that sometimes echoed from Bjorn's chambers, no longer just a reminder of her isolation, but a sound that sent shivers of dread down her spine. It was a soundtrack to her own subjugation, a mocking echo of the joy she was denied. She began to associate pleasant sounds with danger, to flinch at raised voices, to anticipate the worst in every interaction.

Her reflection in the rare polished surface of a shield, or the still water of a basin, was often a stranger. The eyes that stared back were shadowed, haunted, devoid of the spark that had once defined her. They were the eyes of a survivor, yes, but a survivor who had been irrevocably broken. The constant emotional degradation had taken its toll, chipping away at her sense of self-worth until only a hollow shell remained. She questioned her own thoughts, her own feelings, wondering if they were even her own, or merely a distorted echo of Bjorn's contempt.

She would often sit by the hearth, the flickering flames casting dancing shadows on the stone walls, and try to recall moments of happiness from her past. But the memories were like distant stars, faint and elusive, often overshadowed by the ever-present darkness of her current reality. The warmth of the fire, so welcome against her chilled skin, could not penetrate the icy grip that had taken hold of her heart. It was a peculiar kind of torment, to remember what joy felt like, only to be reminded of its utter absence in her life.

The concept of trust had become a foreign language. Bjorn's betrayal was not a singular event, but a constant, gnawing presence. Every kind word from another, every gesture of concern, was met with suspicion. Was it genuine, or a trap? Was it a fleeting moment of human connection, or a calculated move to gain her favor, only to exploit her vulnerability later? She had learned that kindness was a weakness, and vulnerability a sure path to further pain. This made forming any kind of bond with the other servants nearly impossible. They, too, lived under Bjorn's shadow, their lives a precarious balancing act of survival and self-preservation. Their averted gazes, their carefully neutral expressions, were a constant reminder of their shared fear, a fear that prevented any true solidarity.

Her own emotions became a source of confusion and shame. Anger, a natural response to injustice, was a dangerous luxury she could not afford. It would flare within her, a hot ember of defiance, only to be quickly extinguished by the cold dread of repriction. Instead, it often morphed into a dull, pervasive sadness, a weariness that settled deep within her bones. Fear was her constant companion, a coiled serpent in her gut, ready to strike at any unexpected sound or sudden movement. And joy? Joy was a distant memory, a fragile wildflower that had long since withered in the harsh landscape of her existence.

She began to see the world through a lens of perpetual gloom. The vibrant colors of the tapestries seemed muted, the grandeur of the keep an oppressive weight rather than a display of power. Even the changing seasons offered little respite. The harsh bite of winter mirrored the coldness within her, and the fleeting warmth of summer brought only a painful reminder of the life she was missing, the freedom she was denied. The world outside the keep's walls, a world she once yearned to explore, now seemed as alien and as unattainable as the stars.

Bjorn's abuse had achieved a terrible, insidious victory: it had begun to convince her that she deserved it. The constant barrage of his disdain, his casual cruelty, had seeped into her subconscious, eroding her belief in her own inherent worth. She would replay his words in her mind, searching for the fault in herself, the reason for his wrath. It was a futile exercise, born of desperation, a desperate attempt to find logic in the illogical, to impose order on the chaos of his violence. This internal dialogue was a torment all its own, a self-inflicted wound that ran deeper than any he had inflicted.

The physical pain, at least, was straightforward. It was a tangible consequence, a direct result of his actions. But the emotional scarring was a far more complex and devastating wound. It was the quiet erosion of her spirit, the slow, agonizing disintegration of her sense of self. The laughter of the women, the clinking of goblets, the heavy tread of Bjorn's boots on the stone – these were all sounds that had become associated with her suffering. They were the background noise of her imprisonment, the soundtrack to her ongoing torment.

She would find herself staring into the hearth for hours, her mind a battlefield of fragmented memories and suffocating anxieties. The heat of the flames was a comfort, a small solace in the vast emptiness of her life. But even that comfort was fleeting, a temporary reprieve before the crushing weight of her reality returned. The scars on her body were a visible testament to Bjorn's brutality, but the scars on her soul were invisible, deeper, and far more profound. They were the wounds of a spirit that had been battered and bruised, a soul that had been stripped bare, and in the nine years of night, Iris was slowly, agonizingly, learning to live with them, forever marked by the darkness that had consumed her. The reflection she saw was not of a woman, but of a ghost, haunted by the specter of Bjorn and the lingering echoes of his cruelty.

The relentless cycle of Bjorn's dominion had, for nine long years, sought to extinguish every member of Iris's former self. Yet, deep within the shadowed recesses of her spirit, a faint, almost imperceptible warmth persisted. It was a warmth born not of hope, for hope had long since been a casualty of her despair, but of an instinct as primal as breathing – the instinct to resist. These acts of defiance were not grand gestures, nor were they born of a belief in victory. They were the subtle, almost unconscious reactions of a spirit that refused to be entirely subsumed. They were flickers, quickly extinguished, but flickers nonetheless.

One such flicker manifested in the quiet tending of her meager garden patch, a small, sun-starved rectangle of earth behind the servant's quarters. Bjorn, in his capricious cruelty, had allowed her this small task, perhaps as a further means of humiliation, to demonstrate that even her most basic endeavors were subject to his whim. He decreed what could be planted, when it could be watered, and when it could be harvested. He relished watching her stoop to the earth, her hands, once accustomed to the delicate art of embroidery, now stained with soil. But within the rigid confines of his rules, Iris found a sliver of autonomy. When the overseer was not looking, she would sometimes plant a single, forbidden wildflower – a vibrant bluebell, a hardy daisy – amongst the gruel-giving roots and bitter greens. These were seeds pilfered from the pockets of passing merchants, or gleaned from the hedgerows on the rare occasions she was sent on errands. They were tiny acts of rebellion, yielding no practical benefit, offering no tactical advantage. They were simply a defiance of the prescribed order, a silent declaration that her eyes still saw beauty beyond the grey palette of her existence. Bjorn, when he discovered them, would often rip them out with a sneer, his boot grinding them into the mud. Yet, the act of planting them, of coaxing life from the soil with a secret knowledge of its potential for color and joy, was an act that belonged solely to her. It was a fleeting whisper of her own will, a refusal to let his decree dictate the entirety of her world, however small and insignificant the canvas.

Another flicker would ignite in the hushed moments before dawn. While the other servants slept, their bodies exhausted by the day's labor and their minds dulled by fear, Iris would sometimes steal away to the old, disused chapel at the edge of the keep's grounds. The roof was partially collapsed, the stained-glass windows were shattered, and the air within was thick with the scent of decay and damp earth. It was a place of forgotten rituals and abandoned faith, a place where Bjorn's oppressive presence did not quite reach. Here, in the semi-darkness, with the first slivers of light attempting to penetrate the gloom, Iris would sometimes hum. Not songs of joy, for those were too painful to recall, but fragments of old lullabies her mother had sung, or the mournful melodies of the village folk. The sounds were barely audible, a soft murmur against the stones. It was an assertion of her own voice, a refusal to let silence become the sole occupant of her being. Bjorn detested any hint of sentimentality, any expression of inner life that was not directly tied to his service. He had forbidden singing, had banned any display of emotion that was not sorrow or fear. But in the anonymity of the ruined chapel, her voice, however fragile, was her own. Sometimes, a passing guard, his footsteps echoing on the flagstones, would hear the faint sound, and his approach would send Iris scrambling back to her duties, her heart pounding like a trapped bird. The momentary freedom of song, the brief reclaiming of her own melody, was swiftly replaced by the familiar surge of dread. Yet, the act of singing, however ephemeral, had occurred. The sound had been made.

Even in the mundane tasks of the keep, subtle resistances would emerge. When forced to polish Bjorn's armor, a duty she loathed with a visceral intensity, Iris would sometimes, when she believed herself unobserved, meticulously trace the patterns of the engravings on his breastplate. These were not gestures of admiration, but of intimate acquaintance. She would study the intricate lines of the mythical beasts, the sharp edges of the war banners, committing them to memory with a detached curiosity. It was an act of dissecting his power, of understanding the symbols he held so dear, not to appease him, but to demystify him. In this quiet observation, she was not merely a servant polishing metal; she was a scholar of his vanity, a collector of the iconography of his tyranny. She would recall the texture of the metal under her cloth, the precise angle of a dragon's scale, the way the light caught the edge of a sculpted sword. This meticulous examination was a form of intellectual defiance, a refusal to be merely a passive observer of his grandeur. It was her way of asserting that her mind was not enslaved, even if her body was. When Bjorn himself would occasionally inspect her work, his shadow falling over her as she knelt, her focus would immediately shift to the task, her hands moving with a feverish efficiency, her face a mask of subservience. But the images, the details, were already cataloged, stored away in the silent archives of her mind, a small collection of knowledge that was entirely her own.

There were also the stolen moments of connection, however fleeting and fraught with peril. The other servants, bound by a shared fear and a deep-seated mistrust, rarely spoke of anything beyond the immediate demands of their labor. Their eyes, when they met Iris's, were usually averted, their faces carefully blank. But sometimes, a shared glance would linger a fraction too long, a subtle tightening of a jaw, a nearly imperceptible nod. These were not expressions of solidarity, but of a shared understanding of their mutual plight. Once, a younger kitchen girl, Elara, her hands perpetually chapped and red from scrubbing pots, had dropped a tray of pastries meant for Bjorn's table. The clatter of the crockery and the scattering of the sweet cakes had sent a wave of panic through the servants. Bjorn's roar of displeasure was immediate. While others froze, Iris, with a speed that surprised even herself, had swiftly gathered the fallen items, murmuring reassurances to Elara, her voice low and steady. She took the brunt of the verbal abuse that followed, her own body instinctively shielding the terrified girl. Later, when Bjorn had stormed away, Elara had pressed a bruised apple into Iris's hand, her eyes filled with a gratitude that was both profound and dangerous. It was a small act of kindness, a silent acknowledgment of shared humanity in a place designed to strip it away. This, too, was a flicker – a testament to the fact that even in the harshest environments, the capacity for compassion, for empathy, could survive. It was a dangerous act, for Bjorn punished any perceived alliance between his servants with particular relish. But the warmth of the apple in her palm, the silent language of Elara's eyes, was a brief, precious respite from the suffocating isolation.

These flickers of defiance were not acts of rebellion in the conventional sense. They were not attempts to overthrow Bjorn, nor were they fueled by any belief that such an outcome was possible. Instead, they were the quiet, desperate assertions of an individual spirit that refused to be wholly extinguished. They were the tiny, almost invisible threads that Iris wove into the fabric of her subjugated existence, threads of color and sound and knowledge that Bjorn could not entirely unravel. Each wildflower planted, each whispered lullaby, each meticulously observed detail, each act of shared humanity, was a testament to the resilience of the human will. They were the small, persistent reminders to herself that even in the deepest night, a spark could still endure, buried perhaps, but not entirely gone. It was in these hidden acts, these secret affirmations of self, that the possibility of transformation lay dormant, waiting for the right moment to ignite. The internal struggle was paramount; it was a silent war waged within the confines of her own being, a war where even the smallest victory was a profound assertion of existence. Bjorn's cruelty aimed to break her mind, to shatter her sense of self, but these flickers, however faint, were the cracks in his armor, the proof that his dominion was not absolute. They were the quiet whispers of a soul that, though deeply wounded, was not yet dead.

The dust motes danced in the meager shafts of light that dared to pierce the perpetual gloom of Bjorn's keep, each one a tiny, indifferent world in motion. For Iris, these suspended particles were not merely atmospheric phenomena; they were a constant, almost suffocating reminder of the relentless passage of time, and with it, the ever-deepening chasm between the life she now endured and the life she had once known. Nine years. Nine years of nights that bled into days, each indistinguishable from the last in its oppressive monotony, each marked by the gnawing emptiness that Bjorn's tyranny had carved into her soul. Yet, within this barren landscape of her existence, certain memories, like stubborn wildflowers in a scorched field, refused to wither and die. They were the most dangerous of possessions, these memories, for they were the only vestiges of a self that Bjorn had tried so assiduously to obliterate.

The face of Julius. It was the first to surface, always. Not the Julius of grand pronouncements or heroic deeds, but the Julius who would steal away with her to the whispering woods on the edge of their village, his hand warm and calloused in hers. She remembered the scent of pine needles crushed beneath their boots, the dappled sunlight filtering through the dense canopy, painting ephemeral patterns on his earnest features. He had spoken of dreams then, of a future bright with promise, of a life built on mutual respect and shared laughter, a life a thousand leagues removed from the brutal reality of her present servitude. He had described their home, a small cottage with a thatched roof, a garden overflowing with herbs and climbing roses, a hearth that always held the comforting glow of a fire. He had even sketched it for her, not with ink and parchment, but with words, each syllable a brushstroke painting an image so vivid, so tangible, that she could almost feel the rough-hewn wood of the doorframe beneath her fingertips.

These recollections were not gentle whispers; they were often violent intrusions, tearing through the carefully constructed walls she erected around her heart. The stark contrast between the sun-drenched innocence of those stolen moments and the perpetual shadow of the keep was a wound that never truly healed. She would find herself in the scullery, her hands raw from scrubbing, her back aching from the unremitting labor, and suddenly, she would be there again, under the rustling leaves, listening to Julius's quiet assurances. The sweetness of his voice, the unwavering belief in his eyes, would flood her senses, only to be brutally extinguished by the clang of a pot, the bark of an overseer, or the chilling echo of Bjorn's distant laughter. The bitterness that would rise in her throat then was almost as potent as the taste of the bitter greens she was forced to cultivate. It was the taste of what had been stolen, of what had been irrevocably lost.

He had promised her a life where her hands, now rough and chapped, would be free to pursue her embroidery, to create beauty from silk and thread. She remembered the intricate patterns she had once woven, the vibrant hues of indigo and crimson, the delicate depiction of birds in flight and blooming flowers. Julius had admired her work, had often held her creations with a reverence that made her blush, calling them "tapestries of the soul." Now, her fingers were stained with grime, her nails broken, her skin scarred by the harsh detergents and rough fabrics she was forced to handle. The memory of the silken threads, so smooth and yielding, felt like a phantom caress, a cruel mockery of her present existence. The contrast was a constant, searing pain, a testament to the life Bjorn had stolen not just from her, but from the very essence of who she was.

And the music. Oh, the music. Before the nine years of night, music had been the very air she breathed. Her mother's voice, a clear, bell-like soprano, had filled their small home with melodies that spoke of joy, of sorrow, of the ancient rhythms of the earth. She remembered dancing in the village square, her feet light, her heart soaring, Julis's strong hand guiding her. She remembered the joyous clamor of festivals, the mournful refrains sung at wakes, the simple, heartfelt ballads that wove the community together. Now, any hint of song was swiftly and brutally suppressed. Bjorn abhorred any expression of unbridled emotion, any sound that was not an echo of his own commands or the cowering whimpers of his subjects. Yet, in the deepest hours of the night, when the keep was shrouded in a silence so profound it felt like a physical weight, Iris would sometimes recall a particular melody. It was a lullaby her mother had sung, a gentle, flowing tune that spoke of starlight and moonbeams and the quiet peace of sleep. As she lay on her straw pallet, the cold seeping into her bones, she would hum it under her breath, a sound so faint it was barely audible even to herself. This forbidden music, this echo of a happier time, was a double-edged sword. It brought a fleeting, ethereal comfort, a momentary respite from the crushing despair, but it also served as a stark reminder of the silence that now reigned, a silence imposed by fear and brutality. The memory of her mother's voice, once a source of solace, now became a haunting lament for all that had been lost.

The dreams she had shared with Julius felt like fragile, iridescent bubbles, born of pure, unadulterated hope. They had spoken of a small family, of children with his kind eyes and her inquisitive spirit, of quiet evenings by the fire, of a life lived in gentle rhythm with the seasons. They had envisioned a world where their love was a sanctuary, a bulwark against the harshness of the outside. Now, those dreams lay shattered, scattered like broken glass across the cold, unforgiving flagstones of her reality. The image of a future filled with warmth and light had been replaced by the stark, unyielding contours of Bjorn's fortress, a monument to his power and her subjugation. The laughter of children, a sound she had once longed to hear, was now a distant, almost alien concept. The silence of her sterile existence was broken only by the sounds of servitude and the ever-present threat of violence.

These memories, so precious and so painful, became her secret hoard, her hidden treasure. She would revisit them in the stolen moments, in the quiet pauses between the endless tasks, in the darkness of her cell-like room. She would replay Julius's words, the cadence of his voice, the warmth of his touch, the earnestness of his gaze. She would trace the lines of the imaginary cottage, the blooming roses, the flickering hearth. She would hum the forbidden lullabies, her voice a thread of defiance woven into the fabric of her despair. These were not conscious acts of remembrance; they were the desperate, instinctive acts of a soul fighting for survival. They were the embers of her former self, carefully fanned in the hidden corners of her mind, lest they be entirely extinguished by the suffocating darkness.

But with each recollection, a new layer of bitterness began to form. The sweetness of the memories was irrevocably tainted by the grim reality of their absence. The stark contrast between the life she had been promised and the life she was forced to live fueled a slow, smoldering anger. It was not the fiery rage of rebellion, for such an emotion was too dangerous, too exhausting. It was a cold, calcifying resentment, a hardening of her spirit that began to gnaw at the edges of her former gentleness. The memory of Julius's love, once a beacon, now served to highlight the profound loneliness that had become her constant companion. The idealized vision of their future, once a source of comfort, now served as a sharp reminder of the vast, unbridgeable gulf between what could have been and what was.

She began to see the world through a different lens, one tinged with the stark hues of her loss. The kindnesses of the other servants, once a source of fragile hope, now seemed fleeting and ultimately futile. How could a bruised apple, a whispered word of encouragement, truly matter when weighed against the enormity of their collective suffering? Even her own small acts of defiance, the planting of forbidden flowers, the humming of silent songs, felt increasingly hollow. They were temporary reprieves, momentary assertions of self that were quickly swallowed by the relentless tide of Bjorn's control. The seeds of bitterness, once sown, began to sprout, their roots digging deeper into the barren soil of her heart.

The idealized memories of Julius and their shared dreams, once a source of comfort, were now becoming a heavy burden. They were too bright, too beautiful to exist in the grim reality of her present. They served not to sustain her, but to accentuate her desolation. The ghost of what might have been haunted her waking hours, a constant, gnawing ache that no amount of physical hardship could truly compare to. The dreams of a life filled with love and light were now twisted into spectral visions of what had been snatched away, each vivid detail a fresh stab of grief. This internal landscape, once a refuge, was becoming a battlefield, where the specter of happiness warred with the suffocating reality of her present. The weight of these memories, far from being a source of strength, was beginning to crush her, an ever-increasing burden that threatened to extinguish even the faintest flicker of her former spirit. The past, once a sanctuary, was transforming into a prison of its own making, its gilded bars forged from the very dreams she had once cherished.

Chapter 4:
The Tenth Anniversary

The tenth anniversary of Bjorn's ascension was not merely a date on a calendar; it was a fulcrum upon which the brittle balance of his reign teetered. It was a declaration, etched in stone and gilded with the blood of his vanquished rivals, that he was not a transient conqueror, but an enduring sovereign. The preparations, therefore, were not born of joy, but of a chillingly calculated need to project an image of unshakable power and prosperity. The keep, a monolithic entity of dark stone that seemed to bleed into the perpetually bruised sky, underwent a grotesque transformation. Its grim ramparts, usually adorned with the tattered banners of subjugation, were draped in rich, heavy velvets of crimson and obsidian. This stark, funereal splendor whispered of death even as it proclaimed dominion. Torches, generally reserved for the bleakest of nights, were ignited in their hundreds, their flames casting flickering, monstrous shadows that danced with a life of their own against the cold stone, transforming familiar corridors into labyrinthine passages of dread.

For Iris, this enforced gaiety was a fresh torment, a perverse continuation of the agony that had become her daily bread. Her days, already a relentless cycle of brutal labour, became an even more demanding choreography of servitude, orchestrated by the sneering overseers who now patrolled the halls with an even greater sense of self-importance. She, along with the other servants, was a mere cog in the vast, intricate machinery of this macabre celebration. Her hands, perpetually chapped and aching, were now tasked with tasks that mocked her former life with an exquisite cruelty. She was ordered to polish the silver until it gleamed with a blinding intensity, each buffing stroke a painful reminder of the delicate artistry she had once practiced. The intricate carvings on the candelabra, meant to depict scenes of Bjorn's supposed triumphs, were cleaned with painstaking diligence, her fingers tracing over the stylized depictions of vanquished foes, her mind a silent, screaming witness to the perversion of history.

The grand hall, the very heart of Bjorn's dominion, became the focal point of this forced magnificence. Banners, woven with gold thread that seemed to mock the poverty of the land, depicting the snarling wolf crest of Bjorn's lineage, were hung from the vaulted ceilings. Long, heavy tables, usually reserved for the sparse, utilitarian meals of the garrison, were draped with the finest linens, embroidered with such intricate detail that they appeared to be woven from moonlight and shadow. The air, usually heavy with the scent of damp stone and stale sweat, was now thick with the cloying perfume of exotic flowers, their vibrant hues a jarring contrast to the keep's perpetual gloom, their potent fragrance failing to mask the underlying scent of fear. These blooms, brought from distant, sun-drenched lands by merchant ships that paid heavy tolls to Bjorn's coffers, were arranged in colossal vases, their beauty a stark testament to the wealth extracted from the suffering of countless souls.

Iris found herself tasked with the meticulous arrangement of these floral tributes. Her fingers, clumsy and raw, struggled to coax the wilting petals into place, each movement a silent prayer for them to wither and fade, to mirror the dying hope within her. The overseer, a burly man named Grigor with eyes as cold and hard as the iron he usually hammered, watched her every move, his heavy boots echoing on the flagstones like the approach of doom. "Faster, wretch!" he would bark, his voice a grating sound that scraped against her raw nerves. "Do you wish to be a decoration on the feast table yourself?" His words, laced with the ever-present threat of violence, spurred her on, her movements becoming more frantic, more desperate. She felt like a trapped bird, forced to decorate its own cage.

The kitchens, usually a cacophony of clanging pots and hurried shouts, were transformed into a hive of frantic, almost feverish activity. The air was heavy with the aroma of roasting meats – boar, venison, and fowl, all destined for the gullets of Bjorn's sycophants. Spices, rare and expensive, were ground with a ferocity that spoke of the desperation to impress. Sweets, elaborate and rich, were being molded and glazed, their sugary surfaces glinting under the harsh light of the torches. Iris, along with a dozen other women, was assigned the task of preparing the smaller delicacies: candied fruits, honeyed nuts, and delicate pastries that would be offered as tantalizing morsels. It was a task that required precision, a steady hand, a delicate touch, all qualities that Bjorn's reign had systematically stripped from her.

As she worked, her mind would often drift, her gaze falling upon the intricate patterns of the pastry dough. She remembered, with a pang that was both physical and spiritual, the way her own hands, before this nightmare, had once moved with effortless grace, shaping dough into delicate flowers and playful animals for the village festivals. Her mother, a woman whose touch was as light as a summer breeze, had taught her these skills, her laughter a constant melody in their humble cottage. Now, her hands were rough, her nails broken and stained, incapable of such delicate work. The fine flour that dusted her apron was a cruel imitation of the soft, silken texture she remembered.

The wine, a dark, potent vintage that flowed freely for Bjorn's guests, was decanted in cavernous cellars, the air thick with the musty scent of age and fermentation. Iris found herself tasked with ensuring each goblet, crafted from thick, hand-blown glass, was spotlessly clean. She would hold each one up to the flickering torchlight, scrutinizing it for any blemish, any trace of the grime that clung to her own existence. The liquid, dark as a shadowed

forest, represented everything that was denied to the likes of her –
warmth, celebration, forgetfulness. It was a liquid of power, a
lubricant for alliances and a balm for weary consciences, and its
very presence in the keep was a constant, bitter reminder of her
own parched existence.

The music, too, was a significant element of the forced
revelry. Bjorn, a man who abhorred any expression of genuine
emotion, had nonetheless commissioned a troupe of musicians.
Their instruments, finely crafted lutes, harps, and violins, were
polished to a high sheen, ready to fill the oppressive silence of the
hall with a semblance of merriment. The melodies they were
expected to play were not the joyous, unrestrained folk tunes of
the villages, but rather stately, formal pieces designed to impress
and intimidate. Iris, while arranging decorative silks along the
walls, would sometimes catch a snatch of their practice, the notes
sharp and precise, lacking the soul and warmth she associated with
actual music. It was a sound designed to lull, not to stir.

Amidst the flurry of activity, whispers circulated amongst the
servants, hushed tones of apprehension and reluctant excitement.
The lords and ladies from neighboring territories, many of them
rivals brought low by Bjorn's machinations, were expected to
attend. Their presence was a testament to his dominance, a public
acknowledgement of his iron grip. Each arrival would be a
carefully orchestrated spectacle, a parade of bowing heads and
forced smiles, all converging upon Bjorn, the wolf at the apex of
the blood-soaked pyramid. The air thrummed with an unspoken
tension, a collective holding of breath, as if the very stones of the
keep anticipated the volatile atmosphere that would soon fill its
halls.

The servants were instructed on their roles with a
meticulousness that bordered on obsessive. They were to be
invisible, yet ever-present, anticipating every need, fulfilling
every unspoken command. They were to maintain an expression

of humble servitude, their faces devoid of any emotion that might betray the fear or resentment simmering beneath the surface. Any deviation, any misplaced glance, any stumble, would be met with swift and brutal punishment. Iris felt a knot of dread tighten in her stomach with each passing hour. This was not a celebration; it was a demonstration of power, a charade designed to solidify Bjorn's authority, and she, like all the others, was a pawn in his grand, cruel game. The opulence was not a sign of prosperity, but a gilded cage, its bars forged from fear and decorated with the stolen wealth of a broken land. The beauty of the flowers was a lie, their fragrance a deceptive cloak for the stench of despair that permeated the very stones of the keep. And she, Iris, once a weaver of dreams, was now tasked with tending to the thorns of Bjorn's reign, her every action a silent, agonizing capitulation. The tenth anniversary was not a milestone of celebration, but a grim marker of her continued subjugation, a testament to the suffocating darkness that had claimed her life.

The heavy oak doors of the keep, their iron studs glinting like malevolent eyes in the torchlight, groaned open, admitting a figure who, to Iris, was more specter than man. Bernard. The name itself was a phantom that haunted her waking hours, a venomous whisper in the quiet of her despair. He stood silhouetted against the muted grey of the autumn sky, a man etched with the harsh lines of time and, she suspected, something far more corrosive. His cloak, a serviceable but unremarkable wool, was dusted with the remnants of travel, a stark contrast to the opulent silks and velvets that now adorned the keep's interior. Yet, it was not his attire that struck her, but the subtle shift in his bearing, the way he held himself as if bracing for an invisible blow.

Iris, her hands still faintly stained with the dark dye of the ornamental banners she'd been forced to help prepare, froze amidst the throng of servants hurrying about their tasks. Her breath hitched, a ragged, involuntary sound that was quickly swallowed by the clamor of preparation. Her gaze was locked onto him, a morbid fascination holding her captive. This was the man who had once smelled of sawdust and pipe tobacco, who had taught her the names of the stars and the proper way to mend a torn seam. This was her father, the man who had bartered her innocence, her freedom, her very soul for… what? A fleeting promise? A comfortable lie? The question had gnawed at her for years, a festering wound that refused to heal.

His eyes, when they finally found her, were a source of immediate, suffocating pain. They were the same shade of faded blue as hers, but dulled, clouded with a weariness that went beyond mere physical exhaustion. There was a flicker of something there – recognition, perhaps, or a shadow of regret – but it was swiftly extinguished, replaced by a practiced blankness. He offered no sign, no overt gesture of greeting, as if acknowledging her publicly would be an act of reckless endangerment. Instead, his gaze slid away, sweeping past her as if she were just another shadow flitting in the periphery.

A bitter laugh, silent and internal, threatened to bubble up within her. He had always been a man of caution, a man who navigated the treacherous currents of life with a careful, almost fearful, precision. But this… this was a new level of self-preservation. He had come for the tenth anniversary, for Bjorn's grand spectacle, and in doing so, he had cemented his complicity. He was not merely an observer; he was a participant, a testament to Bjorn's reach, a living embodiment of the pact that had bound Iris to this gilded prison.

As Bernard was escorted deeper into the keep by a burly guard, his shoulders stooped slightly, a posture that spoke volumes about his station, or lack thereof, in Bjorn's court. He was not a guest of honour. He was a supplicant, a shadow granted permission to tread the hallowed ground of his daughter's torment. Iris watched him go, the heavy tread of his boots on the flagstones echoing the hollowness that had taken root in her own chest. He was a living monument to her shattered past, a painful reminder of the love that had curdled into betrayal.

The proximity of her father, a man she had once idolised, was a more potent poison than any of Bjorn's threats. It was a visceral agony, a physical manifestation of her deepest fears. She had always harboured a desperate, illogical hope that her father had been deceived, that he had acted out of ignorance or under duress. But his presence here, at this celebration of Bjorn's brutality, in this subservient posture, shattered that fragile illusion. He knew. He understood. And he had chosen to align himself with the architect of her misery.

She felt a primal urge to flee, to lose herself in the labyrinthine passages of the keep, to become one with the shadows she so often inhabited. But her feet remained rooted to the spot, her body betraying her will. She was a moth drawn to a flame, compelled to witness the unfolding tragedy, even as it consumed her. The air grew thick with unspoken accusations, a palpable tension radiating from her very being. Every breath she took felt heavy, laden with the weight of years of unspoken grief and burning resentment.

The servants around her continued their frantic preparations, oblivious to the silent drama unfolding at the edge of their awareness. Their world was one of immediate tasks, of appeasing their superiors, of surviving another day. Iris, however, was trapped in a moment that stretched and warped, time itself seemingly bending to the gravity of her father's return. She saw him again, not as the man who had walked through the doors, but as the man who had stood on their doorstep, his face a mask of forced stoicism, handing her over like chattel. The memory, always a sharp shard in her consciousness, now felt like a gaping wound, fresh and bleeding.

His subservience was almost palpable. He moved with a careful deference, his eyes rarely meeting the gaze of those in Bjorn's employ. There was no arrogance, no pride in his bearing. He was a man diminished, stripped of whatever agency he might have once possessed. It was a sight that should have brought some twisted sense of satisfaction, a vindication of her pain. Instead, it was merely a confirmation of the pervasive rot that Bjorn's reign had sown. Even men like her father, men who had once held a semblance of pride, were reduced to this.

A wave of nausea washed over her. She squeezed her eyes shut, trying to banish his image, but it was futile. His presence was a brand seared into her memory. She could feel the phantom weight of his hand on her shoulder, the sound of his voice – or rather, the absence of it, the deafening silence where words of comfort should have been. The anniversary was meant to celebrate Bjorn's power. Still, for Iris, it had become a grim commemoration of her own utter desolation, amplified tenfold by the chilling return of the man who had set her on this path. The air, once merely thick with the cloying perfume of exotic flowers and the metallic tang of fear, now carried a new, unbearable scent: the bitter aroma of her father's betrayal, a smell that clung to her like a shroud. She wondered, with a despair that chilled her to the bone, if he saw the same despair reflected in her eyes, and if, in the deepest recesses of his heart, he felt even a fraction of the pain he had inflicted. But the cold, practiced neutrality of his gaze offered no such comfort. He was here, a ghost from her past, a silent accuser, and a stark reminder that her suffering was a legacy he had willingly embraced. The weight of his presence was a physical burden, pressing down on her chest, making each breath a conscious, agonizing effort. He was not simply a visitor; he was a living embodiment of the compromise that had damned her. The forced gaiety of the anniversary, the opulent decorations, the feigned merriment – all of it felt like a mockery, a grotesque pantomime played out on the stage of her ruined life. And at the center of it all, a silent, spectral figure stood her father, Bernard, a testament to the darkness that had consumed them both.

The murmuring crowd, a tapestry woven from silks and furs, hushed as Bjorn entered the great hall. His presence was not merely an arrival; it was an event, a gravitational pull that drew every eye, every breath. Iris, positioned near the shadowed alcove where she had retreated after her father's disquieting appearance, felt the familiar prickle of dread. Bjorn's gaze, sharp and predatory, swept across the assembled guests, a subtle acknowledgement of their fleeting loyalty before settling on her. It was a look that could flay skin from bone, a possessive stare that branded her as his, eternally. Tonight, the tenth anniversary of his ascension, was to be a testament to his absolute dominion, and Iris understood, with a cold certainty that settled deep within her marrow, that she was to be the centerpiece of his grim pronouncement.

He moved with a languid grace that belied the iron will beneath, a predator surveying his domain. His laughter, when it finally broke the strained silence, was a deep, resonant sound that echoed the hollowness of the celebrations. It was a laughter that promised no mirth, only the chilling anticipation of a coming storm. He circled her slowly, the rustle of his velvet doublet a whisper against the tense quiet. His eyes, the color of a winter sky before a blizzard, held no warmth, only a chilling amusement. He paused before her, close enough that she could feel the heat radiating from his skin, a stark contrast to the icy dread that encased her.

"My dear Iris," he purred, his voice a silken caress that sent shivers down her spine. The endearment, so utterly devoid of genuine affection, was a mockery. "You have graced my celebration with your presence, as you always do." His words were punctuated by a slow, deliberate blink, as if the act of acknowledging her required immense effort. "Ten years. A decade since I took this fortress, and a decade since you… became mine." The emphasis on 'mine' was a possessive claim, a declaration that echoed the chains that bound her.

He circled her once more, his shadow engulfing her. The scent of expensive spices and something darker, something akin to old blood and forgotten rituals, clung to him. He leaned in, his voice dropping to a conspiratorial whisper, though it was clearly audible to those nearest. "Many have questioned my judgment, my methods. They have whispered of my… acquisitions." A cruel smile played on his lips. "But I say to you, the greatest prize, the most enduring testament to my power, is not this keep, not these lands, but you. A queen in name, a captive in spirit."

Iris's breath caught in her throat. She knew what was coming. Some new cruelty had always marked the anniversary, some fresh humiliation designed to solidify his control. But this felt different. This felt like a culmination, a final pronouncement of her fate. His fingers, long and unnaturally pale, brushed against her cheek, a touch that felt less like a caress and more like a brand. She flinched involuntarily, a tiny movement that did not escape his notice.

"Ah, still so spirited," he mused, his thumb tracing the curve of her jawline. "A shame to break such a beautiful, defiant thing. But then, that is half the pleasure, is it not?" He straightened, his eyes glittering with an almost manic intensity. "Tonight, we celebrate my reign. And what better way to ensure its legacy than to forge a new bond, a bond that will tie you even closer to my bloodline, to my future?"

A collective intake of breath rippled through the hall. Bjorn's pronouncements were rarely mundane. His decrees were etched in stone, his pronouncements carried the weight of death. The anticipation in the air was thick, a palpable entity that pressed down on Iris, stealing her breath. Her father, Bernard, stood among the other onlookers, his face a mask of grim resignation. His presence was a constant, agonizing reminder of the man who had delivered her into this gilded cage. He was a silent witness to her ongoing torment, a living embodiment of her father's failed promises.

Bjorn's gaze, now fixed on the assembled lords and ladies, grew colder, more commanding. He relished the fear, the deference he inspired. "For ten years, Iris has been the jewel in my crown. A symbol of my victory. But a jewel, however precious, remains... separate. Tonight, that changes." He gestured towards the towering fireplace, where the flames danced with an almost sentient fury. "The celebrations are grand; the feasting will be lavish. But the true commemoration, the decree that will echo through the ages, is this: Iris is to be wed."

The announcement landed like a thunderclap. Murmurs erupted, quickly silenced by Bjorn's sharp glance. Iris felt a dizzying wave of nausea. Wed? To whom? She looked to her father, but his eyes were cast down, unable to meet her desperate plea. Then Bjorn's gaze returned to her, and the answer, in all its horrifying glory, dawned on her. He wasn't offering her a husband from a neighboring court, not a political alliance. He was offering her to himself, in a manner more profound, more binding than any ceremony had yet achieved.

He smiled, a slow, unsettling revelation of teeth. "You are my prize, Iris. And a prize is meant to be... claimed. Fully and irrevocably." His eyes raked over her, a possessive, devouring gaze that left her feeling stripped bare. "You have been my captive, my pet, my symbol. Tonight, you become my wife. A wife in truth, bound to me not just by conquest, but by sacred vow. A vow that will ensure no man, no god, no fate can ever pry you from my grasp."

The silence that followed was deafening, broken only by the crackling of the fire and the frantic thumping of Iris's own heart. This was not a marriage; it was an execution of her spirit. It was Bjorn's ultimate act of dominance, a decree that erased any semblance of her former life, any hope of escape. He was not simply claiming her as property; he was absorbing her, making her an indelible part of his dark legacy. He reveled in her despair, in the dawning horror that painted her face. His power was absolute, his cruelty boundless. He had taken everything from her, and now, he was taking her very name, her very future, to be etched into his own insatiable ambition. The cheers that began to rise from the assembled crowd sounded like the cawing of carrion birds, celebrating the final consumption of a soul. Iris stood frozen, a sacrificial lamb before the altar of Bjorn's insatiable ego, the dark decree sealing her fate with an unshakeable finality.

The air in the great hall grew thick with an unspeakable tension, a tangible shroud woven from the fear of those present and the predatory glee of the man at its center. Bjorn's announcement that Iris was to become his wife sent a tremor through the gathered nobility, a ripple of shock that quickly settled into a dreadful understanding of his absolute power. But the vows, the ceremony, the public spectacle – these were merely preludes. The actual, savage consummation of his decree was to unfold in a more private, more brutal theatre.

He had led her away from the murmuring throng, not with a gentle escort, but with a grip that bruised, a silent promise of the violation to come. The chamber into which he dragged her was not one of comfort, but of stark, unforgiving austerity. It was a room stripped of adornment, its stone walls damp and cold, echoing the desolation that was rapidly consuming Iris's soul. A single, flickering torch cast long, dancing shadows that distorted the already grim contours of the space, as if the very architecture recoiled from the darkness that was about to be unleashed within it. Her father, Bernard, stood in the doorway, a spectral, pathetic figure cloaked in shadow, his face a mask of utter, soul-crushing impotence. He did not move, did not speak, did not even meet her eyes, his silence a deafening testament to his utter failure, his profound betrayal. He was a statue carved from despair, a monument to a father's lost honor and a daughter's doomed innocence.

Bjorn's laughter, a low, guttural sound that vibrated in the very stones, filled the oppressive silence. It was not the laughter of a man anticipating marital bliss, but the triumphant roar of a conqueror reveling in the final subjugation of his prey. He turned to her, his eyes burning with an unholy fire, a fire that promised not warmth, but utter annihilation. "You thought you were merely his prisoner, my pet," he rasped, his voice laced with a cruel amusement that stripped away the last vestiges of her dignity. "But you were always mine. And tonight, my ownership becomes absolute, etched into the very fabric of our existence. No longer will you be merely a symbol, a prize to be displayed. You will be consumed. You will be made one with me, in a way that transcends mere flesh and blood."

He moved towards her, his steps measured, deliberate, each one a hammer blow against the fragile walls of her resistance. The air crackled with his malevolence, a palpable force that pressed in on her, stealing her breath, her will. She tried to recoil, to scramble away, but the room was small, and his presence filled every inch of it. Her back met the cold, unyielding stone, trapping her, making her a willing participant in her own undoing. His hands, once a source of chilling curiosity, now felt like instruments of torture. They moved with a chilling efficiency, tearing at her garments, each rip and tear a fresh wound inflicted not just upon her body, but upon her very essence. The rough weave of his tunic scraped against her skin, a coarse reminder of the brutal intimacy that was being forced upon her.

"Look at you," he breathed, his face inches from hers, his breath a foul wind that scorched her skin. "So terrified. So... pure. It's a shame, truly. But a necessary sacrifice, wouldn't you agree? The purity of your spirit will fuel the power of my bloodline for generations to come. A fitting end for the daughter of a fallen lord, wouldn't you say? To be the vessel through which true power is reborn." He pressed himself against her, his weight a crushing burden that threatened to break her. Her pleas, thin and reedy at first, were swallowed by the guttural sounds of his ascendancy. She could feel his strength, his primal ferocity, battering against her defenses, eroding them piece by piece.

Across the chamber, her father remained a silent sentinel, his bowed head a stark image of his complicity. Did he hear her stifled cries? Did the faint, choked gasps of her struggle pierce the fog of his self-imposed blindness? Or had he, too, been consumed by Bjorn's influence, his will dissolved into the ambient darkness of the keep? Iris could not tell. All she could perceive was the suffocating presence of Bjorn, the encroaching oblivion, and the chilling finality of her father's passive gaze, or lack thereof. It was a silence that screamed louder than any accusation, a void where paternal protection should have been.

Bjorn's touch was no longer a caress, but a violation. He moved with a brutal intent, systematically dismantling her defenses, her personhood. Each thrust, each grind, was a declaration of his absolute ownership, a branding that seared itself onto her very soul. The pain was a searing inferno, eclipsing all thought, all feeling, leaving only a raw, primal instinct for survival that was swiftly being extinguished. She felt her spirit, once a vibrant flame, begin to flicker and wane, consumed by the relentless onslaught. Her life force, that precious ember of existence, was being siphoned away, leaving behind only an aching void.

As his final, desperate exertion wracked his body, Iris felt a strange stillness descend upon her. The pain, the terror, the outrage – it all receded, leaving a vast, echoing emptiness. It was not the peace of surrender, but the chilling quiet of something irrevocably broken. Her breath, shallow and ragged, hitched in her throat, and with a final, soft sigh, the last vestiges of her consciousness slipped away. Her body remained, a still, violated vessel, but the light that had defined Iris was gone, extinguished by the brutal, avaricious hands of Bjorn.

He withdrew from her, his chest heaving, his eyes blazing with a triumphant, almost divine satisfaction. He surveyed his handiwork with the detached pride of an artist completing a masterpiece, a masterpiece born of agony and despair. The torchlight flickered across her pale, still face, illuminating the utter cessation of life, the final silencing of her defiance. A single tear, a tiny, crystalline testament to her lost existence, traced a slow path from the corner of her eye, disappearing into the dark stain on the rough stone floor.

Bjorn let out a low, satisfied groan, a sound that was more animal than human. He did not weep. He did not show remorse. Why would he? He had achieved his ultimate goal, the final act of possessive subjugation. He had not merely conquered a woman; he had consumed her very essence, absorbing her into his own dark being. He stood over her, a colossus bathed in shadow and the fading echoes of his own brutal victory, the ultimate abuser, the final destroyer. And in the doorway, her father, Bernard, still stood, a silent witness to the complete and utter annihilation of his daughter, his inaction a more damning indictment than any spoken word. The pact was sealed, not with vows, but with the extinguishing of a soul, a dark sacrament performed in the heart of Bjorn's unforgiving domain. The tenth anniversary had indeed brought a new bond, a final, fatal intertwining of their fates, though not in the way any would have conceived. It was a bond forged in blood and despair, a testament to Bjorn's unyielding cruelty and the crushing weight of a father's betrayal. The darkness had claimed its prize, and the silence that followed was the most profound abuse of all.

The flickering torchlight, once a dancing harbinger of dread, now seemed to cast a funereal pallor over the scene. Iris's breath, a shallow, ragged thing, grew ever more tenuous, each exhalation a whisper of surrender to the encroaching dark. The brutal act that had been inflicted upon her body had not merely wounded flesh; it had sundered the very thread of her being. A chilling stillness had begun to settle, not the peace of acceptance, but the terrifying calm of a spirit being systematically unraveled, its essence leached away like water from a shattered vessel. The pain, a searing inferno moments before, had receded, leaving behind a vast, echoing emptiness that swallowed all sensation, all thought. It was a profound and absolute void, a canvas upon which the last, desperate hues of her existence were being painted.

Her vision, already blurred by tears and the violent upheaval, began to dim further. The rough-hewn stones of the chamber, the leering shadows cast by the torch, the spectral form of her father in the doorway – all these warped and blurred, coalescing into an indistinct tapestry of her final moments. Yet, amidst this dissolution, a single, crystalline shard of consciousness remained, sharp and intensely focused. It was not a thought of forgiveness, nor of resignation. It was a burning ember of pure, unadulterated rage. A furious injustice, a primal scream of 'why?'. Why this indignity? Why this betrayal? Why this utter obliteration of a life that had barely begun to bloom? Her spirit, so recently vibrant with hope, with love, with the promise of a future stolen by brute force, now seethed with a potent, venomous fury. It was the final, incandescent flare of a soul refusing to be extinguished without leaving its mark, its echo of protest against the monstrous cruelty that had rendered her thus.

And then, a flicker. Not of vision, but of memory. A face, so achingly familiar, so full of warmth and light, swam into the periphery of her fading awareness. Julius. His smile, his gentle touch, the whispered promises of a shared future – these were the anchors that had tethered her to life, the beacon that had guided her through the encroaching darkness. In these final, fleeting seconds, as her physical form surrendered to the inevitable, it was to him that her soul reached out, a desperate, inarticulate plea, a silent farewell carried on the dying currents of her breath. She saw not the desolation of her surroundings, but the sunlit glades of their shared dreams, the laughter that had once echoed between them, the quiet comfort of his presence. It was a fleeting glimpse of paradise, a stark contrast to the hell she was leaving, a poignant reminder of all that had been so brutally snatched away.

The lifeblood, so vital and vibrant, continued its slow, inexorable drain. Each pulse, a faint tremor against the cold stone, carried away another fragment of her spirit. She felt herself dissolving, becoming one with the dust and shadows of this desolate place. It was a terrifying alchemy, a transformation from a living, breathing soul into an ephemeral whisper, a phantom on the edge of oblivion. The rage, so potent moments before, began to ebb, replaced by a profound weariness, a profound sadness that settled over her like a shroud. It was the sorrow of a song cut short, of a story left unfinished, of a tapestry torn before its pattern was complete. The injustice of it all was a bitter, lingering taste on her tongue, a final, silent testament to a life extinguished before its time.

Her body, a broken vessel, lay still. The delicate curves of her form were stark against the rough, unforgiving stone, a brutal testament to the violence it had endured. The vibrant spark that had animated her – the quick wit, the gentle kindness, the fierce spirit that had refused to be easily cowed – had been systematically extinguished. Where there had been light, there was now only shadow. Where there had been life, there was a chilling, profound stillness. Her eyes, once pools of vibrant color reflecting the world with curiosity and joy, were now vacant, staring with a heartbreaking emptiness at the indifferent ceiling.

They held no glimmer of recognition, no trace of the woman who had once possessed them. They were the windows to a soul that had departed, leaving behind only a hollow shell, a mournful monument to a life brutally concluded.

The air, which had moments before thrummed with the raw power of Bjorn's triumph and the suffocating presence of Bernard's complicity, now seemed to hold a new kind of silence. It was a silence that was not merely the absence of sound, but a palpable weight, a void where a vibrant life had once been. It was the silence of finality, the deafening quiet that follows a scream, the echoing emptiness that speaks of a profound and irreparable loss. The torch sputtered, casting long, distorted shadows that danced like specters on the walls, as if even the inanimate objects of the chamber recoiled from the profound stillness that had descended. The very essence of Iris, her laughter, her tears, her hopes, her dreams – all had been leached away, leaving behind only this stark, desolate emptiness. Her spirit, it seemed, had been utterly extinguished, her soul's last breathe a sigh of despair, a final surrender to the overwhelming darkness that had claimed her. The tenth anniversary, meant to signify a union, had instead brought about the ultimate severance, the complete and utter annihilation of a life, leaving behind only the chilling echo of what once was.

Chapter 5:
The Year in the Grave

The silence descended not as a gentle lullaby, but as a suffocating shroud, a tangible entity that pressed against what remained of Iris's senses. The ragged breaths that had punctuated her final moments ceased, not with a sigh of release, but with an abrupt, terrifying cessation. The flickering torch, its wild dance now extinguished, had plunged the chamber into an absolute, unyielding blackness. It was a darkness that did not merely obscure vision, but seemed to possess a texture, a viscous, inky quality that coated the inside of her eyelids and seeped into the very pores of her being. There was no longer the faint warmth of the flame, no longer the rough texture of the stone beneath her, only an all-encompassing, profound void.

The abrupt shift from the agonizing awareness of her body to this absolute nothingness was a disorienting plunge. It was as if the world, with all its pain, its light, its very substance, had ceased to exist. But existence, in its most primal form, stubbornly persisted. A chilling stillness, colder than any winter wind, permeated her. It was a stillness that was not the absence of motion, but a profound lack of internal vitality. Her heart, that relentless drummer of life, had fallen silent. The rush of blood, the warmth that had coursed through her veins, was gone, replaced by a creeping, icy numbness that began to spread from her extremities inward, a slow, inexorable march of oblivion.

The transition from the violent rupture of her life to this inert state was not instantaneous. Even as the last vestiges of her spirit seemed to cling to the world, a new awareness began to bloom, or perhaps, to fester. It was the awareness of the grave. The heavy thud of earth, the scraping sounds of shovels, the muffled voices – these had been the last external echoes of her transition. Now, they were replaced by an oppressive silence, punctuated only by the imagined, or perhaps real, creaks and groans of the earth settling around her. She was entombed. The word itself was a cold, hard knot in the dwindling core of her consciousness. Buried. Forgotten.

The darkness was absolute, and within it, the senses began to play their morbid tricks. The absence of light did not equate to the lack of perception. Instead, the internal landscape of her awareness became hypersensitive, picking up alien and horrifying sensations. The feeling of pressure, immense and unwavering, bore down on her. It was the weight of the soil, the stones, the very earth itself, a crushing embrace that offered no solace, only suffocation. The air, what little there was, was stagnant, heavy with the scent of damp earth, of decay, of things long buried and forgotten. It filled her nonexistent lungs with a miasma that was both suffocating and strangely intoxicating, a perfumed harbinger of the inevitable.

Loneliness became a more profound and terrifying entity than any spectral presence she might have imagined in life. There was no one. No one to hear her silent screams, no one to acknowledge her existence, no one even to remember that she had ever drawn breath. The cold was not merely a physical sensation; it was an existential state. It seeped into her very core, a constant, gnawing chill that seemed to extinguish any lingering spark of warmth or hope. It was the cold embrace of the earth, a final, unyielding rejection of life.

Time, as she had known it, ceased to have meaning. The passage of sunrises and sunsets, the rhythm of days and nights, were lost to her. There was only an eternal, unchanging present of darkness and stillness. Yet, within this timeless void, a subtle, insidious change began to take place. The body, that vessel that had so recently housed her vibrant spirit, was beginning its slow, relentless surrender to the primal forces of decomposition.

It started subtly, a faint tenderness that morphed into an unsettling ache. The skin, once supple and warm, began to tighten, to lose its elasticity. The vibrant color drained away, leaving behind a pallor that no amount of moonlight could ever illuminate. The tiny capillaries, so full of life and blood, began to break, leaving faint, ghostly mottens beneath the surface. It was a slow, insidious unmaking, a gradual dismantling of the physical form.

The odor, at first merely the scent of damp earth, began to shift. A faint, cloying sweetness, the initial breath of decay, began to mingle with the mustiness. It was a scent that was deeply unsettling, a testament to the fact that even in this state of utter stillness, life, in its most base and primal form, was still at work, consuming and transforming. The bacteria, unseen and relentless, were beginning their feast, breaking down the intricate structures of cells and releasing gases that would bloat and swell the once-familiar contours of her flesh.

There were moments, fleeting and nightmarish, when a phantom sensation would flicker through her. A phantom itch that could not be scratched, a phantom warmth that hinted at the lost circulation, a phantom tremor that suggested a muscle twitching in the grip of rigor mortis. These were not the echoes of life, but the distorted whispers of a body in its death throes, a final, morbid dance of biological processes continuing in the absence of conscious control.

She felt, or rather, her decaying form felt, the relentless pressure of the earth. Worms, blind and purposeful, began their burrowing journeys, their tiny bodies creating intricate networks through the softening flesh. The delicate tissues, the skin, the muscles, the organs – all were being systematically broken down, their complex forms yielding to the simple, elemental building blocks of organic matter. It was a gruesome, silent process, an unholy communion between the dead and the living earth.

The darkness remained, but it was no longer just the absence of light. It became a canvas upon which the grotesque tapestry of her own decomposition was being painted. She was aware, in a way that transcended mere sensory input, of the liquefaction of internal organs, the softening of bones, the disintegration of tissues. It was a horror that defied description, a violation of the most fundamental sense of self. Her body, the instrument through which she had experienced the world, was now betraying her in its most intimate and horrifying fashion.

The terror was not the sudden, sharp fear of a living being facing a threat. It was a more profound, more existential dread, a gnawing awareness of utter helplessness and insignificance. She was being erased, not just from the minds of the living, but from her very physical being. Her essence, that intangible spark that had defined her, was systematically stripped away, leaving only a decaying husk.

She was a ghost in her own tomb, a disembodied consciousness trapped within a rapidly deteriorating vessel. The memories of warmth, touch, laughter, and sunlight grew increasingly distant, like fading dreams. The monochromatic palette of decay was replacing the vibrant hues of her life. The rich scent of flowers, the taste of sweet fruit, the sound of music – all were receding, overshadowed by the damp, earthy smell and the silent, internal symphony of decomposition.

The silence of the grave was profound, but it was not empty. It was filled with the quiet industry of decay, with the inexorable march of time as it eroded the physical form. It was a silence that screamed of abandonment, of being cast into the most bottomless abyss, forgotten by the world and by herself. Each infinitesimal shift of the soil, each microscopic breakdown of a cell, was a testament to her utter isolation.

She longed for the pain, the agony that had been so vivid in her final moments. At least that had been a sign of life, a testament to her body's refusal to succumb. This was worse. This was the quiet, passive surrender of flesh to the earth, the slow, ignominious disintegration into dust and slime.

There were no specters, no ghouls, no supernatural visitations to break the monotony of her torment. The horror was far more intimate, far more insidious. It was the horror of witnessing one's own undoing, the slow, agonizing dissolution of the self. She was a prisoner of her own decaying body, entombed not just in earth, but in the very process of her own unmaking. The cold seeped deeper, not just into her flesh, but into the very fabric of her soul, a chilling testament to the unforgiving nature of the grave. In this place, even the memory of warmth was eventually consumed by the eternal, silent darkness. The year in the grave had begun, and it promised an eternity of such cold, silent decay.

The silence, once an oppressive blanket, began to hum with a new, discordant frequency. It was not a sound audible to mortal ears, but a vibration that resonated deep within the decaying matrix of what had been Iris. The utter stillness, the profound absence of life, was being subtly, insidiously, disturbed. It was as if the earth itself, having claimed her body, was now beginning to stir with a strange, unbidden vitality. This was not the gentle settling of soil, nor the industrious burrowing of worms; this was something far more... deliberate.

Within the suffocating press of the grave, a nascent awareness, fractured and primal, flickered into being. It was a consciousness divorced from the elegant architecture of a living mind, a raw, untamed energy that clung to the tattered remnants of her former self. The despair that had been a heavy cloak during her conscious demise, the incandescent rage that had burned against the injustice of her fate – these were not extinguished by death. Instead, they had simmered, coalescing in the void, transforming into potent, volatile fuel. This was the genesis of a resurrection, not born of divine intervention or benevolent magic, but of the sheer, visceral refusal to cease.

The earth around her was not merely a tomb, but a crucible. The damp soil, rich with the detritus of countless lives and deaths, acted as a conductor, channeling an unseen current. Whether this current was an intrinsic property of the land itself, a lingering echo of ancient rites performed on this very ground, or an emanation from the raw, untamed emotions Iris had so powerfully projected in her final moments, remained a mystery. What was undeniable was its effect. It was as if the earth, sensing the potent, unspent energy trapped within her decaying form, was drawing it out, weaving it into a new, terrifying synthesis.

The first inklings of this awakening were imperceptible, so subtle as to be mistaken for the phantom sensations of a dying body. A tremor, too faint to register as motion, would pass through the stiffened limbs. A strange warmth, alien to the perpetual cold of the grave, would bloom briefly in the cavernous hollows of her chest, only to recede, leaving a phantom ache. It was the nascent stirring of life force, or a dark imitation of it, beginning to coalesce, to knit together the frayed edges of her existence.

Iris, or what remained of her consciousness, was not merely a passive recipient of these stirrings. Her own despair, a boundless ocean, began to imbue the process with a desperate urgency. Her rage, a wildfire consuming the last vestiges of her humanity, fed the nascent energies with a furious intensity. She was no longer buried; she was being reformed, reassembled not by memory or by the continuity of self, but by the sheer, unyielding force of her will to be. The boundaries of her decaying form became porous, allowing the earth's strange energies to seep in and mingle with the residue of her potent emotions.

It was a slow, disquieting awakening, like the unfurling of a poisonous bloom in the deepest, darkest soil. The delicate tissues, already succumbing to the inevitable processes of decay, began to exhibit an unnatural resilience. Where putrefaction had begun its insidious work, a strange, almost luminous quality began to manifest, a faint phosphorescence that pulsed with a life of its own. The process of decomposition was not being halted; instead, it was being twisted and rechanneled. The very elements that should have broken her down were now being used as building blocks for something new, something that bore the imprint of her past but was irrevocably altered by the present circumstances.

The air within the coffin, once thick with the cloying sweetness of decay, began to thrum with a different sort of energy. It was a palpable pressure, a silent hum that seemed to emanate from the very core of her being. It was the gathering of her will, the slow, agonizing assembly of her shattered essence. The phantom itches that had tormented her, the illusory warmth and tremors, were no longer mere tricks of a dying body. They were the first, tentative movements of a will reasserting itself against the crushing weight of oblivion.

The sensation was akin to being slowly drawn from a deep, cold sleep, but without the clarity of waking. It was a groggy, terrifying awareness of oneself as a separate entity, distinct from the inert matter that encased it. The earth pressed in, not as a tomb, but as a womb. And within this earthen womb, something was stirring, something that had been forged in the fires of despair and the ice of death, something that was slowly, inexorably, coming to life.

The process was not without its horror. Each nascent throb of this reanimated force sent a jolt of agonizing awareness through the decaying flesh. It was a symphony of discord, the sound of creation and destruction playing out in a macabre duet. The worms that had begun their work now found their paths disrupted, their instinctual drives subtly warped by the encroaching energy. Some recoiled, their blind bodies shuddering against the unnatural vibrations. Others, perhaps drawn by an instinctual hunger for this new, potent source, burrowed deeper, their minuscule journeys through the softening flesh becoming a conduit for the coalescing life force.

Iris's rage, once a purely human emotion, began to take on a more elemental quality. It was no longer just anger at her tormentors, but a primal fury against the very concept of death, against the silencing of her voice, against the theft of her future. This rage, so potent in life, had become a formidable force in death. It was a dark sun, drawing in the dissipated fragments of her being, concentrating them, refining them into a singular, burning purpose.

The despair, too, played its part. It was the deep, aching void left by the cessation of her life, a vast emptiness now being filled. It was not filled with hope or with peace, but with a grim determination, a desperate clinging to existence. This despair was the foundation upon which the new edifice of her being was being built, a testament to the tenacity of the spirit, even when stripped bare and cast into the abyss.

The land itself responded to this burgeoning power. The soil above her burial site, which had been unremarkable, began to exhibit subtle anomalies. Unseasonal wilting and then an unnatural, vibrant resurgence of nearby flora. A faint, persistent chill that clung to the air even on the warmest days, emanating from the earth. The animals, sensitive to the unseen currents, would skirt the area, their instincts screaming of something profoundly wrong, something ancient and powerful awakening.

Within the grave, the transformation was a slow, agonizing ballet. The rigidity of death began to soften, not into the flaccidity of decay, but into a new kind of suppleness, a tautness that spoke of contained power. The skin, once pale and lifeless, began to regain a semblance of color, a deep, bruised hue that pulsed with an inner light. The eyes, hollow and vacant, started to shift subtly, a faint, almost imperceptible luminescence flickering within their depths.

This was not a gentle return to life, but a violent, unsettling birth. It was the re-emergence of Iris, not as she was, but as something new, something shaped by the darkness and the despair, something forged in the crucible of the grave. The year in the grave was far from over, but its nature had irrevocably changed. The passive suffering had given way to an active, albeit agonizing, process of becoming. The silence was broken, not by a shout, but by a deep, resonant hum, the sound of something ancient and terrible stirring beneath the earth, ready to reclaim its own. The stirring in the earth was the first tremor of a storm, a prelude to a darkness that would soon engulf the world, a darkness born of a soul that refused to be buried.

The oppressive silence of the grave, once a deafening void, had begun to thrum with a low, persistent vibration. It was not a sound that ears could perceive, but a sensation that resonated through the very marrow of Iris's reawakening form. This was not the gentle sigh of the earth settling, nor the frantic scrabbling of subterranean life; this was a deliberate, insidious stirring, a nascent awareness coalescing within the decaying matrix of her once-living self. The profound stillness, the utter absence of life, was being systematically, terrifyingly, disturbed. It was as if the earth, in its cold embrace, was not merely a tomb, but a crucible, and the lingering essence of Iris was the raw ore being refined within its depths.

Within the suffocating press of the grave, a consciousness, fractured and primal, flickered into being. It was an awareness divorced from the elegant architecture of a human mind, a raw, untamed energy clinging to the tattered remnants of her former existence. The despair that had been a heavy cloak during her conscious demise, the incandescent rage that had burned against the injustice of her fate – these were not extinguished by death.

Instead, they had simmered, coalescing in the void, transforming into potent, volatile fuel. This was the genesis of a resurrection, not born of divine intervention or benevolent magic, but of the sheer, visceral refusal to cease, a desperate clinging to a spectral semblance of self. The earth around her was not merely a burial site; it was a conduit, channeling an unseen current, a dark energy that seeped into the very fabric of her reanimating being.

The first inklings of this awakening were subtle, so faint as to be mistaken for the phantom sensations of a dying body. A tremor, too minute to register as actual movement, would pass through limbs stiffened by rigor mortis. A strange warmth, utterly alien to the perpetual cold of the grave, would bloom briefly in the cavernous hollows of her chest, only to recede, leaving a phantom ache that hinted at the returning tide of sensation. It was the nascent stirring of a life force, or perhaps a dark imitation of it, beginning to coalesce, to knit together the frayed edges of her existence. Iris, or what remained of her consciousness, was not merely a passive recipient of these stirrings. Her own despair, a boundless ocean that had threatened to drown her in life, now began to imbue the process with a desperate urgency. Her rage, a wildfire that had consumed the last vestiges of her humanity, fed the nascent energies with a furious intensity. She was no longer buried; she was being reformed, reassembled not by memory or by the continuity of self, but by the sheer, unyielding force of her will to be. The boundaries of her decaying form became porous, allowing the earth's strange energies to seep in and mingle with the residue of her potent emotions.

The process of decomposition, once an inexorable march towards oblivion, was being twisted, rechanneled. The very elements that should have broken her down were now being used as building blocks for something new, something that bore the imprint of her past but was irrevocably altered by the circumstances of her burial. The air within the coffin, once thick with the cloying sweetness of decay, began to thrum with a different sort of energy. It was a palpable pressure, a silent hum that seemed to emanate from the very core of her reanimated being. It was the gathering of her will, the slow, agonizing assembly of her shattered essence. The phantom itches that had tormented her, the illusory warmth and tremors, were no longer mere tricks of a dying body. They were the first, tentative movements of a will reasserting itself against the crushing weight of oblivion. The sensation was akin to being slowly drawn from a deep, cold sleep, but without the clarity of waking. It was a groggy, terrifying awareness of oneself as a separate entity, distinct from the inert matter that encased it. The earth pressed in, not as a tomb, but as a womb, and within this earthen womb, something was stirring, something that had been forged in the fires of despair and the ice of death, something that was slowly, inexorably, coming to life.

This was not a gentle awakening; it was a violent, unsettling birth. Each nascent throb of this reanimated force sent a jolt of agonizing awareness through the decaying flesh. It was a symphony of discord, the sound of creation and destruction playing out in a macabre duet. The worms that had begun their work now found their paths disrupted, their instinctual drives subtly warped by the encroaching energy. Some recoiled, their blind bodies shuddering against the unnatural vibrations. Others, perhaps drawn by an instinctual hunger for this new, potent source, burrowed deeper, their minuscule journeys through the softening flesh becoming a conduit for the coalescing life force. Iris's rage, once a purely human emotion, began to take on a more elemental quality. It was no longer just anger at her tormentors, but a primal fury against the very concept of death, against the silencing of her voice, against the theft of her future. This rage, so potent in life, had become a formidable force in death. It was a dark sun, drawing in the dissipated fragments of her being, concentrating them, refining them into a singular, burning purpose. The despair, too, played its part. It was the deep, aching void left by the cessation of her life; a vast emptiness now being filled. It was not filled with hope or with peace, but with a grim determination, a desperate clinging to existence. This despair was the foundation upon which the new edifice of her being was being built, a testament to the tenacity of the spirit, even when stripped bare and cast into the abyss.

The land itself responded to this burgeoning power. The soil above her burial site, which had been unremarkable, began to exhibit subtle anomalies. Unseasonal wilting and then an unnatural, vibrant resurgence of nearby flora. A faint, persistent chill that clung to the air even on the warmest days, emanating from the earth. The animals, sensitive to the unseen currents, would skirt the area, their instincts screaming of something profoundly wrong, something ancient and powerful awakening. Within the grave, the transformation was a slow, agonizing ballet. The rigidity of death began to soften, not into the flaccidity of decay, but into a new kind of suppleness, a tautness that spoke of contained power. The skin, once pale and lifeless, began to regain a semblance of color, a deep, bruised hue that pulsed with an inner light. The eyes, hollow and vacant, started to shift subtly, a faint, almost imperceptible luminescence flickering within their depths. The year in the grave was far from over, but its nature had irrevocably changed. The passive suffering had given way to an active, albeit agonizing, process of becoming. The silence was broken, not by a shout, but by a deep, resonant hum, the sound of something ancient and terrible stirring beneath the earth, ready to reclaim its own. The stirring in the earth was the first tremor of a storm, a prelude to a darkness that would soon engulf the world, a darkness born of a soul that refused to be buried.

As the spectral fragments of Iris's consciousness began to coalesce, they were not illuminated by the gentle glow of fond remembrance. Instead, they were seared by the scorching flame of recollection, each memory a brand applied to her reanimating soul. The idyllic pastures of her childhood, once a sanctuary of innocence, were now viewed through a haze of bitter resentment. The sun-drenched days, filled with the laughter of children and the scent of honeysuckle, were now tainted by the chilling whisper of what was lost, what was stolen. She remembered the warmth of her mother's embrace, the comforting rhythm of her lullabies, but the memory was no longer a solace. It was a stark reminder of the love that had been ripped away, the tenderness that had been brutally extinguished. The image of her father's proud smile, once a beacon of paternal pride, now twisted into a grotesque caricature, a testament to the faith that had been shattered, the protector who had failed to protect. These were not cherished echoes; they were shards of glass, sharp and glittering, embedded in the raw wound of her returning awareness.

The betrayal, a venom that had poisoned her final days, festered with a terrifying potency. The faces of those who had wronged her, once etched with malice and deceit, now swam before her spectral eyes with the clarity of a waking nightmare. She saw them in their moments of supposed triumph, basking in the afterglow of their cruel victory, and a searing hatred, cold and absolute, bloomed in the void where her heart once beat. The casual cruelty, the calculated manipulation, the utter disregard for her life – these were not simply memories; they were fuel, igniting the nascent darkness within her. The sweet words of affection, twisted into instruments of torment, now replayed in her mind with a mocking echo, each syllable a lash against her reawakening spirit. The abuse, a relentless tide that had battered her into submission, now surged with a renewed ferocity, each instance of degradation a hammer blow, forging her into something more challenging, something colder, something infinitely more terrible.

Her spectral existence was a torment of distorted perception. The gentle caress of a summer breeze was no longer a bomb, but a phantom touch that hinted at the violation she had endured. The chirping of birds, once a joyful chorus, now sounded like the shrill cries of her own suffering, amplified and distorted by her monstrous metamorphosis. Even the natural world, in its indifferent beauty, seemed to mock her. The vibrant bloom of a rose, a symbol of beauty and fragility, now appeared to her as a blood-soaked testament to her own violent end. The dewdrop clinging to a spider's web, once a delicate marvel, now resembled a tear, a single, crystalline drop of sorrow shed for a life brutally extinguished. Her idyllic past was now a distorted landscape, a cruel mirage that served only to underscore the depth of her present despair and the ferocity of her vengeful rage.

The sweetness of honey, a flavor she had once adored, now evoked the cloying sweetness of decay, the phantom taste of the grave. The scent of rain on parched earth, a perfume of renewal, now reminded her of the tears she had wept, a smell that clung to the world that held her prisoner. Every sensory input was reinterpreted through the lens of her burgeoning monstrous nature. The comforting embrace of moonlight, once a gentle lullaby, now casts long, skeletal shadows, hinting at the horrors that lurked just beyond the veil of perception. Her memories were no longer anchors to her former self, but chains that bound her to her pain, each link forged in the fires of her betrayal and the icy grip of her loss.

She recalled moments of joy, fleeting and fragile, but now they were tinged with a profound sadness, a grief that transcended mere loss. It was the grief of understanding that such light could exist, and yet be so cruelly extinguished. The laughter of children, once a pure and unadulterated sound, now resonated with a hollow echo, a reminder of the innocence stripped from her and the future stolen. These were not memories that offered comfort or solace; they were fuel for the inferno of her hatred. They sharpened the edges of her rage, giving it focus and purpose. The idyllic scenes of her past were now rendered in shades of blood and shadow, a macabre tapestry woven from the threads of her broken life and her terrifying rebirth. The gentle stream that had once flowed peacefully through her childhood memories now churned with a dark, viscous current, carrying the debris of her shattered dreams. The trees that had once provided shade and shelter now stood like gnarled, skeletal fingers, reaching out to grasp and ensnare anything that dared to stray too close to the darkness that now enveloped her.

The psychological torment was profound. Her mind, a battlefield where sanity and monstrosity clashed, struggled to reconcile the woman she had been with the entity she was becoming. The remnants of her human empathy warred with the cold, calculating fury that was taking root. She remembered acts of kindness, gestures of love. Still, now they were viewed with cynical suspicion, a grim understanding of the inherent darkness that lurked beneath the surface of even the most benevolent acts. The abuse she had suffered had eroded the foundations of her trust, leaving behind a wasteland where only suspicion and hatred could take root. The faces of her tormentors, once figures of dread, were now etched into her consciousness with an almost unbearable clarity, each cruel word, each violating touch, a vivid imprint that fueled her desire for retribution. She was a ghost haunted not by the spectres of the past, but by the distorted echoes of her own life, a life that had been stolen, defiled, and now painstakingly reassembled into something far more sinister. The sweetness of memory had curdled, leaving a bitter aftertaste of vengeance.

And then, a new sensation, alien and absolute, began to assert itself. It was a hollow ache, a gnawing emptiness that spread from the newly formed core of her being outwards, a void that demanded to be filled. It was not the familiar pang of hunger that had once signaled a need for sustenance, for bread or fruit or the simple warmth of a shared meal. This was something far more profound, a primal craving that clawed at the edges of her awareness, a desperate thirst that promised oblivion if left unquenched. It pulsed with an urgency that eclipsed even the burning fires of her rage and the crushing weight of her despair. It was a physical demand, raw and undeniable, a signal that the transformation was not merely spiritual or emotional, but intensely, terrifyingly physical.

This thirst was a tangible presence, a constant thrumming beneath the surface of her reanimated consciousness. It was a sensation that seeped into every fiber of her being. This demanding presence whispered of a need so fundamental it threatened to shatter the fragile scaffolding of her returning self. It felt like a furnace had been stoked within her chest, a relentless fire that consumed her very essence, leaving behind only the desperate yearning for… what? She didn't know. The concept of food, of drink, felt distant and inadequate, like a faded echo from a forgotten life. This was a hunger of a different order, a craving that spoke of a more profound need, a more primal form of sustenance.

The remnants of her human physiology, still present in their decaying state, responded to this new imperative with a horrifying alacrity. The decaying flesh seemed to tighten, to draw inwards, as if seeking to contain this internal conflagration. A phantom dryness settled upon her spectral tongue, a parched sensation that intensified with every passing moment. Her nonexistent lungs felt tight, constricted, as if struggling to draw in air that would offer no relief. It was a torment that surpassed even the agonizing process of her reanimation. Each breath, each phantom beat of her spectral heart, was a reminder of this insatiable need, a constant, unbearable reminder that she was alive, but not in any way that resembled life as she had once known it.

The earth, her tomb, her crucible, now seemed to mock her with its sterile indifference. It offered no solace, no nourishment. It was a tomb, and she was its prisoner, a prisoner consumed by a thirst that could not be slaked by the dew of dawn or the coolness of the grave's damp soil. The worms, those mindless architects of decay, now seemed like a perverse parody of her own predicament, their ceaseless burrowing a futile search for sustenance in a barren landscape. But their hunger was a simple, biological need; hers was something far more complex, far more terrifying. It was a hunger born of unnatural creation, a craving that hinted at the monstrous nature of her rebirth.

She instinctively understood, with a clarity that cut through the fog of her reawakening, that this thirst was not for water. It was not for the nourishing juices of the earth or the life-giving essence of rain. No, this craving was far more specific, far more terrifyingly singular. It was a thirst that whispered of warmth, of vitality, of something that pulsed with a life force that was not her own. The realization settled upon her like a shroud, chilling her spectral form even as the internal inferno raged. This was not a hunger that could be satisfied by mere survival. This was a hunger that spoke of consumption, of a need that demanded the very essence of life itself. The desperate gnawing within her intensified, driving her toward a primal instinct, a hopeless, almost overwhelming urge to seek out that which could quell this infernal craving. The year in the grave was etching new, horrific lessons onto her soul, and this thirst was the most immediate, the most terrifying.

The crushing weight of the earth had been a constant, suffocating presence, a testament to her final, desperate moments. But now, something was different. A faint, insidious pressure began to build behind her eyelids, a sensation so alien it was as if the very membranes were being stretched from within. It was not a gentle awakening, nor a gradual awareness of light. It was a violent expulsion, a tearing as if the darkness itself was being rent asunder. And then, they were open.

Her eyes, no longer the lifeless orbs that had been sealed in the finality of death, now registered the world with a terrifying clarity. A blinding, searing white replaced the dim, earthy gloom of the coffin. It was the pale, watery light of dawn, filtering through the dense soil above, a light that felt less like a herald of life and more like an accusation. It was harsh, brutal, and it burned. Her vision, once accustomed to the soft hues of the living world, now perceived the spectrum with a stark, predatory intensity.

The faint phosphorescence of decaying matter, the subtle shifts in shadow that hinted at the burrowing creatures of the deep, all were laid bare to her newly awakened sight. The world was not just seen; it was assessed. It was a landscape of potential prey and lurking threats, a stark and brutal tableau painted in shades of nascent hunger.

The air, or what passed for it within the confines of her earthen tomb, was no longer stagnant. It was alive, thrumming with an unseen energy, a current that vibrated against her reanimated skin. It tasted of damp earth, of the cloying sweetness of decay, but beneath it all, there was something else – a sharp, metallic tang, like the coppery scent of spilt blood. This was not the air of the living, but something wilder, something ancient and elemental, a breath that carried the whispers of the abyss. It filled her nonexistent lungs with a strange, invigorating chill, stirring the embers of her rage into a roaring inferno.

The first coherent thought that pierced the fog of her rebirth was not one of relief, or of wonder, or even of the profound disorientation one might expect from a soul returning from the void. It was a searing, incandescent fury. It was not the slow burn of anger that had simmered in life, but a white-hot explosion, a primal scream that echoed not in the air, but in the very marrow of her reanimated bones. The injustices of her past, the cruelties inflicted upon her, the sheer, unadulterated malice of those who had orchestrated her demise – these memories, once painful recollections, now coalesced into a singular, all-consuming rage. It was a storm brewing within the confines of her grave, a tempest of vengeance that threatened to shatter the very foundations of her being.

The faces of her tormentors swam before her renewed sight, more precise and more vivid than any living memory. Their smug smiles, their casual cruelty, the dismissive flick of their wrists as they sealed her fate – these images were not mere recollections; they were fuel. Each perceived insult, each act of betrayal, each moment of suffering she had endured, was a spark igniting the tinder of her awakened soul. The gentle hand that had once soothed her tears was now a memory of a fist that had struck her down. The voice that had whispered promises of love was now a viperous hiss, spitting venom and deceit. The world she remembered was a lie, and the truth, the chilling, horrifying truth, was now laid bare.

This was not a resurrection in the sense of a divine miracle, nor a gentle return to a life unlived. This was a violent, brutal birth, a tearing away from the embrace of death, not for redemption, but for retribution. The woman who had been Iris was gone, buried beneath layers of pain and betrayal. What remained was something else entirely, something forged in the crucible of despair and tempered in the fires of an unquenchable rage. The victim had been entombed, but the predator was now stirring, its eyes fixed on the world above, not with longing, but with a chilling, predatory intent.

The earth, which had so recently been her tomb, now felt like a cage. The soil, once a symbol of finality, now represented an obstacle, a barrier that needed to be breached. Her spectral limbs, still bound by the constraints of her decaying form, began to twitch with an unnatural strength. It was not the weak, involuntary spasms of a body struggling against rigor mortis, but a deliberate, potent flexing of unseen muscles, a testing of the limits of her new existence. The worms, once oblivious passengers on her descent into oblivion, now seemed like insignificant annoyances, their slow, deliberate movements a stark contrast to the urgent, almost frantic energy that now pulsed within her.

She felt a new kind of hunger, not for sustenance, but for something far more profound, something that clawed at the edges of her consciousness. It was a thirst that demanded to be quenched, a gnawing emptiness that whispered of a need for… more. More than the meagre existence she had been granted, more than the fleeting moments of joy that had been so brutally snatched away. It was a hunger for retribution, a craving for the very life force of those who had wronged her, a desire to feel their fear, to taste their despair.

The soft, earthen confines of the coffin began to groan under the strain of her burgeoning power. The wood, once a solid barrier, now felt brittle, yielding. The nails that had sealed her fate seemed to stretch and bend, their metallic grip weakening against the relentless force of her will. The air, thick with the scent of decay, now carried a new, potent aroma – the smell of her own reawakening, a dark perfume that spoke of a power far older and more terrible than life itself. The year in the grave had not been an end, but a gestation, a period of terrifying transformation. And now, the chrysalis was breaking, revealing not a delicate butterfly, but a creature of shadow and rage, ready to descend upon the unsuspecting world. The dawn that filtered through the soil was not a harbinger of a new day, but a dim illumination of a nightmare that had just begun. The first light had brought not peace, but the raw, unadulterated fury of a soul reborn into vengeance. The world above remained ignorant, oblivious to the monstrous force about to claw its way from the earth, its first conscious act not a plea for mercy but a silent, burning vow of utter devastation. The earth trembled, not with the tremors of nature, but with the suppressed roar of a predator awakened. The silence of the grave was broken, not by a cry of pain, but by the first, nascent thrum of a heart that had died and been reborn, fueled by a hatred that would consume all.

Chapter 6:
The Dearg Due Rises

The wood of the coffin groaned, a pained, splintering protest against the unnatural force that assailed it from within. It was not the slow decay of time, nor the gnawing of vermin, but a violent exertion of will made manifest in flesh and bone, a will that had been honed to a razor's edge in the cold, silent darkness of the earth. Iris, or what had once been Iris, was no longer a passive recipient of her earthen shroud. The grave, once a symbol of her final surrender, was now a battleground, and she was the victor, clawing her way back into a world that had so callously discarded her.

Her fingers, stiff and unnaturally cold, dug into the rotting timber of the coffin lid. They were no longer the delicate digits of a woman, but instruments of pure, unadulterated power, tipped with nails that had grown long and sharp in the stillness of her tomb, like the talons of a raptor. Each contraction of her muscles sent tremors through her reanimated limbs, a symphony of cracking joints and protesting sinews that drowned out the fainter sounds of the night. The earth, which had cradled her in death, now seemed to recoil from her reawakening. It was as if the very soil, infused with the life force of the world above, sensed the alien intrusion, the unnatural resurrection of something that had been deemed irrevocably lost.

A low, guttural sound, more of a growl than a human cry, escaped her lips as she heaved upwards. It was the sound of a primal beast, of something ancient and terrible breaking free from its bonds. The coffin lid, already weakened by the damp and the passage of years, cracked further, a jagged fissure appearing near the edge where her desperate fingers had found purchase. Dust and debris rained down as the wood warped and buckled, the nails that had sealed her away groaning under the immense pressure. They were designed to keep the dead in their resting places and to prevent the restless from disturbing the slumber of the departed. But they were no match for the sheer, unyielding force of her rage.

The air around her, thin and cloying within the confines of her tomb, seemed to thicken with a palpable sense of dread. It was as if the very atmosphere was resisting her ascent, a final, futile attempt to keep her buried beneath the weight of her past. The moon, a sliver of bone-white against the velvet expanse of the night sky, cast an ethereal, chilling glow that barely penetrated the dense earth. But even this faint illumination seemed to flicker and wane as she strained, as if the celestial body itself was shrinking away from the unholy spectacle unfolding below. The night air, already unnaturally cold, seemed to plummet further, carrying with it the scent of grave-damp and something else, something metallic and acrid, the unmistakable aroma of fresh blood – though no blood had yet been shed. It was the scent of her own reanimation, the dark perfume of a life violently repossessed.

With a final, agonizing surge, a surge that felt as though her very soul was being ripped from the embrace of the earth, the coffin lid gave way. It splintered with a thunderclap, chunks of rotten wood flying outwards. Her head, then her shoulders, broke through the opening, her hair, matted with soil and clinging to her face like seaweed, obscuring her eyes for a fleeting moment. But then, her head snapped up, and her eyes, now fully open, burned with an incandescent fury. They were no longer the soft, gentle eyes of Iris, but the cold, calculating gaze of something far more predatory, reflecting the faint moonlight with an unsettling, unnatural gleam. The pupils, dilated to an almost black abyss, seemed to drink in the limited light, revealing no trace of humanity, only a burning, unquenchable thirst.

The loose soil cascaded around her as she pulled herself further out of the shattered coffin. Her movements were not fluid, not graceful, but jerky, almost mechanical, yet imbued with a terrifying strength. It was the strength of a predator that had been starved, denied its rightful place, and was now determined to reclaim what had been stolen. The grave, a pit of despair and decay, was now her launching pad. She pushed against the sides of the hole, her hands finding purchase in the yielding earth. The soil was cold, damp, clinging to her skin like a second shroud, but she barely registered it. Her focus was entirely on the world above, the world that had betrayed her, the world that would now pay the price.

The moon, as if emboldened by her emergence, shone a little brighter, illuminating the scene with a spectral radiance. The graveyard, a collection of silent, sombre monuments to the departed, was now imbued with a new, sinister energy. The wind, which had been a gentle sigh moments before, now whipped through the ancient yew trees that stood sentinel around the cemetery, their branches rustling like the dry bones of the forgotten. It carried whispers on its breath, not of the wind itself, but of the unquiet spirit that had just broken free, a whisper of vengeance that promised to echo through the lives of those who had put her here.

Her body, still clad in the tattered remnants of her burial gown, felt heavy, awkward, a vessel still adapting to its new, unholy purpose. Yet, with each movement, a strange vitality surged through her. It was not the warmth of life, but a chilling, invigorating cold, the very essence of her undeath. The worms, disturbed by her violent awakening, wriggled away from her form, their blind, instinctual fear a testament to the unnatural aura that now emanated from her. They were the natural denizens of the grave, yet even they recoiled from the monstrous force that had usurped their domain.

She hauled herself out of the earth, her body a testament to the brutal struggle. Dirt clung to her in clumps, obscuring the pallor of her skin, a stark contrast to the deep, almost bruised colour of her lips, which were drawn back in a grimace of exertion and rage. Her eyes, however, remained fixed on the heavens, as if seeking guidance, or perhaps, a target. The world above was bathed in the cold, uncaring light of the moon, a world that had moved on, oblivious to the horror that was now crawling from its soil.

The act of breaking free was not merely a physical exertion; it was a defiance of natural law, a tearing of the veil between life and death. The earth seemed to bleed around the edges of the grave, a dark, viscous liquid seeping from the disturbed soil, a grim testament to the unnatural violence of her resurrection. It was as if the very ground mourned the violation, acknowledging the monstrous birth that had occurred within its silent depths. The air, already thick with the scent of decay, now carried a new, sharp edge, a hint of the power that was being unleashed.

She stood, finally, on shaky legs, the shattered remains of the coffin a grim monument to her struggle. Her gaze swept across the desolate graveyard, each tombstone a potential reminder of the passage of time, of the lives that had ended while hers had been cruelly, unjustly stolen. The cold night air bit at her exposed skin, but she felt no discomfort, only a growing sense of power. It was as if the very elements were bending to her will, the chill of the night a reflection of the coldness that now resided in her heart.

The moonlight, catching the strands of her unbound hair, made them shimmer with an unearthly luminescence. Her form, once frail, now possessed a stark, skeletal grace, her bones seeming to hum with a dark energy. The injustice of her past, the years of suffering, the ignominy of her burial – all of it coalesced into a singular, burning purpose. She was not reborn to forgive, nor to repent. She was reborn for retribution, a creature forged in the fires of despair and exhaled into the cold, unforgiving night. The grave had been her crucible, and the moon, her witness to the monster she had become. The silence of the graveyard was no longer a sanctuary for the dead, but a hunting ground for the newly awakened. And the Dearg Due had risen.

The moonlight, that spectral herald of the night, traced the contours of Iris's newly formed being, a silent testament to the profound metamorphosis that had seized her. Gone was the soft, rounded visage of the peasant girl, the lines of her face now honed to an unsettling sharpness, as if carved from alabaster by the hand of a cruel deity. Her cheekbones, once subtly prominent, now stood out with an almost avian delicacy, lending her features an aristocratic, predatory elegance that was both beautiful and deeply disquieting. The curve of her jaw, previously defined by a gentle softness, had become a more pronounced, angular line, hinting at a strength and resilience that belied her spectral pallor. Even the delicate shell of her ears, once almost hidden by strands of humble brown hair, now seemed more defined, catching the scant light with a pearlescent sheen, as if sculpted from moonlight itself.

Her eyes, however, were the genuine windows into the abyss that had claimed her. They were no longer the warm, earth-toned pools that had once reflected the simple joys and sorrows of village life. Now, they were vast, obsidian depths, holding within them an ancient, glacial coldness that seemed to freeze the very air around her. The pupils, once capable of dilation and contraction in response to light and emotion, were now permanently widened, vast expanses of inky blackness that absorbed the moonlight rather than reflecting it. Within their unfathomable depths, one could glimpse not the fleeting reflections of the present, but the echoes of aeons, of forgotten ages, and of unspeakable deeds. There was no flicker of recognition, no spark of warmth, only the unwavering, calculating gaze of a predator that had shed the cumbersome baggage of humanity. The whites of her eyes, once a clean canvas, were now streaked with faint, venous lines, a delicate tracery of crimson that pulsed with a faint, internal luminescence, a sign of the unnatural lifeblood that now coursed through her veins.

And then there was the aura, the invisible mantle that she now wore. It was a palpable presence, a chilling emanation that spoke of power both ancient and terrifying. It was not the aggressive, overt display of a brute, but a subtle, suffocating pressure, like the stillness before a storm, or the hushed anticipation in a predator's lair. This aura of predatory power was a constant hum, a subtle vibration that seemed to resonate with the very fabric of the night. It whispered of silent hunts, of swift and brutal endings, and of a hunger that would never be truly sated. Those who might have chanced upon her in this nascent stage of her undeath would have felt an instinctive urge to flee, a primal fear that bypassed reason and burrowed deep into the subconscious. It was the instinctive recoil from something fundamentally *other*, something that defied the natural order of things.

Her movements, once the hesitant, earthbound steps of a mortal, had undergone a profound transformation. They were now fluid, possessed of an unnerving grace that spoke of years, or perhaps centuries, of honing her physical form. Each step was deliberate, yet impossibly silent, her feet gliding over the damp earth as if she were suspended inches above it. There was no rustle of disturbed leaves, no crunch of gravel, only the faintest whisper of displaced air. It was as if the very ground had learned to hold its breath in her presence, yielding to her passage without a sound. Her limbs moved with a liquid economy of motion, each gesture precise and economical, devoid of any unnecessary exertion. The subtle tension in her shoulders, the almost imperceptible sway of her hips as she walked – these were the hallmarks of a hunter, of a creature that understood the exquisite art of movement and stealth.

The tattered remnants of her burial shroud, clinging to her form, seemed to accentuate rather than conceal the stark, almost skeletal beauty that had emerged. The pale fabric, stained with the earth and the tears of grief, now served only to highlight the alabaster smoothness of her skin, a skin that seemed to possess its own subtle luminescence in the moonlight. The hollows beneath her cheekbones and the delicate arch of her clavicle were now more pronounced, lending her a fragile, ethereal appearance that was a chilling counterpoint to the immense power that radiated from her. Her hands, once stained with the honest grime of labour, were now impossibly delicate, her fingers long and slender, tipped with nails that had not only grown but had also hardened, acquiring a subtle, polished sheen, like slivers of obsidian. They moved with a disturbing dexterity, capable of both the most tender caress and the most lethal strike.

The very air around her seemed to hum with this latent energy. It was not the vibrant warmth of living breath, but a fabulous, crisp presence, like the breath of winter that could freeze the sap in the trees. This coolness was an extension of her being, a palpable manifestation of the chilling power that now court.

The chill in the air wasn't merely the late autumn breeze whistling through the skeletal branches of the ancient oaks. It was the palpable aura of something ancient and predatory that had taken root in the place where Iris once stood. Her transformation was more than skin profound; it was a primal awakening, a shedding of mortal frailty for an immortal hunger. Her steps, once hesitant and earthbound, now carried an unnerving grace, silent and swift as a whisper of wind through dry leaves. Each footfall was deliberate, deliberate in its purpose, a controlled descent upon her target.

She moved through the familiar paths of her childhood home, now alien territory. The moon, her sole companion and witness, cast long, distorted shadows that danced like specters in her wake. She saw the manor house ahead, its dark silhouette stark against the bruised twilight sky. It was a place of memory, of laughter, and of betrayal. Tonight, it would be the stage for retribution.

Her father, Bernard, was inside. She knew it without seeing him, could feel the thrum of his lifeblood, a distant beacon in the oppressive stillness of the night. He was oblivious, safe in his ignorance, unaware that the daughter he had forsaken was now a force of nature, a harbinger of his reckoning.

She reached the imposing oak door, its heavy wood groaning slightly as she pushed it open. The sound, amplified in the silence, was a jarring intrusion. She didn't bother with subtlety; subtlety was a luxury afforded to the living, the unaware. Her arrival was meant to be an announcement, a pronouncement.

Inside, the grand hall was dimly lit, shadows clinging to the corners like cobwebs. The scent of old wood, beeswax, and something else… fear. Faint, but present. She moved through the cavernous space, her spectral form gliding effortlessly across the polished floorboards. The portraits on the walls seemed to watch her, their painted eyes wide with a frozen horror, as if they too sensed the unnatural presence that now inhabited their ancestral home.

She found him in his study, a room that smelled of stale pipe tobacco and old paper. He sat slumped in his leather armchair, a half-empty glass of amber liquid resting on the mahogany desk beside him. The fire in the hearth had died down to embers, casting a weak, flickering glow. He looked older, frailer than she remembered, his face etched with lines that spoke of worry, perhaps even regret, but not the kind she craved.

He looked up, startled by the faint sound of her arrival. His eyes, dimmed by age and perhaps drink, widened slightly as they focused on her. Recognition flickered, then disbelief, followed by a wave of sheer terror.

"Elara?" The name was a rasp, barely a whisper. He scrambled back in his chair, his hands rising defensively, trembling. "No... it can't be... you're... dead."

A slow, cold smile spread across Elara's face, a smile that didn't reach her unnaturally bright eyes. "Did you think I would simply fade away, Father? Did you think your betrayal would go unanswered?" Her voice was no longer the soft lilt of the girl he had known, but a low, resonant hum, imbued with an ancient power that vibrated in the very air. It was the sound of the grave, of the earth reclaiming what was hers.

He scrambled to his feet, backing away, his breath coming in ragged gasps. "This is a nightmare. A dream. I must be dreaming." He reached for the decanter on his desk, his hand shaking so violently that he spilt some of the amber liquid.

Elara took a step forward, her movements fluid, unnervingly silent. "No dream, Father. This is reality. Your reality, now." She extended a hand, her fingers unnaturally long and pale, her nails sharp and dark. A faint, ethereal glow emanated from them.

He flinched, stumbling back against a bookshelf, sending volumes tumbling to the floor. "Stay away from me!" he croaked; his eyes wide with primal fear. He looked like a cornered animal, stripped of all defense, his bravado vanished like smoke in the wind.

She continued her advance, relentless, inevitable. "You took everything from me, Father. My life, my future, my innocence. You thought you could bury me and forget? You thought wrong." Her voice dropped to a whisper, laced with ice. "The debt must be paid."

She reached him. He tried to push her away, but his hands passed through her spectral form, leaving him grasping at air. The futility of his struggle was evident in his terrified eyes. He was trapped, not by physical restraints, but by the supernatural force she now commanded.

Her gaze locked onto his, drawing him in. He felt a chilling coldness spread through him, a draining sensation that started in his core and radiated outwards. It wasn't just the cold of fear, but a deeper, more profound chill, the cold of life itself being leached away.

"You fed on my life," she whispered, her voice inches from his ear, her spectral lips brushing against his skin, sending shivers down his spine. "Now, I will feed on yours."

A faint tremor ran through him as she leaned closer. Her eyes seemed to deepen, the blackness within them swirling like a vortex. He felt a strange pull, an irresistible force drawing him towards her, even as his body screamed in terror. His limbs felt heavy, his breath shallow.

He saw her lips part, revealing not teeth, but something sharper, more predatory. A faint red glow emanated from her throat, pulsing like a second heart. A low hum vibrated in the air, a sound that seemed to resonate deep within his bones.

A scream died in his throat as he felt a sharp, piercing sensation, not physical, but deeper, at the very essence of his being. It was as if she were drinking not just his blood, but his life force, his memories, his very soul. A profound weakness washed over him, rendering him incapable of movement, barely capable of thought.

He could feel his vitality draining away, leaving him cold, weak, and terrified. The room seemed to spin, the shadows deepening, swirling around them. He could feel his strength ebbing, his life force seeping away like sand through cupped hands.

Her grip, though unseen, tightened, anchoring him. Her eyes, once familiar, were now alien, filled with an ancient hunger that mirrored the void within her. He saw a flicker of something else within them – not malice, but a cold, calculating necessity. This was not revenge as humans understood it; this was a primal act of sustenance, a reclaiming of what was unjustly taken.

He felt a final, searing emptiness as the last vestiges of his life force were drawn from him. His body slumped, a hollow shell. The light in his eyes flickered and died, replaced by the same vacant darkness that now resided within her.

Elara released him, and he crumpled to the floor, a lifeless husk. She stood over him, her form shimmering slightly, a faint crimson glow pulsing beneath her skin. The cold air in the room seemed to intensify, a testament to the life that had just been extinguished.

A sigh escaped her lips, a sound that was both relief and a chilling emptiness. The hunger was momentarily sated, and the gnawing emptiness eased. But she knew it was only temporary. The thirst would return, stronger perhaps, demanding more.

She looked at the man who was her father, the man who had betrayed her, and felt no triumph, no remorse. Only a cold, detached understanding of the natural order. She had been wronged, and nature demanded balance. She had restored it, in her own way. The scent of spilt wine mingled with the faint, metallic tang of newly spilt blood – or rather, the essence that had sustained her—a chilling, yet strangely satisfying aroma. The taste of vengeance was potent, a dark nectar that fueled her nascent existence. She turned, her movements still unnaturally fluid, and glided towards the open door, leaving the shadowed room and its occupant behind. The night awaited, and with it, new hungers to satisfy.

The spectral chill that had seeped into the very bones of the manor house, a chilling testament to the recent demise of Bernard, now coalesced into a more focused, predatory intensity. Elara, or what remained of her, the husk animated by an ancient, insatiable thirst, turned her attention from the hollow shell of her father to the architect of her deepest despair. Bjorn. The name echoed in the cavernous silence of her newly awakened consciousness, not as a whisper of memory, but as a guttural, primal need. He was the fulcrum of her suffering, the venom that had poisoned her existence and birthed this horrific rebirth. Her vengeance would not be swift or merciful. It would be a slow, deliberate unravelling, a mirroring of the agony he had inflicted upon her, amplified by the timeless hunger that now gnawed at her.

The hunt for Bjorn was not a frantic chase, but a methodical pursuit, guided by an instinct honed in the eternal night. She did not need maps or compasses; the scent of his fear, a cloying, metallic perfume, drew her like a moth to a dying flame. He would be in his usual haunts, she surmised, his opulent chambers within the oldest wing of the estate, a place he considered his impregnable fortress. He would be surrounded by the trappings of his wealth and power, oblivious to the storm that had gathered and was now poised to break upon him. She glided through the manor's shadowed corridors, her movements a silent ballet of retribution. The very air seemed to recoil from her passage, growing colder, heavier. The portraits of her ancestors, their painted eyes now seeming to hold a morbid fascination, watched her glide past, their silent witness a grim approval of the coming reckoning.

She felt him before she saw him, a discordant tremor in the otherwise hushed symphony of the night. His presence was a foul stain, an affront to the house's ancient stillness. He was in his study, a room that had always reeked of self-satisfaction and the cloying scent of expensive, cheapened indulgence. The heavy oak door, intricately carved with scenes of supposed velour and conquest, stood ajar. He had never been one for proper security, his arrogance a constant, blinding shield. He believed himself untouchable, a god in his own gilded cage. Elara paused, a phantom sentinel on the threshold, savoring the moment, the anticipation a dark, heady wine.

Bjorn was slumped in his high-backed chair, a posture of casual dominion that spoke volumes of his hubris. A decanter of ruby-red liquid, likely his favored brandy, stood within easy reach, a testament to his ingrained habits. A half-burned cigar smoldered in a heavy crystal ashtray, its acrid smoke a thin veil between him and the encroaching darkness. The room was lit by the warm glow of a dying fire and a single, ornate desk lamp, its golden light casting long, dancing shadows that seemed to writhe with an unnatural life of their own. He was humming a tuneless melody, a sign of his utter complacency. He looked older than Elara remembered, his features coarsened by a life of excess and ruthless ambition, but the glint of avarice and cruel intelligence remained sharp in his eyes. He was the master of his domain, or so he believed.

Elara stepped into the room, her presence a sudden, icy draft that extinguished the false warmth of the fire. The humming stopped. Bjorn's head snapped up, his eyes, accustomed to the dim light, narrowing in confusion, then widening in dawning horror. The confusion was a fleeting thing, a flicker of disbelief quickly consumed by the raw, unadulterated terror that began to bloom on his face. He knew, with a certainty that chilled him to the marrow, that this was no living soul who had entered his sanctuary.

"Who... who's there?" His voice was a thick, uncertain rasp, a far cry from the booming arrogance she had always despised. He fumbled for the brandy decanter, his hand trembling so violently that it threatened to spill its contents. His eyes darted around the room, searching for the source of the oppressive cold, the encroaching dread.

Elara remained in the shadows for a beat longer, letting the fear fester. It was a potent elixir, a prelude to the feast. She savored the exquisite tension, the palpable unravelling of his composure. Then she stepped fully into the lamplight, her form coalescing from the ethereal haze into a shape at once familiar and monstrous. Her spectral pallor was pronounced, her eyes, once the warm hazel of a beloved daughter, now burned with an unholy, crimson light, as embers plucked from the most bottomless abyss. Her features, though still bearing a semblance of Elara's beauty, were sharpened, ethereal, and utterly devoid of human warmth. The long, dark hair cascaded around her like a shroud, framing a visage that was a chilling testament to her transformation.

"Father," she purred, the sound a low, resonant vibration that seemed to thrum through the very floorboards, shaking the brandy glass on the desk. It was a sound that held no affection, no hint of the daughter he had once known. It was the sound of the grave, awakened and demanding its due.

Bjorn let out a choked gasp, his hand flying to his chest as if to ward off a physical blow. "Elara? No... it cannot be. You are... gone. Dead." He staggered to his feet, his legs unsteady, knocking over a stack of leather-bound ledgers with a resounding thud. The sound echoed in the sudden, suffocating silence. "This is a trick! A hallucination! The drink..." He reached for the decanter again, his fingers clumsy and desperate.

A slow, unnerving smile, devoid of any mirth, spread across Elara's lips. It was a predatory baring of teeth, a promise of what was to come. "Dead? Oh, Father, I am more alive now than I have ever been. And you, you will soon understand the true meaning of mortality." Her voice was a silken whisper, yet it carried the weight of ages, the cold authority of the earth itself. She took a step forward, her feet making no sound on the thick Persian rug.

Bjorn stumbled backwards; his eyes wide with a terror that was rapidly eclipsing any semblance of reason. He saw the unnatural glow in her eyes, the unearthly pallor of her skin, the way her form seemed to shimmer at the edges, as if struggling to remain tethered to the mortal realm. This was no ghost, no mere apparition. This was something far more terrible, something ancient and ravenous.

"Stay away from me!" he shrieked, his voice cracking. He scrambled for a heavy brass letter opener on his desk, a pathetic weapon against the spectral horror before him. He brandished it wildly, his hand shaking uncontrollably. "I have done nothing to you!"

Elara's smile widened, a cruel, knowing expression. "Nothing? You took everything, Father. You bartered my life, my future, my very soul for your own selfish gain. You thought you could bury me, forget me, and escape the consequences. But some debts, Father, are not so easily erased. They fester. They grow. They return." She advanced, her movements fluid and inexorable, like a tide of encroaching darkness. The air around her grew perceptibly colder, frost blooming on the edges of the desk and the spines of the books.

Bjorn backed away, his breath coming in ragged, desperate gasps. He was trapped between the spectral apparition and the solid, unyielding furniture of his study. His eyes darted frantically, searching for an escape that did not exist. "This is madness! You were weak, frail! I did what I had to do!"

"Weak? Frail?" Elara's voice dropped to a low, dangerous growl. "You thought my suffering would break me. Instead, it forged me. It awakened me. You gave me the gift of this eternal hunger, Father. And now, it must be fed." She was closer now, close enough for him to feel the unnerving chill radiating from her, close enough to see the swirling vortex of darkness within her eyes.

He could feel a strange weakness seeping into his limbs, a draining sensation that began in his core and spread outwards like a creeping paralysis. It wasn't just the fear; it was something more profound, a leaching of his very vitality. His knees buckled, and he dropped the letter opener with a clatter. It landed on the floor, a futile testament to his lost power.

"What... what are you doing?" he stammered, his voice barely audible. He felt a profound lassitude wash over him, his thoughts becoming sluggish, his will dissolving like mist in the morning sun.

Elara reached out a translucent hand, her fingers unnaturally long and pale, tipped with sharp, dark nails that seemed to absorb the lamplight. She didn't touch him, not in the conventional sense. Her spectral fingers hovered inches from his chest, yet he felt a searing cold penetrate his skin, his very flesh, and burrow deep into his being. It was the touch of the grave, the kiss of oblivion.

"I am reclaiming what is mine," she whispered, her voice inches from his ear. He felt a phantom breath, colder than any earthly wind, stir his hair. "The life you stole, the years you denied me. I will take them back. Every drop. Every breath."

He felt a tug, a profound and terrifying pull from the very center of his being. It was as if an invisible cord had been attached to his soul, and Elara was slowly, deliberately, drawing it out of him. His vision began to blur, the opulent study swirling around him like a storm-tossed sea. The fire seemed to recede, the lamplight dimming, as if the very sources of light and warmth in his life were being extinguished.

His mind, clouded and sluggish, registered a terrifying realization: she was not merely killing him; she was consuming him. She was drinking him, not of blood, but of essence, of life force, of the very spark that made him Bjorn. The years of ambition, of cruelty, of self-serving machinations, all were being siphoned away, leaving him hollow, a mere husk.

He tried to cry out, to beg for mercy, but the words caught in his throat, choked by the overwhelming lethality of her presence. He felt his strength draining away, his consciousness flickering like a dying candle flame. He could feel the years of his life being peeled away, each stolen moment a searing agony, yet also a strange, detached numbness. He saw, in the swirling darkness that was consuming his vision, Elara's face, no longer contorted in rage, but serene, almost peaceful, as she drank him in.

The crimson glow in her eyes intensified, pulsing with a nascent power that was both terrifying and strangely captivating. He felt a final, agonizing emptiness as the last vestiges of his vitality were ripped from him. His legs gave way completely, and he collapsed onto the floor, not with a thud, but with a soft, sighing sound, like a deflating balloon. His eyes, vast and vacant, stared up at the ceiling, reflecting only the encroaching darkness.

Elara withdrew her hand, a faint, ethereal luminescence fading from her fingertips. She stood over his lifeless form, her spectral outline shimmering with a faint, crimson aura. The air in the study was now frigid, the silence absolute, save for the faint, almost inaudible hum that emanated from her. The gnawing hunger that had driven her was momentarily appeased, a deep, resonant satisfaction settling within her. It was not the triumphant exhilaration of revenge, but the primal contentment of a predator sated.

She looked down at the ruined form of Bjorn, the man who had orchestrated her torment, and felt no remorse, no triumph, only a cold, detached understanding. He had been a predator in his own right, and now, he had become the prey. The cycle had come full circle. The balance had been restored in a way that only the ancient, unforgiving laws of nature could dictate. The scent of spilt brandy mingled with the faint, metallic tang of released life force, a dark, potent perfume that now clung to her. It was the aroma of a debt paid in full, a dark nectar that sustained her nascent, horrifying existence. Turning away from the empty vessel that had once been Bjorn, Elara glided towards the open doorway, the spectral chill trailing in her wake, ready to embrace the endless night and the new hungers it promised.

The frigid emptiness that had been her tomb, the suffocating embrace of the grave, was no longer a place of despair but a cradle, a sanctuary where her actual existence had begun. The spectral chill that had clung to her, a testament to her transition, now felt like a familiar caress, a comforting cloak woven from the threads of the night. She, Elara, the broken daughter, was no more. In her place stirred something ancient, something ravenous, a creature forged in the crucible of betrayal and resurrected by a thirst that transcended mortal understanding. The blood, warm and vibrant, that now coursed through her ethereal veins was not just a sustenance; it was a declaration of rebirth, a visceral affirmation of her terrifying new reality.

The act itself had been a primal imperative, a desperate clawing from the suffocating darkness of oblivion towards a semblance of being. The initial shock of Bernard's spent life force, a lingering echo in the stillness of his final resting place, had been a mere prelude. It had been a chilling appetizer, a taste of the power that lay dormant within the very fabric of her awakened state. But it was Bjorn, the architect of her most profound suffering, whose essence had truly ignited the inferno within her. His lifeblood, still pulsing with the arrogance and avarice that had defined his existence, had been a potent elixir, a torrent of stolen years and corrupted vitality.

She remembered the sensation with a clarity that was both exquisite and horrifying. It was not a simple drinking, but a taking. Her spectral form, still tethered precariously to the mortal plane, had reached out, not with flesh and bone, but with tendrils of pure, unadulterated need. The air around Bjorn had crackled with an unseen energy as she drew him in, the very life force that animated him siphoned away like water from a dying well. It was a violation, a communion of the damned, and it had been utterly, intoxicatingly, profound.

The warmth that flooded her was unlike anything she had ever known. It was not the gentle heat of a summer's day or the comforting glow of a hearth. This was a raging inferno, a molten core of power that pulsed and thrummed through her being, banishing the eternal cold of the grave. Each beat of her reanimated heart, a sound that was more felt than heard, sent ripples of potent energy through her. The spectral pallor of her skin seemed to recede, replaced by a faint, unearthly luminescence, a testament to the vitality she had claimed.

Her senses, once dulled by the slow decay of death, were now sharpened to an almost unbearable degree. The faint scent of spilt brandy and the metallic tang of Bjorn's lifeblood, which had mingled in the aftermath of his demise, now assaulted her nostrils with an astonishing intensity. She could discern the faint scent of decaying leaves from the garden outside, the musty odor of ancient times in the study, and the very breath of the night itself. It was a symphony of smells, overwhelming and exhilarating, each note a testament to the vibrant, living world from which she had been so cruelly severed, and which she now, in her new form, could perceive with such startling clarity.

The shadows that had once been her companions, her silent witnesses to her grief and her suffering, now seemed to recede, their oppressive darkness diminished by the internal light that blazed within her. She could see the intricate carvings on the heavy oak door, the minute details of the woven rug beneath her feet, the dust motes dancing in the dying lamplight – all rendered with a clarity that was both a gift and a burden. This heightened perception, this acute awareness of the world around her, was a direct consequence of the life she had consumed.

The realization of what she had done, of what she had become, settled upon her not as a wave of horror, but as a profound, almost serene understanding. She was no longer Elara, the innocent victim. She was the Dearg Due, the red, or blood, guest, a creature of nightmare, a being sustained by the very essence of life. The word itself, ancient and terrible, resonated within her, a label that perfectly encapsulated her newfound identity.

This hunger, this insatiable craving that had driven her from her grave, was not quenched. It had been momentarily sated, a beast temporarily pacified, but the embers of its fiery appetite still glowed, promising a future of perpetual yearning. It was a constant, gnawing presence, a reminder that her existence was now irrevocably bound to the act of taking. The life she had absorbed from Bernard and Bjorn was a reprieve, a balm on a wound that would never truly heal, but would only ever be temporarily closed.

She felt a strange duality within her. On one hand, there was the chilling echo of Elara, a faint whisper of the innocent girl she had once been, a ghost of her former self recoiling from the monstrous act. This spectral remnant mourned the loss of her humanity, the innocence she had irrevocably shed. But the dominant force quickly drowned this out, the primal instinct that now governed her very being. This was the Dearg Due, the blood-drinker, reveling in its newfound power, its eternal potential.

The taste of blood, still lingering on her spectral lips, was a potent reminder of her transformation. It was not the coppery, metallic taste of spilt gore one might imagine. It was richer, more complex, imbued with the very essence of the life it had sustained. It held the warmth of passion, the sting of ambition, the sweetness of regret – a chaotic yet intoxicating blend that spoke of a life lived, now irrevocably hers. She found herself drawn to it, not with revulsion, but with a strange, burgeoning desire, a craving that was both terrifying and exhilarating.

She glanced at the fallen form of Bjorn, his eyes staring blankly at the ceiling, a testament to his final, pathetic end. There was no pity, no remorse. Only a cold, detached observation. He had been a predator, a taker of lives, and in the cruel, unforgiving tapestry of existence, he had become the prey. His fate was a grim, yet fitting, conclusion to his perfidy. The house, once a symbol of his power and his cruelty, now held the silent testament to his demise, a monument to the vengeance of the wronged.

The shadows in the study deepened, to writhe with a newfound energy, mirroring the turmoil and transformation within her. The silence was no longer empty, but filled with the faint hum of her own spectral energy, a resonant vibration that spoke of power and of eternity. She was a creature of the night, a denizen of the darkness, and the darkness now embraced her, not as an enemy, but as a welcoming mother.

The weight of her transformation was immense, a cosmic shift in her very being. The concept of death, once an inevitable end, was now a distant memory, a realm she had transcended. Immortality, an idea previously confined to myth and legend, was now her stark, chilling reality. This eternity stretched before her, a vast, uncharted expanse, filled with the promise of both wonder and terror. The hunger, the insatiable thirst, was the key that unlocked this endless existence, the price she had paid for her resurrection.

She raised a hand, her spectral fingers extended, and watched as the faint, crimson aura that now clung to her shimmered and pulsed. It was the mark of her new life, the undeniable evidence of the power she now wielded. This was not the gentle, ephemeral glow of a spirit, but the potent, dangerous luminescence of a predator, a being fueled by the very lifeblood of the world.

The chilling realization that this hunger would never truly abate, that it would be a constant companion on her eternal journey, began to dawn. It was a terrifying prospect, yet strangely invigorating. It meant she would continue to exist, to experience, to *be*. The alternative, the eternal oblivion of the grave, was far more terrifying. She had been given a second chance, a horrifying, blood-soaked rebirth, and she would not squander it.

The manor house, the silent witness to her transformation, now felt like a cage too small to contain her burgeoning power. The confines of its ancient walls, once a source of her sorrow and her despair, now felt like a mere stepping stone. The world beyond its shadowed corridors beckoned, a vast expanse teeming with life, with prey, with the sustenance she now craved. The scent of fear, the intoxicating aroma of life's vital essence, would guide her, drawing her out from the darkness and into the unsuspecting world.

Her spectral form, no longer tethered solely to the immediate vicinity of her victims, began to solidify, to gain a tangible presence, albeit one of ethereal grace and terrifying power. The transformation was not just internal; it was a visible manifestation of the life she had consumed. The residual warmth of Bjorn's stolen vitality seemed to imbue her with a semblance of solidity, a chilling echo of the man she had destroyed.

She felt a profound connection to the night itself, to the moon that hung like a spectral eye in the inky sky, to the rustling leaves of the ancient trees that surrounded the manor. They were her kin now, fellow creatures of the darkness, bound by the same primal instincts, the same silent pursuit of survival. The folklore she had once dismissed as fanciful tales now held a chilling resonance, a mirror to her own grotesque reality. The legends of the nightwalkers, the blood-drinkers, the ancient evils that lurked in the shadows – they were no longer stories; they were her brethren.

The thought of other souls, other lives waiting to be consumed, sent a shiver of anticipation through her. It was a morbid curiosity, a hunter's instinct awakened, a testament to the monster she had become. The memory of Elara, the daughter who had yearned for love and belonging, was now a faint, almost insignificant echo, overshadowed by the all-consuming hunger of the Dearg Due. She had been reborn, not into life, but into an existence defined by the absence of it, an existence fueled by the very thing she now craved more than anything else. The first blood had been shed; the first transformation complete. The age of the Dearg Due had begun.

Chapter 7:
Centuries of Solitude

The passage of years, then decades, then centuries, became a concept as fluid and meaningless as the mist that clung to the ancient forests of her early existence. What was once measured by the turning of seasons, the cycles of the moon, or the predictable rhythms of human life, now bled into an indistinguishable expanse. For Iris, or rather, for the entity she had become, time was no longer a river flowing towards an inevitable ocean of oblivion, but a stagnant, unfathomable pool, within which she was an isolated, unmoving island. Her initial, desperate clinging to the memory of mortality, to the sharp, painful edges of human experience, had slowly, inexorably, softened. The sharp sting of loss, the fleeting joy of connection, the gnawing ache of loneliness – these were sensations that belonged to a different existence, a life lived under the tyranny of a ticking clock. Now, her awareness stretched across an unimaginable span, each moment a single, unblinking eye in an eternity of vision.

She observed the world, not with the eager curiosity of a newcomer, but with the detached weariness of a perpetual witness—landscapes, once vibrant and distinct, blurred into a continuous panorama. The towering oaks that had sheltered her in her early years of anguished solitude eventually succumbed to rot and wind, replaced by saplings that grew, matured, and withered in the blink of her unseeing gaze. Forests gave way to fields, fields to villages, villages to sprawling cities that clawed at the sky with their relentless, glittering spires. She saw the slow, agonising crawl of human civilisation, a species forever teetering on the precipice of self-destruction, yet always, inexplicably, enduring. Their triumphs were brief sparks against the encroaching darkness, their follies a recurring, tiresome echo.

The people themselves became spectral figures in her grand, unending theatre. Their lives, so vibrant and charged with emotion to them, were to her mere blips on a vast, temporal canvas. A generation's rise and fall was less than a single breath for her. She saw lovers meet, their whispered vows echoing in her perception as a fleeting sigh, their eventual parting a faint ripple in the vast stillness. She witnessed the birth of children, their cries a momentary disturbance in the quiet hum of her being, their eventual deaths a silent fading, like embers cooling in the hearth of existence. Each face, each name, each story was a fleeting inscription on a page that was constantly being rewritten. There was no space for attachment, for the investment of her spectral essence, when all she observed was destined to crumble and fade.

The sheer, unyielding isolation was the most profound torment of her immortal existence. It was a solitude that gnawed not at her spirit, for her spirit, in the mortal sense, had long since been eroded, but at the very core of her being. To exist without a companion, without shared experience, without even the simple comfort of a sympathetic gaze, was to exist in a state of perpetual, profound emptiness. She was an echo in a void, a solitary star in an infinite, unpopulated cosmos. She could recall the warmth of human touch, the resonance of shared laughter, the comforting weight of a hand on her shoulder. Still, these memories were like faded tapestries, their vibrant colours leached away by the relentless erosion of time and solitude. They offered no solace, only a haunting reminder of a world from which she was irrevocably exiled.

She had tried, in the early centuries, to engage. To interact. To find some semblance of connection in the ephemeral lives that pulsed around her. She would walk amongst them, a silent wraith, observing their customs, their rituals, their fleeting passions. She saw the rise and fall of empires, the birth of new technologies that promised to reshape their world, only to be replaced by even more advanced marvels that rendered the old obsolete. She witnessed the ebb and flow of belief, the fervent adherence to gods and dogmas that, in her timeless perspective, seemed like childish fancies. She learned their languages, their histories, their philosophies, absorbing them not for understanding, but for the fleeting distraction they offered from the crushing weight of her own unending existence.

Yet, every connection attempt was met with an insurmountable barrier. Her presence, subtle as she tried to make it, often unnerved them. A flicker of unease in their eyes, a sudden chill in the air, a sense of being watched by something ancient and unknowable. They were creatures of the tangible, of the finite, and her spectral nature, the very essence of her being, was alien to them. When she did find those rare souls who seemed more attuned to the unseen, who felt her presence not as a threat but as something… different, their lives were always too short. Their understanding is too limited. They would glimpse the vastness of her existence, the profound gulf that separated them, and their mortal minds, unable to comprehend, would often fracture or recoil in fear, leaving her more isolated than before.

The world's evolution became a spectacle she could not participate in, only observe. The dusty roads gave way to paved highways, the flickering torchlight to the incandescent glare of electricity. She saw the horseless carriages that roared with unnatural speed, spewing foul smoke into the air, and the flying machines that defied gravity, carrying fragile mortals through the heavens. She saw the development of tools that could communicate across vast distances instantaneously, yet the people using them often seemed more disconnected than ever. It was a dizzying, relentless march of progress, driven by a species that seemed perpetually dissatisfied with its lot, always seeking something more, something different, something… beyond.

She remembered one particularly poignant period, perhaps the fifth or sixth century of her solitary vigil. The world was entering a period humans called the Renaissance. Art and science flourished, and there was a palpable surge of intellectual curiosity. She found herself drawn to the burgeoning centres of learning, to the libraries filled with ancient texts and the workshops where ingenious minds experimented with new ideas. For a time, she almost felt a flicker of what might have been kinship. She watched artists painstakingly render the human form, capturing fleeting expressions with an astonishing fidelity. She listened to philosophers debate the nature of reality, their words, though grounded in mortality, echoing some of the fundamental questions that had plagued her own existence.

But even then, the gulf remained. She could observe the delicate brushstrokes, the intricate carvings, the elegant equations, but she could not truly *feel* the artist's passion, the inventor's triumph, the philosopher's doubt. Her appreciation was intellectual, a detached analysis of form and function, devoid of the emotional resonance that made these creations meaningful to their creators. She was a ghost at the feast, an unseen observer in a world teeming with life and creation, forever an outsider looking in. The very intensity of their human experience, the very thing that made their lives so tragically brief, was also what made them so vibrant, so compelling, and so utterly unattainable for her.

The passage of time had also brought about a profound change in her own nature, or rather, in her perception of it. The initial raw hunger, the primal need that had driven her from her grave, had evolved. It was no longer a ravenous beast at her throat, but a constant, low hum, a persistent awareness of her own spectral existence and the life force that sustained it. She had learned to subsist on the fringes of existence, to draw sustenance not just from the direct consumption of life, but from the ambient energy of the living world. The vibrant pulse of a bustling city, the raw, untamed energy of a storm-ravaged landscape, the silent, steady growth of a primordial forest – all contributed to her unending sustenance, albeit in far less potent and direct ways. This allowed her to exist without the constant, desperate need for direct feeding, which had been the source of so much terror and revulsion in her early centuries.

However, this prolonged existence, devoid of the natural cessation that defined mortal life, had also brought about a peculiar detachment from her own being. She no longer felt the sharp, defined edges of self that humans possessed. Her consciousness was like a vast, amorphous sea, encompassing centuries of observation, of experience, of non-experience. She was the sum of all she had witnessed, yet paradoxically, she felt less and less like a distinct individual. The memories of Elara, the human girl, were like scattered fragments, shards of coloured glass in the immense ocean of her being. They were present, undeniably, but they no longer formed a coherent picture, no longer defined the totality of who she was.

The concept of "loneliness" itself began to lose its sharp, painful edge, morphing into a pervasive state of being. It was not an emotion she actively felt, but rather the fundamental condition of her existence. She was an entity that existed, that perceived, that endured, but she did not *connect*. The vibrant tapestry of human interaction, with its intricate threads of love, hate, joy, and sorrow, was a spectacle she could appreciate from afar, but never participate in. She was like a lighthouse keeper, eternally vigilant, sending out beams of light into the darkness, but never receiving a response, never sharing the quiet solitude of her watch with another soul.

And so, she continued to drift through the ages, a silent, eternal spectre. The changing world was her backdrop, the ephemeral lives of mortals her fleeting entertainment. She was a witness to history, a creature unbound by its dictates, forever observing, forever enduring, forever alone. The vastness of her existence was both a curse and a strange, terrifying freedom. She was free from the constraints of mortality, from the inevitable march towards oblivion. But this freedom came at a terrible price: an eternity of silent observation, a never-ending vigil in the lonely theatre of time. The landscapes shifted, the cities rose and fell, the faces changed, but she remained, an unchanging constant in a world of flux, a monument to an existence that transcended the very meaning of life and death. The centuries passed, each one indistinguishable from the last, a slow, inexorable tide washing over the shores of her unending solitude.

The ancient standing stones, weathered and cloaked in a shroud of perpetual twilight, marked the boundaries of her dominion. They were not erected by mortal hands in memory of kings or heroes, but born of a primal magic, their jagged silhouettes against the bruised sky a testament to forces long forgotten. Here, upon a plateau that offered a commanding, yet desolate, view of the world that had moved on without her, lay Iris's resting place. It was a grave, yes, but not one of earth and worms. It was a nexus, a heartwood of her endless existence, a place steeped in the very essence of her sorrow and her power.

The air here was thin, sharp with the tang of decay and something far older, far more primal. A constant wind, a mournful sigh that never truly ceased, scoured the barren ground, whipping wisps of mist from unseen hollows and swirling them about the base of the monoliths like restless spirits. There was no birdsong to break the oppressive silence, no scurrying of small creatures to betray the presence of life. The very soil seemed leached of vitality, a grey, stony dust that clung to the boots of any who dared trespass. This was no patch of hallowed ground, no sanctuary for peace. It was a wound upon the earth, a place where the veil between worlds wore perilously thin, and Iris was its self-appointed guardian, its eternal inhabitant.

Her lair was not a crypt carved into the earth, but the very landscape itself. The rough-hewn rocks, slick with a perpetual dampness that felt more like cold sweat than dew, formed alcoves and shadowed recesses where she could coalesce, where her spectral form could find a semblance of anchor in the ethereal currents that swirled around her. The wind, her constant companion, would sometimes carry the faintest whispers of her thoughts, a chilling murmur that could freeze the marrow of any who heard it. The mist, thick and cloying, was more than just atmospheric moisture; it was an extension of her will, a veil that obscured and disoriented, a silent alarm that alerted her to the approach of the unwary.

This desolate expanse was not chosen by chance. It was a place that resonated with the emptiness that had become her constant state. The sheer isolation of the moor, its unyielding terrain, its stark beauty that verged on the terrifying, all mirrored the landscape of her own soul. It was a place that repelled life, that discouraged habitation, and that was precisely its appeal. Here, she could exist without the constant, jarring intrusion of mortal presence, without the fleeting warmth of their vibrant existence that, in her earlier centuries, had been a source of torment. Now, it was a resource, a distant hum that she could draw upon, but at this distance, it was no longer an immediate temptation.

The standing stones, imbued with an ancient, untamed energy, pulsed with a subtle resonance that was intrinsically linked to her own being. They were conduits, drawing power from the earth and the ceaseless, often brutal, dance of the celestial spheres. In the heart of this circle, where the stones stood closest, was the focal point of her power, the place she considered her actual grave. It was a depression in the ground, not deep, but profoundly unsettling, as if the earth itself had recoiled from something buried there, leaving a scar of desolation. Moss, a sickly, pallid green, clung to the edges, the only concession to organic life in the immediate vicinity. The air here was always colder, the wind's lament more pronounced, and a tangible sense of watchful malevolence permeated the atmosphere.

Centuries of solitude had etched themselves into the very fabric of this place. The stones had witnessed her endless vigil, her silent suffering, her gradual transformation from a tormented soul to an ancient, predatory force. They absorbed the echoes of her despair, the faint tremors of her unfettered power, and projected them outwards, creating an aura that was both repellent and, to a particular kind of soul, inexplicably alluring. It was a beacon, not of hope, but of a dark fascination, a magnet for those who strayed from the well-trodden paths, those who carried their own burdens of grief or desperation, those who, consciously or unconsciously, sought out places where the world's harsh realities were amplified, not softened.

The remoteness of her resting place was its most potent defence, and its most insidious lure. Far from the bustling centres of human activity, where the clamour of life could mask her presence and dilute her power, this barren plateau offered an unvarnished canvas for her existence. To reach it, one had to navigate treacherous bogs that swallowed the unwary whole, traverse forests so dense that sunlight was a forgotten memory, and climb slopes that offered little purchase for tired feet. Yet, it was precisely this arduous journey that filtered her prey. Those who arrived were already weakened, their spirits frayed, their senses dulled by hardship. They were ripe for the picking, their desperation a fragrant invitation that drifted on the wind, reaching her with unfailing accuracy.

The sky above was rarely clear. More often than not, it was a canvas of bruised purples and oppressive greys, the sun a pale, distant disc struggling to break through the perpetual haze. Storms were frequent visitors, not the cleansing downpours of gentler climes, but violent tempests that lashed the land with fury.

Lightning would illuminate the stark landscape in fleeting, terrifying flashes, revealing the skeletal forms of ancient, gnarled trees that clawed at the sky like desperate hands. Thunder would roll and rumble, a primal roar that seemed to emanate from the very core of the earth, a symphony that Iris found profoundly comforting, a testament to the raw, untamed forces that mirrored her own.

The ground itself was a mosaic of lichen-covered rocks, thorny scrub, and patches of coarse, wiry grass that offered little sustenance to any but the hardiest of creatures – creatures that rarely ventured into this blighted domain. Pockets of stagnant water, their surfaces scummed with a dark, iridescent film, lay scattered across the plateau, breeding grounds for unseen things that skittered and writhed in the perpetual gloom. The scent of ozone, particularly after a storm, mingled with the pervasive aroma of damp earth and decaying vegetation, creating an olfactory tapestry that was both unsettling and deeply familiar to Iris. This was the scent of her domain, the perfume of her eternity.

The isolation was not merely physical; it was spiritual. There were no ancient ruins of forgotten civilisations here, no whispers of past glories or tragic falls that might imbue the land with a sense of history or human resonance. It was a place that seemed to exist outside of time, a pocket of primordial desolation touched by something ancient and dark, then left to fester. The stones, the wind, the mist, the very earth – they were all extensions of her own unending solitude, her own deep-seated power.

She would often find herself drawn to the periphery of her domain, to the edge of the plateau where the land began its descent into the shadowed valleys below. From these vantage points, she could observe the distant, fleeting lights of human settlements, mere pinpricks in the vast darkness. She saw their hurried lives, their brief passions, their inevitable ends, and felt no connection, no longing. They were like fireflies, their brief illumination a stark contrast to the eternal night that was her existence. They were the potential, the sustenance, the occasional distraction, but they were not kin.

Her grave was a place of perpetual twilight, a realm where the sun's rays seemed to falter, unable to pierce the veil of ancient sorrow that hung heavy in the air. It was a testament to her unending existence, a monument to her profound solitude, and a silent, chilling invitation to those who, by fate or by folly, found themselves drawn to its desolate embrace. It was her hunting ground, her sanctuary, her eternal lair, where the echoes of centuries of solitude coalesced into a palpable, predatory presence.

The solitude was a shroud, a comfort woven from threads of ice and absence. Yet, beneath its chilling embrace, another sensation, far more insistent and agonising, pulsed with a relentless rhythm. It was the hunger, an inferno that raged within the hollowed chambers of her spectral form, a constant, gnawing emptiness that no amount of ethereal sustenance could ever truly quell. It was the curse of her undeath, the unyielding thirst that bound her to the cycle of predator and prey, a fundamental truth of her existence as the Dearg Due.

This was not the pang of a mortal stomach, a temporary discomfort to be soothed by a meal. This was a cosmic void, a craving that reached into the very marrow of her being, demanding to be filled. It was a sensation that had begun as a subtle ache in her earliest centuries, a vague disquiet that had gnawed at the edges of her awareness. With each passing epoch, it had deepened, its tendrils wrapping around her consciousness, shaping her every thought and action. It had become the leitmotif of her eternity, the soundtrack to her ceaseless vigil.

The hunger was a physical manifestation of her spectral essence, a thirst for the vital force that flowed through mortal veins. It was the antithesis of her own desiccated existence, a stark reminder of the vibrant life she had once possessed and now, by necessity, consumed. When it grew acute, a phantom ache would bloom in her chest, a sensation akin to a thousand tiny blades scraping against her spectral ribs. Her senses would sharpen, not with the clarity of waking life, but with a predatory focus, tuning into the distant thrum of lifeblood, the faint scent of fear that wafted on the wind.

Psychologically, the hunger was a torment of its own making. It stripped away the layers of contemplation, of philosophical musings that had once occupied her long stretches of isolation. It reduced her to her most primal state, a creature driven by an insatiable need. Memories of mortal sensations, of warmth and connection, would sometimes surface, only to be twisted and perverted by the gnawing void within. The thought of companionship, of shared existence, was no longer a solace but a temptation, a tantalising possibility that the hunger warped into a desire for consumption. To be close to another was to be close to the source of her relief, a dangerous proximity that often led to her undoing.

The ebb and flow of this hunger dictated the rhythm of her existence. There were periods, after a particularly potent feeding, when a deceptive calm would settle over her. The gnawing emptiness would recede, allowing a semblance of clarity to return. In these moments, she could observe the world from her desolate plateau, her ancient stones standing as silent witnesses to the passage of time. She could ponder the ephemeral nature of mortal lives, the fleeting joys and sorrows that occupied their brief sojourn. But these interludes were always temporary, fragile bubbles of peace that the ever-present hunger would inevitably shatter.

As the stolen vitality began to wane, the hunger would awaken, a slow burn at first, then a searing blaze. It was a primal instinct, as deeply ingrained as the desire to breathe for any living creature. But for Iris, it was a curse, a constant reminder of the monstrous transformation she had undergone. It was the infernal engine that drove her, the inescapable imperative that propelled her from the solitary heights of her dominion to the shadowed fringes of the mortal world.

The transformation was always the most harrowing part. It was a descent, a shedding of the ethereal and an embrace of the predatory. Her spectral form would solidify, the mist and wind coalescing into a more tangible, albeit still unearthly, shape. Her eyes, once pools of sorrow, would blaze with a feverish light, reflecting the inferno within. Her limbs, usually languid and spectral, would grow taut with a coiled energy, ready to spring. The very air around her would thicken, charged with an unseen tension, a silent warning to any who might be in her path.

The scent of fear became her siren song, a perfumed whisper on the night air that drew her inexorably towards its source. It was a scent that spoke of vulnerability, of weakness, of an imminent feast. She learned to distinguish the subtle nuances of mortal emotions – the raw panic of a traveller lost in the woods, the quiet despair of a soul contemplating its end, the fleeting terror of a sudden, unexpected encounter. Each held a unique flavour, a distinct resonance that the hunger craved.

The process of feeding was not merely an act of survival; it was an act of consumption that left an indelible mark. The stolen life force, the very essence of her victims, would seep into her being, temporarily sating the raging inferno. But it was a fleeting satiation, a borrowed peace that could never last. The hunger was immortal, and the sustenance it craved was ultimately beyond its grasp. The more she consumed, the deeper the void seemed to become, a testament to the insatiable nature of her curse.

This constant yearning also bred a peculiar form of desperation. It gnawed at her resolve, chipping away at the stoicism she had cultivated over centuries of solitude. There were times, in the depths of a particularly acute craving, when her carefully constructed control would fray. She would find herself lingering in the shadows of human settlements, the distant laughter and music a cruel mockery of her own desolate existence. The vibrant pulse of life, so close yet so unattainable in its proper form, would become an almost unbearable temptation.

The desperation was a dangerous companion. It dulled her innate caution, making her more reckless, more prone to leaving traces of her passage. It was the whisper of the beast within, urging her to abandon the subtleties, to embrace the raw, brutal efficiency of her true nature. In earlier centuries, this desperation had led to numerous mistakes, to periods of intense scrutiny and near-discovery. But with time, she had learned to temper it, to channel it into a more refined form of predation.

Yet, even with her newfound mastery, the hunger remained the master. It was the constant, unseen puppeteer, pulling the strings of her eternal existence. It was the shadow that stretched long behind her, even in the deepest twilight. It was the silent scream that echoed in the vast emptiness of her solitude, a testament to the unquenchable thirst of the Dearg Due. And it was the promise, the inevitable certainty, that the cycle would always continue, that the hunger would always return, demanding its due. The centuries of solitude were defined not just by her isolation, but by this unceasing, voracious need, a gnawing emptiness that was the very heart of her monstrous eternity. It was a thirst that could never be quenched, a hunger that would always remain, an unending testament to the darkness that had claimed her.

The spectral shroud of her solitude, once a balm, now served as a chilling camouflage. Iris, the Dearg Due, was not merely a passive entity of sorrow and isolation; she was a predator honed by the long, unyielding arc of centuries. The hunger, that ceaseless, infernal ache within her spectral core, had long ago sculpted her into a master manipulator, an artisan of deception.

Her ancient grave, nestled within the desolate crags of the accursed mountains, was not merely a tomb but a nexus of her power, a place where the veil between worlds thinned, allowing her to weave her insidious lures.

Her most potent weapon, however, was not forged of spectral energy or arcane power, but of a sound that resonated with the deepest, most primal chords of the mortal heart: her mournful cry. It was a melody born of an eternity of loss, a lament that carried on the wind, a siren song for souls adrift. It wasn't a shriek of agony, nor a wail of despair, but something far more subtle, far more seductive. It was the sound of profound loneliness, a resonant echo of every unfulfilled longing, every unspoken ache that festered in the human spirit. She modulated it with an instinctual understanding of mortal frailty, weaving into its melancholic tapestry the subtle undertones of yearning, of a shared experience that transcended the physical.

When the hunger began its insistent gnawing, Iris would emerge from the shadowed embrace of her sepulchre. She would ascend to the highest promontory, her translucent form shimmering against the bruised twilight sky. Then, she would sing. The sound would spill forth, not a torrent, but a carefully curated stream, designed to drift on the night air, to find its way to the ears of those who were most susceptible. It was a sound that could reach a solitary shepherd tending his flock under a canopy of indifferent stars, a hunter lost in the labyrinthine woods as dusk bled into night, or a weary traveller seeking respite from a harsh journey, his heart heavy with the weight of his solitude.

The cry was a promise, unspoken yet deeply understood. It spoke of a kindred spirit, of an understanding that the mundane world could not offer. It was the sound of a heart that had known profound sorrow and, therefore, could empathise with the sorrow of another. For the lonely, it was a beacon, a fragile hope in the vast expanse of their isolation. For the lost, it was a guide, a whisper of solace in the encroaching darkness. For those burdened by grief, it was a testament to their pain, a validation of their suffering.

But the mournful cry was only the overture. Iris was a composer of a far more complex symphony of deception. Her spectral presence, when she chose to manifest it more tangibly, was a masterpiece of ethereal allure. She did not appear as a grotesque aberration, a creature of pure horror, not at first. Instead, she would condense her spectral essence, coalescing into a form that hinted at the beauty she once possessed, a beauty now tinged with an otherworldly melancholy. Her features would be sculpted from mist and shadow, her eyes pools of an ancient, sorrowful light that seemed to gaze not just at her victim, but into the very depths of his soul.

She would often appear on the periphery of a traveller's vision, a fleeting glimpse that sparked curiosity and disbelief. Was it a trick of the fading light? A phantom born of exhaustion? Or was it something more? This ambiguity was crucial. It allowed the seed of fascination to take root, to blossom into a desire to investigate, to understand the apparition that haunted the desolate landscapes.

When her chosen prey, drawn by the haunting melody or the tantalising glimpses of her form, ventured closer to her desolate domain, Iris would subtly amplify her presence. She would manifest more fully, yet still veiled in an ethereal grace. Her movements would be fluid, silent, as if she floated rather than walked. Her voice, when she spoke, was a hushed whisper, a silken caress against the ear, imbued with the same sorrow and understanding that characterised her cry, but now more intimate, more personal.

"You are far from home," she might murmur, her voice a soft echo in the stillness. "Or perhaps, you seek what you cannot find there."

Her words were never accusatory, never demanding. They were observations, gentle probes into the heart of her victim's desolation. She would listen not just to their words but to the unspoken anxieties and hidden fears that lay beneath the surface. She would mirror their loneliness, validating their feelings, making them feel seen and understood in a way they had likely never experienced before.

"The road is long," she might sigh, her spectral form shimmering, "and the nights are cold. It is a comfort, is it not, to know one is not entirely alone in the vastness?"

She played upon the innate human need for connection, for companionship. She offered not just solace, but a promise of belonging. Her desolate grave, a place of death and decay, became, through her subtle enchantments, a sanctuary, a haven from the harsh realities of the mortal world. The air around her would grow strangely still, the usual sounds of the wilderness muted, as if nature itself held its breath in deference to her spectral presence. This unnatural calm was another layer of her deception, creating a surreal atmosphere of peace that lulled her victims into a false sense of security.

Curiosity was a powerful motivator, but Iris understood that a more potent bait was often needed. She would subtly hint at her supposed plight, weaving tales of ancient sorrow, of a love lost, of an eternal vigil. Her story was always one of profound tragedy, designed to elicit sympathy and a protective instinct. She presented herself not as a monster, but as a victim, a soul trapped by circumstance, yearning for release, for understanding.

"I have waited here for so long," she might lament, her gaze fixed on some unseen point in the distance, "for a soul who could hear my song, a soul who might understand the weight of centuries."

She would allow her victims to believe they were the chosen one, the rare individual capable of piercing her veil of sorrow. This sense of specialness, of being singled out by such an ethereal and enigmatic being, was a potent aphrodisiac for the ego, especially for those who felt overlooked or insignificant in their everyday lives. They would feel a sense of purpose, a noble quest to offer comfort to this spectral beauty, to perhaps even free her from her eternal torment.

The more they engaged with her, the more she would subtly draw them closer to the heart of her domain. She would guide them, not with forceful commands, but with soft suggestions, with a gentle turn of her misty head, a lingering gaze in a particular direction. The path would lead deeper into the desolate landscape, away from the familiar world, into a realm where her influence was most decisive. The air would grow colder, not a biting, physical cold, but a chilling resonance that seeped into the bones, a primal warning that was easily dismissed as the natural consequence of venturing into such a remote and forsaken place.

She would offer them respite from their journey, a place to rest within the spectral embrace of her surroundings. It was a calculated gesture, designed to disarm them further. The ground beneath their feet softened, the jagged rocks appearing to recede, as if the very earth itself was bending to her will, preparing a welcoming bed for her guest. She would conjure phantom comforts – the illusion of a gentle breeze, the scent of a long-forgotten flower, the soft glow of a spectral fire – all designed to lull them into a state of profound relaxation.

Her touch, when it came, was like the caress of moonlight, cool yet strangely alluring. She would brush a spectral hand against their cheek, her touch sending shivers not of fear, but of an intoxicating sensation that blurred the lines between danger and desire. Her eyes, filled with an ancient sorrow, would hold them captive, drawing them deeper into her otherworldly gaze. They would see in her not a predator, but a lost soul, a beautiful tragedy, and their mortal hearts, so prone to both compassion and a misguided sense of heroism, would be irrevocably ensnared.

She preyed on their deepest vulnerabilities: their loneliness, their yearning for meaning, their desire for connection. She offered them a fleeting illusion of solace, a seductive whisper of understanding in the vast, uncaring silence of the world. And as they drew closer, captivated by her mournful song and ethereal beauty, they unknowingly stepped onto the precipice of an eternal darkness, their very life force a beacon that the insatiable hunger of the Dearg Due would ultimately extinguish. Her desolate grave was not just her prison, but a meticulously crafted trap, a silent monument to the unwary souls who had dared to answer her mournful call.

The spectral shroud of her solitude, once a balm, now served as a chilling camouflage. Iris, the Dearg Due, was not merely a passive entity of sorrow and isolation; she was a predator honed by the long, unyielding arc of centuries. The hunger, that ceaseless, infernal ache within her spectral core, had long ago sculpted her into a master manipulator, an artisan of deception. Her ancient grave, nestled within the desolate crags of the accursed mountains, was not merely a tomb but a nexus of her power, a place where the veil between worlds thinned, allowing her to weave her insidious lures.

Her most potent weapon, however, was not forged of spectral energy or arcane power, but of a sound that resonated with the deepest, most primal chords of the mortal heart: her mournful cry. It was a melody born of an eternity of loss, a lament that carried on the wind, a siren song for souls adrift. It wasn't a shriek of agony, nor a wail of despair, but something far more subtle, far more seductive. It was the sound of profound loneliness, a resonant echo of every unfulfilled longing, every unspoken ache that festered in the human spirit. She modulated it with an instinctual understanding of mortal frailty, weaving into its melancholic tapestry the subtle undertones of yearning, of a shared experience that transcended the physical.

When the hunger began its insistent gnawing, Iris would emerge from the shadowed embrace of her sepulchre. She would ascend to the highest promontory, her translucent form shimmering against the bruised twilight sky. Then, she would sing. The sound would spill forth, not a torrent, but a carefully curated stream, designed to drift on the night air, to find its way to the ears of those who were most susceptible. It was a sound that could reach a solitary shepherd tending his flock under a canopy of indifferent stars, a hunter lost in the labyrinthine woods as dusk bled into night, or a weary traveller seeking respite from a harsh journey, his heart heavy with the weight of his solitude.

The cry was a promise, unspoken yet deeply understood. It spoke of a kindred spirit, of an understanding that the mundane world could not offer. It was the sound of a heart that had known profound sorrow and, therefore, could empathise with the sorrow of another. For the lonely, it was a beacon, a fragile hope in the vast expanse of their isolation. For the lost, it was a guide, a whisper of solace in the encroaching darkness. For those burdened by grief, it was a testament to their pain, a validation of their suffering.

But the mournful cry was only the overture. Iris was a composer of a far more complex symphony of deception. Her spectral presence, when she chose to manifest it more tangibly, was a masterpiece of ethereal allure. She did not appear as a grotesque aberration, a creature of pure horror, not at first. Instead, she would condense her spectral essence, coalescing into a form that hinted at the beauty she once possessed, a beauty now tinged with an otherworldly melancholy. Her features would be sculpted from mist and shadow, her eyes pools of an ancient, sorrowful light that seemed to gaze not just at her victim, but into the very depths of his soul.

She would often appear on the periphery of a traveller's vision, a fleeting glimpse that sparked curiosity and disbelief. Was it a trick of the fading light? A phantom born of exhaustion? Or was it something more? This ambiguity was crucial. It allowed the seed of fascination to take root, to blossom into a desire to investigate, to understand the apparition that haunted the desolate landscapes.

When her chosen prey, drawn by the haunting melody or the tantalising glimpses of her form, ventured closer to her desolate domain, Iris would subtly amplify her presence. She would manifest more fully, yet still veiled in an ethereal grace. Her movements would be fluid, silent, as if she floated rather than walked. Her voice, when she spoke, was a hushed whisper, a silken caress against the ear, imbued with the same sorrow and understanding that characterised her cry, but now more intimate, more personal.

"You are far from home," she might murmur, her voice a soft echo in the stillness. "Or perhaps, you seek what you cannot find there."

Her words were never accusatory, never demanding. They were observations, gentle probes into the heart of her victim's desolation. She would listen not just to their words but to the unspoken anxieties and hidden fears that lay beneath the surface. She would mirror their loneliness, validating their feelings, making them feel seen and understood in a way they had likely never experienced before.

"The road is long," she might sigh, her spectral form shimmering, "and the nights are cold. It is a comfort, is it not, to know one is not entirely alone in the vastness?"

She played upon the innate human need for connection, for companionship. She offered not just solace, but a promise of belonging. Her desolate grave, a place of death and decay, became, through her subtle enchantments, a sanctuary, a haven from the harsh realities of the mortal world. The air around her would grow strangely still, the usual sounds of the wilderness muted, as if nature itself held its breath in deference to her spectral presence. This unnatural calm was another layer of her deception, creating a surreal atmosphere of peace that lulled her victims into a false sense of security.

Curiosity was a powerful motivator, but Iris understood that a more potent bait was often needed. She would subtly hint at her supposed plight, weaving tales of ancient sorrow, of a love lost, of an eternal vigil. Her story was always one of profound tragedy, designed to elicit sympathy and a protective instinct. She presented herself not as a monster, but as a victim, a soul trapped by circumstance, yearning for release, for understanding.

"I have waited here for so long," she might lament, her gaze fixed on some unseen point in the distance, "for a soul who could hear my song, a soul who might understand the weight of centuries."

She would allow her victims to believe they were the chosen one, the rare individual capable of piercing her veil of sorrow. This sense of specialness, of being singled out by such an ethereal and enigmatic being, was a potent aphrodisiac for the ego, especially for those who felt overlooked or insignificant in their everyday lives. They would feel a sense of purpose, a noble quest to offer comfort to this spectral beauty, to perhaps even free her from her eternal torment.

The more they engaged with her, the more she would subtly draw them closer to the heart of her domain. She would guide them, not with forceful commands, but with soft suggestions, with a gentle turn of her misty head, a lingering gaze in a particular direction. The path would lead deeper into the desolate landscape, away from the familiar world, into a realm where her influence was most decisive. The air would grow colder, not a biting, physical cold, but a chilling resonance that seeped into the bones, a primal warning that was easily dismissed as the natural consequence of venturing into such a remote and forsaken place.

She would offer them respite from their journey, a place to rest within the spectral embrace of her surroundings. It was a calculated gesture, designed to disarm them further. The ground beneath their feet softened, the jagged rocks appearing to recede, as if the very earth itself was bending to her will, preparing a welcoming bed for her guest. She would conjure phantom comforts – the illusion of a gentle breeze, the scent of a long-forgotten flower, the soft glow of a spectral fire – all designed to lull them into a state of profound relaxation.

Her touch, when it came, was like the caress of moonlight, cool yet strangely alluring. She would brush a spectral hand against their cheek, her touch sending shivers not of fear, but of an intoxicating sensation that blurred the lines between danger and desire. Her eyes, filled with an ancient sorrow, would hold them captive, drawing them deeper into her otherworldly gaze. They would see in her not a predator, but a lost soul, a beautiful tragedy, and their mortal hearts, so prone to both compassion and a misguided sense of heroism, would be irrevocably ensnared.

She preyed on their deepest vulnerabilities: their loneliness, their yearning for meaning, their desire for connection. She offered them a fleeting illusion of solace, a seductive whisper of understanding in the vast, uncaring silence of the world. And as they drew closer, captivated by her mournful song and ethereal beauty, they unknowingly stepped onto the precipice of an eternal darkness, their very life force a beacon that the insatiable hunger of the Dearg Due would ultimately extinguish. Her desolate grave was not just her prison, but a meticulously crafted trap, a silent monument to the unwary souls who had dared to answer her mournful call.

Over the span of centuries, the tales of Iris and her melancholic domain began to coalesce, to solidify from hushed whispers into the robust sinews of legend. What had once been a personal, primal need for sustenance had, through countless retellings and the fertile ground of mortal imagination, transformed into something far more potent and far-reaching. The initial encounters, stark and terrifying in their raw, predatory nature, were gradually softened, embellished, and reshaped by the human tendency to find meaning and moral instruction in the face of the inexplicable.

The initial victims, those who had stumbled too close to her sepulchre, lost to the gnawing hunger and the chilling embrace of her spectral essence, were no longer simply unfortunate souls. They became cautionary tales, their disappearances woven into the fabric of local folklore. The desolate mountains, already a place of ill repute, became synonymous with the Dearg Due, the "Red Lady" or the "Sorrowful Spirit," depending on the region and the particular emphasis of the storytellers. Children were warned not to stray too far from the hearth after dusk, lest the Lady of Sorrow hear their lonely cries and beckon them into the eternal night.

The legend of Iris evolved. The raw predator, the being driven by an insatiable, ancient hunger, became a more complex figure in the collective consciousness. She was the embodiment of lost love, a spectral maiden forever weeping for a stolen heart, her tears staining the very air with sorrow. Her mournful song, once a direct lure, was reinterpreted as a lament for a world that had forgotten her, a heartbroken plea for remembrance. This romanticised version, while still terrifying, carried a different weight. It spoke not just of immediate danger, but of a profound, existential sadness that resonated with the very human experience of loss.

Bard and storyteller alike would weave verses about her ethereal beauty, a beauty now tinged with the melancholy of centuries. They spoke of her shimmering form, appearing as a mist-wreathed maiden on moonlit nights, her eyes reflecting an ancient grief. They recounted tales of brave, or perhaps foolish, youths who had sought her out, not for her spectral essence, but to offer solace, to try and break the curse that bound her to her desolate mountain. These narratives, while acknowledging her spectral nature, often cast her victims as more active participants, driven by a noble, albeit doomed, quest to offer compassion to a tormented soul.

The practicalities of her feeding, the brutal efficiency with which she extinguished lives to sate her spectral hunger, were subtly elided. Instead, the focus shifted to the psychological torment, the way she ensnared her victims with promises of love and understanding, only to lead them to their doom. This emphasis on emotional manipulation rather than raw physicality made her legend more palatable for the masses, transforming her into a figure that could be discussed, debated, and feared in the relative safety of lit taverns and cosy hearths.

The Dearg Due became a boogeyman of sorts, a spectral guardian of the wild, untamed places. She was the reason for the sudden chill in the air, the unexplained rustling in the undergrowth, the eerie silence that descended upon the forest when darkness began to creep. She was the reason why specific paths were avoided after sunset, why lone travellers were urged to stay on well-trodden roads, and why the mountain peaks were viewed with a mixture of awe and dread.

Her mythos is also intertwined with older, more primal fears. She was the embodiment of the uncanny valley, a being that was both familiar in its human-like form and utterly alien in its spectral nature. She represented the unknown dangers that lurked beyond the fringes of civilisation, the ancient powers that held sway in the wild places that humanity had yet to conquer. The stories served as a societal pressure valve, a way to externalise anxieties about the wild, the unknown, and the ever-present spectre of death.

One recurring motif in the evolving legends was the idea that she was not entirely malevolent but rather a victim of her tragic circumstances. This narrative offered a semblance of comfort to the fearful populace; if she was a victim, then perhaps she could be reasoned with, or possibly her torment was so profound that it warranted a degree of pity, even as she was feared. This sympathetic portrayal, however, was a double-edged sword, often leading to the very foolish bravery she preyed upon. The legends would speak of those who believed they could "save" her, who thought their mortal love could break the chains of her spectral existence. These well-intentioned fools, the stories would invariably conclude, met the same fate as the others, their noble intentions dissolving into the cold, spectral embrace.

The very act of telling her story became a ritual, a way for communities to reinforce their shared understanding of the world and its dangers. The Dearg Due was the ultimate symbol of the uncanny, the entity that blurred the lines between the living and the dead, the natural and the supernatural. Her myth served as a constant reminder that the world was not as it seemed, that beneath the veneer of everyday reality lay ancient forces and beings that operated by rules entirely alien to mortal comprehension.

In the hushed chambers of nurseries, the tales of the Dearg Due were often employed to ensure compliance. The spectral maiden, with her sorrowful eyes and her haunting song, was far more effective than any earthly threat. "Be good," mothers would whisper to their unruly children, "or the Dearg Due will hear you and come to take you away." The chilling melody that once lured unsuspecting travellers was now reimagined as a lullaby of dread, a sombre serenade designed to instil a healthy fear of the dark and the unknown. Her legend had transcended its origins, becoming a cultural touchstone, a shared narrative that bound communities together in their collective fear and their whispered fascination.

The stories would evolve with each passing generation, adapting to society's changing fears and anxieties. Sometimes she was a vengeful spirit, driven by a thirst for retribution for past wrongs. Other times, she was a lonely entity, forever searching for a connection she could no longer experience. Yet, regardless of the specific narrative thread, the core of the legend remained: a beautiful, sorrowful, and terrifying spectral being dwelling in the desolate reaches of the mountains, a constant reminder of the fragility of life and the enduring power of ancient, supernatural forces. The Dearg Due was no longer just a solitary hunter; she was a myth, a legend, a cornerstone of the dark folklore that clung to the shadowed corners of the human world.

Chapter 8:
The Lure of the Howl

The sound that drifted from the desolate crags was not the savage shriek of a beast of prey, nor the guttural roar of a creature driven by pure malice. It was something far more insidious, something that burrowed into the very marrow of the soul. Iris's lament was a melody spun from the finest threads of despair, a tapestry woven from the countless centuries of her solitary existence. It was a sound that held within it the hollow echo of every forgotten joy, the phantom touch of every lost embrace, and the crushing weight of an eternity spent in the chilling silence of death.

This was no mere cry for sustenance, no primal urge made audible. Instead, it was a distillation of pure sorrow, a resonant ache that vibrated with the collective loneliness of a world that had long since moved on, leaving her ensnared in its lingering shadows. The lament was a symphony of unanswered questions, a chorus of unspoken goodbyes. It carried on the biting wind, not with the force of a gale, but with the subtle, pervasive insistence of a persistent memory. It found its way into the ears of those who already carried a burden of sadness, those whose hearts were already open to the melancholic embrace of solitude.

The sound quality was profoundly unnatural. It possessed a hypnotic allure, a siren's call that was far more subtle than any overt threat. It was neither loud nor demanding. Instead, it was a delicate weaving of tones, a carefully modulated frequency that seemed to bypass the ear and resonate directly within the listener's psyche. It whispered of shared suffering, of a profound understanding that transcended the superficial interactions of mortal life. It was the sound of a kindred spirit, a spectral soul adrift in an ocean of time, yearning for a connection, a flicker of recognition in the vast, indifferent expanse of existence.

For the shepherd, huddled against the encroaching chill of night, his flock a huddled mass of silent wool, the lament was a reminder of his own isolation. It spoke of long nights, of the quiet gnawing of solitude that often accompanied his solitary profession. He would pause, his hand instinctively reaching for his crook, his gaze drawn toward the sound, a vague sense of recognition stirring within him, as if the melody itself were a forgotten lullaby from his own childhood, tinged with an unfamiliar sadness.

For the hunter, lost in the deepening twilight of the ancient woods, the rustling leaves and snapping twigs suddenly fell silent, giving way to a deeper quiet, broken only by that ethereal, mournful sound. It wasn't the desperate cry of a wounded animal, which might inspire a surge of adrenaline or a renewed sense of purpose. Instead, it was a sound that spoke of a weariness so profound it bordered on apathy, a soul so steeped in sorrow that the world beyond its immediate pain ceased to exist. The hunter, his own journey fraught with the quiet anxieties of navigating the encroaching darkness, would find himself inexplicably drawn to the source of that sound, a flicker of curiosity warring with a primal, unarticulated unease.

And for the weary traveller, his back bowed under the weight of his pack and the heavier burden of his own private griefs, the lament was a balm, a spectral embrace that promised solace. It spoke not of grand pronouncements or boisterous camaraderie, but of the quiet understanding that came from shared pain. It was the sound of a soul that had known loss and, therefore, could empathise with the losses of another. The traveller, his heart heavy with unspoken regrets and unfulfilled desires, would find his steps faltering, his destination momentarily forgotten as he strained to hear the source of that hauntingly beautiful, achingly sad melody.

The lament was a siren's call, but not one that promised earthly delights or fleeting pleasures. It promised something far more profound, far more intoxicating to a soul already burdened by the mundane realities of existence: the promise of being understood. It was the sound of a being who had existed beyond the transient concerns of mortal life, a being whose sorrow was so ancient and so profound that it had transcended mere emotion and become a fundamental aspect of her existence. It was the sound of the eternal feminine, forever waiting, forever mourning a love that was lost to the mists of time, a sorrow so profound that it echoed through the ages, seeking a sympathetic ear.

Iris's cry was a manifestation of her unique nature as a Dearg Due. She was not merely a ghost, a lingering echo of a life extinguished. She was a creature of immense power, her spectral essence interwoven with the very fabric of the desolate mountains she inhabited. Her hunger was a constant companion, a gnawing emptiness that drove her existence. But this hunger was not a simple biological imperative; it was a spectral thirst, a yearning for the vital essence of life, a sustenance that could temporarily quell the gnawing void within her.

The lament was a crucial tool in her predatory arsenal. It was the bait, carefully crafted to ensnare the unwary. It was a melody that spoke of deep, personal suffering, and in doing so, it resonated with the hidden wounds of those who heard it. It was a reminder of their own loneliness, their own unfulfilled longings, their own quiet despairs. It was a sound that whispered, "You are not alone in your suffering." And for those who felt adrift, lost in the vastness of existence, that whisper was a powerful, irresistible lure.

The spectral nature of her song meant conventional sound limitations did not bind it. It could penetrate stone, bypass distance, and seep into the very consciousness of its listeners. It was a song that could be heard even in the most profound silence, a melody that seemed to emanate from within the listener's own mind, as if their own suppressed sorrows had finally found an outward voice. The wind, a fickle messenger, would carry it with an uncanny precision, guiding it to the ears of those most receptive to its sorrowful tune.

The sorrow embedded within the lament was not a fleeting sadness, but an eternal ache. It was the collective grief of centuries, the lament of a soul that had witnessed the rise and fall of empires, the birth and death of generations, all while remaining trapped in her own spectral purgatory. This profound depth of sorrow gave the lament a weight, a gravity that no mortal sound could replicate. It was the sound of a soul perpetually on the verge of dissolution, yet held together by the sheer force of its unending grief.

And within this ocean of sorrow, Iris wove threads of something else entirely: a subtle, almost imperceptible hope. It was the hope of connection, the hope of finding another soul who could understand her suffering, a soul who could offer a moment of respite from her eternal torment. This was not a conscious offering of hope, but rather an inherent byproduct of her existence, a projection of her own yearning that became an irresistible lure to those who also yearned for something more than the mundane reality they inhabited.

The lament was a paradox. It was a sound emanating from a being driven by insatiable hunger, yet it spoke of profound sadness and a desperate need for connection. It was a song that promised solace, yet it led to utter oblivion. It was the sound of the Dearg Due, a melody of despair that echoed through the desolate mountains, a haunting testament to the power of loneliness and the allure of a siren's mournful song. It was the sound that marked the threshold between the mortal world and the spectral abyss, a chilling invitation to step into an eternal night from which there was no return. The lament was not just a sound; it was a promise, a confession, and ultimately, a carefully orchestrated trap, designed to ensnare the unwary heart and consume its vital essence. It was the very embodiment of her being, a spectral song sung for an audience of one, yet heard by many, each note a carefully placed step on the path to damnation.

The desolate moors were Iris's dominion, vast expanses of heather and gorse that stretched towards a perpetually bruised sky. Here, under the indifferent gaze of a sun that seemed perpetually reluctant to break through the shroud of mist, her lament found its most potent resonance. The wind, a constant, mournful sigh across the undulating landscape, seemed to conspire with her sorrow, weaving her spectral voice into its own melancholic symphony. It was on these barren plains, where the earth itself seemed to weep with a perpetual dampness, that the land felt most alive with her grief. The stunted trees, gnarled and twisted like arthritic fingers, clawed at the heavens, their silhouettes stark against the dying light, mirroring the tormented form of the Dearg Due. Each gust of wind that swept across the moors carried not just the scent of peat and decaying foliage, but also the faint, chilling echo of Iris's eternal despair. The very air seemed heavy with unspoken sadness, as if the land absorbed and amplified the anguish emanating from its spectral inhabitant.

When the fog descended, thick and cloying like a shroud cast over the world, the moors transformed into an even more terrifying realm. Visibility dwindled to mere feet, and the familiar contours of the land dissolved into an ethereal, dreamlike landscape. In such moments, Iris's lament became disembodied, a disquieting presence that seemed to emanate from everywhere and nowhere at once. The fog muffled other sounds, rendering the world unnervingly silent, save for that one, haunting melody. It was as if the mist itself was a living entity, drawn to her sorrow, and in turn, amplifying its reach. The isolation intensified, a tangible entity that pressed in on all sides, making the listener feel utterly alone in a world that had ceased to exist beyond the immediate, chilling embrace of the spectral song. The ancient standing stones, monolithic sentinels that dotted the moors, seemed to absorb the lament, their weathered surfaces weeping with condensation, their silent presence adding to the aura of timeless despair. The ground beneath one's feet, often sodden and treacherous, felt like the very tears of the earth, a constant reminder of the pervasive sorrow that clung to this place.

Beyond the open moors, Iris's voice would sometimes drift from the edges of ancient forests, where the canopy was so dense that sunlight rarely touched the forest floor. Here, the trees stood like silent witnesses to centuries of sorrow, their roots deeply embedded in the earth, their branches intertwined in a perpetual, sombre embrace. The air within these woods was perpetually cool, carrying the scent of damp earth, decaying leaves, and the subtle, musky aroma of the wild. When Iris's lament echoed through these hushed depths, it seemed to awaken the slumbering melancholy of the woods. The rustling leaves would fall silent, the chirping of birds would cease, and the forest would hold its breath, captivated by the spectral sorrow. The tangled undergrowth, choked with ferns and moss-laden branches, created a labyrinthine environment, where shadows danced and played tricks on the eyes, mirroring the deceptive nature of Iris's song. The ancient trees, some bearing the scars of lightning strikes and the ravages of time, seemed to stoop lower, their limbs heavy with the weight of centuries, as if sharing in the spectral creature's endless grief. The very silence of these ancient woods was profound, a deep, resonant quietude that made Iris's mournful cry all the more piercing, all the more terrifying. It felt as though the trees themselves were weeping, their sap akin to tears, their creaking branches the mournful groans of ancient beings burdened by an unseen sorrow.

Crossroads, too, held a particular allure for the lament. These liminal spaces, where paths diverged and fates were often decided, became imbued with an even greater sense of unease when touched by Iris's song. A fog-shrouded crossroads, especially under the cloak of night, was a place where the veil between worlds felt thinnest, and Iris's spectral voice served as a potent lure, a chilling invitation to step into the unknown. The air at these intersections often felt heavy, charged with an unseen energy, a palpable tension that seemed to precede the spectral sound. The crossroads, stripped of their daytime purpose, became stages for spectral dramas, their familiar markers – a weathered signpost, a solitary, gnarled hawthorn tree – transformed into ominous symbols under the influence of Iris's mournful lament. The mist would coil and writhe around the intersecting paths, obscuring the way forward and backwards, leaving the listener stranded in a temporal and spatial void, with only the siren call of the Dearg Due for company. It was at these places, where decisions hung in the balance, and the future was uncertain, that Iris's song seemed to find its most susceptible audience, promising a form of understanding that transcended the mundane anxieties of mortal choice.

The atmosphere that permeated these locales when Iris's lament was heard was one of profound isolation. It was an isolation that went beyond mere physical solitude; it was a spiritual and emotional severance from the world. The listener felt as though they were the only living soul left on a desolate earth, adrift in an ocean of despair. The land itself seemed to recoil from the touch of the living, its very essence saturated with the ancient grief of the Dearg Due. The silence was not peaceful, but expectant, a suffocating stillness that amplified the internal tremors of fear and loneliness. Even the natural world seemed to conspire in the spectral creature's mournful song. The wind, usually a traveller's companion, became a harbinger of dread, its whispers carrying the chilling echoes of Iris's sorrow. The shadows deepened not just with the setting of the sun, but with a deeper, existential darkness that seemed to emanate from the very soil.

The dread that permeated these places was not the sudden, visceral terror of a confrontation, but a creeping, insidious unease that seeped into the bones. It was the dread of the unknown, the fear of a presence that was both ancient and powerful, yet intangible and unseen. It was the dread of being utterly alone, yet paradoxically, feeling the undeniable weight of another's eternal suffering pressing in. The landscape, in these moments, became a reflection of Iris's own tormented soul. The desolate moors, the ancient forests, the fog-shrouded crossroads – they were all, in their own way, desolate, haunted places, perfectly attuned to the spectral resonance of her lament. The very earth seemed to sigh with a collective weariness, a silent acknowledgement of the sorrow that had become an intrinsic part of its being. Each sigh of the wind, each rustle of unseen movement in the undergrowth, each distant, mournful cry of a night bird – all seemed to be woven into the tapestry of Iris's grief, amplifying its reach and its insidious power. The air itself felt colder, thinner, as if the spectral entity was drawing the warmth and vitality from the surroundings, leaving behind only a chilling emptiness. The stars, when they managed to pierce the perpetual gloom, seemed to wink out of existence as her lament swelled, as if even the celestial bodies recoiled from the profound sadness that emanated from this corner of the world. It was a place where despair had taken root, and the lament of the Dearg Due was its perpetual bloom, a deadly flower of sorrow that lured the unwary into its eternally shadowed embrace. The silence that followed her song was perhaps the most terrifying aspect, a vacuum filled not with peace but with a deafening echo of her unending pain, leaving the listener with the gnawing certainty that they had stumbled upon a place where sorrow had become eternal.

The lament, a spectral siren song woven from the threads of eternal sorrow, did not discriminate in its selection of victims. It did not seek out the strong, nor the wise, nor the seasoned warriors who might possess the fortitude to resist its chilling allure. Instead, it resonated most powerfully with those whose own lives were shrouded in a similar, albeit mortal, despair. The lament was a beacon for the lost, a whisper of companionship for the utterly alone, and an irresistible invitation for those who courted danger with a reckless abandon born of emptiness.

Foremost among those drawn into the spectral embrace were travellers caught unawares by the encroaching darkness. The moors, vast and unforgiving, offered little in the way of shelter once the sun dipped below the horizon, and the mist, a treacherous thief of direction, could disorient even the most experienced guide. These souls, their faces etched with the fatigue of a long journey, their bodies chilled by the night air, would often find themselves adrift in a sea of heather and shadow. It was in such moments of profound disorientation, when the familiar world receded and the oppressive weight of isolation pressed in, that Iris's lament would begin to filter through the swirling fog. It started as a faint, almost ethereal melody, easily dismissed as the sighing of the wind or the distant cry of a night bird. But as their fear and desperation deepened, so too did the clarity of the sound. It was a voice, undeniably, a voice that seemed to speak directly to the gnawing anxiety in their chests. They would strain their ears, their hearts thrumming with a mixture of dread and an inexplicable flicker of hope. Could it be another traveller? A sign of habitation? Or, in their most desperate, delirious moments, a succour for the profound loneliness that had begun to consume them? This burgeoning hope, however fragile, was the initial spark, the tiny ember that the spectral lament fanned into an inferno. They would veer from their intended path, drawn by the promise, however faint, of a human (or perhaps, something more) connection, a respite from the crushing solitude of the wild. The lament offered a destination, a focal point in the disorienting void, a lure that preyed on their most primal need: not to be alone.

Then there were the lonely souls, the outcasts and the melancholic, who found themselves in the remote, windswept reaches of Iris's domain. These were individuals who carried their own internal desolation, their spirits burdened by loss, by unrequited love, by the sheer weight of existence. They sought not necessarily solace, but perhaps understanding, a reflection of their own inner turmoil in the external world. The moors, with their brooding skies and desolate beauty, often served as a sanctuary for such spirits. They would wander the heather-clad hills, their thoughts a tangled mess of regret and longing, their footsteps aimless. It was to these souls, whose inner landscape mirrored the outer desolation, that Iris's lament sang with a particular poignancy. Her sorrow, amplified by centuries of existence, seemed to harmonise with their own burgeoning despair. The spectral melody was not just a sound; it was an emotional resonance. It spoke of loss so profound that it transcended mortal understanding, of a pain so deep that it became eternal. For those already teetering on the precipice of despair, this amplified sorrow served both as a comfort and a condemnation. It was a confirmation that their own suffering was not unique, that there existed a sorrow on an epic scale. This realisation could be intoxicating, a perverse form of validation. They might find themselves drawn to the source of the sound, not necessarily with a conscious desire for death, but with an unconscious yearning for an end to their own pain, an end that the lament seemed to promise through absorption into something greater, something all-encompassing. The spectral inhabitant of the moors mirrored the isolation they felt, and this shared solitude, however terrifying, was a powerful, albeit destructive, bond. They were drawn to the lament because it seemed to understand them, to speak the unspeakable language of their own hearts. It was an echo of their own internal landscape, made manifest in a haunting melody.

A third, and perhaps the most disturbing, category of individuals susceptible to Iris's lure were those driven by a morbid curiosity. These were the romantics of the macabre, the thrill-seekers who courted danger like a lover, drawn to the edge of the abyss with an almost irresistible fascination. They heard tales of the spectral lament, whispered in hushed tones in smoky taverns, passed down through generations as cautionary folklore. But instead of heeding the warnings, these individuals saw an opportunity for an experience that transcended the mundane. They were drawn to the forbidden, to the uncanny, to the very essence of fear itself. They would venture into the moors, not necessarily lost or lonely, but with a deliberate intent to confront the legendary spectral entity. They might carry charms or talismans, believing their preparation would offer protection, but these were often mere tokens against a power that operated on a far deeper, psychological level. The morbidly curious were usually intellectually detached, viewing the spectral lament as a phenomenon to be observed, a mystery to be unravelled. However, the very act of seeking it out, of willingly immersing oneself in a place known for its spectral inhabitant, was an act of profound vulnerability. Their curiosity became a form of psychological opening, a deliberate exposure to the uncanny. The lament, sensing this willingness to engage with the spectral, would become more potent, more insidious. It would play upon their fascination, weaving threads of dread and allure into an irresistible tapestry of sound. They might initially feel a thrill, a sense of exhilaration at being so close to the legendary. But as the lament enveloped them, that intellectual curiosity would erode, replaced by the primal terror of being utterly out of one's depth. The allure of the unknown would give way to the crushing reality of an ancient, inescapable sorrow. They had sought a ghost story and found themselves becoming a part of one. Their detachment would shatter, their bravado would crumble, leaving them exposed and vulnerable to the same despair that had claimed so many others. Their curiosity was a dangerous dance with a predator, and in the end, the predator always won.

The psychological vulnerabilities that made these individuals susceptible were varied, yet interconnected. For the lost traveller, it was the primal fear of death in isolation, the desperate need for any sign of rescue or companionship, however spectral. Their vulnerability lay in their immediate, life-threatening predicament, their senses heightened by fear, making them more attuned to the subtle, yet insistent, call of the lament. They were already adrift in a sea of uncertainty, and the lament offered a false shore.

For the lonely souls, it was a more profound, more existential vulnerability. Their isolation was not situational, but a part of their very being. They yearned for connection, for an understanding that the mundane world seemed incapable of providing. Iris's lament, born of an eternal, profound isolation, offered a mirror to their own souls. It was a dangerous form of validation, a siren song that promised to absorb their pain into a greater, eternal suffering, a perverse form of belonging. Their subconscious yearning for connection, even a perilous one, made them fertile ground for the spectral lure. They were already seeking an escape from their own loneliness, and the lament offered the ultimate, albeit fatal, escape.

The morbidly curious, on the other hand, were vulnerable not out of fear or yearning, but out of an overestimation of their own control and intellectual prowess. They believed they could engage with the spectral on their own terms, observing and analysing without succumbing. Their vulnerability lay in their hubris, in their underestimation of the profound, primal power of Iris's lament. They sought a thrill, an experience, but found themselves consumed by a force that defied rational understanding. They were drawn in by the promise of the forbidden, the allure of the dangerous, but their fascination closed their eyes to the true nature of the entity they sought. The lament did not require fear or sadness to ensnare; it could exploit any opening, any deviation from the path of cautious reason.

In each case, the lament acted as a catalyst, amplifying pre-existing vulnerabilities and transforming them into an irresistible force. It was the whisper in the dark that promised an answer, the echo in the silence that offered a response, the phantom hand that reached out from the mist. It was the ultimate seduction, preying on the deepest, most fundamental aspects of the human psyche: the fear of being alone, the yearning for connection, and the dangerous allure of the unknown. The lament did not create these vulnerabilities, but it found them, nurtured them, and ultimately, exploited them with a chilling, eternal precision. The individuals drawn into its mournful melody were not simply lost; they were actively, though often unconsciously, seeking something that only the spectral sorrow of the Dearg Due could, in its own tragic way, provide. They sought an end to their own suffering, and found it in the infinite, unending suffering of another.

The very essence of Iris's mournful cry was a masterpiece of deception, a delicate tapestry woven from threads of genuine desolation and cunning predatory intent. It was not a simple howl of pain, though pain was undoubtedly its foundation, but a carefully constructed symphony of despair designed to ensnare the unwary. The lament, as it drifted through the mist-shrouded moors, was a deceptive balm, a promise of shared suffering that drew souls closer to the precipice. It spoke to the lonely, the lost, and the morbidly curious, not with an outright threat, but with an invitation to witness, to understand, perhaps even to empathise with an ancient, profound sorrow. This auditory lure, however, was merely the prelude to a far more sinister performance. Beneath the guise of shared anguish lay a hunter's keen awareness, a predatory instinct honed over centuries of solitude and blood.

The sound itself was a testament to Iris's supernatural nature. It was not merely an acoustic phenomenon; it was an extension of her will, a spectral tendril reaching out to caress and then to bind. When the lament began its mournful ascent, it seemed to emanate from the very heart of the moor, from the stones, the heather, the weeping willows that lined the forgotten paths. But its source was always elusive, shifting, as if the landscape itself were sighing with a grief that mirrored the spectral melody. This inherent ambiguity was crucial to its effectiveness. Those who heard it were not presented with a clear, identifiable enemy, but with an enigma, a haunting mystery that beckoned investigation. The sound would eddy and flow, sometimes sounding as if it were just over the subsequent rise, at others seeming to whisper from the very depths of the earth. This spatial deception served to disorient, to draw victims further and further off their intended course, deeper into the heart of Iris's domain, a place where the veil between worlds was thinnest and her power most absolute.

The duality of Iris's cry was its most potent weapon. The lament was undeniably steeped in a sorrow so profound it could curdle the blood, a grief that had festered and grown with the passing of centuries. It resonated with the deepest wells of human sadness, with the quiet despair that gnawed at the edges of mortal lives. This genuine pain was not feigned; it was the very fabric of her spectral existence, a constant ache born of betrayal and eternal isolation. Yet, this same pain served as a veil for her predatory nature. The raw, unadulterated sorrow emanating from the lament acted as a potent masking agent, obscuring the sharp edges of her hunger, dulling the senses of those who fell under its spell. A traveller, lost and chilled, might hear the lament and believe it to be the cry of another soul in distress, an echo of their own predicament. A lonely heart might interpret it as a kindred spirit, an entity that understood the weight of existence. A thrill-seeker might see it as the validation of their belief in the supernatural, a spectral performance staged for their personal edification. None of them truly grasped that the sorrow they heard was not an invitation to solace, but a dinner bell, a mournful announcement of a predator's intent.

The lament's power lay not just in its sound, but in its resonance. It tapped into the victim's deepest vulnerabilities, amplifying their existing fears and desires until they became an overwhelming force. For the lost, it was the promise of guidance, however spectral. For the lonely, it was the illusion of companionship. For the curious, it was the ultimate unravelling of a forbidden mystery. Iris did not simply howl; she wove a narrative of despair and longing into her cries, a narrative that each individual, in their own isolated state, would unconsciously complete with their own specific needs and fears. The sound was a mirror, reflecting to each listener what they most desperately wished to see or hear, all while subtly nudging them towards her desolate lair.

Her resting place, a forgotten hollow shrouded in perpetual twilight, became a focal point for the lament. The melody drew energy from the very earth around it, coalescing into a beacon for the lost. The air around this place grew heavy, charged with an ancient, melancholic energy that pulsed in time with Iris's spectral song. The lament acted as a homing signal, a psychic beacon that guided the susceptible, their wills eroded by the pervasive sorrow, towards the source of the sound. They would find themselves walking, as if in a dream, towards the desolate hollow, their steps no longer their own, their minds filled with the lingering echoes of the mournful melody.

The transformation from lament to lure was a gradual, insidious process. It began with a whisper, a sigh carried on the wind, and escalated into a full-throated cry that resonated with the very soul. Iris, the Dearg Due, did not possess crude fangs and claws in the conventional sense. Her predatory tools were far more ancient and psychological. Her howl was a weapon of mass emotional destruction, a sonic key that unlocked the gates of reason and ushered in the reign of primal need. The sound would penetrate the deepest recesses of the mind, bypassing conscious thought and speaking directly to the id. It offered a false sanctuary, a promise of understanding that was, in reality, a promise of consumption.

The sounds that accompanied the lament were as crucial as the melody itself. The soft rustling of unseen things in the heather, the snap of a twig in the distance, the chilling sigh of the wind – these were all orchestrated by Iris to enhance the spectral illusion. They were the subtle embellishments that made the lament more than just a sound; they were the sensory cues that painted a picture of a desolate, yet potentially inhabited, landscape. The crunch of leaves underfoot, the distant call of a nocturnal bird, the almost imperceptible shifting of the mist – all were part of the auditory theatre. These ambient sounds, amplified and distorted by the lament, created an atmosphere of profound isolation, an environment where the spectral song became the only point of reference, the only perceived source of potential connection.

Iris's ability to manipulate sound was not limited to her lament. She could, when the need arose, weave other auditory illusions into her hunt. The distant cry of a lost lamb, the faint echo of a child's laughter, the murmur of voices that never coalesced into discernible words – these were all subtle variations on her theme, each designed to play upon a specific emotional chord. The cry of the lamb would appeal to the compassionate, the innocent. The laughter of a child would invoke a protective instinct, a desire to rescue. The murmuring voices would sow confusion, doubt, and a desperate need for clarity. All these variations, however, ultimately served the same purpose: to draw her prey closer, to lull them into a false sense of security, and to close their eyes to the true horror that awaited.

The spectral hollow where Iris rested was more than just a physical location; it was a nexus of sorrow, a place where the veil between worlds thinned to a whisper. The lament, in its most potent form, seemed to emanate from this place, drawing the very essence of the moor into its mournful cadence. The mist, thick and cloying, would swirl around the hollow, a spectral shroud that concealed the true nature of its inhabitant. The trees, gnarled and ancient, seemed to weep, their branches twisted into agonising contortions, their leaves rustling with a sound that mimicked hushed lamentations. This was Iris's domain, and the lament was its voice, its invitation, and its trap.

The psychological impact of the lament was profound. It bypassed the rational mind, sinking its spectral tendrils directly into the limbic system, the seat of emotion and primal instinct. It was a form of sonic hypnosis, a gradual erosion of willpower and critical thinking. The more one listened, the more susceptible they became, their own internal struggles and despairs resonating with the spectral sorrow, creating a feedback loop of ever-increasing despair. A fading of the external world often accompanied this descent. The sounds of the moor would recede, the visual details would blur, and the only reality that remained was the haunting, all-encompassing melody.

Iris's howl was not a chaotic outburst; it was a meticulously crafted tool. The pitch, the rhythm, the subtle shifts in tone – all were employed to maximise its allure. She could modulate her lament, making it softer, more intimate, as if whispering secrets of shared pain, or amplify it, filling the desolate landscape with a tidal wave of despair. The variations were endless, each tailored to the individual listener and the specific circumstances of their vulnerability. A traveller on the verge of succumbing to the elements would hear a lament that offered the promise of warmth and shelter, a phantom hearth. A soul consumed by heartbreak would listen to a cry that spoke of eternal love and loss, a spectral echo of their own shattered romance.

The hunting grounds of the Dearg Due were vast, but the lament always drew her prey towards the desolate hollow. It was as if the sound itself created an invisible tether, a spectral cord that bound the victim to the source. As they drew closer, the lament would intensify, becoming more personal, more direct. The whispers of sorrow would morph into distinct phrases, seemingly spoken directly to the listener, acknowledging their specific pain, their deepest fears. "You are not alone," the lament might seem to sigh, "for I too have suffered." Or perhaps, "Your burden is too great; let me share it with you." These were not words spoken aloud, but impressions, thoughts planted directly into the mind, further eroding their autonomy.

The prey, trapped in this auditory hallucination, would find their resolve weakening with each passing moment. The initial flicker of curiosity or hope would be extinguished by the overwhelming tide of sorrow, replaced by a desperate, almost masochistic, yearning to surrender. The lament offered an end to their pain, an absorption into something greater, something that promised to alleviate their individual suffering by submerging it into an eternal ocean of grief. This promise, however deceptive, was irresistible to those already teetering on the brink.

The predatory nature of the howl was thus masked by its apparent vulnerability. It was a cunning inversion of expectation, a reversal of the natural order. The victim believed they were approaching a source of comfort, a kindred spirit in their despair, when in reality, they were walking directly into the jaws of a predator. The lament was the bait, the irresistible allure of shared sorrow, and the hollow was the trap, the desolate maw that awaited its next meal. Iris, the spectral mistress of the moors, had perfected the art of the predatory melody, a symphony of sorrow that heralded not rescue, but eternal consumption. Her howl was both her lament and her lure, a perfect, terrifying fusion of her own eternal pain and her unyielding predatory hunger, a haunting testament to the darkness that lurked beneath the surface of the world, forever seeking to draw the unwary into its cold, unforgiving embrace. The echo of her cry was not a call for help, but a death knell, a final, mournful melody that signalled the end of one soul's journey and the continuation of her own unending, spectral existence.

The wind, a spectral hand, tugged at Silas's threadbare cloak, its icy breath whispering forgotten names through the skeletal branches of the ancient hawthorn. He hunched his shoulders, the meagre warmth of his dwindling fire long since leached away by the encroaching twilight. The moor, a vast, bruised canvas of fading heather and sodden peat, stretched out before him, a familiar but increasingly disquieting expanse. For weeks, he had traversed its desolate beauty, seeking the solitude that his restless soul craved, a balm for wounds inflicted not by steel, but by the gnawing erosion of human betrayal. He had found a measure of peace in the relentless silence, broken only by the bleating of distant sheep or the melancholic cry of a curlew. But tonight, a new sound had begun to weave its way into the tapestry of the moorland night, a sound that unsettled him to his very bones.

It began as a faint tremor in the air, a harmonic dissonance that prickled the hairs on his arms. At first, he dismissed it as the wind playing tricks, the mournful sigh of the moor itself. Yet, it persisted, growing in clarity and intensity, resolving itself into a sound that was both achingly familiar and utterly alien. A lament. It was a cry of such profound sorrow, such unutterable desolation, that it seemed to emanate not from any single throat, but from the very earth, from the weeping stones and the spectral mist that clung to the low-lying hollows. It was a sound that bypassed his ears and resonated directly within the cavern of his chest, awakening a phantom ache, a buried grief he thought long interred.

Silas, a man more accustomed to the blunt realities of the world – the bite of frost, the weight of a tool, the sting of a lie – found himself disarmed by the sheer emotional force of the sound. It spoke of loss on a scale that dwarfed his own petty heartbreaks. It hinted at an ancient suffering, a cosmic despair that had seeped into the very marrow of this desolate place. He stood frozen, the wind whipping his thin hair across his face, his gaze fixed on the swirling grey veils that obscured the horizon. His rational mind, a well-worn tool he usually wielded with precision, did not explain. There were no wolves on these moors, no lost travellers to be heard. This was something else, something primal and elemental.

Yet, despite the chill that traced its icy path down his spine, a strange curiosity began to bloom within him, a morbid fascination that warred with his innate caution. The lament, for all its sorrow, held a peculiar allure. It was a siren song of sadness, a whispered promise of understanding to a soul adrift in loneliness. He found himself leaning into the sound, straining to discern its nuances, to decipher the hidden narrative within its mournful cadence. It was as if a part of him, the part that had always felt a kinship with the shadows, recognised a kindred spirit in the spectral wail.

He took a hesitant step, then another, his worn boots sinking slightly into the damp earth. The lament seemed to swell in response, as if acknowledging his approach. It shifted, becoming more distinct, a tapestry of interwoven sighs and keening notes. It painted a picture in his mind of a solitary figure, bowed by an immense burden, lost in an endless night of grief. He imagined a spectral woman, perhaps, her face etched with an eternal sorrow, her voice the conduit for the moor's collective heartbreak. The thought, though morbid, brought a strange solace, a feeling of connection to something larger than himself, something that shared his own deep-seated melancholy.

His initial hesitation began to ebb, replaced by an almost compulsive need to draw closer, to witness the source of such profound despair. The mist, which had seemed a mere atmospheric phenomenon moments before, now took on a more ominous character. It swirled with a deliberate, almost sentient grace, its tendrils reaching out to enfold him, muffling the sounds of the moor and amplifying the haunting melody. The path ahead, dimly visible, seemed to curve and twist, beckoning him deeper into the spectral embrace. He knew, with a chilling certainty that settled in the pit of his stomach, that he was venturing into territory unknown, guided by a sound that was both a lament and a lure.

Each step was a surrender. The rational voice that urged him to turn back, to seek the meagre safety of his dying fire, grew fainter, a distant echo drowned out by the rising tide of the spectral song. He found himself mirroring its rhythm, his heartbeat falling into a slow, deliberate cadence that seemed to pulse with the mournful vibrations. His senses, usually sharp and observant, began to dull, his focus narrowing to the ethereal sound that now seemed to fill the world. The biting wind, the damp chill, the rough texture of his cloak – all receded, replaced by the all-consuming presence of the lament.

He imagined it was a lost soul, trapped in the desolate expanse, crying out for release. Perhaps it was a spirit wronged, its grief so profound it echoed through the ages, a testament to a betrayal that had shattered its very existence. The idea resonated deeply with Silas, a man who carried his own quiet resentments, his own ghosts of affection betrayed. He felt a surge of empathy, a desire to offer what little comfort he could, even if it meant venturing into the heart of this spectral sorrow. He pictured himself finding the source, a spectral presence, and offering a silent acknowledgement, a shared moment of grief that transcended words.

The landscape around him began to shift, the familiar contours of the moor blurring into an indistinct, twilight realm. The heather, once a rich tapestry of muted purples and browns, now seemed to shimmer with an unnatural luminescence, as if illuminated by an unseen, spectral moon. The gnarled shapes of the ancient trees twisted into grotesque caricatures, their branches reaching out like skeletal fingers, beckoning him forward. Yet, Silas pressed on, his eyes fixed on a point in the distance where the mist seemed to coalesce, where the lament sounded most pure, most potent.

He was not moving of his own volition, he realised, not entirely. There was a force at play, a subtle but undeniable pull that guided his steps, that coaxed his feet along the unseen path. It was as if an invisible thread had been attached to his very soul, drawing him inexorably towards the heart of the lament. He tried to resist, to anchor himself to the fading memories of the rational world, but the sound was too potent, its sorrow too overwhelming. It spoke of an end to loneliness, an absorption into something vast and sorrowful, a permanent peace that transcended mortal suffering.

He stumbled over a hidden root, catching himself on a moss-covered stone as his hand brushed against the cold, damp surface. A jolt, not of pain, but of spectral energy, coursed through him. The lament seemed to surge, its volume increasing, its tone shifting from a mournful cry to something more akin to a welcoming embrace. He felt a sudden, overwhelming urge to lie down, to let the mist enfold him, to let the sorrow consume him, to become one with the endless lament of the moor.

His mind, clouded by the pervasive melancholy, began to conjure images. He saw a phantom cottage, its windows glowing with a warm, inviting light, smoke curling from its chimney. He heard the phantom murmur of voices, the faint clinking of crockery, the illusion of a life lived in peaceful solitude. It was a mirage, a spectral mirage woven from his deepest desires, designed to draw him further into the heart of the snare. He knew, on some primal level, that it was not real, yet the allure was almost irresistible.

He could almost taste the phantom warmth, feel the imagined comfort of a hearthside fire. The lament, in its infinite cunning, had tapped into his most desperate needs, crafting an illusion of sanctuary that was nothing more than a prelude to consumption. He was no longer walking; he was being drawn, his will eroded, his senses dulled, his very being succumbing to the spectral embrace. The mournful melody was no longer just a sound; it was a palpable force, a current that carried him, a prisoner of his own longing, towards an unseen, but undoubtedly terrifying, destination. The wind still tugged at his cloak, but now it felt less like a caress and more like the insistent tug of spectral fingers, guiding him towards his inevitable, sorrowful end. The mist, once a veil of atmospheric mystery, had become a suffocating shroud, its tendrils wrapping around him, promising oblivion cloaked in the guise of eternal peace.

Chapter 9:
Fleeting Glimpses

The mist, thick as a phantom's shroud, coiled around Silas, each swirling tendril a caress that left a phantom chill upon his skin. He stumbled, his boot catching on an unseen rise in the sodden earth. It was not the mist alone that disoriented him, but the way it seemed to distort the very fabric of reality, bleeding the edges of the world until all that remained was a grayscale canvas of unsettling ambiguity. Sounds, too, were muffled and distorted, as if the moor itself was holding its breath, listening. The lament that had drawn him so inexorably forward now seemed to recede, its mournful cadence dissolving into the damp air, leaving behind a void that felt even more profound than the sorrow it had conveyed.

It was in this sudden, unnerving silence that he first perceived it—a movement, a fleeting impression at the very edge of his vision. Not the rustle of an animal, nor the swaying of the sparse, stunted heather, but something far more deliberate, far more unsettling. A ripple in the greyness, a shadow detaching itself from the deeper gloom of a low-lying gully. He blinked, his eyes straining against the pervasive dimness. For a fraction of a second, he thought he saw the faint, almost phosphorescent outline of a figure, impossibly slender, impossibly still. It was gone before his mind could fully process the image, swallowed by the mist as if it had never been.

A shiver, unrelated to the damp cold, traced its icy path down his spine. His breath hitched in his throat. He told himself it was a trick of the light, a hallucination born of exhaustion and the disquieting allure of the spectral lament. Yet the memory of that fleeting glimpse lingered, an unwelcome seed of doubt planted in the fertile ground of his apprehension. He had sought solitude, but this felt like a violation of that solitude, an intrusion by something that defied natural explanation.

He continued to move, though the certainty that had propelled him forward moments before had begun to wane, replaced by a gnawing unease. The mist seemed to press in on him, a tangible weight that stole his breath and blurred his senses. He found himself glancing constantly to his left and right, his gaze sweeping across the indistinct landscape, searching for any further sign of the anomaly. He saw nothing but the undulating, featureless expanse of the moor, punctuated by the skeletal silhouettes of ancient, wind-battered trees.

Then it happened again. This time, the impression was stronger, more distinct, though still maddeningly ephemeral. He was passing a cluster of weathered standing stones, their ancient forms softened by centuries of rain and wind. In the deep shadow cast by the largest stone, something stirred. It was a presence, an almost palpable aura of stillness that felt incongruous with the restless, swirling mist. He froze, his heart hammering against his ribs like a trapped bird. He saw it more clearly this time: a woman's form, cloaked and hooded, her posture one of profound, almost statuesque sorrow. Her face was obscured, lost in the deep cowl, but he felt, with a certainty that bypassed logic, that she was looking at him.

The sight was so stark, so unexpected, that it momentarily arrested his movement—his very breath. He was a man who had seen hardship, who had witnessed the brutal realities of life and death. But this was different. This was an apparition, a ghost conjured from the very fabric of the moor's melancholy. And yet there was no fear, only a profound sense of pity and a strange, disquieting recognition. He felt a kinship with this spectral mourner, a shared understanding of loss and loneliness that transcended the boundaries of the living and the dead.

Before he could take a step, before he could even form a coherent thought, she vanished. Not with a sudden movement, but as if the shadows themselves had reclaimed her, or as if she had simply dissolved into the mist, leaving no trace of her passing. The space where she had stood was now empty, the shadow beneath the stone indistinguishable from the surrounding gloom.

Silas stood there for a long moment, the silence of the moor pressing in on him. He ran a trembling hand over his face, his mind struggling to reconcile what his eyes had seen with the rational world he knew. It was a phantom, he told himself again, a product of his overwrought imagination. The lament, the isolation, the pervasive atmosphere of sorrow—it had all conspired to create a vision. Yet the lingering impression of her sorrow, of her silent gaze, remained etched in his mind, a haunting testament to something he could not explain.

He forced himself to move on, his steps now heavier, more hesitant. The encounter, brief as it was, had shifted something within him. The moor, which had once offered a solace of its own bleak kind, now felt imbued with a deeper, more profound mystery. He was no longer merely a man seeking solitude; he was an intruder in a realm where the veil between worlds was thin, where grief could manifest as a visible presence.

The mist seemed to thicken as he ventured deeper, the visibility shrinking to mere yards. The landscape became a blur of indistinct shapes and shifting greys. He kept his gaze fixed on the ground before him, wary of stumbling, but his peripheral vision remained unnervingly active. He saw flickers of movement, subtle shifts in the texture of the mist, that his logical mind dismissed as optical illusions, yet his instincts screamed otherwise.

He found himself caught in a peculiar state of heightened awareness, where his senses were both dulled by the oppressive atmosphere and sharpened by an unshakeable feeling of being watched. He felt eyes upon him, unseen gazes that tracked his every move. He would catch a glimpse of something at the edge of his sight—a swirl of darker grey against the lighter mist, a fleeting outline that suggested a form—only for it to dissipate the moment he turned his head. It was like trying to grasp smoke, an elusive presence that danced just beyond his reach, always present, yet never truly there.

This constant, subtle sense of being observed was more unsettling than any overt threat could have been. It was the insidious nature of it, the way it played on his nerves, chipping away at his composure. He imagined her, the spectral woman, moving through the mist with a silent grace, her presence a constant echo of the lament he had first heard. Was she the source of the sorrow, or merely a manifestation of it? He had no way of knowing.

He recalled fragmented tales from his childhood, whispers of spirits that haunted these desolate moors, of lost souls who could not find rest. He had always dismissed them as folklore, the fanciful imaginings of superstitious minds. But now, standing in the heart of this spectral fog, with the echoes of a mournful song still resonating within him, those old tales took on a chilling new relevance.

He paused, listening intently. The wind had died down, and the only sound was the soft, sibilant hiss of the mist itself. In that profound quiet, he thought he heard it again—a faint, almost inaudible sigh, seemingly emanating from the air around him. He turned, his gaze sweeping the immediate vicinity. For an instant, a fleeting, heart-stopping instant, he saw her again. This time, she was closer, standing at the edge of a shallow depression in the land. She was silhouetted against the slightly lighter grey of the mist, her form impossibly delicate, her head bowed. He could discern the faint curve of her cheek, the delicate line of her jaw, though her features remained lost in shadow.

He felt a powerful urge to call out to her, to ask her name, to offer whatever comfort he could. But his throat was tight, his voice caught somewhere between his fear and his profound sympathy. The moment stretched, suspended in the heavy, damp air. He watched, mesmerized, as she slowly, almost imperceptibly, raised a hand. It was a gesture of profound despair, a reaching out to nothingness.

And then she was gone. Not a gradual fading this time, but an abrupt disappearance, as if a curtain had been drawn or a light extinguished. The space where she had stood was empty, the mist reclaiming its formless anonymity. Silas stood alone, the silence now a deafening roar in his ears. The lingering impression of her sorrow, of her phantom hand reaching out, was almost unbearable.

He realized then that her appearances were not meant to be solid, tangible encounters. They were fleeting glimpses, ephemeral manifestations designed to unsettle, to sow seeds of doubt and unease. She was a creature of shadow and mist, her presence as transient as the fog that clung to the moor. She appeared at the periphery of his vision, in the deepest shadows, in moments of profound silence, only to vanish as quickly as she had materialized, leaving him to question the validity of his own senses.

He continued his journey, though the phantom woman had become a constant companion, a spectral observer in the desolate landscape. He would catch her in his peripheral vision—a fleeting impression of movement, a subtle distortion in the mist, a dark shape coalescing for a heartbeat before dissolving back into the ether. Each sighting, however brief, left him with a deeper sense of disquiet. It was the uncertainty that gnawed at him, the inability to firmly grasp what he was seeing, or if he was seeing anything at all.

He found himself anticipating these glimpses, a morbid curiosity overriding his fear. He would pause, his breath held, his eyes scanning the gloom, hoping for another ephemeral appearance and dreading it in equal measure. He was caught in a peculiar dance with the unknown, drawn forward by an unseen force, haunted by the ghost of a woman whose sorrow seemed to permeate the very air he breathed. The mist, once a mere atmospheric phenomenon, had become a canvas upon which his deepest fears and his most profound sense of empathy were painted in fleeting, spectral strokes. He was lost, not just in the fog, but in the disquieting reality of Iris's elusive presence.

The air itself seemed to grow heavy, not with the usual dampness of the moor, but with an unnatural, biting cold that pierced through Silas's thick woolen cloak as if it were mere linen. It was a chill that bypassed the skin, settling deep within his bones, a profound and unsettling sensation that spoke of something far more ancient and malevolent than the elements. It was the cold of the grave, the frigid breath of death made manifest. This was not the slow, creeping frost of a winter night, but an abrupt, suffocating plunge into an icy abyss. He shivered, not from exertion, but from a primal instinct that screamed danger.

He had felt it before, a subtle shift in the atmosphere when the spectral woman had appeared, a mere whisper of cold that he had attributed to the pervasive mist. But this was different. This was a tangible presence, a palpable aura of frigid despair that clung to him like grave dirt. It was as if the very warmth of life had been leached from the surrounding moor, leaving behind a void of absolute, unyielding cold. His breath plumed in ragged bursts, each exhalation a desperate, futile attempt to ward off the encroaching frost. His fingers, encased in leather gloves, felt numb, the circulation sluggish, as if his very blood had turned to ice water.

He paused, his heart thudding a frantic rhythm against his ribs. His gaze swept the indistinct landscape, searching for the source of this unholy chill. He saw nothing but the shifting, ethereal curtains of mist, the muted browns and greys of the desolate moorland. Yet the cold was undeniable—an invisible hand that squeezed the life from him, a chilling prelude to an encounter he was beginning to dread with a ferocity that surprised him. He had sought out the desolation of the moors for a measure of peace, a respite from the clamor of the world. But this was a desolation of a different order, a chilling emptiness that promised no solace, only a grim, inescapable truth.

The sensation was akin to standing on the edge of a frozen precipice, the air so thin and frigid that each breath felt like inhaling shards of ice. It was a cold that had no business being present on this temperate, albeit damp, evening. It was a testament to an unnatural power, a force that could twist the very atmosphere to its grim will. He felt an overwhelming urge to turn back, to flee from this encroaching, deathly frigidity. But a morbid fascination, a desperate need to understand, held him rooted to the spot. He had seen her, glimpsed her ethereal form, and now this profound cold announced her proximity, a herald of her dark, vampiric essence.

He remembered the old tales, the whispers of the Dearg Due, the blood-red maiden, whose touch was said to bring an icy death, whose very presence drained the warmth from the living. He had dismissed them as mere folklore, the superstitious ramblings of a bygone era. But the bone-chilling cold that now enveloped him was no myth. It was a stark, undeniable reality, a physical manifestation of a horror that transcended the natural world. This was the chill of her passing, a lingering echo of her unholy existence that seeped into the very marrow of his being.

He noticed it now, the way the mist itself seemed to condense and shimmer with an unnatural frost around him, as if the very air were recoiling from an unseen taint. Tiny ice crystals, impossibly delicate, seemed to form and dissipate in the space around his head, catching the faint, diffused light of the unseen sun in fleeting, spectral glints. The heather underfoot, which had been damp from the mist, now seemed brittle, each stalk rimed with a delicate, almost crystalline frost—a stark contrast to the surrounding sodden earth. It was as if a miniature blizzard had descended upon his immediate vicinity, an isolated pocket of arctic desolation in the heart of the moor.

This was not merely a drop in temperature; it was an active, aggressive draining of heat. He felt a weakness spreading through his limbs, a lethargy that threatened to drag him down into the sodden earth. His thoughts, usually sharp and incisive, felt sluggish, clouded by the pervasive cold. It was as if his very life force were being siphoned away, a slow, agonizing surrender to the unholy frigidity. The world around him, previously cloaked in a uniform grey, now seemed to take on a more defined, sharper outline, as if the extreme cold were somehow enhancing his vision, forcing him to perceive every detail with a chilling clarity. The gnarled branches of the wind-battered trees appeared stark and skeletal, each twig etched with an unnerving precision against the swirling mist. The very stones beneath his feet seemed to gleam with a cold, impassive light.

He pressed on, driven by a mixture of fear and desperate resolve. The chill, though unnerving, was also a sign, a confirmation that he was on the right path, or at least in the vicinity of whatever spectral entity had captured his attention. It was a terrifying beacon, a warning that the Dearg Due was near, her vampiric essence a palpable force that could alter the very fabric of the world. He tightened his grip on the stout staff he carried, its familiar weight a small comfort against the encroaching desolation. He knew, with a certainty that chilled him more than the air, that this was no ordinary spectral manifestation. This was something ancient, something predatory, and its cold embrace was a prelude to a far more profound danger.

The silence, too, was different now. It was not the peaceful quiet of solitude, but a heavy, oppressive stillness, as if the very air were holding its breath, anticipating a horrific revelation. The distant bleating of sheep, which had been a faint but persistent sound earlier, had completely ceased. The chirping of unseen insects, the rustle of unseen creatures in the heather—all had fallen silent, as if even the hardy wildlife of the moors understood the primal danger that emanated from this unnatural cold. It was a silence born of primal fear, a reverence for the terrifying presence that had imposed its frigid will upon the landscape.

He found himself scanning the ground with renewed intensity, not just for unseen obstacles, but for any sign of the woman, for any glimpse of the creature that could command such a chilling aura. He recalled the legends of her hunger, her insatiable thirst, and the cold was a direct reflection of that unholy desire. It was the cold of a tomb, the cold of a heart that had long ceased to beat, filled only with the dark, predatory instinct of a creature sustained by the very lifeblood of others.

He stumbled, his foot catching on a root hidden beneath the frost-rimed heather. The sudden jolt sent a wave of icy pain through his ankle, and for a moment, he feared he might fall. As he regained his balance, his gaze swept downward, and he saw it—a faint, almost imperceptible crimson stain on the frosted ground, a dark bloom against the white. It was too small to be significant, perhaps a berry from a hardy, frost-bitten bush, but in the context of the unnatural cold, it sent a fresh wave of dread through him. He imagined it was not a berry, but a droplet of blood, a testament to the Dearg Due's recent passage, a subtle warning of the carnage she was capable of.

The chill seemed to intensify with each passing moment, a creeping paralysis that threatened to overtake him. He felt a desperate need to move, to escape this icy grip, but his limbs felt heavy, sluggish. It was as much a psychological battle as a physical one. The cold was a manifestation of her power, an attempt to demoralize, to weaken him before she even revealed herself fully. He had to fight it, to push back against the encroaching dread, to maintain his clarity of mind. He focused on his breathing, forcing deep, steady breaths into his lungs, trying to rekindle the warmth within.

He thought of the stories of those who had encountered the Dearg Due, their fates often ending in unexplained disappearances, their bodies found drained of life, their skin cold and pale. He understood now why. The cold was not just a warning; it was a weapon, a silent, insidious killer that sapped the very essence of life. It was the antithesis of warmth, of vitality, of everything that made existence bearable.

A sudden gust of wind, unnervingly devoid of any warmth, whipped around him, carrying with it a faint, metallic scent. It was the scent of blood, he realized with a sickening lurch—sharp and coppery, mingled with the damp, earthy smell of the moor. It was a scent that spoke of recent violence, of a life brutally extinguished. The cold deepened, a physical manifestation of the horror that the scent evoked. He could feel the frost creeping up his legs, a visible condensation clinging to the rough wool of his trousers.

He knew he was approaching something ancient, something terrifyingly real. The folklore was not just stories; it was a warning, a desperate attempt by those who had survived to imbue future generations with the knowledge of the dangers that lurked in the shadows. The chill was her signature, the icy imprint of a creature that fed on the warmth of life, leaving behind only the desolate cold of death. And as he ventured deeper into the mist, the chilling embrace of the Dearg Due tightened around him, a stark and terrifying reminder of the spectral danger that lay hidden within the heart of the desolate moors. The cold was not just around him; it was within him, a persistent, bone-deep ache that promised to linger long after he had, hopefully, escaped her spectral grasp.

The moor, so recently a canvas of muted greys and swirling mist, now seemed to sharpen, each detail etched with an almost painful clarity by the unnatural cold. It was as if the very air, leached of its warmth, had become a lens, magnifying the desolate beauty of the landscape and, by extension, the terrifying presence that stalked it. Silas found himself catching these fleeting glimpses, moments where the veil of mist seemed to thin, offering him fractured, horrifying insights into the entity he pursued. These were not mere impressions of shadow and cold; they were brief, brutal affirmations of the legend, confirmations of the Dearg Due's monstrous reality.

The first such glimpse came when Silas paused, his breath snagging in his throat, the frigid air searing his lungs. He had rounded a cluster of gnarled hawthorns, their skeletal branches clawing at the sky, and there, not twenty yards ahead, the mist swirled and parted. For a fraction of a second, he saw her. It wasn't the spectral, almost translucent figure he had glimpsed before, but something far more corporeal, far more terrifying. Her skin, even in the dim light, possessed an unnerving pallor—not the healthy flush of life, but the waxy, almost porcelain hue of death. It was a stark, unnatural whiteness that seemed to absorb the scant light rather than reflect it.

Her eyes, when they met his, were not the sorrowful pools he had briefly seen. Instead, they were pools of obsidian, devoid of any warmth or recognition, yet burning with an intelligent, predatory hunger. There was a glint within them, a sharp, almost reptilian sheen that spoke of ancient instincts and a profound disregard for the lives of mortals. It was a look that bypassed politeness, that saw him not as a fellow being, but as sustenance, as a potential victim. The pupils seemed unnaturally dilated, swallowing the irises, and in that terrifying instant, Silas felt a primal fear bloom in his chest, a terror that clawed at his very sanity. This was no lost soul; this was a hunter.

And her movements— even that briefest of moments revealed an unnerving grace, a fluidity that defied the harsh terrain and the biting cold. She moved with an unearthly elegance, her slender frame seeming to glide over the uneven ground as if walking on air. There was no hesitation, no awkwardness, just a smooth, controlled motion that hinted at immense power held in reserve. It was the predatory grace of a snake, the silent, deadly stalk of a wolf, amplified and distorted into something far more sinister. Her posture was unnaturally erect, her head held high, exuding an aura of regal, chilling dominance.

Then, as swiftly as it had appeared, the mist closed in again, swallowing her from view. Silas was left gasping, his heart hammering against his ribs like a trapped bird. The cold seemed to bite deeper, a physical manifestation of the fear that now coursed through him. That was no mere ghost. That was the Dearg Due, the blood-red maiden of legend, and her vampiric form was a chilling testament to the darkness that dwelled within the human heart, twisted and corrupted by an insatiable thirst. The pallor of her skin was not sickness; it was the absence of life's vital warmth. The glint in her eyes was not madness; it was the predatory gleam of a creature that had mastered the art of the hunt over centuries, perhaps millennia.

He pressed on, driven by a desperate need to understand, to witness more, even as every instinct screamed at him to flee. The cold was his constant companion, a reminder of her proximity, but now it was laced with the vivid, terrifying image of her. He began to notice subtle changes in the landscape around him, anomalies that seemed to be a direct result of her passage. The heather, where it had been touched by the edge of the mist that still clung to her wake, seemed to wither and blacken, the vibrant purple of the late bloom turning to a brittle, ashen grey. The very earth seemed to recoil, the soil appearing drier, more cracked, as if her presence leached the moisture and life from everything it touched.

Another glimpse came near a stunted, ancient oak, its branches contorted into grotesque shapes by years of relentless wind. He had been drawn by a sudden, unnerving silence, the absence of even the wind's mournful howl. He looked up, and through a momentary rift in the swirling fog, he saw her again, this time perched impossibly on one of the oak's thickest branches. She was not struggling for purchase; she seemed to be a part of the tree itself, her pale form blending eerily with the grey bark.

This time, he focused on her hands. They were long and slender, her fingers unnaturally tapered, tipped with nails that seemed to have a faint, pearlescent sheen, like shards of polished bone. He could almost feel the chill radiating from them, a cold that could freeze flesh with a touch. He imagined those fingers, delicate yet impossibly strong, sinking into the soft flesh of her victims, draining them of their lifeblood, leaving behind only the hollowed shells that the legends spoke of. The detail was so stark, so horrific, that it felt as if he were seeing through her eyes, experiencing the world as she did—a world of eternal hunger and cold.

There was a subtle, almost imperceptible elongation of her canine teeth, a sharpness that was not present in the face of a living human. It was a subtle detail, easily missed, but in the context of the other observations, it painted a chilling picture. These were the tools of her trade, the instruments of her eternal curse. They were not merely fangs; they were symbols of her predatory nature, a constant reminder of the violence inherent in her existence.

Her lips, a pale, almost bloodless red, were drawn back slightly in what might have been a smile, but it held no mirth, no warmth. It was a chilling baring of teeth, a silent promise of the pain and terror to come. The pallor of her skin was so profound that the faint color of her lips seemed unnatural, a stark contrast that only served to emphasize the emptiness of her being. It was the color of a rose that had been left to wilt in the frost, its vibrant life leached away, leaving behind a faded, mournful hue.

He noticed, too, the subtle way her hair seemed to shimmer, not with the healthy luster of living locks, but with an almost metallic sheen, like spun moonlight or frost-laden silk. It was dark, so dark it seemed to absorb the very light, and it flowed around her with an unnatural stillness, even when the wind tugged at the mist. It seemed to possess a life of its own, a dark halo that framed her spectral visage.

These glimpses were like shards of ice piercing his composure, each one a stark reminder of the horror he faced. He found himself scrutinizing every shadow, every eddy in the mist, his senses heightened to an almost unbearable degree. He was no longer just a scholar pursuing a legend; he was a prey animal, acutely aware of the predator that hunted him. The folklore spoke of the Dearg Due's hypnotic gaze, her ability to ensnare the minds of mortals with a single look. He now understood the power behind those tales, the sheer force of will and malevolent intent that could be conveyed through those obsidian eyes.

He recalled a particular passage from an old text, describing the Dearg Due as having a "body cold as a corpse, yet animated by a hunger that never ceased." The images he was witnessing were the living embodiment of that description. The unnatural pallor, the predatory glint, the chilling grace—they all spoke of a being that existed outside the natural order, a creature sustained by the antithesis of life itself. The cold was not just an atmospheric phenomenon; it was the outward manifestation of her inner emptiness, the frigid core of a creature that had long since forfeited its humanity.

He saw her again, a fleeting apparition across a shallow gully. She was crouched low, her movements now less graceful, more animalistic. Her body was tensed, coiled like a spring, her gaze fixed on something in the mist ahead. He couldn't see what it was, but the intensity of her focus, the predatory stillness, sent a tremor of fear through him. It was a stark reminder of her true nature, a being driven by primal urges that transcended human morality. The ethereal beauty he had glimpsed earlier was a façade, a thin veneer over the ravenous beast that lay beneath.

Her form seemed to ripple slightly, as if the edges of her being were not entirely solid, but constantly shifting, a testament to her spectral nature. Yet there was a palpable solidity to her presence, a weight that could be felt even at a distance. It was a paradox that defied logic, a being of mist and shadow that could exert such a tangible, chilling influence on the world.

The details he was gathering were terrifying, yet invaluable. They were solidifying the legend, transforming the whispers of folklore into a concrete, horrifying reality. He was not chasing a phantom; he was tracking a creature of nightmare, a creature that had walked the earth for untold centuries, feeding on the lifeblood of the unwary. Each glimpse, however brief, served to deepen his understanding of her power, her nature, and the profound danger she represented.

He felt a strange, almost perverse fascination intertwining with his fear. To witness such a creature, to see the physical manifestation of ancient evils, was a privilege of a sort, a macabre education in the darkest corners of existence. But the price of this knowledge was steep, measured in the ever-deepening chill that permeated his soul and the increasingly vivid images of horror that now haunted his mind's eye. He knew, with a certainty that settled like a shroud of ice around his heart, that these fleeting glimpses were merely the prelude. The true encounter, the true test of his resolve, was yet to come. And with each chilling vision, his dread grew, not just of her power, but of the chilling truth she represented: that the monsters of legend were not always confined to the pages of old books. Sometimes, they walked the moors, their breath the cold of the grave, their eyes burning with an eternal hunger.

The moor, so recently a canvas of muted greys and swirling mist, now seemed to sharpen, each detail etched with an almost painful clarity by the unnatural cold. It was as if the very air, leached of its warmth, had become a lens, magnifying the desolate beauty of the landscape and, by extension, the terrifying presence that stalked it. Silas found himself catching these fleeting glimpses, moments where the veil of mist seemed to thin, offering him fractured, horrifying insights into the entity he pursued. These were not mere impressions of shadow and cold; they were brief, brutal affirmations of the legend, confirmations of the Dearg Due's monstrous reality.

The first such glimpse came when Silas paused, his breath snagging in his throat, the frigid air searing his lungs. He had rounded a cluster of gnarled hawthorns, their skeletal branches clawing at the sky, and there, not twenty yards ahead, the mist swirled and parted. For a fraction of a second, he saw her. It wasn't the spectral, almost translucent figure he had glimpsed before, but something far more corporeal, far more terrifying. Her skin, even in the dim light, possessed an unnerving pallor—not the healthy flush of life, but the waxy, almost porcelain hue of death. It was a stark, unnatural whiteness that seemed to absorb the scant light rather than reflect it.

Her eyes, when they met his, were not the sorrowful pools he had briefly seen. Instead, they were pools of obsidian, devoid of any warmth or recognition, yet burning with an intelligent, predatory hunger. There was a glint within them, a sharp, almost reptilian sheen that spoke of ancient instincts and a profound disregard for the lives of mortals. It was a look that bypassed politeness, that saw him not as a fellow being, but as sustenance, as a potential victim. The pupils seemed unnaturally dilated, swallowing the irises, and in that terrifying instant, Silas felt a primal fear bloom in his chest, a terror that clawed at his very sanity. This was no lost soul; this was a hunter.

And her movements. Even that briefest of moments revealed an unnerving grace, a fluidity that defied the harsh terrain and the biting cold. She moved with an unearthly elegance, her slender frame seeming to glide over the uneven ground as if walking on air. There was no hesitation, no awkwardness, just a smooth, controlled motion that hinted at immense power held in reserve. It was the predatory grace of a snake, the silent, deadly stalk of a wolf, amplified and distorted into something far more sinister. Her posture was unnaturally erect, her head held high, exuding an aura of regal, chilling dominance.

Then, as swiftly as it had appeared, the mist closed in again, swallowing her from view. Silas was left gasping, his heart hammering against his ribs like a trapped bird. The cold seemed to bite deeper, a physical manifestation of the fear that now coursed through him. That was no mere ghost. That was the

Dearg Due, the blood-red maiden of legend, and her vampiric form was a chilling testament to the darkness that dwelled within the human heart, twisted and corrupted by an insatiable thirst. The pallor of her skin was not sickness; it was the absence of life's vital warmth. The glint in her eyes was not madness; it was the predatory gleam of a creature that had mastered the art of the hunt over centuries, perhaps millennia.

He pressed on, driven by a desperate need to understand, to witness more, even as every instinct screamed at him to flee. The cold was his constant companion, a reminder of her proximity, but now it was laced with the vivid, terrifying image of her. He began to notice subtle changes in the landscape around him, anomalies that seemed to be a direct result of her passage. The heather, where it had been touched by the edge of the mist that still clung to her wake, seemed to wither and blacken, the vibrant purple of the late bloom turning to a brittle, ashen grey. The very earth seemed to recoil, the soil appearing drier, more cracked, as if her presence leached the moisture and life from everything it touched.

Another glimpse came near a stunted, ancient oak, its branches contorted into grotesque shapes by years of relentless wind. He had been drawn by a sudden, unnerving silence, the absence of even the wind's mournful howl. He looked up, and through a momentary rift in the swirling fog, he saw her again, this time perched impossibly on one of the oak's thickest branches. She was not struggling for purchase; she seemed to be a part of the tree itself, her pale form blending eerily with the grey bark.

This time, he focused on her hands. They were long and slender, her fingers unnaturally tapered, tipped with nails that seemed to have a faint, pearlescent sheen, like shards of polished bone. He could almost feel the chill radiating from them, a cold that could freeze flesh with a touch. He imagined those fingers, delicate yet impossibly strong, sinking into the soft flesh of her victims, draining them of their lifeblood, leaving behind only the hollowed shells that the legends spoke of. The detail was so stark, so horrific, that it felt as if he were seeing through her eyes, experiencing the world as she did – a world of eternal hunger and cold.

There was a subtle, almost imperceptible elongation of her canine teeth, a sharpness that was not present in the face of a living human. It was a subtle detail, easily missed, but in the context of the other observations, it painted a chilling picture. These were the tools of her trade, the instruments of her eternal curse. They were not merely fangs; they were symbols of her predatory nature, a constant reminder of the violence inherent in her existence.

Her lips, a pale, almost bloodless red, were drawn back slightly in what might have been a smile, but it held no mirth, no warmth. It was a chilling baring of teeth, a silent promise of the pain and terror to come. The pallor of her skin was so profound that the faint color of her lips seemed unnatural, a stark contrast that only served to emphasize the emptiness of her being. It was the color of a rose that had been left to wilt in the frost, its vibrant life leached away, leaving behind a faded, mournful hue.

He noticed, too, the subtle way her hair seemed to shimmer, not with the healthy luster of living locks, but with an almost metallic sheen, like spun moonlight or frost-laden silk. It was dark, so dark it seemed to absorb the very light, and it flowed around her with an unnatural stillness, even when the wind tugged at the mist. It seemed to possess a life of its own, a dark halo that framed her spectral visage.

These glimpses were like shards of ice piercing his composure, each one a stark reminder of the horror he faced. He found himself scrutinizing every shadow, every eddy in the mist, his senses heightened to an almost unbearable degree. He was no longer just a scholar pursuing a legend; he was a prey animal, acutely aware of the predator that hunted him. The folklore spoke of the

Dearg Due's hypnotic gaze, her ability to ensnare the minds of mortals with a single look. He now understood the power behind those tales, the sheer force of will and malevolent intent that could be conveyed through those obsidian eyes.

He recalled a particular passage from an old text, describing the *Dearg Due* as having a "body cold as a corpse, yet animated by a hunger that never ceased." The images he was witnessing were the living embodiment of that description. The unnatural pallor, the predatory glint, the chilling grace – they all spoke of a being that existed outside the natural order, a creature sustained by the antithesis of life itself. The cold was not just an atmospheric phenomenon; it was the outward manifestation of her inner emptiness, the frigid core of a creature that had long since forfeited its humanity.

He saw her again, a fleeting apparition across a shallow gully. She was crouched low, her movements now less graceful, more animalistic. Her body was tensed, coiled like a spring, her gaze fixed on something in the mist ahead. He couldn't see what it was, but the intensity of her focus, the predatory stillness, sent a tremor of fear through him. It was a stark reminder of her true nature, a being driven by primal urges that transcended human morality. The ethereal beauty he had glimpsed earlier was a facade, a thin veneer over the ravenous beast that lay beneath.

Her form seemed to ripple slightly, as if the edges of her being were not entirely solid, but constantly shifting, a testament to her spectral nature. Yet, there was a palpable solidity to her presence, a weight that could be felt even at a distance. It was a paradox that defied logic, a being of mist and shadow that could exert such a tangible, chilling influence on the world.

The details he was gathering were terrifying, yet invaluable. They were solidifying the legend, transforming the whispers of folklore into a concrete, horrifying reality. He was not chasing a phantom; he was tracking a creature of nightmare, a creature that had walked the earth for untold centuries, feeding on the lifeblood of the unwary. Each glimpse, however brief, served to deepen his understanding of her power, her nature, and the profound danger she represented.

He felt a strange, almost perverse fascination intertwining with his fear. To witness such a creature, to see the physical manifestation of ancient evils, was a privilege of a sort, a macabre education in the darkest corners of existence. But the price of this knowledge was steep, measured in the ever-deepening chill that permeated his soul and the increasingly vivid images of horror that now haunted his mind's eye. He knew, with a certainty that settled like a shroud of ice around his heart, that these fleeting glimpses were merely the prelude. The true encounter, the true test of his resolve, was yet to come. And with each chilling vision, his dread grew, not just of her power, but of the chilling truth she represented: that the monsters of legend were not always confined to the pages of old books. Sometimes, they walked the moors, their breath the cold of the grave, their eyes burning with an eternal hunger.

Silas was not the first to claim such encounters, nor would he be the last, though few had the fortitude to persist, let alone record their experiences. The scattered testimonies, often dismissed as the ramblings of the addled or the fanciful tales of superstitious folk, painted a disquieting, fragmented portrait of the

Dearg Due. These were the whispers from the fringes of sanity, the echoes of terror that the rational mind sought to silence.

There was the account of Old Man Hemlock, a hermit who lived on the desolate western edge of the moor, a place where the peat bogs swallowed the unwary and the wind sang dirges through the skeletal remains of ancient trees. He was found one bone-chilling autumn morning, huddled by his meager fire, his eyes wide with an unseeing terror, his skin like parchment stretched taut over brittle bone. He spoke, in fevered, disjointed whispers, of a woman with eyes like a winter sky and hair black as a starless night. She had, he claimed, stood at the edge of his small clearing, bathed in the spectral moonlight, her form ethereal yet undeniably present. He described a cold so profound that it seeped into his very marrow, a chill that had nothing to do with the biting wind. He spoke of her voice, a melody that promised solace, a siren's call that lured him toward the moor's treacherous embrace. But when he described her mouth, her words turned to a strangled gasp; he had seen, he swore, teeth that were not human, teeth that gleamed with a hunger he could only equate to that of a starved wolf. The village doctor pronounced him suffering from exposure and a touch of madness, a common affliction, he'd noted, for those who lived too close to the wild. Hemlock died a week later, his final days spent whimpering about the "cold kiss" and the "eyes that stole the light."

Then there was the tale of Elara, a young woman from a hamlet nestled in the shadow of the moors, a place where stories of the "Lady of the Mists" were woven into lullabies and cautionary rhymes. She had, in her youth, wandered too far from home one twilight, chasing a will-o'-the-wisp, a common enough folly. She claimed to have stumbled upon a figure draped in shadows, standing beside a moss-covered standing stone. Elara remembered only a chilling stillness, a silence so absolute that the chirping of crickets and the distant bleating of sheep vanished as if by magic. The figure, she said, turned to her, and though her face was obscured by the encroaching darkness and the swirling vapors, Elara felt an intense gaze upon her, a gaze that felt ancient and sorrowful, yet held a hidden current of something predatory. She spoke of an overwhelming urge to approach, to offer comfort to this seemingly lost soul. But as she took a step forward, the figure raised a hand, a hand that seemed impossibly pale in the gloom, and a wave of profound melancholy washed over Elara, a despair so potent it nearly buckled her knees. It was only the sudden, piercing cry of a hawk overhead that broke the spell, jolting her back to her senses. When she looked again, the figure was gone, leaving behind only the damp scent of ancient earth and a lingering, unbearable sorrow that clung to her for days, a shadow of the

Dearg Due's despair. Her family, embarrassed by the tale that was deemed a fanciful ghost story, ensured she never spoke of it again, but Elara, as she grew older, would often stare out at the moors with a haunted look in her eyes, a silent testament to the glimpse of something ancient and terrible she had witnessed.

From a different village, further to the north, came the story of a shepherd who swore he saw a woman bathing in the icy waters of a high mountain tarn, even in the depths of winter. He had been seeking a stray ewe, venturing into territory rarely trod by man. He heard no splash, no disturbance of the water, yet there she was, submerged up to her neck in the frigid depths. Her skin, he recounted with a shudder, was the colour of unbleached linen, and her dark hair fanned out around her like a raven's wing on the water's surface. She looked towards him, and he claimed her eyes held an impossible depth, like peering into a moonless night. He felt no immediate threat, but rather an overwhelming sense of pity, as if she were trapped in an eternal, agonizing cold. He turned to find his ewe, and when he glanced back, she had vanished, leaving the tarn undisturbed, the ice unbroken. He was ridiculed by his neighbours, who attributed it to the potent local brew and the solitude playing tricks on his mind. Yet, he never again ventured that high into the moors, and his sheepdogs, usually fearless, would whimper and refuse to go near the tarn, their instincts sensing an ancient wrongness that logic could not explain.

These accounts, though disparate, shared common threads: the unnatural pallor, the piercing gaze, the overwhelming cold, and a profound sense of something ancient and sorrowful, yet undeniably dangerous. They were the fractured reflections of a truth that many refused to acknowledge, the inconvenient realities that challenged the orderly world. Each narrative, however brief and often dismissed, contributed to the growing tapestry of fear and mystery that surrounded the

Dearg Due. They spoke of encounters that left an indelible mark, not just on the witness, but on the very landscape they inhabited, a subtle corruption of the natural order, a chilling reminder that some legends were more than just stories. They were warnings. The folklore, often relegated to the realm of childish superstition, was beginning to whisper its own chilling truths through these fragmented, fear-laden testimonies. Each dismissed witness was, in their own way, a stone laid upon the foundation of Silas's grim understanding.

The chilling visions Silas had endured were not unique, nor were they entirely unprecedented. History, as he was discovering, was littered with the hushed whispers of those who had brushed against the spectral hem of the *Dearg Due*, their encounters dismissed, their warnings unheeded. It was a grim testament to the human capacity for denial, a collective turning of blind eyes to the monstrous truths that lurked just beyond the veil of the mundane. The folklore, with its stark pronouncements of vampiric dread, was not merely a collection of ancient fears; it was a tapestry woven with the threads of real, terrifying experiences, often rationalized into oblivion by those who feared to believe.

Consider the case of the miller, Thomas, who worked his days by the sluggish, peat-stained river that snaked its way through the moorland's heart. For weeks, the village gossips had whispered of his growing melancholy, his once jovial laughter replaced by a haunted silence. He spoke, in fractured confessions to the village priest, of a pervasive chill that clung to him even by his hearth, a cold that seemed to emanate from a pale, impossibly beautiful woman he'd seen on the riverbank at dusk. He described her tears, like droplets of frozen dew, and a sorrow in her eyes that mirrored his own burgeoning despair. He'd felt an overwhelming compulsion to offer her solace, to draw her into the warmth of his own life, and she, in turn, had seemed to offer him an escape from his earthly burdens. The priest, a man steeped in the dogma of the Church and the practicalities of harvest, attributed Thomas's state to a bout of "vapours" and a touch of hypochondria, exacerbated by the damp and the loneliness of his profession. He prescribed tonics and prayer, urging Thomas to focus on his work and to avoid the melancholic ramblings of the local elders who still clung to tales of the old ways. But Thomas's condition worsened. He began to wander from his mill at night, drawn by an unseen force to the river's edge, where he claimed to hear a mournful melody, a song that promised oblivion and release. One morning, his wife found his mill wheel still, the sacks of flour untouched. Thomas was gone, and the only trace of his passing was a single, impossibly pale lily floating serenely on the dark water, a bloom that should not have been able to survive the season's frost. His disappearance was eventually attributed to an accidental drowning, a tragic but not uncommon end for a man plagued by melancholy, his whispered warnings about the spectral woman of the river lost to the practical explanations that best suited the living.

Then there was the story of the young shepherdess, Isolde, who tended her flock on the higher, more desolate reaches of the moor. She was known for her unusual affinity with the wild, often seen conversing with the wind and the stoic grey stones as if they held the secrets of the universe. One late autumn afternoon, as the sky bled into bruised shades of purple and orange, she reported seeing a woman standing on a distant tor, her silhouette stark against the fading light. Isolde described her as impossibly slender, her hair a cascade of midnight darkness that seemed to flow with a life of its own, untouched by the biting wind that whipped Isolde's own hair about her face. She felt an immediate, inexplicable dread, a primal instinct screaming at her to turn her flock and flee. Yet, she was also drawn by a strange fascination, a morbid curiosity that held her rooted to the spot. The woman, though impossibly distant, seemed to turn her head, and Isolde felt a piercing gaze, a silent communication that spoke of ancient hunger and a profound weariness. She saw no features, no discernible face, only the impression of eyes that held the cold emptiness of a winter's night. Isolde recounted this experience to her family, her voice trembling with the residual fear. Her father, a pragmatic farmer who understood the value of good wool and sturdy fences, dismissed her fears as the fanciful imaginings of a lonely girl who spent too much time communing with the spirits of the moor. He warned her against believing such tales, reminding her that the moor held its own dangers, but they were of the earthly kind – treacherous bogs, sudden storms, and the occasional lost wolf, not spectral ladies with eyes like the abyss. Isolde, chastened but unconvinced, learned to heed her own instincts. She began to keep her flock closer to the village, and when the mists rolled in thick and heavy, she would hum a protective chant her grandmother had taught her, a series of nonsensical syllables that she felt, deep in her bones, offered a shield against unseen perils. Years later, a traveller stumbled upon a small, weathered cairn on that very tor, marked by a single, frost-bitten rose. The cairn, he noted in his journal, seemed to emanate a profound sadness, a palpable aura of loss that clung to the air like a shroud. Isolde herself, though she lived a long life, was said to have never fully shaken the chill of that encounter, forever casting a wary eye towards the desolate heights of the moor.

The pattern was undeniable, a tragic echo resonating through the fragmented accounts: the subtle signs, the intuitive warnings, the chilling glimpses, all invariably met with skepticism, rationalization, or outright disbelief. The folklore, rather than being a source of guidance, often became a point of ridicule. Those who dared to speak of the unnatural were dismissed as superstitious fools, their experiences relegated to the realm of imagination or the ravings of the mentally unsound. This dismissal was, in itself, a form of danger, blinding individuals to the genuine threats that stalked their isolated communities.

Consider the tale of the scholar, Alistair Finch, who had journeyed to the region years before Silas, seeking to document local legends. He was a man of empirical observation, a firm believer in the power of reason to dispel the shadows of superstition. He dismissed the tales of the

Dearg Due as mere elaborations on old fears of disease and the unknown, perhaps influenced by the harsh realities of the unforgiving landscape. He interviewed villagers, gathering snippets of folklore, but filtered them through his rationalistic lens, seeking logical explanations for every alleged supernatural event. He heard the stories of the chilling cold, the unnatural pallor, the predatory glint in the eyes, but he attributed them to factors like poor circulation, malnutrition, and the psychological effects of isolation and fear. He documented the story of a trapper named Silas Thorne (a name that struck Silas, the current investigator, with a chilling premonition), who had claimed to have seen a woman of impossible beauty emerge from a swirling mist, her skin like moonlight on snow, her eyes holding the depth of a starlit night. Thorne had described her singing a song that promised eternal peace, a melody that had lulled him into a near-trance. He'd felt an overwhelming urge to follow her into the fog, a desire to escape the harshness of his existence. However, he recounted how his loyal hunting dog had suddenly bristled, barking ferociously at the apparition, its guttural snarl breaking the spell. Thorne, jolted by the dog's terror, had seen a fleeting glimpse of something sharp and unnatural about her teeth before she vanished into the mist. Finch, in his journals, meticulously noted this account but dismissed the "sharp teeth" as a trick of the light or the trapper's overwrought imagination, focusing instead on the potential for hypothermia and hallucination induced by prolonged exposure and the isolation of his profession. Thorne, a man of the wild, a man who trusted his instincts and the primal warnings of his animal companion, was rendered a cautionary tale of overactive imagination, his genuine encounter with the vampiric entity conveniently explained away by the scholar's insistence on mundane causes. Finch returned to civilization, his academic reputation intact, leaving behind a region where the whispers of the *Dearg Due* continued to circulate, unacknowledged by the halls of learned men.

The tragedy lay in this persistent refusal to acknowledge the possibility of the impossible. The folklore was not just a set of stories; it was a repository of ancestral knowledge, a survival guide etched in the collective memory of communities that had lived in close proximity to forces beyond their comprehension. The tales of the

Dearg Due were warnings, passed down through generations, detailing the signs, the dangers, and the methods of avoidance. Yet, for every soul who heeded these whispers, there were many more who scoffed, who clung to the comforting illusion of control and rationality.

Silas found himself wrestling with this very dilemma. The fragmented accounts he unearthed, the chilling folklore he meticulously pieced together, were all pointing towards a terrifying reality. Yet, he understood the immense psychological barrier that separated belief from disbelief. He saw how the elders, their faces etched with the wisdom of years spent on the moor, spoke in hushed tones of the "Mist Maiden" and the "Cold Lady," their words carrying the weight of genuine fear. But when these same stories reached the ears of the younger generation, or the visiting outsiders, they were often met with eye-rolls and dismissive chuckles. The rational mind, so adept at dissecting the tangible world, struggled to accommodate the supernatural. It sought patterns, logic, and scientific explanations, and when none were readily apparent, it created them, often in the form of denial.

He thought of the local innkeeper, a portly man named Barnaby, who would laugh heartily when the

Dearg Due was mentioned, attributing all the disappearances and strange occurrences to the treacherous terrain, the harsh weather, or simply the escapades of restless souls seeking to escape their mundane lives. "Ghosts and ghouls," he'd declare, wiping ale from his beard, "are for children and fools. Give me a good stout ale and a warm fire, and I'll face any phantom that dares cross my path." Yet, Silas had observed Barnaby's hand tremble when he poured a drink on particularly foggy nights, his gaze often darting towards the darkened corners of the common room, as if expecting something to materialize from the shadows.

Barnaby, for all his outward bravado, was not immune to the underlying fear that permeated the region. He simply chose to confront it with a barrage of denial and forced merriment, a defense mechanism as old as time itself. His cheerful dismissal served to further erode the authority of the old tales, making it even harder for genuine warnings to be heard.

The irony was a bitter draught: the very people who were most susceptible, those whose lives were intertwined with the moor's unforgiving nature, were often the most likely to disregard the warnings that might have saved them. The fisherman who ventured out on mist-shrouded mornings, the shepherd who strayed too far from the beaten path, the solitary traveller caught out after dusk – these were the potential victims, the ones most vulnerable to the

Dearg Due's predatory allure. And yet, they were often the ones most eager to dismiss the old wives' tales, to embrace the modern world's embrace of the rational, leaving themselves open to the ancient dangers that thrived in the liminal spaces between belief and disbelief.

Silas felt the weight of this tragic pattern settling upon him. He was not merely pursuing a creature of myth; he was battling against a tide of ingrained skepticism, a collective amnesia that allowed ancient horrors to persist. The fleeting glimpses he had witnessed were not just personal revelations; they were echoes of countless forgotten warnings, each one a testament to the

Dearg Due's enduring presence and the tragic, often fatal, consequence of ignoring the signs. The mist that swirled across the moor was not just a meteorological phenomenon; it was a veil, and behind it lay a truth that many were too afraid, or too rational, to see. And it was precisely this blindness, this willful ignorance, that made the *Dearg Due* so terrifyingly effective, allowing her to continue her silent, deadly hunt, one unheeded warning at a time.

Chapter 10:
The Cycle of Blood

The hunger was a constant, a gnawing emptiness that no amount of earthly sustenance could ever assuage. It was the foundational truth of Iris's existence, the very bedrock upon which her millennia of undeath were built. Not a mere craving, but a visceral, all-consuming need that dictated the rhythm of her immortal life, a ceaseless demand that echoed in the hollow chambers of her spectral heart. It was the thirst that had driven her from the mortal coil, a fevered desperation that had stripped away the last vestiges of her humanity, leaving behind only the primal instinct for blood.

This thirst was more than just a biological imperative; it was a profound spiritual malady, a curse woven into the very fabric of her being. Each drop of crimson she consumed was a temporary balm, a fleeting respite from the gnawing void, but never a cure. The blood did not merely sustain her; it was the essence of her unlife, the raw energy that fueled her unnatural existence, allowing her to defy the natural decay of flesh and bone. Without it, the slow, inexorable process of her undeath would assert itself, her form would begin to wither, her strength would wane, and the spectral luminescence that clung to her like a shroud would dim, eventually fading into utter nothingness. This terrifying prospect was a constant shadow, a silent threat that propelled her relentless pursuit of sustenance.

Her senses, honed to an unnerving degree by centuries of predation, were perpetually attuned to the subtle, intoxicating scent of life. The faint aroma of warm blood, carried on the wind from miles away, could set her nerves alight, a symphony of promise that drowned out all other sensations. It was a perfume of life, a siren's call that lured her from her shadowed solitude, drawing her inexorably towards her prey. The very air seemed to thicken with the scent when a mortal walked nearby, each thrum of a human heart a distinct beat in the chaotic symphony of the night, a beat that resonated with a primal echo within her own stilled breast. The world, for Iris, was a landscape painted in shades of crimson and grey, the vibrant hues of life only truly appreciated in their potential to quench her unending thirst.

The act of feeding was a complex ritual, a blend of necessity and a perverted form of intimacy. It was not simply about the intake of nourishment; it was about the transference of vitality. As she drank, she felt the life force of her victim flow into her, a warm, vital current that momentarily filled the void within. It was a sensation both exquisite and agonizing, a brief period of ecstatic fullness before the inevitable emptiness began to reassert itself, the gnawing hunger slowly, inevitably, returning. This ebb and flow defined her existence, a perpetual cycle of temporary satiation followed by renewed, desperate craving. The intimacy of the act, the close proximity to the warm, pulsing life she so desperately needed, was a cruel mockery of the human connection she had lost, a poignant reminder of the humanity she had sacrificed at the altar of her vampiric nature.

Her immortality, far from being a gift, was a gilded cage, and the bars were forged from her insatiable thirst. She had witnessed empires rise and crumble, seen civilizations bloom and wither, all while trapped in this eternal cycle of need. The passage of time, so devastating to mortals, meant little to her, save that it offered her more opportunities to hunt, more chances to prolong her tormented existence. Seasons changed, generations passed, but the hunger remained, a constant, unchanging companion. The world evolved, its peoples adapting and changing, yet her fundamental nature, her unyielding thirst, remained precisely the same as it had been in the shadowed past. She was a relic of a bygone era, an anachronism fueled by the lifeblood of the present, a living testament to a curse that defied the march of progress.

The psychological toll of this unending hunger was immense. It gnawed at her resolve, tempting her to abandon the carefully constructed facade of control she had maintained for centuries. There were nights, particularly when the thirst was at its most potent, when the predatory instincts threatened to overwhelm her, when the very concept of restraint became a distant, fading memory. The faces of her victims, the fleeting expressions of terror and confusion, were often blurred by the overwhelming haze of her need, mere conduits for the life-giving fluid she craved. Yet, even in the throes of her hunger, a remnant of her former self, a ghost of compassion, would sometimes stir, a faint whisper of guilt that she would quickly suppress. This internal conflict, this war between her primal needs and the tattered remnants of her conscience, was an ongoing torment, a burden as heavy as her immortality itself.

She had learned, over the long centuries, to orchestrate her existence around this fundamental requirement. Her movements were dictated by the availability of prey, her periods of activity dictated by the ebb and flow of her thirst. She sought out isolated communities, places where the scent of life was strong and the potential for discovery was minimal. She developed an uncanny ability to anticipate the movements of mortals, to understand their routines and vulnerabilities, all in service of her hunt. Her very environment became a tool, the shadows her cloak, the silence her ally. The moon, so often a symbol of romantic allure, was for her a celestial guide, its pale light illuminating her path through the darkened world, a beacon that drew her ever onward in her endless quest.

The chilling folklore that Silas was unearthing was, in essence, a testament to this eternal thirst. Each whispered tale, each hushed warning, was a ripple effect from her relentless pursuit. The disappearances, the unexplained chills, the unnerving encounters in the mist – all were the direct consequence of her unending need. The

Dearg Due was not merely a creature of supernatural power; she was a manifestation of a primal hunger, an eternal embodiment of the desire to survive at any cost. Her existence was a constant reminder that in the darkest corners of the world, life and death were inextricably intertwined, and that sometimes, the most terrifying forces were those driven by the most fundamental of all instincts: the need to live, no matter the price. Her curse was to live forever, not in peace or fulfillment, but in a perpetual state of yearning, a constant, agonizing reminder of what it meant to be alive, a state she could only experience vicariously, one stolen drop of blood at a time. The cycle was unbroken, the thirst unquenchable, and the night was her eternal hunting ground.

The selection was never a matter of random chance, nor was it dictated by a capricious whim. It was a precise, almost scientific art honed over countless nights, a ballet of predator and prey orchestrated by an instinct as old as the shadows themselves. Iris did not hunt indiscriminately. Her quarry was chosen with a discerning eye, a predatory acumen that could discern the subtlest vulnerabilities from across the vast, moonlit expanse. The forest, for her, was not a chaotic tangle of life and death, but a meticulously cataloged larder, each rustle of leaves, each distant cry, a whisper of potential.

Her gaze, often described as ancient and unnerving, was not simply a passive observation of the night. It was an active interrogation, a silent probe that sifted through the mundane realities of the mortal world, seeking the threads of isolation and despair that would inevitably unravel. She favored those who had already begun to drift from the safety of the collective. The solitary traveler, venturing beyond the flickering lamplight of a village, their path illuminated only by the cold, indifferent moon.

The hunter, lured too deep into the untamed wilderness by the promise of a prize, their senses dulled by ambition and the thrill of the chase. These were the ones who had already, in a sense, surrendered a portion of their safety, who had stepped onto the precipice of the unknown, making them ripe for her descent.

There was a particular resonance, a subtle hum of recognition, when her ancient eyes fell upon those who carried the burden of secrets. Not the trivial gossip that flitted through bustling towns, but the deep, soul-crushing secrets that festered in the darkness of the human heart. The illicit affair, the hidden debt, the unacknowledged sin – these were the invisible chains that bound individuals to their own private prisons. And when such a soul found themselves adrift, a solitary figure in the vast expanse of the night, the chains of their secrets often rendered them even more susceptible, their minds preoccupied with their own internal torment, less attuned to the external dangers that lurked. Iris found a strange, melancholic kinship in these souls. Their hidden sorrows, their quiet despair, often mirrored the deep, unhealing wound of her own lost humanity. It was a dangerous empathy, a dark reflection that drew her in, the whisper of their fear a siren song to her own ancient loneliness.

The instinct that guided her choices was a complex tapestry woven from millennia of survival and an intimate understanding of mortal frailty. It was a predatory gaze that could perceive the subtle tremors of fear even before they manifested as outward signs. The slight hesitation before crossing a shadowed stream, the furtive glance over a shoulder, the quickening of a breath – these were the tell-tale signs of a mind already steeped in apprehension. And where there was fear, there was often a vulnerability, an opening through which her own spectral hunger could insinuate itself.

She could sense the subtle scent of despair, a perfume that clung to certain individuals like a shroud. It was not the fleeting sadness of a lost day, but the ingrained melancholy of a life that had been chipped away by hardship, disappointment, and the crushing weight of loneliness. These were the souls who had learned to expect little from the world, whose hopes had long since withered and died, leaving behind a barren landscape of resignation. For them, the ultimate oblivion, the final silencing of their pain, might even hold a perverse sense of release. This was a dangerous realization, a chilling insight that she sometimes wrestled with in the quiet hours between hunts. The thought of offering a cessation of suffering, even through her own predatory act, was a dark temptation, a twisting of her curse into something that bordered on a morbid mercy.

Her ancient eyes, pools of obsidian that seemed to absorb the very light of the moon, would sweep across the darkened landscape. They were not merely seeing; they were

reading the night. She could discern the subtle patterns of life and movement, the faint trails of those who had strayed from the beaten path. The faint shimmer of a campfire, too far from any settlement, spoke of an isolation that was ripe for intrusion. The lonely cry of a lost child, a sound that would stir a primal protective instinct in most mortals, for Iris was a stark reminder of a different kind of vulnerability, a helpless entity adrift in a dangerous world. It was the quiet hum of a lone cabin nestled deep within a forgotten wood, the soft glow of a single lamp against the impenetrable darkness, that drew her attention like a moth to a phantom flame.

She observed the lone traveler, their silhouette stark against the rising mist, their pace faltering as the path grew indistinct. Her senses, sharpened by the eternal hunt, could detect the tremor of their fear, the subtle quickening of their pulse that sang a melody of delicious anticipation to her. She did not need to see their faces clearly; their posture, the way they hugged themselves against the encroaching chill, the hesitant steps that betrayed a growing unease – these were enough. They were already entering her domain, and in doing so, they had accepted, however unconsciously, the unspoken risks of the wild.

Then there were those whose secrets manifested as a certain wildness in their eyes, a desperate hunger that mirrored her own, albeit on a far more mundane scale. The poacher, risking the ire of the law for a meager gain, their senses on high alert, not for her, but for the game warden. The runaway, their heart pounding with the fear of recapture, their eyes darting into every shadow, seeking phantom pursuers. These individuals, already living on the edge, their lives dictated by a constant state of vigilance and a deep-seated anxiety, often possessed a certain recklessness that made them alluring. They were already accustomed to a life lived in the liminal spaces, the fringes of society, and thus, their transition into her shadowy realm felt less like an abduction and more like an inevitable, albeit terrifying, culmination of their existing circumstances.

Iris did not revel in their terror, not in the raw, visceral sense that some might imagine. Her predatory satisfaction was a more subtle, more profound thing. It was the quiet affirmation of her power, the validation of her ancient existence. It was the knowledge that even in a world that had moved on, a world that had largely forgotten the old ways and the old fears, she, the

Dearg Due, remained. Her continued existence was a testament to the enduring power of the primal, the undeniable truth that beneath the veneer of civilization, the ancient instincts of survival and predation still held sway.

The choice, then, was an intricate dance between opportunity and an almost uncanny understanding of the human psyche. She sought not just life, but life that was already teetering on the edge, life that was already imbued with a certain melancholic hue. Her ancient eyes scanned the darkness, not with malice, but with an ancient, unyielding need, seeking the perfect confluence of isolation, vulnerability, and the subtle, irresistible scent of despair. It was a selection process as old as time itself, a chilling testament to the enduring power of the predator and the fragile nature of mortal existence when faced with the eternal night.

The forest, usually a symphony of rustling leaves and chattering creatures, fell into an unnatural silence. It was a hush that spoke not of peace, but of anticipation, a collective breath held by the ancient trees as Iris moved through their shadowed depths. Her senses, honed by centuries of existence, had pinpointed a tremor in the night, a discord in the nocturnal harmony that signaled the presence of her chosen prey. It was a young man, barely more than a boy, who had strayed from the faint, winding path that snaked its way through the ancient woods. The scent of his fear, a sharp, metallic tang that cut through the damp earth and decaying foliage, reached her long before her spectral form even breached the treeline.

He moved with a frantic haste, his boots crushing fallen leaves with a clumsy, desperate urgency. His form was a dark silhouette against the opalescent glow of the full moon, his shoulders hunched, his gaze darting erratically into the impenetrable darkness that pressed in on all sides. He was clearly lost, his breath coming in ragged gasps, each exhale a visible cloud in the crisp night air. The faint, flickering light of a torch he carried cast wild, dancing shadows that distorted the familiar shapes of the trees, transforming them into monstrous, grasping figures. This, Iris noted with a flicker of predatory satisfaction, was a soul already adrift, his mind consumed by the immediate terror of his predicament, his awareness of the deeper, more ancient terrors of the night dulled by his more immediate, mortal anxieties.

Her movements were a study in absolute stealth. She did not run, nor did she stride. She flowed, a manifestation of the darkness itself, her spectral form phasing through the dense undergrowth as if it were mere mist. The thorns that would have snagged and torn at mortal flesh passed through her without resistance. The gnarled roots that would have tripped an unwary traveler offered no impediment to her ethereal passage. She was a whisper in the wind, a phantom wisp gliding through the moon-dappled glades, her eyes, twin pools of obsidian, fixed unswervingly on her quarry.

The young man stumbled, his foot catching on a hidden root. He cried out, a strangled gasp of fear and pain, the torch flailing wildly, illuminating his pale, sweat-slicked face for a fleeting moment. Iris observed him, not with pity, but with a detached, analytical gaze. His vulnerability was palpable, a raw, exposed nerve in the fabric of the night. He was alone, far from the comforting glow of any hearth, his only companion the wavering flame of his torch and the oppressive silence of the woods. This was the perfect moment, the precipice from which he would inevitably fall into her waiting embrace.

She adjusted her trajectory, her spectral form drifting closer, the air around her growing colder, heavier. The young man, sensing a shift in the atmosphere, a subtle change that even his panicked mind could register, began to run faster, his movements growing more erratic, more desperate. He tripped again, this time falling heavily to the damp earth. The torch clattered from his hand, its flame sputtering and dying, plunging him into near-total darkness, save for the silvered moonlight that filtered through the dense canopy.

Now, the true hunt began. Iris ceased her spectral gliding and began to stalk. She moved with a predatory grace, her steps utterly silent, her form coiled and ready. The young man scrambled to his feet, his eyes wide with terror, his breath coming in shallow, panicked bursts. He called out, his voice a thin, reedy sound that was quickly swallowed by the vastness of the forest. "Is anyone there? Please, I'm lost!"

Iris remained in the shadows, a silent observer. She could have revealed herself then, could have sent a shiver of primal terror down his spine with a mere glimpse of her terrifying visage. But she preferred to prolong the exquisite agony of anticipation. She allowed him to feel the oppressive weight of her presence, the chilling certainty that he was not alone, that something ancient and inimical was watching his every move.

She began to circle him, her movements dictated by an instinct as old as the stars. She used the trees as cover, her spectral form weaving between their ancient trunks, a wraith of the night. She could hear the frantic thumping of his heart, a rapid drumbeat that echoed the rhythm of her own silent pursuit. The scent of his fear, now mingled with the metallic tang of spilled blood from his grazed hands and knees, was intoxicating.

The young man, overwhelmed by the unseen threat, began to sob, his body trembling uncontrollably. He pressed himself against the rough bark of a massive oak, as if hoping to merge with its solid form, to find solace in its steadfastness. But the oak offered no protection against the encroaching darkness. Iris could sense his mind unraveling, his thoughts becoming fragmented, his grip on reality loosening with each passing moment.

She closed the distance, her spectral form now mere yards away. She could feel the residual warmth of his mortal life, a stark contrast to the icy chill of her own existence. She allowed herself a moment of silent contemplation, a fleeting recognition of the life she was about to extinguish. He was so young, so full of a vibrant, ephemeral spark that she had long since lost. But such reflections were fleeting, a minor distraction from the primal imperative that drove her.

Then, with a sudden, swift surge of spectral energy, she moved. It was not a blur, not a rush, but an instantaneous transition from stillness to action. She materialized directly behind him, her incorporeal hand reaching out, not to grasp, but to *infuse*. The young man gasped, a sharp intake of breath, his eyes widening in dawning horror as he felt an icy tendril of energy snake into his very being, draining the warmth, the life, the very essence of his soul.

His body went rigid, his muscles locked in a final, desperate tension. A silent scream contorted his features, a scream that was never uttered, a silent testament to the terror that consumed him. His eyes, wide and unseeing, stared into the impenetrable darkness, reflecting nothing of the moonlit world around him. The vibrant spark that had flickered within him was extinguished, replaced by an echoing emptiness, a void that Iris now filled.

She held him for a moment, absorbing the last vestiges of his life force, a dark, potent energy that pulsed through her spectral form, invigorating her ancient being. The forest, which had held its breath, now seemed to exhale, the rustling of leaves and the chirping of insects slowly returning, as if the natural order had been restored, albeit with a new, silent predator in its midst. Iris released the lifeless husk, which crumpled to the ground with a soft thud, its brief mortal journey concluded. She turned, her form already beginning to dissolve back into the shadows, leaving behind only the silence, the darkness, and the lingering chill of her passage. The hunt was over, the cycle of blood replenished, and the ancient forest, once again, belonged to the darkness.

The spectral hand, now imbued with the stolen vitality, lingered near the fallen form. It was not the physical blood that Iris craved, not the crude crimson fluid that pulsed through mortal veins. Her hunger was far more profound, a gnawing emptiness that yearned for the very essence of life, the bright, ephemeral spark that animates flesh and bone. As the last vestiges of the young man's spirit ebbed, drawn into her like a phantom tide, a wave of warmth, alien and yet deeply familiar, coursed through her ethereal being. It was a fleeting sensation, a mere echo of the vibrant pulse she had just extinguished, but it was enough.

The chill that perpetually clung to her, a shroud woven from the threads of eternity and isolation, receded ever so slightly. The suffocating thirst, a constant, rasping torment that had plagued her for centuries, eased into a dull ache, a promise of respite rather than a desperate craving. For a brief, precious interval, the sharp edges of her immortal existence were softened, her perception sharpened by the infusion of mortal life. The moonlight, which had seemed a cold, indifferent observer, now shimmered with a newfound luminescence. The ancient trees, their bark etched with the hieroglyphs of forgotten ages, seemed to breathe with a subtle, resonant energy.

This was the paradox of her existence: to subsist, she had to extinguish. To find solace, she had to inflict despair. The act, though born of a fundamental need, carried with it a dark ecstasy, a forbidden communion that was both reviled and reveled in. As the energy settled within her, a potent elixir that temporarily banished the gnawing void, Iris felt a surge of power, a clarity of being that was rarely afforded to her. The oppressive weight of her eternal curse lifted, replaced by a sense of vibrant, albeit temporary, fullness.

She could feel the echoes of the young man's final moments, the desperate fear, the bewildered realization, the ultimate surrender. These impressions, so raw and potent, were not a source of guilt but rather a testament to the power she wielded, the potent life force she had absorbed. It was a brutal transaction, a cosmic imbalance rectified by the primal law of predator and prey. The forest floor, now stained with the faint trace of spilled blood, a mere physical marker of a far deeper exchange, held no judgment. It was a silent witness to the timeless cycle, the ebb and flow of life and death, of consumption and renewal.

Her spectral form, usually indistinct and wavering, solidified for a moment, imbued with the borrowed luminescence of the absorbed spirit. The obsidian depths of her eyes, which had been pools of perpetual shadow, now held a fleeting, almost imperceptible glint, a reflection of the life force that had so recently been extinguished. This brief period of satiation was a fragile shield against the encroaching despair that was her constant companion. It was a fleeting reprieve, a momentary triumph over the relentless erosion of her own being.

She lingered there, absorbing the last echoes of the stolen life, letting the borrowed vitality seep into her very essence. The world around her seemed to hum with a renewed vibrancy, a testament to the energy that now coursed through her. The air grew still, as if the forest itself paused to acknowledge the potent exchange that had just transpired. This was not merely the consumption of flesh and blood; it was the assimilation of existence, a dark, intimate embrace that bound her to the ceaseless rhythm of life and death. The raw, primal nature of the act was undeniable, a fundamental truth of her cursed immortality. The satisfaction was not a gentle warmth, but a fierce, intoxicating fire that burned away the gnawing emptiness, if only for a precious, fleeting time. She drew strength from the stolen spark, a stark reminder of the vibrant, ephemeral nature of mortal life, a life she could only borrow, never truly possess. The silence that followed the frenzied moments of the hunt was now pregnant with a different kind of energy, the quiet hum of sustenance, the deep satisfaction of a hunger momentarily appeased.

The stolen essence, still warm and vibrant within her spectral form, was more than just a balm against the gnawing emptiness. It was the very scaffolding upon which her continued existence was precariously built. Each life extinguished, each vital spark absorbed, served as a brick laid in the eternally crumbling edifice of her undeath. This was not mere survival; it was a conscious, albeit grim, act of self-perpetuation. The vitality she siphoned was a potent elixir, not just for her physical (or rather, un-physical) being, but for the very fabric of her cursed immortality. It was the currency of her existence, paid out in the coin of mortal lives to purchase another span of time, another turn of the desolate wheel.

The transaction was stark, devoid of sentiment or remorse. The primal law of predator and prey played out in the shadowed glades and forgotten hollows of her domain, a ritual as ancient as the blood that flowed in mortal veins. Life for undeath. Sustenance for an eternity of barren existence. The young man's fear, his bewilderment, the faint flicker of hope that had been so brutally extinguished – these were not specters of guilt that haunted her. Instead, they were testament to the power she commanded, the potent life force that flowed through her, temporarily banishing the chill of her eternal solitude. This stolen vigor was the fuel that kept the infernal engine of her being running, a monstrous heart beating with borrowed rhythm.

Without this perpetual replenishment, she would fade. The edges of her spectral form, already prone to dissipation, would fray and unravel, scattering her essence to the winds like so much dust. Her consciousness, a fragile ember in the vast darkness of her curse, would flicker and die. The world, already muted and distant to her senses, would become an impenetrable void. The borrowed vitality, therefore, was not a luxury, but a necessity. It was the intricate, cruel mechanism that allowed her to persist, to observe, to endure the endless, agonizing passage of centuries. The brief moments of satiation were merely a reprieve, a temporary bulwark against the inevitable erosion of her being.

She felt it acutely now, this borrowed strength. The world, which had seemed a desaturated watercolor before the consumption, now held a sharper, more vibrant hue. The moonlight, no longer a cold, sterile glare, seemed to caress her spectral form with a soft, almost benevolent glow. The ancient trees, their gnarled branches reaching like skeletal fingers towards the heavens, exuded an aura of patient, enduring power, a power she could now, in a small measure, tap into. It was as if the very life of the forest, amplified by the stolen essence of the mortal, resonated with her own renewed being. This amplified perception was a fleeting gift, a testament to the raw power she had assimilated.

This cycle, this grim exchange, was the defining characteristic of her existence. It was not a choice, but a mandate, woven into the very fabric of her cursed immortality. To exist was to consume. To endure was to prey. The act was as natural to her as breathing was to the mortals she hunted, though infinitely more profound and terrifying in its implications. Each life she claimed was a sacrifice laid upon the altar of her continued existence, a necessary evil that allowed her to remain a sentient entity in a world that had long forgotten her. The desolate beauty of her domain, the ancient forests, the crumbling ruins, the mist-shrouded moors – they were the stage upon which this eternal drama of consumption and survival played out, a silent testament to her monstrous perpetuity.

The satiation she felt was not a passive state, but an active regeneration. It was the mending of spectral tears, the reinforcing of ethereal bonds, the rekindling of a consciousness that constantly threatened to gutter and fade. Her senses, dulled by the prolonged absence of vitality, sharpened. The faintest whisper of wind through the leaves, the distant hoot of an owl, the subtle shift of earth beneath unseen roots – all became acutely discernible. This heightened awareness, born of replenished life force, was a double-edged sword. It allowed her to better navigate her domain, to anticipate threats, and to more effectively pursue her next quarry. But it also underscored the profound isolation of her existence, highlighting the stark contrast between the vibrant tapestry of mortal life and the monochromatic stillness of her own eternal present.

The nourishment she received was not merely physical; it was a spiritual and existential revitalization. It was the infusion of purpose into a being that had, for all intents and purposes, been stripped of it by the curse of her immortality. The act of feeding, however brutal, provided a temporary focus, a directive that kept the abyss of ennui at bay. The young man's life, so carelessly extinguished, had provided not just sustenance, but a brief, intoxicating sense of agency. It was a stark reminder that even in her desolate state, she was not entirely powerless, that she could still influence the ephemeral lives of those who shared the mortal coil with her.

The energy settled within her, a potent reservoir that would sustain her for a time. It was a flickering flame against the encroaching darkness, a defiant spark in the vast emptiness of her perpetual night. This replenished strength was the foundation of her continued vigilance, the silent promise that she would be there, a predator in the shadows, for as long as the cycle demanded. The spectral hand, now infused with the borrowed warmth, slowly receded, its ethereal fingers unclasping from the phantom echo of the life it had just consumed. The warmth was already beginning to dissipate, a reminder that this respite was fleeting, that the gnawing hunger would inevitably return, and with it, the grim necessity of another hunt. Her existence was a testament to this brutal truth: to live, she must take life. To remain was to continue the cycle, an endless, desolate echo in the halls of eternity.

Chapter 11:
Memories of Julius

The stolen essence, a temporary effervescence against the deep, abiding chill of undeath, had receded, leaving behind not a void, but a hollow ache that resonated with a forgotten melody. It was a familiar sensation, this ebb and flow of borrowed vitality, a cycle that defined her eternal existence. Yet, even as the spectral arteries pulsed with renewed, albeit borrowed, life, another sensation, more ancient and far more profound, began to stir. It was a whisper from the depths of her fractured memory, a phantom limb reaching out from a past she had desperately tried to bury beneath centuries of darkness—the memory of Julius.

It was a memory that defied the very nature of her curse. Her vampiric transformation, a voracious predator of life and spirit, had claimed much of her former self. The vibrant hues of her mortal days had long since faded, replaced by the muted palette of eternal twilight. The sharp edges of joy and sorrow had been blunted, smoothed over by the vast expanse of time and the constant need to feed. Yet, the memory of Julius, her first love, her Julius, remained. It was not a ghostly apparition that flickered at the edges of her vision, nor a spectral voice whispering temptations in the dead of night. It was something far more insidious, a deep, abiding sadness that clung to her like the grave-dust on a long-forgotten shroud.

She remembered the warmth of his hand in hers, a searing contrast to the perpetual cold that now resided within her. His laughter, a sound so full of unadulterated joy, echoed in the silent chambers of her mind, a cruel mockery of her own soulless existence. His eyes, the color of a summer sky just before a storm, had held a promise of a future, a future she had once believed in, a future that had been irrevocably stolen. These were not mere fragments of remembrance, but vivid, visceral sensations that pierced through the protective layers of her immortal shell. It was as if the very act of drawing life, of clinging to existence, had, paradoxically, reawakened the slumbering embers of her lost humanity, forcing her to confront the profound depth of her loss.

The stolen vitality, while a necessary balm, was a temporary distraction. It could fortify her spectral form, sharpen her senses, and briefly push back the encroaching ennui. But it could not erase the indelible imprint of a love that had once burned so fiercely. This memory was a shard of ice embedded in the heart of her spectral being, a constant, chilling reminder of the man she had been, the woman she had loved, and the life she had lost. It was a testament to the fact that even the most ancient and potent curses could not entirely extinguish the echoes of the human heart.

She would walk through the moon-drenched forests, her ethereal form gliding silently over the dew-kissed earth, and the scent of night-blooming jasmine would suddenly, inexplicably, bring his face to mind. The rustling of leaves in the wind would transform into the murmur of his voice, speaking words of endearment she hadn't heard in centuries. These were not summoned images, not deliberate conjurations of a fading past. They were intrusions, unbidden guests that arrived unannounced, forcing her to relive moments of tenderness and shared dreams that were now as foreign to her as the sun was to the deepest abyss.

The contrast between her current existence and the life she had shared with Julius was a torment all its own. He had been a creature of the light, his spirit as vibrant and untarnished as a freshly minted coin. He had spoken of grand adventures, of building a future, of a life filled with simple joys and unwavering love. Her vampiric nature, a creature of shadow and decay, was the antithesis of everything he represented. She had once been human, capable of love and laughter, but that woman was now a ghost within a ghost, a spectral echo of a life long extinguished.

And Julius, her beloved Julius, was the anchor that tethered her to that lost world, the painful proof that she had once possessed a soul worth saving.

This specific memory, the memory of Julius, was a unique torment. It was not the fleeting regret of a stolen life, nor the gnawing hunger for sustenance. It was a deep, melancholic ache, a sorrow that transcended the boundaries of undeath. It was the persistent reminder that even in her immortal state, a part of her remained irretrievably human, forever yearning for a love she could no longer experience, a warmth she could no longer feel. The very essence of her vampiric existence was the antithesis of the life she had shared with him. His was a life lived in the sun, filled with the breath of life, the beat of a mortal heart. Hers was an eternity in shadow, a silent existence sustained by the stolen vitality of others, a constant battle against the oblivion that threatened to claim her.

She recalled the way he would smile, a slow, genuine unfolding that could chase away any shadow. His hands, calloused from his work, were surprisingly gentle as they traced the lines of her face. He had seen her, truly seen her, not as a curiosity or a prize, but as a soul to be cherished. That recognition, that profound connection, was something her vampiric nature could never replicate. The lives she consumed offered only a temporary surge of power, a fleeting illusion of vitality. They provided no solace, no genuine connection, no echo of the love she had once known.

There were nights when the silence of her existence became unbearable, when the weight of her immortality pressed down upon her spectral form like a tombstone. On those nights, the memory of Julius would come to her unbidden, a phantom caress, a whispered promise. She would see them again, young and vibrant, walking hand-in-hand beneath a sky painted with the colors of dawn. She would feel the phantom weight of his arm around her shoulders, hear the rumble of his contented sigh. These were not the nightmares that haunted the dreams of mortals; they were the spectral echoes of a happiness so profound that its absence now felt like a physical wound.

Her vampiric existence was a constant negotiation with oblivion. Each life she claimed was a desperate act of defiance against the inevitable dissipation of her being. But the memory of Julius was a different kind of threat. It was a threat to the very structure of her undeath, a reminder of the vibrant, loving woman she had once been. Her curse had stripped her of her humanity, but it had not, and perhaps could not, entirely strip her of her capacity for love, or rather, for the profound sorrow that followed its loss.

She would stand at the precipice of ancient ruins, the wind whipping around her like a mournful dirge, and she would imagine his presence beside her. He would have marveled at the stories held within the crumbling stones, his eyes alight with wonder. She, too, had once possessed such a spirit, such a capacity for awe. Now, she saw only the passage of time, the inevitable decay, the silent testament to mortality. The world, once a place of wonder, had become a vast, empty stage upon which her lonely existence played out.

The ritual of feeding, while essential for her survival, was a stark reminder of her divergence from the mortal realm. She took life; she did not share it. She consumed, she did not create. This fundamental difference separated her irrevocably from the world Julius had inhabited, the world of warmth, of growth, of burgeoning life. He had been a beacon of that vitality, and her existence was now a perpetual twilight, forever cast in the shadow of his memory.

Sometimes, in the deepest hours of the night, when the moon hung like a pale, spectral eye in the heavens, she would allow herself to immerse herself in the memory fully. She would recall the first time he had kissed her, the tentative brush of his lips, the sudden, overwhelming surge of emotion that had left her breathless. It was a sensation she could no longer replicate, a pure, unadulterated human experience that her vampiric form had rendered impossible. The borrowed life force could mimic the physical sensations of warmth and strength, but it could never rekindle the fire of true human emotion.

The act of remembering Julius was a painful, yet strangely necessary, ritual. It was a defiance against the utter erasure of her past. Her vampiric nature sought to consume all, to reduce everything to the primal drive for survival. But the memory of Julius was a stubborn ember, refusing to be extinguished. It was a testament to the profound impact one soul could have on another, an impact so deep that even the jaws of undeath could not entirely obliterate its echo. It was a lingering ghost, not of his presence, but of her own lost self, a self that had once known love and been loved in return, a self that now existed only in the bittersweet landscape of memory.

The stolen essence, the warmth that pulsed within her spectral form, was a fleeting comfort. It was a temporary shield against the gnawing emptiness, a momentary illusion of strength. But it could not fill the cavernous void left by the absence of Julius. His memory was a constant, melancholic counterpoint to the primal hunger that drove her. It was a shard of her lost humanity, a painful reminder of a life vibrant with love and laughter, a life that now existed only in the desolate halls of her eternal remembrance. This persistent echo was the true haunting, a sorrow as deep and unending as her own cursed immortality, a silent lament for the love that had been, and would never be again.

The gilded cage of her mortal dreams stood in stark opposition to the cold, iron bars of her current reality. She remembered the whispered promises made under a sky alive with fireflies, the scent of honeysuckle heavy on the night air. Julius, with his earnest gaze and a heart brimming with a future they would build together, had painted pictures of a life so achingly simple, so profoundly beautiful. Their vows, spoken softly in the quietude of a sun-dappled meadow, had promised a shared hearth, the gentle rhythm of daily existence, and the comforting weight of his hand in hers through the long arc of years. He had envisioned a cottage nestled by a murmuring brook, children with eyes like his, their laughter echoing through sun-drenched days. The world, then, had been a canvas of endless possibility, splashed with the vibrant hues of hope and devotion.

Now, the meadow was a place of cold, damp earth, the fireflies replaced by the phosphorescent glow of decay. The honeysuckle's sweetness was a distant, mocking echo, lost to the metallic tang of blood that now perfumed her nights. The vows she had once cherished were like brittle parchment, crumbling to dust in the face of her eternal hunger. The simple happiness Julius had offered was a phantom limb, a sensation of warmth in a body forever consumed by an unquenchable cold. Her nights were no longer filled with the murmur of shared dreams and the gentle breathing of a beloved beside her. Instead, they were a predatory ballet, a silent hunt through shadowed landscapes, the only music the frantic thrum of mortal hearts. The stolen essence, the borrowed vitality, offered a fleeting simulation of life, but it was a hollow imitation, devoid of the genuine connection that had once been the very foundation of her existence.

The contrast was a shard of glass lodged in the heart of her spectral being. She had once yearned for the sunrise, for the simple act of waking beside the man she loved, to greet the day with a kiss and a shared cup of tea. Now, the sun was anathema, a searing brand that threatened to consume her very essence. Her awakening was a descent into the ever-present twilight of undeath, a ritualistic preparation for the hunt. The intimacy of shared mornings had been replaced by the primal instinct of survival, the quiet communion of souls supplanted by the brutal necessity of feeding.

The image of Julius, his brow furrowed in concentration as he carved a wooden bird for her, or his eyes crinkling with mirth as they shared a simple meal, was a cruel mirage against the backdrop of her vampiric reality.

He had spoken of growing old together, of their hair turning silver, of watching their grandchildren play in the garden. He had seen her, not as a fleeting beauty, but as a woman who would walk with him through every season of life. That vision of a shared future, so complete and so full of life, was now a grotesque parody. Her existence was an unbroken chain of seasons, each one identical in its eternal chill. There would be no silvering of hair, no gentle descent into old age. There would only be the relentless cycle of hunger and satiation, the unending march of centuries with no companion but the echoes of her own despair. Her immortality, once a distant, abstract concept that held no fear, had become a gilded prison, its walls adorned with the faded frescoes of a life she had lost.

The idyllic visions of marriage and simple happiness were now like the delicate wings of a long-dead butterfly, beautiful in their fragility but utterly divorced from the harsh reality of her present. The scent of wedding bells had been replaced by the cloying aroma of decay, an invisible shroud that clung to her. The tenderness of his touch, the assurance of his embrace, had been supplanted by the cold, calculating precision of a predator. He had offered her a home, a sanctuary built on love and trust. She now dwelled in mausoleums and forgotten ruins, her only companions the shadows and the specter of her own past. The life she had once yearned for, the life of warmth, of shared laughter, of a love that deepened with time, was now a cruel joke played by fate, a poignant testament to the profound depth of her fall.

Her current existence was a perversion of those deepest desires. She had craved connection, a soul to intertwine with, a hand to hold through the darkness. Instead, she was condemned to a solitude so profound it ate at the very edges of her being. The stolen vitality, the very fuel that sustained her monstrous form, was a constant, bitter reminder of what she had become. It was a parasitic existence, a life taken from others to perpetuate her own damnation. Julius had dreamed of a life built on shared abundance, on the mutual creation of joy. Her life was built on depletion, on the silent, unmaking of others.

She remembered the way his eyes would soften when he looked at her, a profound tenderness that spoke volumes without a single word. He had seen the best of her, the nascent soul that was reaching for the light. Now, when she glimpsed her reflection, it was a creature of the night, her eyes reflecting a predatory gleam, her features sculpted by an ancient, insatiable hunger. The woman he had loved was a ghost, a spectral memory haunting the hollow shell of her vampiric form. The stark juxtaposition of those innocent dreams and her grim reality was a torment that never ceased, a constant gnawing ache that reminded her of the immeasurable distance between the woman she had been and the monster she had become. The silence of her eternal nights was filled not with the gentle lullaby of love, but with the silent screams of her lost humanity, a perpetual lament for the life that had been so cruelly, so irrevocably, stolen. The simple happiness Julius had promised was now a tale from a forgotten land, a fable of a life she could only glimpse in the tattered remnants of her shattered memory.

The spectral tendrils of memory, once a comforting shroud, now felt like chains, binding her to a phantom warmth that only accentuated the chilling void of her present. Each recollection of Julius, once a balm to her sorrow, was now a sharpened shard, grating against the raw edges of her eternal existence. He had been the sun to her nascent dawn, the steady rhythm of a heartbeat that promised continuity, a future woven from shared breaths and whispered intimacies. His love, a tangible thing, had been a sanctuary, a place where the world's harsh edges softened, and her own spirit felt safe to unfurl. The simple, domestic tapestry he had envisioned – a hearth fire casting dancing shadows, the scent of baking bread, the murmur of children's voices – was a cruel irony now. For her heart was the cold, echoing expanse of crypts, the only bread she knew was stolen life, and the only voices that echoed were the silent screams of her victims, a constant, agonizing chorus to her monstrous lullaby.

Was it truly solace she sought in these phantoms? Or was it merely a deeper plunge into the abyss of her loss, a perverse indulgence in the agony of what could never be?

The ember of humanity, she sometimes feared, had long since been extinguished, choked by the very darkness that now defined her. Yet, in the deepest, most guarded chambers of her spectral heart, a flicker persisted. It was a dangerous thing, this persistence, this faint yearning for the touch of sunlight on her skin, for the comforting weight of a human hand clasped in hers, for the simple, unadulterated joy of a shared glance that spoke of a love that transcended the mortal coil. But that ember was guarded fiercely, for to acknowledge it was to court a pain so profound it threatened to unravel the very fabric of her being, to shatter the fragile facade of control she had painstakingly constructed over centuries of undeath.

The question gnawed at her, a persistent, unseen worm. Could these memories, these fragments of a life lived in light, offer a path away from the predatory dance that had become her existence? Or were they merely fuel for the inferno of her despair, a constant reminder of the innocence irrevocably lost, the humanity devoured by the insatiable hunger? Julius had loved the woman she was, the woman who laughed freely, who wept with genuine sorrow, who found beauty in the fleeting moments of a mortal life. He had seen her soul, a luminous thing that reached for the heavens. Now, when she looked into the depths of her own being, she saw only the predatory gleam, the ancient hunger that had consumed her, leaving behind a hollow echo of the woman he had cherished.

The desire for vengeance, a cold and sharp-edged blade, had been her constant companion, the driving force behind her centuries of existence. It had been a purpose, a singular focus that allowed her to navigate the endless expanse of her damnation. But the memories of Julius, they complicated this singular purpose. They introduced a nuance, a whisper of a different path, one that led not through the scorched earth of retribution, but perhaps, impossibly, towards a flicker of redemption. It was a thought so alien, so terrifyingly fragile, that she usually recoiled from it, pushing it back into the deepest recesses of her awareness.

For what was redemption to a creature of eternal night?

What was a soul to a being that had no body to truly inhabit, no life to truly live?

She remembered the way he would trace the lines of her palm, his brow furrowed in concentration, as if deciphering the very secrets of her future.

"You have a spirit that burns brighter than any star," he had whispered, his voice a low hum against her skin.

"A heart that beats with the rhythm of the world." His belief in her, so absolute, so unwavering, was a stark contrast to the self-loathing that now festered within her. He had seen a vessel of light; she was now a chalice of darkness, filled with the bitter dregs of her eternal curse.

Could that light, however faint, still exist?

Could the memory of his love, so pure and untainted, offer a guide through the perpetual twilight of her existence?

It was a seductive, yet perilous, notion. To seek solace in his memory was to invite the pain of his absence anew, to reopen wounds that had long since calcified into a permanent ache. Yet, the alternative was a descent into a bleak, unthinking predation, a life devoid of any semblance of meaning beyond the primal urge to survive. And in those quiet moments, when the roar of her hunger subsided to a low growl, she found herself drawn to the spectral warmth of his love, a moth to a flame that promised both destruction and a fleeting, exquisite warmth.

The very essence of her current being was antithetical to the life Julius had envisioned. He had dreamed of a shared existence, a partnership built on mutual respect and affection. She was now a solitary predator, her existence defined by the silent, brutal act of taking. The stolen vitality, the very substance of her continued existence, was a constant, sickening reminder of the chasm that separated her from the woman he had loved. It was a life built on the unmaking of others, a stark perversion of the life-giving love he had offered.

Perhaps, she mused, the memories were not meant to offer solace, but rather to serve as a mirror, reflecting the profound depth of her fall. They were a testament to the immeasurable distance between the woman she had been and the monster she had become. And in that stark reflection, there was a grim, unsettling truth: the pursuit of vengeance, while a powerful motivator, had also become a form of imprisonment, trapping her in a cycle of violence that mirrored the very curse she sought to escape.

The whispers of her former self, the echoes of Julius's love, were a dangerous siren song, calling her towards a shore she dared not approach. For what if, in embracing that fragile hope, she found herself utterly consumed by the darkness? What if the ember, when exposed to the harsh winds of her reality, was simply snuffed out, leaving her with nothing but the cold, hard certainty of her monstrous nature? The very thought sent a shiver through her spectral form, a cold that had nothing to do with the temperature of her surroundings.

Yet, the alternative was to continue this endless, solitary hunt, to exist as a specter of her former self, driven by a hunger that could never be truly sated, haunted by the ghosts of a life she could no longer claim. The memories of Julius, in their bittersweet cruelty, offered a tantalizing glimpse of a different path, a possibility of something more than eternal damnation. Whether she had the strength, or indeed the desire, to pursue it remained the most profound and agonizing question of her unending existence. The path of vengeance was clear, a well-trodden road paved with the tears of her victims. But the path hinted at by Julius's memory was shrouded in mist, uncertain and fraught with peril, a whisper of hope in the overwhelming darkness. And in the silence of her eternal nights, that whisper, however faint, was beginning to hold a dangerous, compelling allure.

The Julius she now held in her mind was a creature sculpted by centuries of longing, a monument built from the fragments of a time when the world was painted in hues of sunlight and laughter, not the perpetual twilight that had become her domain. This idealized Julius, the one who occupied the hushed chambers of her spectral heart, was a far cry from the man he had been in life, yet paradoxically, he was more vivid, more potent. His hands, once warm and calloused from honest labor, now possessed a gentle, ethereal touch, capable of soothing the restless demons that clawed at her immortal soul. His voice, a deep baritone that had once rumbled with affection and quiet strength, now echoed with a celestial resonance, a melody that promised an unending peace. He was the steadfast anchor in the churning tempest of her existence, the unwavering lighthouse beam cutting through the fog of her predatory instincts.

She replayed their shared moments with an almost religious fervor, each memory polished and perfected until it gleamed with an unnatural luminescence. Their walks through sun-dappled meadows, the scent of wildflowers heavy on the air, were now imbued with a profound significance, each rustle of leaves a whispered promise of forever. The simple act of him reading poetry aloud by the hearth, his brow furrowed in concentration, his voice a soft cadence against the crackling flames, had been elevated to an exquisite ballet of shared understanding. The laughter, oh, the laughter! It was no longer a fleeting sound, but a crystalline chime that hung suspended in the air, a testament to a joy so pure, so unadulterated, that it seemed to have been drawn from the very essence of creation. In these curated recollections, there were no shadows, no imperfections, no hints of the mundane realities that had once existed alongside their love. The petty squabbles, the minor irritations, the quiet anxieties that had colored their mortal lives – these were meticulously excised, leaving behind a pristine, unblemished tableau of perfect devotion.

This meticulous reconstruction served a purpose, a desperate, silent plea against the encroaching darkness. By elevating Julius and their past to an almost divine status, she was creating a bulwark, a sanctuary against the gnawing self-loathing that threatened to consume her. If their love was a perfect, untarnished thing, then perhaps, by extension, the woman he had loved – the woman she had been – was also untainted. This was, of course, a dangerous delusion, a delicate edifice built upon the shifting sands of denial. Yet, it was also a potent defense. It allowed her to compartmentalize, to relegate the monstrous aspects of her current existence to a separate, sealed chamber, a place where the light of Julius's memory could not penetrate.

The man who had loved her had seen only the light within her, a nascent flame that he had carefully fanned. He had been blind to the potential for darkness, the inherent fragility of her mortality, and the primal urges that lay dormant beneath her civilized veneer.

Or perhaps, more truthfully, he had chosen not to see. His love had been a conscious act of faith, a deliberate embrace of her goodness, a refusal to acknowledge any possibility of corruption. And in her grief, in her desperate need to cling to some vestige of that untarnished love, she had amplified his faith, turning it into an absolute, unwavering certainty in her own inherent purity.

She recalled the way he would speak of their future, his eyes alight with the earnestness of a man who believed in the enduring power of love and commitment. Their envisioned home, a modest cottage nestled in a verdant valley, a place where children's laughter would echo through sunlit rooms, where the scent of baking bread would mingle with the perfume of roses climbing the trellises – this was the dream she now clung to with a ferocity that bordered on obsession. It was a dream untarnished by the harsh realities of her transformation, a vision of domestic bliss that existed in a realm utterly divorced from the cold, echoing crypts that had become her resting place. The children, so vital to his vision, were now mere phantoms in her memory, their innocent faces a stark contrast to the pallor of the victims whose lifeblood sustained her. The hearth fire, once a symbol of warmth and domesticity, had been replaced by the chilling glow of moonlight filtering through ancient stained glass, illuminating a chamber of perpetual, solitary vigil.

This idealization, however, was a double-edged sword. While it offered a reprieve from the crushing weight of her current reality, it also served as a constant, agonizing reminder of what had been irrevocably lost. The perfection she attributed to Julius and their past highlighted the profound ugliness of her present. The man who had cherished her purity was now inextricably linked to the monster she had become, and the dissonance was a constant, internal torment. She was a living, breathing testament to the corruption of innocence, a walking embodiment of the stark truth that even the purest love could not shield one from the abyss.

The more radiant Julius's memory became, the deeper the shadows of her own existence grew.

The romanticized vision of their life together also served to distance her from the brutal truth of her transformation. It allowed her to construct a narrative where her current state was an anomaly, a temporary affliction rather than an intrinsic part of her being. By focusing on the idealized past, she could pretend that the monster was an intruder, a temporary tenant in a soul that still belonged to the woman Julius had loved. This was a fragile illusion, of course, one that the slightest tremor of self-awareness could shatter. Yet, it was an illusion she clung to with all the spectral strength she possessed.

The memories were not simply a source of comfort; they were a weapon, wielded against the encroaching despair. They were the shimmering threads with which she wove a tapestry of denial, a beautiful lie that shielded her from the whole, unadulterated horror of her eternal damnation. The Julius of her memories was not the man who had lived and breathed, who had felt the warmth of the sun on his skin and the sting of cold rain. He was a symbol, an archetype, a representation of everything she had lost and could never reclaim. He was the embodiment of a perfect world, a world that had existed before the darkness descended, before the hunger took root, before the curse irrevocably altered the landscape of her soul.

She found herself selectively editing her recollections, carefully curating the moments that would serve her narrative. The arguments that had, in reality, been mere blips on the radar of their affection, were now erased. The moments of doubt, the fleeting insecurities that had, in life, been overcome by their shared love, were now nonexistent. What remained was a distilled essence of their happiness, a concentrated elixir of pure, unadulterated bliss. This was not a truthful recollection; it was a desperate act of self-preservation, a spectral artist meticulously retouching a masterpiece that had long since been marred by the ravages of time and the gnawing corruption of undeath.

The idealized Julius also served as a justification for her continued existence, in a twisted sort of way. By clinging to the memory of his pure, untainted love, she could convince herself that there was still something within her worth saving, something that deserved to exist, however monstrous her current form. If he had loved the woman she was, then perhaps that woman, however deeply buried, still held a flicker of life. This was a dangerous game, a gamble with her very sanity, but it was a game she felt compelled to play. The alternative was to embrace the full horror of her being, to acknowledge the monstrous reality of her eternal hunger, and to accept that the woman Julius had loved was gone, irrevocably lost, replaced by something ancient and predatory.

The perfection of these memories, however, also underscored the utter impossibility of her redemption. If their past was a flawless diamond, then her present was a gaping wound, festering and incurable. How could she possibly bridge the chasm that now separated her from that pristine state? How could the creature who now stalked the night, driven by an insatiable thirst, ever hope to reclaim the purity that Julius had so ardently adored? The idealized past, in its very perfection, highlighted the horrifying finality of her fall. It was a beacon of light that served only to illuminate the profound depth of the darkness she now inhabited. It was a constant, silent lament for a lost innocence, a perfect world shattered into a million glittering shards, shards that now reflected only the monstrous visage of her eternal damnation. The memory of Julius was no longer a source of solace; it was a mirror, reflecting a lost paradise that only amplified the desolation of her present.

The silence that had descended upon their shared world after Iris's transformation was palpable, a suffocating shroud that Elara could almost taste. It had settled over Julius, she imagined, like the first frost of a relentless winter, chilling him to the bone. He had lost not just a lover, but the very essence of the future they had so meticulously woven together. The meadows they had walked, the hearth by which they had shared whispered secrets, the dreams of a bustling, laughter-filled cottage – all had been plunged into an unimaginable void with her sudden, brutal alteration. How could he have possibly navigated such a cataclysm? Had the vibrant tapestry of their life together simply unraveled, thread by thread, leaving him with only the gaping holes where joy and shared anticipation once resided?

She pictured him alone in their small dwelling, the scent of her absence clinging to the very air, an olfactory phantom more potent than any lingering perfume. The sunrise, once a herald of shared beginnings, would have been a cruel mockery, a reminder of a dawn that no longer held the promise of her waking smile.

Had he spent his days in a fog of disbelief, his nights haunted by the echoes of her voice, the phantom touch of her hand?

Or had the relentless march of time, that indifferent balm, begun to smooth the sharp edges of his grief?

The thought was a fresh agony, a new layer of torment to the already unbearable weight of her eternal existence. The possibility that he had, in some way, found solace, that his life had continued, however diminished, was a betrayal of the magnitude of what they had shared. It suggested that the light he had held for her, the unwavering belief in their shared destiny, had ultimately proven stronger than the darkness that had claimed her.

And what of moving on?

The phrase itself felt like a sacrilege. Could a heart that had known the profound, soul-deep connection she had shared with Julius ever truly beat for another?

She imagined him, perhaps years later, his hair silvered by the passage of seasons, his eyes holding a perpetual shadow.

Had he met someone new, someone whose laughter was a present melody, not a fading echo?

Had he found a different hand to hold, a different voice to whisper his dreams into?

The images that flickered through Elara's mind were indistinct, like figures seen through a thick mist. She could conjure no concrete details, no sharp lines of a new reality for him. This vagueness was not an accident; it was the manifestation of her own profound isolation. She could not conceive of him finding happiness without her, because her own existence was so utterly defined by his absence, by the memory of what had been.

The uncertainty surrounding Julius's fate was a constant, gnawing ache, a hollow space within her spectral heart that no amount of stolen life could ever fill. She could replay their moments together, polish them until they gleamed with an unearthly light, but she could never truly know what had become of him after she was no longer his Iris. Had he ever truly understood the nature of her transformation? Had he been driven away by fear, by revulsion, or had his love been so profound that it transcended even the grotesque reality of her undeath? The latter was a comforting fiction, one that her idealized memories readily embraced, but the former was a chilling possibility that could not be entirely dismissed. The man who had loved her so fiercely might have been terrified, his adoration curdling into abject horror at the sight of the monster she had become.

This was the cruellest irony of her eternal damnation: to be forever bound to the memory of a love that she could never truly revisit, to a man whose future was a closed book, an unknowable enigma. Her existence was a perpetual echo chamber of their past, yet the present and future of the man who had been its very foundation remained an inaccessible mystery. She was adrift in an ocean of memory, surrounded by the spectral remnants of their shared life, yet utterly alone in her inability to comprehend his journey beyond the moment of her fall. This ignorance was a form of torment, a constant reminder that even the most cherished bonds could be severed, leaving one irrevocably isolated.

The weight of this unanswered question pressed down on her, a suffocating blanket of eternal sorrow. It was the ultimate testament to her isolation, a chilling confirmation that even the most potent love could not guarantee a shared destiny, a unified future. She was a creature of shadows and echoes, her existence a testament to what had been lost, while Julius, if he still lived, was a creature of the continuing world, his life a narrative she could never access. His fate, therefore, was not merely a personal tragedy for him, but a profound source of eternal torment for her. It was the ultimate proof that her transformation had not just stolen her life, but had irrevocably severed her from the very world that had once held her dear, leaving her with a void where her beloved's future should have been, a void that echoed with the chilling finality of her unending solitude.

She would never know if he had found peace, if his laughter had returned, if his eyes had ever again held the sparkle of untroubled joy. She could only speculate, weaving phantom narratives that served only to highlight the stark reality of her own eternal grief. The Julius of her memories was forever frozen in time, a perfect, untarnished image of the man he had been, and the man she had loved. But the man who had lived, who had breathed and aged and potentially loved again, remained lost to her. This gnawing uncertainty was a constant companion, a silent witness to the futility of her eternal vigil. It was the final, cruel twist of the knife, a chilling reminder that even in the realm of the undead, where time held little sway, some doors remained irrevocably closed, some questions forever unanswered, leaving her in a state of perpetual, sorrowful longing. The knowledge that she would never receive an answer, that the truth of Julius's life after her own ceased to be was forever beyond her reach, was a more profound torment than any physical suffering. It was the ultimate distillation of her isolation, the chilling realization that even the deepest love could not bridge the chasm between life and undeath, between memory and reality, between her eternal sorrow and his unknowable fate.

Chapter 12:
The Weight of Eternity

The endless march of time, once a gentle rhythm marking the blooming of flowers and the turning of seasons, had become a deafening roar, an implacable tide that swept away all that Elara held dear. Her existence, a cruel anomaly preserved by the very magic that had cursed her, rendered her a spectator to a world that perpetually shed its skin. Mortals, in their ephemeral brilliance, burned brightly, only to be extinguished with a speed that bordered on the absurd. Their generations, a mere flicker in the grand, indifferent expanse of her own unending vigil, rose and fell with a monotonous regularity that gnawed at the edges of her sanity.

She had seen empires crumble to dust, their monumental architectures reduced to forgotten rubble by the relentless winds of change. She had witnessed the birth of gods and their subsequent dethronement, the fervent prayers of one era morphing into the scoffing disbelief of the next. The same sun that had warmed Julius's skin, that had glinted off the laughter in his eyes, had risen and set countless times since their last embrace, each dawn a fresh insult to the permanence of her sorrow. The faces of those she had known, their hopes and fears, their loves and losses, were now less than faint impressions on the winds of memory. They were ghosts of ghosts, phantoms of phantoms, their vibrant lives reduced to a whispered legend, a forgotten nursery rhyme.

The sheer insignificance of mortal endeavors became a source of profound weariness. Their struggles, their triumphs, their heartbreaks – all were played out on a stage so minuscule, so fleeting, that it felt like watching ants scurrying across a vast, unfeeling plain. What was the desperate cry of a king for his dying kingdom when that kingdom itself would be a forgotten footnote in the annals of geological time? What was the passionate declaration of love between two souls when their entire lineage would vanish like dew in the morning sun? Elara found herself adrift in an ocean of existential ennui, the vibrant hues of life muted to a uniform, dull grey.

The world changed, and yet she remained the same, a static monument to a moment long past. She was a living anachronism, a relic of a forgotten age, her very presence a defiance of the natural order. This eternal sameness, this inability to ebb and flow with the currents of existence, became her most profound torment. While the world mutated and evolved, shedding its old forms for new, she was a prisoner of her own unchanging state. Her body, a vessel of undeath, refused to betray the passage of years; her heart, long stilled, beat with a phantom rhythm that mocked the vitality of the world around her.

She recalled the thrill of discovery, the eager anticipation of learning, the simple joy of experiencing something for the first time. Now, even the most novel of events felt like a rehash, a predictable permutation of patterns she had witnessed a thousand times before. A new philosophy would emerge, only to be superseded by another, its followers convinced of its ultimate truth, oblivious to the fact that their 'ultimate truth' was merely another fleeting dogma destined for the dustbin of history. A new artistic movement would blossom, its creators pouring their souls into their work, their creations hailed as revolutionary, only to be dismissed as quaint and archaic by the next generation.

The people she encountered were like fleeting characters in a play she had seen performed endlessly. Their hopes and dreams, their loves and hatreds, were all variations on themes she had long since memorized. She could predict their reactions, anticipate their desires, and often, her predictions were chillingly accurate. This foresight, born not of wisdom but of sheer, repetitive exposure, robbed her of any genuine connection. How could she truly empathize with a joy she had witnessed countless times, or mourn a sorrow that echoed a thousand previous laments? It bred a profound detachment, a cold, clinical observation of the human condition.

She found herself staring at the stars, their ancient light reaching her across unimaginable distances, a distance that mirrored her own isolation. The constellations, the very patterns that had guided sailors and inspired poets for millennia, were her only constant companions. They shifted, of course, their slow, inexorable dance across the celestial sphere a testament to the vastness of time, but their forms, their enduring presence, offered a strange sort of solace. They, too, had witnessed the rise and fall of civilizations, the birth and death of stars, yet remained a silent, majestic testament to endurance.

The conversations of mortals often became a tedious drone. Their concerns, so urgent and all-consuming to them, seemed trivial to her. The anxieties of a merchant over a fluctuating market, the petty rivalries of nobles, the impassioned speeches of politicians – they were all fleeting ripples on the surface of a deep, unchanging ocean. She would listen, her spectral ears attuned to the nuances of their voices, but her mind would often drift, cataloging the variations of their folly, the infinite ways in which they repeated the same mistakes.

This detachment was a necessary shield, a way to preserve what little sanity she had left. To fully engage with the fleeting lives around her would be to invite a constant barrage of grief. Each smile would be a reminder of Julius's lost smile, each embrace a ghost of his embrace. Each burgeoning hope would be a precursor to inevitable disappointment. So, she retreated, building walls of indifference around her heart, a heart that had long since ceased to beat with a living warmth.

She had tried, in her early centuries, to find meaning in the grand sweep of history. She had sought to understand the underlying currents that shaped human destiny, to find patterns in the chaos, to glean some profound lesson from the relentless churn of existence. But the lessons, if they existed, were perpetually obscured by the sheer volume of data, by the overwhelming sameness of the human experience. It was like trying to discern a single melody from a cacophony of a million competing instruments, each playing a slightly different version of the same tune.

The concept of progress, so cherished by mortals, often seemed like a mirage. They would invent new tools, develop new technologies, build grander cities, only to find themselves facing new problems, new challenges, new ways to inflict suffering upon themselves and each other. The tools of war became more sophisticated, the methods of oppression more refined, the capacity for cruelty seemingly limitless. While their outward forms changed, the core of their nature – their capacity for both great love and profound wickedness – remained stubbornly constant.

This realization brought a peculiar sort of melancholy, a deep-seated sadness for the inherent limitations of their existence. They were caught in a cycle, their lives a series of recurring themes, their progress often illusory, their ultimate fates sealed by the very nature of their mortality. She, who was no longer bound by such limitations, could see the grand, tragic arc of their story with a clarity that was both a gift and a curse.

Sometimes, in the deep quiet of the night, when the world was asleep, and the stars held their silent vigil, she would find herself whispering Julius's name into the emptiness. It was a reflex, an ingrained habit, a desperate attempt to conjure the warmth of a love that had been consumed by the fires of eternity. But the name, spoken into the void, returned to her as an echo, a hollow sound that only emphasized her isolation. His world, his life, had continued, a vibrant, unfolding narrative that she could no longer access. He was a closed book, a chapter in her life that had ended abruptly, leaving the rest of his story a blank page, forever beyond her reach.

The weight of this unknowable future was a constant companion, a silent, ever-present ache. It was the ghost of a future that might have been, a testament to the life that had been stolen from her, and the life that had continued without her. She was a creature of the past, forever anchored to the moments she could no longer touch, while the man she had loved was a creature of the present, a mystery she could never hope to unravel. And in that unresolvable mystery lay the true, chilling expanse of her eternal march.

The passage of centuries, each one a slow, deliberate erosion, had worn away the finer contours of Iris's humanity. What remained was a starker, more elemental silhouette, a being defined not by shared feeling or tender connection, but by the primal imperatives of her vampiric existence and the enduring, unhealed wounds of her past. Empathy, once a readily accessible wellspring, had long since dwindled to a brackish pool, its waters muddied by the ceaseless tide of her solitude and the gnawing demands of her predatory nature. Compassion had become a foreign language, its phrases forgotten, its grammar lost to the arid landscapes of her immortal heart. Connection, the delicate, silken thread that bound mortals to one another and, in turn, to their own sense of self, had frayed and snapped countless times, leaving her adrift in an ocean of profound isolation.

Her vampiric form, a vessel sculpted by eternal night and insatiable hunger, had ceased to be a mere shell. It had become an outward manifestation of her inner desolation, a grim testament to the desolation that had taken root within her. The sharp angles of her features, once softened by the flush of mortal life, now held a predatory sharpness, as if carved from obsidian by the relentless chisels of time and despair. Her eyes, once windows to a soul capable of warmth and light, were now twin pools of ancient, chilling darkness, reflecting only the void that had consumed her from within. They held a predatory gleam, a hunter's keenness that could dissect weakness from across a crowded room, but they were devoid of the spark of shared experience, the flicker of understanding that might have bridged the chasm between her and the fleeting mortals she encountered. The pallor of her skin, once indicative of a fragile mortal constitution, now spoke of a perpetual, unyielding chill, the coldness that permeated her being, seeping from her very bones. Her movements, too, had transformed, shedding the natural hesitations and graceful imperfections of humanity for a fluid, almost unnerving precision. She moved with the silent grace of a predator stalking its prey, each step measured, each gesture deliberate, designed for efficiency and the swift execution of her needs. There was no wasted motion, no accidental brush of a limb against another, only the purposeful, predatory ballet of the immortal hunter.

The concept of 'need' itself had become a more brutal, more immediate thing. The subtle hungers of the human spirit – for companionship, for understanding, for purpose – had been brutally overwritten by the singular, all-consuming craving for vitae. This thirst was not merely a physical sensation; it had become a psychological imperative, a constant hum beneath the surface of her consciousness, demanding appeasement. It dictated her thoughts, shaped her interactions, and, most insidiously, eroded the very foundations of her moral compass. The lives of mortals, once rich with individual stories and complex emotions, had been reduced to a singular, stark designation: sustenance. Their hopes, their fears, their loves, their dreams – these were merely ephemeral distractions, the flickering shadows cast by the flame of their brief existence, a flame that ultimately served only to fuel her own unending night. The intricate tapestry of human interaction, with its subtle courtesies and nuanced emotions, had been stripped down to its most basic, brutal transaction. A glance could convey intent, a gesture could signal submission or defiance, but the deeper currents of shared joy or sorrow were lost in the unbridgeable chasm between her immortal, predatory nature and their fragile, mortal existence.

The loneliness, once a sharp, piercing ache, had calcified into a dull, pervasive presence, a shadow that clung to her like a shroud. It was not the fleeting sadness of a missed embrace or an unshared laugh, but a vast, echoing emptiness that spanned millennia. She had witnessed countless individuals forge bonds, share secrets, and build lives together, only to watch those connections dissolve with the inexorable march of time. These ephemeral unions, so vibrant and vital to them, were like fleeting sparks in the vast darkness of her own unchanging existence, and the sight of them, rather than offering solace, only served to underscore her own perpetual state of detachment. She could observe their rituals of courtship, their expressions of affection, and their pledges of fidelity, but the emotional resonance of these acts was lost on her. It was akin to a deaf person observing a symphony, recognizing the movements and gestures of the musicians, but remaining deaf to the music itself. The nuances of human connection, the subtle interplay of vulnerability and trust, were a foreign dialect she could no longer comprehend.

Her interactions with mortals had become transactional, stripped of any genuine affection or lingering regret. When she fed, it was not with the desperate urgency of a starving creature, nor with the melancholic regret of a being forced to extinguish a light it cherished. Instead, it was with a cold, clinical efficiency, a necessary act of biological preservation. The struggle, the fear, the plea for mercy – these were merely incidental details, the brief, fleeting sensations of a dying organism, as irrelevant to her as the buzzing of a fly to a great predator. She had learned to manipulate their hopes and fears with a practiced ease, offering illusions of solace or promises of power that masked her true intentions. This was not born of malice, but of a chilling pragmatism. Why engage in protracted deception when a well-placed word, a carefully constructed lie, could achieve the desired result with far less effort? The art of persuasion had become the art of necessity, honed by centuries of observing mortal fallibility.

The trauma of her own transformation, the violent severance from her mortal life, had left an indelible scar, a festering wound that refused to heal. While the raw agony of the initial loss had long since faded, it had transmuted into a deep, unshakeable cynicism. She had seen the promises of immortality twisted into curses, the blessings of longevity into instruments of torment. She had witnessed the despair of those who outlived all they held dear, their existence stretching into an unbearable, empty expanse. This understanding, gained through her own agonizing experience, had rendered her incapable of offering genuine comfort or hope. To provide such things would be a profound hypocrisy, a betrayal of the very nature of the existence she embodied.

Her predatory instincts, once a source of shame and conflict, had long since become her primary mode of operation. The primal urge to hunt, to track, to overcome and consume, was now as natural to her as breathing was to mortals. It was a constant, low-grade thrum beneath her awareness, a siren song that drew her towards the vulnerability of life. This instinct, unchecked by the moderating influence of compassion or the constraints of a moral code, had sharpened her senses to an almost unbearable degree. She could detect the faintest scent of fear, the subtle tremor of a heartbeat accelerating in anticipation or dread. She could sense the pulse of life like a distant beacon, a promise of satiation in the vast, silent wilderness of her immortality. This heightened awareness, while essential for her survival, also further alienated her from the world of mortals. Their lives, so fragile and easily extinguished, became a constant, tantalizing prospect, a buffet laid out before a creature perpetually on the brink of starvation.

The memories of her mortal life, once a source of bittersweet solace, had become fragmented and distant, like faded frescoes in a crumbling ruin. The faces of loved ones, the echoes of laughter, the warmth of a shared embrace – these were now ghost impressions, phantoms that flickered at the periphery of her consciousness. The pain associated with these memories had dulled, but so too had the joy. They were relics of a self she no longer inhabited, fragments of an experience that had been brutally excised. She could recall the *fact* of love, the *concept* of happiness, but the visceral, lived experience of these emotions had been irrevocably lost, buried beneath layers of undeath and eternal solitude. Sometimes, in the deepest hours of the night, a phantom sensation would surface – the ghost of a caress on her cheek, the echo of a whispered endearment – but these were mere sensory echoes, devoid of the emotional weight that had once given them meaning. They were like echoes in an empty cathedral, the memory of sound without the substance.

The erosion of her humanity was not a sudden cataclysm, but a slow, insidious decay, like a statue left too long in the corrosive rain. Each century chipped away another facet, smoothing sharp edges, blurring vibrant colors, until what remained was a stark, unadorned form, stripped bare of all but the most essential, predatory elements. She was a being sculpted by the unforgiving chisel of eternity, her existence a testament to the relentless power of isolation and the brutal demands of an unending predatory cycle. The monster, once a terrifying transformation, had become her most authentic self, the last vestige of a humanity long since surrendered to the encroaching darkness. The emptiness within her was no longer a void to be feared, but a vast, echoing chamber that had become her natural habitat, a chilling testament to the enduring power of her vampiric nature.

The endless expanse of her existence had, by necessity, woven Iris into the fabric of a world far removed from the fleeting affairs of mortals. It was a realm steeped in shadow and myth, populated by beings who, like her, had shed the comforting constraints of mortality to embrace eternal night. These were not mere specters or illusions, but entities possessing their own ancient histories, arcane powers, and territorial imperatives. Her path, dictated by the relentless hunt and the perpetual need for solitude, had crossed with many of them over the millennia, each encounter etching another scar onto her already-weathered soul.

There were the Sylvani, the ancient tree-folk whose roots delved deeper than any tomb, and whose consciousness stretched across entire forests. They moved with the slow, deliberate grace of growing things, their bodies gnarled and bark-skinned, their eyes like pools of sap reflecting the starlight. Iris had encountered them in the primordial woodlands that predated human civilization, where their groves were sacred, and their anger was as potent as any storm. They viewed all transient beings with a profound disdain, and vampires, with their unnatural hunger and their disregard for the cycles of life and death, were anathema to their very being. One particularly chilling encounter, centuries before the rise of iron cities, had seen her stumble into a Sylvani sacred circle during a rare moonless night. The air had thickened with an unseen energy, and the ancient trees had stirred, their branches like skeletal arms reaching for her. Whispers, like the rustling of leaves in a gale, had slithered from the shadows, speaking of ancient curses and the purging of the 'unnatural'. She had felt the earth beneath her feet writhe, tendrils of moss and vine snaking towards her, attempting to bind her, to draw her into the very soil from which they sprang. It had taken all her speed and a desperate, primal surge of her vampiric strength to break free, leaving a trail of scorched earth and wilting foliage in her wake. The Sylvani, she had learned, did not forget such trespasses. Their vengeance was as slow and inevitable as the turning of seasons, a creeping blight that could wither kingdoms over centuries, and Iris had learned to give their ancient domains a wide berth.

Then there were the Groluk, creatures born of the deepest caverns, their forms sculpted by pressure and eternal darkness. They were beings of raw, elemental earth, their skin like obsidian, their eyes burning with the cold fire of geode crystals. They rarely ventured to the surface, their dominion lying in the crushing depths of the world. But occasionally, driven by some unfathomable urge or drawn by disturbances in the earth's crust, they would emerge. Iris had met a scouting party once, near a network of volcanic caves that pulsed with latent heat. The Groluk were not beings of intellect or malice in the mortal sense; a singular, primal imperative drove their existence: to maintain the balance of the earth, to reshape its very form according to their ancient, geological understanding. They perceived her vampiric essence as a disruption, an impurity that clung to the surface world like a parasitic growth. The encounter was not one of combat, but of profound, terrifying indifference. The Groluk had simply flowed around her, their immense, stony bodies parting like a river around a boulder, as if she were not even present. But as they passed, she felt a chilling resonance, a vibration that seemed to seep into her bones, a silent judgment from a power that operated on scales of time and pressure incomprehensible to her own immortal existence. It was a stark reminder that even among the eternal, she was not the apex predator, nor the sole master of darkness.

Her travels had also brought her into contact with the elusive Fae, the beings of the twilight realms, whose existence danced on the edges of mortal perception. These were not the whimsical sprites of children's tales, but ancient, capricious entities, bound by their own inscrutable laws and driven by desires that were as alien as the stars. Some Fae were curious, their eyes like polished gemstones, their smiles as sharp as slivers of ice. They would observe her from the periphery, their forms flickering like heat haze, their laughter like the chime of distant bells, a sound that could both enchant and unnerve. They seemed to find her predatory nature amusing, a brutal simplification of their own intricate games of manipulation and desire. They were not adversaries in the traditional sense, for they rarely engaged in direct confrontation. Instead, they wove illusions, whispered temptations, and subtly altered the paths of those they deemed interesting, often leading them to their doom, or to Iris herself. She had learned to tread carefully in lands rumored to be touched by the Fae, for their gifts were often poisoned, and their games could ensnare even the most wary.

There were darker entities as well, beings that dwelled in the forgotten places, the shadowed corners of reality where the veil between worlds thinned. The Whispering Ones, for instance, spectral entities that fed on the echoes of forgotten tragedies, had once haunted a ruined abbey where Iris had sought refuge. They were not corporeal, but threads of sorrow and despair woven into the very stone and air, their presence manifesting as a suffocating dread and the phantom sensation of being watched by countless unseen eyes. They had no physical form to rend, no vitae to drain, yet their touch was a chilling emptiness that threatened to unravel her very being, to draw her into their endless tapestry of lament. She had been forced to flee that place, not by physical force, but by the sheer, unbearable weight of their collective grief, a psychic onslaught that threatened to drown her own consciousness in a sea of eternal despair. It was a stark, terrifying lesson that some enemies could not be fought with fang and claw, but only escaped through sheer will and the severing of all emotional anchors.

Even beings as seemingly disparate as the ancient Dragons, though long thought to be creatures of myth by the mortal world, were not entirely gone from the hidden corners of existence. Iris had encountered a solitary one, an elder of immense age and power, slumbering in a mountain caldera. The Dragon's breath was not merely fire, but a primal force that warped reality itself, and its scales shimmered with an ancient, cosmic energy. While it was aware of her presence, a fleeting flicker in the vast panorama of its millennia-long existence, it regarded her with the same detached curiosity it might afford an ant crawling across its colossal form. There was no animosity, no territorial dispute, merely an acknowledgement of another immortal creature, an ephemeral spark in the grand, slow unfolding of aeons. It spoke, not with a voice, but with a resonance that echoed directly in her mind, a consciousness so vast it dwarfed her own. It conveyed no threat, nor offered any comfort, simply a brief, silent exchange of acknowledgement before it turned its awareness back to the slow geological processes it oversaw. It was a humbling, terrifying encounter, a testament to powers that predated even the oldest of the undead, a reminder that her own immortality, while vast, was but a blink in the eye of true cosmic forces.

These encounters, though varied, underscored a crucial truth: Iris was not an anomaly, but a thread in a much larger, far more dangerous tapestry. She was a predator, yes, but within a world of predators. She was immortal, but within a realm of the eternal. Her existence, though long and solitary, was intertwined with the destinies of beings who commanded elements, who shaped realities, and who operated on principles far removed from the simple hunger that drove her. These interactions were not always direct confrontations. More often, they were subtle shifts in the supernatural currents, a brief crossing of paths in the hidden highways of the night, a fleeting awareness of another ancient consciousness in the same desolate landscape. It was a constant, underlying hum of immense, unseen powers, a reminder that the world she inhabited was far stranger, far more perilous, and far more ancient than any mortal could ever comprehend. She navigated this labyrinth of eternal beings with a caution born of experience, understanding that a misstep could lead to oblivion, not at the hands of mortals, but at the whim of powers that had witnessed the birth and death of stars. The weight of eternity was not just the burden of her own unending existence, but the chilling realization of the countless other eternities unfolding in the shadows, each with its own dangers, its own inscrutable goals, and its own ancient, unforgiving power.

The lingering scent of petrichor, the earthy perfume of rain on parched soil, had a way of clawing at the edges of Iris's consciousness. It was a scent that belonged to a world of fleeting sunshine and gentle showers, a world she had long since been severed from. Tonight, the rain was a relentless deluge, pounding against the ancient stones of a forgotten chapel she had sought shelter within, its gothic arches weeping water, its stained-glass windows like vacant eyes staring into the storm. Each drop that cascaded down the crumbling façade, each gust of wind that moaned through the shattered nave, seemed to carry whispers from a time when such sounds were a comfort, a promise of renewal.

It was in these moments, when the primal hunger was momentarily sated, when the immediate threat of discovery or conflict receded, that the ghost of her humanity would stir. It was a spectral presence, an echo of a life lived under the sun, a life where emotions bloomed and faded like wildflowers, where mortality lent a precious urgency to every sunrise. The memory would unfurl, not as a coherent narrative, but as a mosaic of fragmented sensations: the warmth of a lover's hand, the innocent laughter of children, the bitter-sweet taste of a shared meal, the profound peace of a slumber undisturbed by eternal thirst. These were not memories she actively sought, for they were a torment, a stark juxtaposition to the cold, unending existence she now endured. They were uninvited guests, arriving unannounced on the currents of memory, sharp and exquisite in their brief, agonizing appearance.

She found herself standing before a ruined altar, the stone chipped and worn, a single, spectral moonbeam piercing the gloom to illuminate a faded fresco of a celestial scene. The Virgin Mary, her painted eyes serene, her alabaster skin untouched by the ravages of time, seemed to gaze upon Iris with an impossible, gentle understanding. For a fleeting instant, Iris saw not the monstrous creature she had become, but Elara, the woman who had once knelt in places like this, her heart filled with faith and hope. Elara, who had known fear, yes, but also joy, love, and the simple, profound beauty of a life lived in the light. The contrast was a physical blow, an ache that settled deep within her unfeeling chest, a phantom limb of a heart that had long since ceased to beat.

The ghost of Elara would often surface in the most unexpected ways. Sometimes it was a snatch of a lullaby, hummed unconsciously by a mortal mother in a distant village, its melody finding its way to Iris on the night air and twisting itself into a knot of forgotten tenderness. Other times, it was the sight of a wilting rose, its petals bruised and fallen, a mirror to her own decaying spirit, a poignant reminder of beauty's ephemeral nature. Or it could be the simple act of watching the stars, the same stars that had guided Elara, now merely cold, distant beacons in her ceaseless, nocturnal journey. They held no comfort now, only the vast, indifferent silence of eternity, a silence that echoed the hollowness within her.

These moments of reflection were not a respite, but a deeper kind of suffering. They were the moments when the predatory instincts, the insatiable thirst, the cold detachment honed over centuries of survival, receded just enough to allow the raw wound of her lost humanity to bleed. The predatory nature was a shield, a necessary armor against the crushing weight of her unending existence, a way to survive in a world that was both a hunting ground and a tomb. But the ghost of Elara was the shard of glass embedded in that armor, a constant, agonizing reminder of what had been shattered, what could never be reclaimed.

She remembered, with a clarity that burned like a brand, a specific scent: the lavender that grew wild in her mother's garden, its fragrant tendrils climbing the stone walls, its delicate purple blooms a splash of vibrant color against the verdant green. Her mother, with hands calloused from toil but gentle in their touch, would gather the dried sprigs, tucking them into linen sachets to ward off moths and infuse their simple home with a calming aroma. Iris, as Elara, had loved that scent. It had meant peace, safety, the comforting presence of home. Now, the faintest hint of lavender, carried on a phantom breeze or clinging to the tattered remnants of an ancient garment, could send a tremor through her. It was a scent that spoke of belonging, of a time before she was a creature of shadow and blood, a time when she was simply a daughter, a woman, a mortal.

The rain outside intensified, drumming a frantic rhythm against the chapel roof, each peal of thunder a violent punctuation mark in the silence of her thoughts. She closed her eyes, trying to push back the tide of memory, to reinforce the barriers that kept the monster at bay and the human submerged. But the harder she fought, the more vivid the recollections became. She saw the sun on her face, a sensation so alien now it felt like a dream of warmth from a different world. She heard the murmur of voices, a tapestry of sound woven from conversations and laughter, a symphony of life that was now muted by the silence of her own eternal night.

There was a particular memory, sharp and cruel, of her own wedding day. The scent of lilies, heavy and sweet, the soft rustle of her bridal gown, the nervous tremor in her hands. She recalled the earnest gaze of the man she had pledged her life to, a man whose future, like her own, had seemed boundless and bright. And then, the brutal interruption, the sudden descent into darkness, the primal scream that had been ripped from her throat not in pain, but in an agony of transformation. That memory was the deepest scar, the wound that never truly healed, the constant reminder of the violent severing of her life.

The tragedy of her existence lay not just in the unending cycle of hunger and death, but in the persistent, agonizing awareness of what she had lost. The predatory urges were a constant, a thrumming beneath her skin, a gnawing emptiness that demanded to be filled. But between those demands, in the quiet, shadowed spaces of her immortal life, the ghost of Elara would walk, her ethereal form a poignant testament to a stolen life. Iris fought to remain the predator, the creature of the night, for that was the only way she knew to survive. Yet, these moments of reflection, these painful glimpses into a past that was both a sanctuary and a torture, were a reminder that beneath the hardened shell of the vampire, a flicker of the human soul still remained, forever trapped between the memory of sunlight and the reality of eternal darkness.

She ran a hand over the cold, damp stone of the altar, her fingers tracing the worn carvings. They depicted scenes of salvation, of sacrifice, of a love that transcended mortal life. Such concepts were alien to her now, yet a faint resonance, a distant echo, stirred within her. It was the ghost of faith, the faintest whisper of the belief that had once sustained Elara. It was a desperate plea from a soul adrift in the abyss, a silent yearning for something more than this endless, barren existence. The vampire craved blood, the hunter sought prey, but the remnants of the woman yearned for redemption, for a peace that seemed forever out of reach.

The rain began to subside, the drumming softening to a steady patter. The moon, which had been a sliver of spectral light, now seemed to shine with a little more clarity, illuminating the dust motes dancing in the air like miniature spirits. Iris turned away from the altar, her movements fluid and silent, the predatory grace returning, pushing the spectral Elara back into the recesses of her being. The hunger, momentarily dulled by the onslaught of memory, began to stir anew, a low growl in the depths of her unhallowed existence. The moments of reflection were over, the fragile illusion shattered by the unyielding reality of her curse. The hunt would resume, the eternal night would continue, and the ghost of the woman she once was would retreat, waiting for the next scent of petrichor, the next stray lullaby, the next fleeting glimpse of a lost world to call it back from the shadows. But even as she moved towards the broken door, the faint, phantom scent of lavender seemed to cling to her, a subtle, melancholic reminder of the human tragedy woven into the fabric of her eternal night. The weight of eternity was not just the burden of her own unending existence, but the crushing sorrow of the lives she could no longer live, the loves she could no longer feel, the simple human joys that were now only agonizing, spectral memories.

The rain, though abating, still wept down the chiseled stone of the chapel, mirroring the unending tears that fell within the hollowed chambers of Iris's being. Eternity. The word itself was a cruel jest, a mocking whisper from the void that had swallowed her life whole. It was not a gift, this ceaseless march through centuries, but a gilded cage, each golden bar a memory, each polished surface a reflection of a face she could no longer recognize as her own. Her immortality was a punishment, a penance for sins she had not committed and for a fate that had been thrust upon her like a shroud woven from nightmares.

The echoes of Elara, the woman she had once been, were not gentle murmurs of remembrance but the sharp, unbidden cries of a soul perpetually in torment. Each sunrise she could not witness, each season she endured countless times, each generation that bloomed and withered beneath her unblinking gaze, was a fresh lash against her spectral flesh. There was no respite, no sweet oblivion, only the grinding, inexorable passage of time, each moment a testament to her profound isolation. The world spun on, a vibrant, ephemeral dance of life and death, and she, a solitary, unmoving statue, was condemned to witness its fleeting beauty from the desolate shores of unending night.

Her curse was woven into the very fabric of her being, an agonizing inheritance passed down through the tainted blood of her lineage. The sins of her sire, a creature of ancient darkness and unspeakable cruelty, clung to her like grave-dirt, a perpetual stain upon her soul. She was a living monument to his depravity, a testament to the eternal consequence of his actions. Each life she had been forced to extinguish, each flicker of humanity she had ruthlessly snuffed out in her own being, added another brick to the wall of her damnation. There was no absolution, no path to redemption, only the endless, harrowing journey through the wasteland of her immortal existence.

The thirst was a relentless tide, a primal force that clawed at the edges of her consciousness, demanding appeasement. It was a constant, gnawing hunger that eclipsed all other sensation, a physical ache that resonated deep within her unfeeling core. Yet, even in its agonizing grip, there were moments, brief and agonizing, when the ghost of Elara would stir. She would feel the phantom sensation of sunlight on her skin, the distant murmur of laughter, the warm embrace of a love long lost to the grave. These spectral sensations were not a comfort but a cruel mockery, a stark reminder of the vibrant life that had been ripped from her, leaving behind only this hollow shell, eternally driven by a bloodlust that was as much a part of her curse as the unending years.

Peace was a forgotten word, a concept as alien as the dawn. Sleep offered no solace, only a descent into a deeper, more profound darkness, haunted by the specters of her past and the chilling certainty of her future. Her dreams, when they dared to visit, were not of tranquil slumber but of fleeting moments of connection, of shared warmth and whispered promises, all of which inevitably dissolved into the cold, stark reality of her eternal vigil. She remembered the simple joy of a hearth fire, its warmth chasing away the chill of a winter's night, the comforting weight of a loved one's head upon her shoulder. Now, the only warmth she experienced was the fleeting heat of spilled blood, and the only embrace she knew was the cold grip of death she inflicted upon others.

The memories were not curated treasures, but a hoard of sharp, jagged shards, each one a tiny blade that twisted and turned within her soul. The faces of those she had loved and lost, the innocent eyes of children she had inadvertently terrified, the pained expressions of those she had been forced to destroy – they all paraded before her in an endless, agonizing procession. She was a living archive of sorrow, a walking tomb of forgotten lives. Each memory was a whisper of what had been, a poignant reminder of the vibrant tapestry of human experience from which she had been irrevocably severed. The weight of these memories was a crushing burden, heavier than any mountain, more suffocating than any grave.

Her curse was the perpetual awareness of her own monstrosity. Unlike the creatures of myth who reveled in their dark power, Iris was acutely, agonizingly aware of the abyss that separating her from humanity. She saw the fear in the eyes of her prey, the primal terror that fueled her existence, and each flicker of that fear was a reflection of her own lost innocence. She was a predator, yes, but a predator haunted by the ghost of a shepherdess, forever yearning for the lost flock she could never rejoin. The predatory instinct, the cold, calculating efficiency of the hunter, was a necessary armor, a shield against the unbearable truth of her own existence. But beneath that armor, the raw wound of her humanity bled, a constant, throbbing ache that never truly subsided.

Centuries of existence had not dulled the edges of her pain; they had merely polished them into a finer, more exquisite torture. Each passing era brought with it new joys and sorrows for mortals, new triumphs and tragedies, all of which she witnessed from her lonely vantage point. She saw empires rise and fall, landscapes transform, the very stars in the heavens shift in their ancient dance, and through it all, she remained unchanged, a static point in a universe of flux. This unchanging nature, this immunity to the ravages of time, was the cruelest irony. While the world around her embraced change and renewal, she was condemned to an existence of sterile repetition, an endless cycle of hunger, hunt, and the hollow echo of her lost humanity.

The silence of eternity was the most deafening sound of all. It was a silence broken only by the thrum of her own unnaturally steady heart, the whisper of blood in the veins of her victims, and the ever-present clamor of her own tormented thoughts. There were no loving words to fill the void, no comforting laughter to chase away the shadows. Her existence was a desolate landscape, devoid of the warmth and connection that gave meaning to mortal lives. She was adrift in an ocean of time, with no shore in sight, forever bound to the desolate island of her own unending night.

Her immortality was, indeed, a gilded cage. The luxury of endless time, the power that flowed through her veins, the knowledge accumulated over centuries – these were but gilded bars, each one a testament to her imprisonment. She possessed the wisdom of ages, yet it brought her no comfort. She commanded a power that could reshape the world, yet she used it only to sustain her own agonizing existence. This paradox, this stark contrast between her capabilities and her suffering, was the bitterest pill of all. She was a god-like creature, cursed with a mortal's unending heartache, forever trapped between the phantom warmth of the sun and the cold, unforgiving embrace of eternal darkness. The very concept of "life" for her was a grotesque distortion, a constant, unyielding battle against the creeping despair that threatened to consume her entirely. She existed, yes, but she did not *live*. She endured, she survived, she hunted, but the vibrant spark of existence, the simple joy of being, had been extinguished long ago, leaving behind only the ashes of a life that would never truly end.

Chapter 13:
The Folklore of the Dearg Due

The first whispers of Iris's existence were born not from grand pronouncements or scholarly treatises, but from the hushed breaths of terrified villagers. In the hamlets clinging to the shadowed foothills, where the mist coiled like spectral serpents and the ancient forests loomed with a palpable dread, her name, or rather, the chilling descriptions of her passage, began to take root. It started subtly, with a missing sheep, a child's unexplained fever that burned too hot and too fast, a hunter who ventured too deep into the woods and was never seen again. These were the seeds, innocuous enough on their own, but when sown in the fertile ground of fear and superstition, they sprouted into something far more sinister.

The early tales were rooted in the immediate, the tangible. A fleeting glimpse of a pale figure against the moonlit snow, a shadow that moved with unnatural speed between the gnarled oaks, the mournful sigh that seemed to emanate from the very air when darkness fell. These were the raw materials, the fragmented observations of a community grappling with the inexplicable. The fear of the unknown, a primal force as old as humanity itself, twisted these raw impressions into something akin to a predator stalking the edges of their lives. The local priest, a man of stern piety and weathered faith, would speak of the Devil's influence, of ancient curses stirred from their slumber, inadvertently adding a layer of divine dread to the growing folklore. His pronouncements, meant to fortify his flock against true evil, instead lent a certain gravitas to the spectral presence, making it seem not just a random terror, but a force with a purpose, however malevolent.

As generations passed, the village of Oakhaven, the epicenter of these early encounters, became a nexus of fragmented narratives. The stories were passed down from grandparent to child, often around the flickering hearth fire, during long, storm-lashed nights when the wind howled like a banshee. The details, once sharp and immediate, began to blur, to meld with older, more established legends of forest spirits and vengeful fae. Iris, the woman who had become something more, was slowly being reshaped, her solitary tragedy transmuted into a monstrous entity. The scarlet stain that clung to her lineage, the cursed blood that coursed through her veins, became a visual marker. She was the "Crimson Lady," the "Veiled Apparition," the "Night's Thirst." Children were warned to be inside their homes before dusk, to bolt their doors tightly, and never, ever to wander near the ancient standing stones at the edge of the woods, lest the Crimson Lady claim them.

The oral tradition was a fickle artist, and Iris was its canvas. Each retelling was an act of embellishment, a splash of hyperbole, a darkening of the shadows. The missing livestock became entire herds that vanished without a trace, leaving only desiccated husks. The unexplained fevers escalated into a plague that swept through the village, decimating families, all attributed to the "breath of the Night's Thirst" that seeped through cracked window panes. The lone hunter's disappearance evolved into a gruesome tableau, his remains found impossibly drained, his very life force seemingly siphoned away. The truth of her existence, the solitary pain and the relentless hunger were lost in the cacophony of terror. She was no longer Iris, the woman burdened by an eternal curse; she was a predator, a creature of pure malice, a tangible embodiment of every villager's deepest fears.

This transformation was not limited to the immediate vicinity of Oakhaven. As families migrated, as traders and travelers passed through the region, the whispers carried with them. A traveler, seeking shelter in a remote inn miles away, might recount a chilling encounter, a pale figure glimpsed through the fog, and the innkeeper, a repository of local lore, would nod sagely, adding his own embellishments. "Ah, yes," he'd say, his voice low and gravelly, "that sounds like the legend of the Blood Moon Wanderer. They say she walks the lonely roads, seeking solace, or perhaps something more… a thirst that can never be quenched." Thus, Iris's legend began to spread, a creeping vine of fear winding its way through the tapestry of rural folklore.

Her form, too, became a subject of endless debate and horrified speculation. Some described her as impossibly tall and gaunt, her skin stretched taut over bone, her eyes burning with an unholy light. Others spoke of a more ethereal presence, a shimmering silhouette cloaked in shadows, a whisper on the wind. The recurring element, however, was the color red. The crimson hue of her supposed attire, the blood-red lips, the impossibly pale skin that seemed to absorb all light, all contributed to her terrifying persona. The practical details of her existence – the need to feed, the solitary hunts – were reinterpreted as acts of deliberate cruelty. A curse did not drive her, but by a savage delight in torment. She became the boogeyman of parents, the ultimate cautionary tale to young children who dared to stray too far from the light.

The folklore began to adapt across different regions, subtly morphing to fit local superstitions. In the northern territories, where the winters were long and brutal, she became the "Frost Wraith," a creature that stole the warmth from unwary travelers, leaving them frozen and lifeless. In the marshlands to the west, her legend intertwined with tales of will-o'-the-wisps and drowning spirits, becoming the "Bog Hag," who lured lost souls to their watery graves. Each iteration, however, retained the core elements: an ancient, predatory being, driven by an insatiable hunger, an unnerving pallor, and a connection to the night and its attendant terrors. The sheer longevity of her existence, incomprehensible to mortals, became a source of her mythic power. She was not a fleeting specter, but an enduring terror, a constant presence in the shadowed corners of the world.

The tales often served a practical purpose for the villagers. By demonizing Iris, by transforming her into an external, monstrous threat, they could reinforce community bonds and social order. Strict adherence to customs, staying within the perceived safety of the village, and avoiding solitary excursions into the wild were all implicitly encouraged by the dire warnings about the "Crimson Lady." The legend provided a framework for understanding misfortune; any unusual death, any strange occurrence, could be readily attributed to her malevolent influence, absolving the community of any need for deeper introspection or more complex explanations. It was a collective coping mechanism, a way to impose order on a chaotic and often unforgiving world.

There were, of course, dissenting voices, those who, perhaps through direct encounter or an innate skepticism, saw a flicker of something other than pure evil. A hermit living on the fringes of society might speak of a sorrowful creature, glimpsed only in moments of profound despair, a being of immense loneliness rather than predatory rage. These accounts, however, were rare and often dismissed as the ramblings of the eccentric or the disillusioned. The sheer weight of terror and the power of collective fear ensured that the dominant narrative was one of unadulterated horror. Iris, the woman, was long forgotten, buried beneath layers of myth and legend, replaced by the terrifying phantom that stalked the edges of human consciousness. Her curse, once a personal torment, had been externalized, amplified, and weaponized into a universally recognized symbol of primal fear. She was no longer a victim of fate; she was the monster in the dark, a tale whispered to keep the children in their beds and the doors locked.

The enduring power of the Dearg Due's legend lies not in its variability, but in its remarkable consistency. Across scattered hamlets and isolated homesteads, a tapestry of recurring motifs weaves a chillingly unified portrait of this spectral entity. These shared characteristics, passed down through generations like an inherited dread, serve to solidify her mythical status, offering tangible, albeit terrifying, descriptions for those who live under her perceived dominion. They are the brushstrokes that, when applied by countless storytellers, create an unforgettable and terrifying masterpiece of folklore.

Perhaps the most frequently cited and universally recognized element is the mournful howl. It is not the cry of a wolf, nor the lament of the wind, but a sound that seems to emanate from the very heart of despair. This keening wail is often described as an unnerving, drawn-out sound that rises and falls with a profound sorrow, capable of curdling the blood and sending shivers down the spine. It is said to be heard on moonless nights, when the veil between worlds is thinnest, and its appearance is an almost sure harbinger of misfortune. Some accounts suggest the howl is a cry of eternal longing, a lament for a life unjustly stolen, while others believe it is a primal call to her victims, a siren song of death. This vocalization is not a mere auditory phenomenon; it is an emotional resonance, a raw expression of the anguish that fuels her spectral existence, and it has a profound psychological impact on those who claim to have heard it. It is a sound that bypasses rational thought, striking directly at the primal fears that lie dormant within the human psyche. The sheer desolation in the sound, the utter hopelessness it conveys, is often more terrifying than any visual apparition. It speaks of an unending torment, an existence devoid of solace, and this bleakness is what truly unnerves those who hear it. The howl can travel for miles, yet it often sounds as if it is right beside the listener, a disorienting and terrifying effect that adds to the creature's spectral nature. It is the sound of utter isolation, a solitary voice crying out in an eternal, empty darkness.

Complementing the mournful howl is the pervasive, chilling cold that accompanies the Dearg Due's presence. This is not the natural chill of an autumn evening or the biting frost of winter. Instead, it is an unnatural, bone-deep cold that seems to leach the very warmth from the air and the living. Those who have claimed to encounter her speak of the temperature plummeting without explanation, their breath misting before their faces even on the warmest of nights. This frigid aura is more than just a physical sensation; it is often described as a psychic chill, a palpable sense of dread and emptiness that settles upon the soul. It is as if the creature herself is a void, an absence of all life and warmth, and her proximity is a stark reminder of mortality and decay. The cold is a tangible manifestation of her curse, a constant reminder of the life force that has been so brutally extinguished from her. It is a cold that seeps into the marrow, making one feel profoundly vulnerable and exposed. This unnatural frigidity is a signature of her passage, a calling card left upon the fabric of reality. It can manifest as a localized phenomenon, a pocket of intense cold surrounding her apparition, or it can spread like a creeping frost, chilling entire farmsteads. It is said that plants wither and die in her wake, and that any water exposed to her chilling aura will freeze solid, regardless of the ambient temperature. This extreme cold is a stark contrast to the supposed lifeblood she craves, a paradox that only deepens the mystery and terror surrounding her. It suggests a fundamental imbalance, a corruption that has touched the very essence of her being, turning warmth and life into their antithetical opposite.

The spectral appearance of the Dearg Due is another element that surfaces repeatedly in the folklore, though its specifics can vary, the core elements remain remarkably consistent. She is invariably depicted as a pale, ethereal figure, often veiled or cloaked in shadow. Her skin is described as unnaturally white, almost translucent, as if drained of all blood and life. This pallor is not the healthy lightness of a fair complexion, but a sickly, deathly hue that betrays her unnatural state. Her eyes, when visible, are often described as either hollow and dark or burning with a faint, malevolent glow. Her form is typically slender, gaunt, and unnaturally tall, an elongated silhouette that seems to glide rather than walk. Some tales speak of her leaving no footprints, as if she floats just above the earth, a spectral phantom untethered from the physical world. The recurring motif of a veiled or shrouded figure adds to her mystique, obscuring her true features and allowing the observer's imagination to fill in the blanks with their deepest fears. The crimson hue, so central to her name, is often subtly hinted at, perhaps in the unnatural redness of her lips, or in the way her spectral form seems to shimmer with a faint, arterial light, especially when viewed under the moon. This visual dichotomy – the deathly pallor contrasted with the subtle suggestion of blood – is a powerful and disturbing image. Her movements are often described as fluid and unnervingly silent, adding to her ghostly nature. She is a creature of twilight and shadow, a being that exists on the periphery of human perception, glimpsed only in fleeting, terrifying moments. The details of her attire, while varying, often lean toward flowing, dark fabrics, further enhancing her spectral, sorrowful appearance. It is a look that speaks of a mournful past, a tragic end that has left her forever trapped in a state of spectral undeath. The stark contrast between her unearthly paleness and the supposed crimson of her origin is a powerful visual, hinting at a life violently taken and an unnatural hunger that persists.

Central to the legend, and often the focal point of many tales, is the desolate grave from which the Dearg Due is said to emerge. This is not a resting place of peace, but a site imbued with an almost tangible malevolence. The grave is invariably depicted as in a lonely, forgotten place – at the edge of a dark wood, in a neglected corner of a cemetery, or beneath a gnarled, ancient tree. It is said to be perpetually barren, with no flowers or plants daring to grow upon its cursed soil. The earth itself is often described as dark and unnaturally cold, even in the height of summer. The gravestone, if one exists, is usually ancient and weathered, its inscription long since eroded by time and the elements, leaving only an indecipherable marker of a forgotten soul. Some legends claim the grave is never marked at all, a simple mound of earth that radiates an aura of profound despair. The very air around the grave is said to be heavy and oppressive, making it an area that even the bravest villagers shun. It is the point of origin for her spectral journey, the anchor that binds her to the mortal realm. The desolation of her resting place mirrors the desolation of her existence, a physical manifestation of her eternal torment. It is a place that calls to the darkness within her, a beacon that draws her back from her hunts, a silent testament to the tragedy that spawned her. The aura of decay and sorrow that emanates from this desolate grave is said to be palpable, a psychic stain that warns all who approach of the unholy presence that lies beneath. It is a place where the boundary between life and death is not merely blurred, but violently shattered.

The recurring nature of these elements—the mournful howl, the chilling cold, the spectral appearance, and the desolate grave— serves to create a unified and terrifying image of the Dearg Due. They are the threads that bind the disparate tales together, providing a framework for understanding and fearing this supernatural entity. These consistent characteristics allow the legend to transcend its origins, making the Dearg Due a universally recognizable figure of dread within the folklore. They are the tangible markers of her passage, the signs that alert the superstitious to her presence and the dangers that lie in her wake. This consistency transforms her from a mere campfire story into a deeply ingrained archetype of gothic horror, a creature that embodies the primal fears of death, loss, and the uncanny. The collective understanding of these traits amplifies the fear, creating a shared experience of terror that binds communities together in their apprehension. It is this shared mythology, built on a foundation of consistent, terrifying imagery, that allows the Dearg Due to endure as a potent symbol of the supernatural within the shadowed corners of human storytelling. The unwavering uniformity in these descriptors, despite the vast geographical distances and the passage of centuries, speaks to a profound archetypal resonance. It is as if the collective unconscious of the people has conjured a singular, potent image of spectral dread, and this image has been consistently imprinted onto the folklore of the land. The Dearg Due is not merely a creature of legend; she is a manifestation of ancient fears, given form and voice through these enduring, terrifying characteristics.

The spectral figure of the Dearg Due, with her chilling howl and deathly pallor, is a compelling entity within Irish folklore. Yet, like any deep-rooted legend, her story does not exist in a vacuum. The potent imagery and terrifying attributes associated with her are not entirely novel but rather draw on a wellspring of older, more ancient beliefs and superstitions that permeated the Irish landscape for centuries. To truly understand the Dearg Due, one must explore the fertile soil of Irish mythology from which her legend appears to have sprung, examining the echoes of vampires, vengeful spirits, and blood-drinking entities that might have shaped her contemporary form.

Long before the term "vampire" became a widely recognized part of the global lexicon, Ireland harbored its own unique tapestry of beliefs concerning beings that lingered beyond the grave, fueled by a hunger for the vitality of the living. These creatures, often born of tragic deaths, unnatural curses, or a deep-seated resentment, shared specific primal characteristics with their more famous Eastern European counterparts. The concept of a "corp-seir" or "corp-án," a sort of revenant or animated corpse, was prevalent. These beings were often depicted as animated corpses, driven by a malevolent force to roam the earth, their actions fueled by a lingering, earthly attachment or a thirst for vengeance. While not always explicitly blood-drinkers in the manner of Stoker's Dracula, their association with decay and a draining of life force from the living created a conceptual bridge. The Dearg Due, with her insatiable need for blood, can be seen as a particularly potent and focused manifestation of this broader fear of the restless dead, whose spectral existence necessitated a terrible price from the living. The emphasis on the blood, central to her name and nature, sets her apart, suggesting a more specific and visceral form of undead predation than the more generalized vengeful spirits.

Furthermore, the ancient Celts, and by extension the early Irish, possessed a profound understanding of the liminal spaces between life and death, and the entities that might inhabit them. The Tuatha Dé Danann, the mythical divine race of Ireland, while gods and goddesses, were also beings capable of immense power and inspiring fear. Their stories, replete with magic, transformations, and conflicts, sometimes touched upon darker themes that resonated with the populace. While the Tuatha Dé Danann themselves are not depicted as blood-drinkers, the idea of powerful, otherworldly beings with supernatural appetites and the capacity for both creation and destruction was deeply ingrained. The Dearg Due, in her vampiric hunger, could be interpreted as a perversion of these influential figures, a fallen divinity or a corrupted mortal who has embraced a dark power. The legend of the Abhartach, a dwarf king who, according to some tellings, was buried alive and rose again to demand blood from his people, offers a striking parallel. The Abhartach, much like the Dearg Due, is a supernatural being rooted in a specific locale, a cursed figure whose existence is predicated on consuming the living. The cyclical nature of his reanimation and his demand for sustenance echo the persistent, vampiric hunger of the Dearg Due, suggesting a shared ancestral fear of the persistent undead and their parasitic nature.

The belief in the existence of malignant spirits and the necessity of appeasing or warding them off was a cornerstone of ancient Irish superstition. Inevitable deaths, particularly those marked by betrayal, murder, or suicide, were believed to create a spiritual imbalance, leaving the soul restless and prone to malevolence. These spirits, sometimes referred to as "sidhe" in a broader sense when speaking of the fairy folk, could also take on more sinister forms when fueled by negative emotions. The concept of a "Banshee," while typically depicted as a harbinger of death rather than a direct predator, shares the motif of a mournful, spectral cry, and her presence is tied to specific families, implying a lingering spiritual connection or curse. The Dearg Due, however, moves beyond mere prophecy; she is an active agent of death and decay, her presence directly linked to the draining of life. This might suggest a conflation or evolution of beliefs, where the terrifying spectral pronouncements of a Banshee have been merged with the more visceral, predatory nature attributed to other forms of undead. The idea that the Dearg Due emerges from a desolate grave also aligns with the traditional understanding of cursed burial sites as potent sources of spiritual disturbance. These were places where the natural order was deemed to be irrevocably broken, and from which malevolent forces could emanate.

The folklore surrounding various forms of "draugar" or spirits that would rise from their graves in Norse mythology, with which the Celts had significant historical and cultural contact, might also have influenced the development of such legends. While distinct, the shared northern European emphasis on the power of the dead and their potential to interact with or prey upon the living cannot be entirely discounted. Stories of the dead rising to plague the living, to steal their warmth or their life force, were not uncommon in the broader pagan traditions of the region. The Dearg Due's specific attributes, however, firmly anchor her within the Irish context, particularly through the thematic emphasis on blood and the specific rituals that were sometimes believed to be necessary to put such entities to rest permanently, such as the severing of the head or the staking through the heart, which appear in various folk traditions concerning the undead.

The landscape itself also amplified the fear of the unquiet dead. Ireland's ancient burial mounds, its rugged coastlines, and its deep, dark forests provided a natural stage for tales of the supernatural. The isolation of many communities, coupled with the harshness of life, would have made any disruption of the natural order, especially the unnatural animation of the dead, a cause for profound terror. The Dearg Due, as a creature emerging from a lonely grave, embodies this primal fear of the darkness that lurks just beyond the hearth's light, a fear that is amplified by the very geography of the land. The stories of her emergence would have resonated deeply in a culture that held a strong reverence for the land and its ancient, often mysterious, history.

The very name "Dearg Due," meaning "red blood," is a crucial element in understanding her connection to these older traditions. It immediately sets her apart from more generalized ghosts or specters. The emphasis on blood suggests a more primal, visceral hunger, a specific form of vampirism rooted in the life-giving essence that all living creatures possess. This focus on blood aligns with certain ancient beliefs about the power of blood, both as a source of life and as a conduit for spiritual energy or curses. In many mythologies, blood is considered sacred, and its unnatural shedding or consumption is a profound violation of the natural and spiritual order. The Dearg Due's thirst for blood, therefore, is not merely a physical craving but a symbolic one, representing a complete inversion of life's vital force.

One can also draw parallels with the broader concept of the "evil eye" or "evil glance," which was prevalent across many cultures, including Ireland. This superstition held that certain individuals, through envy or malice, could project a harmful influence upon others, leading to illness, misfortune, or even death. While not directly involving blood-drinking, it speaks to a deep-seated belief in the power of the gaze and the intention of the individual to inflict harm. The Dearg Due, with her potentially glowing or hollow eyes, could be seen as an extreme manifestation of this fear, where the harmful intent is amplified and directly drains life force, symbolized by blood.

The folklore surrounding the "mearaí" or mischievous spirits, and the more sinister "púca," which could transform into terrifying shapes, also contributes to the rich tapestry of Irish supernatural beings. At the same time, the púca is often more chaotic and unpredictable; its ability to embody fear and cause distress hints at a broader cultural understanding of entities that operate outside the norms of human experience and can induce terror. The Dearg Due, in her spectral form, embodies a more specific and horrifying predatory role, but the underlying fear of shapeshifting entities or those that feed on fear and vitality can be seen as a common thread in Irish folklore.

In essence, the Dearg Due is not an isolated anomaly but rather a potent synthesis of various ancient fears and beliefs. She is the embodiment of the lingering dread of the restless dead, a spectral revenant whose insatiable thirst for blood taps into primal anxieties about life, death, and the corrupting influence of the unnatural. Her legend, while specific in its details, resonates with broader themes found in Irish mythology: the power of curses, the malevolence of spirits tied to particular locations, the fear of unnatural animation, and the profound significance of blood as the essence of life. She represents a chilling evolution of these older tales, a vampiric entity deeply rooted in the cultural and mythological soil of Ireland, a testament to the enduring power of folklore to reflect and amplify our deepest fears. The recurrence of such themes across different tales suggests a deeply ingrained cultural understanding of the spectral realm and its potential dangers, a tapestry of dread woven over centuries that finds a particularly potent and terrifying expression in the legend of the Dearg Due.

The legend of the Dearg Due, like any enduring myth, does not exist in a monolithic state of unquestioning acceptance. Instead, it thrives in the fertile ground of human perception, dividing communities into those who tremble at its whisper and those who scoff at its very existence. This dichotomy, the chasm between fervent belief and staunch skepticism, is not merely an academic curiosity; it is the very lifeblood that keeps the legend vibrant, shaping behaviour, dictating caution, and fueling the deep, primal anxieties that lie at the heart of the human psyche.

For the believers, the tales of the Dearg Due are not mere campfire stories or quaint folklore. They are gospel, woven into the fabric of their understanding of the world. These are the individuals who, when the wind howls with an unnatural keenness through the ancient ruins or when the moon casts long, skeletal shadows across the bogs, feel a prickle of dread that transcends rational explanation. They are the ones who instinctively avert their gaze from certain desolate, overgrown burial sites, places whispered to be the unquiet resting grounds of the "red blood" creature. The stories, passed down through generations, are not abstract narratives but practical warnings. They speak of the insatiable thirst, the chilling pallor, the unearthly strength, and the way the very air grows cold and heavy in the presence of such a being.

These believers are often found in the older generations, those whose lives have been shaped by a landscape steeped in ancient superstitions and a profound respect for the unseen forces that govern existence. They recall grandparents who warned against straying too far from the safety of the village after dusk, especially near forgotten graveyards or sites of historical tragedy. They speak of rituals, hushed and often unspoken, designed to ward off the creature's malevolent influence. Perhaps it's the careful placement of certain herbs by doorways, the recitation of ancient protective verses, or the avoidance of specific paths known to be favoured by the undead predator. For them, the Dearg Due is not a figment of imagination but a tangible threat, a dark possibility that lurks just beyond the veil of ordinary reality.

The impact of this belief on their daily lives can be profound. Certain areas, even if historically significant or offering the most direct routes, become taboo. Families might choose longer, safer journeys to avoid passing by a known haunt of the Dearg Due. Nights of the new moon, often associated with increased supernatural activity, become periods of heightened vigilance. The sounds of the night – the hoot of an owl, the rustle of leaves, the distant bleating of sheep – are not merely natural occurrences but potential harbingers of something far more sinister. The fear is not necessarily a constant, paralyzing terror, but a low hum of awareness, a cautious respect for the darkness that might hold ancient, terrible secrets. It is a worldview where the boundaries between the living and the dead are permeable, and where the dead, especially those who died violently or unnaturally, can retain a terrifying form of agency.

The legend of the Dearg Due also fosters a sense of community amongst believers, a shared understanding of a common danger. It creates a collective memory of near misses and cautionary tales, reinforcing the belief system through shared experience, even if those experiences are filtered through the lens of folklore. The fear itself becomes a unifying force, a communal thread binding them together in their awareness of the supernatural. The stories are retold, embellished, and reinforced, each telling serving as a ritualistic act of remembrance and a reaffirmation of the ancient warnings. It is in these shared narratives that the Dearg Due gains a tangible presence, a spectral figure that looms large in the collective consciousness, even if no one has directly encountered her. The very fact that the legend persists, that it continues to evoke fear, is seen as irrefutable proof of its truth.

However, standing in stark contrast to the devoted believers are the skeptics. These are the pragmatists, the rationalists, the individuals who view the tales of the Dearg Due as nothing more than antiquated superstition, the fanciful imaginings of a less enlightened age. For them, the world is governed by discernible laws, by science and logic, and there is no room for creatures that rise from the grave to drain the lifeblood of the living. They attribute the stories to fear of the unknown, to misinterpretations of natural phenomena, or simply to the enduring power of human storytelling.

The skeptics often attribute the perceived "haunted" areas to factors such as local geography, historical events that naturally engender unease, or even the deliberate spread of rumors for various purposes. A graveyard may be avoided not because of a spectral occupant but because it is poorly maintained, isolated, or has a history of accidents or illicit activities. A sudden drop in temperature might explain a peculiar chill in the air due to atmospheric conditions, or a draft from an unseen crevice. The howls and moans that fuel the believers' imaginations are easily dismissed as the sounds of the wind whistling through natural formations, the cries of nocturnal animals, or even the creaking timbers of old, abandoned structures.

These individuals often possess a keen intellect and a desire for empirical evidence. They may actively debunk the stories, offering rational explanations for seemingly supernatural occurrences. They might point to the lack of verifiable evidence and the absence of concrete proof despite centuries of alleged existence. They would argue that if such a creature truly existed and posed a genuine threat, there would be undeniable evidence – historical records of mass deaths directly attributable to its feeding, physical remains, or consistent, undeniable encounters that could not be explained away. The absence of such irrefutable proof is, to them, the ultimate refutation.

Furthermore, the skeptics may view the believers' adherence to the legend as a form of mass hysteria or a coping mechanism for dealing with the uncertainties and harsh realities of life. In a world that can be brutal and unpredictable, the idea of a supernatural entity provides a tangible, albeit terrifying, scapegoat for misfortune. It allows individuals to attribute suffering and death to an external force, rather than accepting the often random and impersonal nature of tragedy. The Dearg Due, in this view, becomes a symbol of primal fears, a personification of the darkness that humanity has always struggled to comprehend and control.

The influence of the Dearg Due myth on the skeptics is less about influencing their daily behavior and more about shaping their perception of those who believe. They might view their more superstitious neighbors with a mixture of pity and mild exasperation, seeing their beliefs as an unfortunate adherence to outdated notions. They may engage in debates, attempting to enlighten those who cling to the legend, often with limited success. For the true skeptic, the legend of the Dearg Due, while an interesting artifact of cultural history and a testament to the enduring power of folklore, remains firmly in the realm of fiction, a ghost story with no true substance.

The existence of both believers and skeptics creates a fascinating dynamic within communities where the legend of the Dearg Due holds sway. It fosters a subtle tension, a quiet disagreement about the nature of reality. The believers live with a heightened sense of awareness, their actions guided by caution and a deep-seated respect for the unseen. The skeptics move through the world with a rational certainty, dismissing the whispers of the supernatural as fanciful tales. Yet, even for the most hardened skeptic, there can be moments of unease, fleeting instances where the veil between the rational and the irrational seems to thin. A sudden, inexplicable chill, a shadow that appears to move with a life of its own, or a silence that feels too profound, can sometimes plant a seed of doubt, a tiny flicker of recognition that perhaps, just perhaps, the old stories hold a grain of truth.

This ongoing interplay between belief and disbelief is not just a cultural phenomenon; it is a testament to the power of myth itself. The Dearg Due, whether real or imagined, continues to exert an influence. For the believers, she is a harbinger of dread, a reason for vigilance, and a symbol of the enduring mysteries of the world. For the skeptics, she is an example of how fear and imagination can coalesce into enduring tales, a reminder of the human need to explain the inexplicable. In their differing reactions, both groups, in their own way, contribute to the legend's continued existence, ensuring that the "red blood" creature, in some form, will continue to haunt the edges of human consciousness for generations to come. The very debate she sparks, the division she creates, is a powerful testament to her enduring presence in the folklore of Ireland, a testament to the fact that some stories, once told, refuse to die. The fear she inspires, even in its dismissal by some, is a form of acknowledgement, a subtle nod to the potent imagery and the primal anxieties that the legend of the Dearg Due so effectively taps into. It is this very tension, this unresolved dialectic between acceptance and rejection, that ensures the legend remains a living, breathing entity within the cultural landscape.

The shadow of the Dearg Due stretches far beyond the immediate fear she instills in those who dwell in the superstitious corners of Ireland. Her legend, a testament to the enduring power of primal anxieties and the chilling resonance of betrayal, has seeped into the very fabric of the collective consciousness, becoming an indelible stain upon the tapestry of dark folklore. She is more than just a spectral entity; she is a potent symbol, a living embodiment of vengeance against injustice, and a stark, terrifying reminder of the consequences of severing sacred bonds, particularly those of love and loyalty. Her tale, passed down through hushed whispers and fearful glances, serves as a perpetual admonishment, a spectral guardian at the periphery of our understanding, reminding us that the darkness that lies beyond the comforting veneer of normalcy is not only real but can be profoundly vengeful.

The Dearg Due's legacy is intrinsically linked to the profound sense of unease that permeates certain landscapes, particularly those touched by tragedy or the weight of ancient secrets. Her story serves as a perpetual echo of past wrongs, a spectral accusation against humanity's perceived transgressions. In the desolate moors, the windswept coasts, and the forgotten burial grounds, her legend finds fertile ground, thriving in the shadows of human folly and the enduring specter of mortality. She is a constant reminder that some debts are never truly settled, that the sins of the past can fester and give rise to monstrous forms, forever seeking retribution. This persistence of her myth speaks volumes about the human psyche's fascination with the macabre, our inherent need to confront and articulate our deepest fears, and our enduring belief in a cosmic balance that, when disrupted, can unleash unimaginable horror.

Her enduring presence in folklore is not merely a product of sensationalism or the simple desire for a good scare. It stems from a deeper, more primal resonance, tapping into universal fears of the unknown, the violation of the natural order, and the ultimate vulnerability of human life. The Dearg Due embodies the terror of a predatory force that operates beyond recognized laws of existence, a creature that defies the sanctity of life and death. Her insatiable hunger, her pale, unearthly beauty twisted by malevolence, and her ability to lure unsuspecting victims into her deadly embrace; all contribute to a potent and terrifying image that lingers long after the tale has ended. She is the dark queen of a forgotten realm, her reign established not by decree but by the sheer, unadulterated terror she inspires.

The tale of the Dearg Due, at its core, is a narrative of profound betrayal and the horrifying metamorphosis it can induce. The story of a woman wronged, a lover's infidelity leading to her tragic demise, resonates with a visceral human understanding of hurt and the desperate yearning for justice. However, in the folklore of the Dearg Due, this yearning transcends the mortal realm, transforming into a supernatural curse. Her undead existence is not a passive haunting but an active, relentless pursuit of vengeance. This aspect of her legend speaks to a deep-seated cultural understanding that certain injustices are so profound, so shattering, that they can break the very chains of death, condemning the wronged to an eternity of seeking recompense. The Dearg Due is the ultimate manifestation of this, a specter born from the ashes of a broken heart and a violated trust, forever bound to exact a bloody toll.

Her legacy also serves as a potent cautionary tale, particularly for those who might dismiss the power of ancient beliefs or the sanctity of promises. The Dearg Due's story serves as a stark warning about the consequences of deceit and the potential for supernatural retribution when mortal transgressions are deemed so heinous that they cannot be left unpunished by earthly means. In communities where her legend is deeply ingrained, the tales are not merely a source of morbid fascination but are actively used to instill a sense of moral responsibility and to caution against actions that could invite a darker fate. The very act of recounting her story becomes a ritual, a collective affirmation of the belief that some acts of cruelty carry with them a supernatural price, a debt that will eventually be collected by the forces that dwell in the shadows.

The enduring power of the Dearg Due's myth is also a testament to the human capacity for storytelling, our innate drive to create narratives that explain the inexplicable and to give form to our deepest anxieties. She is a figure born from the fertile ground of folklore, a potent archetype that continues to evolve and adapt, finding new resonance in each retelling. Her spectral form, her vampiric nature, and her tragic origins combine to create a character that is both terrifying and, in a morbid way, compelling. She represents the ultimate transgression against the natural order, a being that defies the boundaries of life and death, and in doing so, she taps into a primal fear that has haunted humanity for millennia. The fact that her legend persists, that it continues to inspire dread and fascination, is a testament to its deep roots within the human psyche and its ability to articulate those fears that lie just beneath the surface of our rational minds.

Furthermore, the Dearg Due's legend, like many enduring myths, acts as a conduit for processing societal anxieties and historical traumas. The specific details of her origin story, often involving betrayal and violence, can be seen as symbolic representations of broader societal issues. Her unending thirst for blood can be interpreted as a metaphor for the destructive nature of unchecked desires or the lingering bitterness of past injustices that continue to drain the lifeblood from communities. In this light, the Dearg Due becomes more than just a monster; she becomes a cultural phenomenon, a dark mirror reflecting the hidden fears and unresolved conflicts that lie at the heart of human society. Her continued presence in folklore suggests that these anxieties, these historical wounds, remain potent and continue to find expression in the spectral forms that haunt our collective imagination.

The psychological impact of the Dearg Due's legend cannot be overstated. She embodies the fear of the predatory other, the unknown entity that lurks in the darkness, waiting to strike. Her vampiric nature, a recurring theme in folklore across many cultures, taps into a fundamental fear of violation and the loss of one's life force. In the context of Irish folklore, her connection to specific landscapes and historical events grounds her terror in a tangible reality, making the abstract fear of the supernatural feel all the more immediate and menacing. The stories reinforce a sense of caution, particularly among those already predisposed to believe in unseen forces that govern the world. The Dearg Due's legacy, therefore, is one of perpetual vigilance, a somber reminder that the darkness can and does manifest in terrifying ways, and that some legends, once born from sorrow and betrayal, refuse to rest in peace. She is the embodiment of a fear that is as ancient as humanity itself, a fear that finds its most potent expression in the chilling whisper of the Dearg Due. Her story is a testament to the enduring power of myth to shape our understanding of the world, to articulate our deepest dreads, and to remind us of the thin, fragile line that separates the living from the spectral horrors that may lie just beyond.

Chapter 14:
Echoes of the Past

The chill that had settled in Iris's spectral heart was not merely the absence of warmth, a typical affliction of the undead. It was a deeper, more pervasive cold, one that seeped from the very memory of her father, Bernard. Even after centuries had elapsed, his phantom presence was a more persistent torment than the physical act of draining his lifeblood had ever been. That act, a desperate, primal eruption of rage and pain, had offered a fleeting, intoxicating release, a moment where her torment was transmuted into his. But the catharsis was as ephemeral as the crimson life he had once possessed. What remained, what truly anchored her to this desolate existence, was the gnawing realization of his treachery, the profound betrayal that had been the genesis of her monstrous transformation.

His memory was a specter that clung to her, a constant, unwelcome companion. It manifested not as a spectral apparition, but as a suffocating atmosphere, a distortion in the ethereal plane that mirrored the rot at the core of her own being. When she looked upon the moon, its silver light that once kissed her skin now seemed to reflect the pallor of his dying face. When the wind wailed through the desolate ruins of her ancestral home, it carried not the lament of lost love but the echo of his whispered lies, the insidious venom he had injected into her very soul. Bernard. The name itself was a wound that refused to scab over. He, her progenitor, the one who should have shielded her from the harsh realities of the world, had instead been the architect of her damnation.

The act of her vengeance, so ravenous and absolute, had been a feverish delirium. In those initial moments, fueled by the unholy thirst that now defined her, the world had narrowed to the singular, all-consuming need to end him, to make him pay for the sin of his manipulation. She remembered the sickening give of his flesh beneath her fangs, the warmth, then the chilling depletion, the final, shuddering gasp that had been both her release and her damnation. It had been a moment of terrible triumph, a violent assertion of her newfound power against the weakness he had exploited. But the satisfaction had been a shallow, fleeting thing, like the taste of blood that offered no true sustenance. It was a temporary dam against an ocean of despair, an ocean that, once breached, had only surged higher.

Now, centuries later, the memory of his betrayal was a more potent poison than any mortal venom. It was the constant hum beneath the roar of her insatiable hunger, the quiet, insidious voice that whispered doubts even in the heat of her predatory frenzy. Her father, the man whose love she had believed in, whose guidance she had trusted, had willingly sacrificed her, not to any greater evil, but to his own selfish desires. He had traded her innocence, her life, for power, for influence, for the fleeting favor of those who saw her not as his daughter, but as a tool, a pawn to be discarded. The realization had shattered her world, and the pieces had been reassembled into something monstrous, something that mirrored the ugliness of his soul.

This internal landscape of resentment and bitterness was a far more intricate prison than any physical confinement. It was a tapestry woven from the threads of her past, each strand a testament to his deceit. When she encountered the naive hopefulness of a young traveler, her father's condescending dismissal of her own youthful dreams would resurface, a phantom echo of his patronizing smile. When she witnessed an act of genuine affection, the memory of his calculated pronouncements of love, so devoid of true feeling, would curdle the sight into something grotesque. Even the most primal of her urges, the insatiable thirst that drove her to hunt, was tinged with his memory. It was as if his own emptiness, his own lack of true substance, had been imprinted upon her, a void that she could never truly fill, no matter how much life she consumed.

The very act of feeding, once a source of terrifying power, now served as a constant reminder of her origins. Each life she took was a flicker of existence extinguished, a stolen moment from a world that had been stolen from her. And in the frantic moments of consumption, when the world would blur into a crimson haze, she would sometimes see his face superimposed upon her victim's, his betrayal a recurring phantom that haunted the edges of her consciousness. It was a cruel irony that the very means of her survival, the sustenance that kept her from fading into the spectral ether, was inextricably linked to the memory of the one who had condemned her to this unending hunger.

The rage, once a raging inferno, had long since settled into a smoldering ember, a deep-seated cynicism that permeated her every thought, her every spectral tremor. She had sought retribution, and she had found it in the most absolute of terms. But the satisfaction had been a mirage. The void within her, carved out by his betrayal, remained. It was a chasm that no amount of spilled blood could ever fill. Her father's memory was the ghost that truly haunted her, not the specter of his physical form, but the spectral residue of his actions, the lingering stain of his treachery that had irrevocably shaped her existence. He was the original wound, and she, the creature born from its festering depths, was forever bound to his memory, a living testament to a father's sin. His echo was her curse, and it was a curse that even death, in its truest form, could not absolve. She was a creature of his making, and in that terrible, undeniable truth lay the most profound and enduring of her torments. The thirst was a symptom; the betrayal was the disease. And the disease, unlike the ephemeral lives she consumed, was eternal.

The frost that clung to Iris's spectral essence was no mere meteorological phenomenon; it was the calcified residue of Björn's touch. His cruelty, a palpable miasma, had seeped into the very marrow of her existence, leaving indelible marks that pulsed with a phantom ache. It wasn't the swift, brutal ending he had promised, nor the prolonged agony of her initial transformation, that haunted her most. It was the insidious, methodical dismantling of her spirit, the systematic erosion of her will, that had truly forged the monster she had become. His memory was not a specter of a man, but a searing brand, a dark constellation of atrocities that guided her vampiric trajectory.

The physical wounds had long since faded, the torn flesh and broken bones having knit themselves into a semblance of wholeness that defied mortal comprehension. Yet, these were the least of the scars. The actual damage was etched onto her soul, a tapestry of torment woven with the threads of Björn's depravity. She remembered the chilling glint in his eyes as he orchestrated her transformation, a cold, scientific detachment that stripped away any semblance of humanity from the act. He had not been driven by passion or rage, but by a perverse curiosity, a desire to dissect, to dissect not flesh, but the very essence of life, to see what remained when the light was systematically extinguished.

His taunts, delivered in a low, sibilant whisper that slithered into her mind like a viper, were more potent than any blade. He had reveled in her fear, in her helplessness, feeding off her escalating terror as if it were a sustenance of its own. He had spoken of her nascent vampirism not as a curse, but as a magnificent experiment, a testament to his own genius, his own dominion over life and death. "See, little bird," he had rasped, his breath smelling of decay and some cloying, unfamiliar spice, "the cage is broken, but the wings you have now are not for flight. They are for rending." Each word had been a drop of acid, corroding the remnants of her former self, stripping away the layers of innocence and hope until only a raw, exposed nerve remained.

The memory of his hands, skeletal and cold, as they had guided her first, agonizing draught, was a recurring nightmare. He had forced the chalice to her lips, the dark liquid within promising oblivion but delivering a searing, unholy rebirth. He had watched, a grotesque smile playing on his lips, as her body convulsed, as her screams tore through the desolate chamber, as the life she had known bled out and was replaced by an insatiable, gnawing emptiness. "Embrace it," he had commanded, his voice a silken whip. "It is your destiny. It is *my* creation." The violation was profound, not merely physical but existential. He had not simply turned her into a creature of the night; he had claimed ownership of her very being, a twisted father figure who had birthed her anew into a world of eternal shadow.

Björn's cruelty was the crucible in which her vampiric nature had been forged. It was the fire that tempered her, the hammer that shaped her nascent monstrosity. Every instinct she now possessed, every surge of predatory hunger, every flicker of unnatural strength, was a direct echo of his influence. He had not merely inflicted pain; he had sculpted it, molded it, until it became the very foundation of her existence. The physical manifestations of his torment were a constant reminder: the subtle tremor that sometimes ran through her limbs when a memory of his touch surfaced, the way her eyes, when reflecting certain lights, held a chilling, predatory gleam that mirrored his own.

She remembered the chilling detachment with which he had dissected her humanity, piece by agonizing piece. He had introduced her to the concept of the hunt not as a necessity for survival, but as a perverse sport, a demonstration of superiority. He had schooled her in the art of deception, the subtle manipulation of mortal minds, teaching her to twist their desires and exploit their weaknesses with a skill that was both terrifying and undeniably effective. "Fear is a potent tool, my dear," he had often said, his voice dripping with a dark amusement. "But desire… desire is the key that unlocks the deepest vaults of the soul. And you, my creation, will learn to wield it like a master."

His legacy was not one of blood spilled in battle, but of whispers in the dark, of seeds of corruption sown into fertile minds. He had taught her to see the world not as a place of wonder, but as a vast hunting ground, filled with prey eager to be ensnared. He had shown her the emptiness that lay beneath the veneer of mortal lives, the hollowness of their aspirations, the fragility of their affections. And in doing so, he had hollowed out a portion of her own being, leaving a void that only the lifeblood of others could temporarily fill.

The memory of Björn was a dark touchstone for her vampiric existence. It was the constant refrain beneath the symphony of her predatory urges, the dark muse that inspired her darkest impulses. When she encountered a particularly vulnerable soul, it was Björn's mocking laughter that echoed in her mind, urging her to exploit their naivete. When she felt the primal urge to rend and tear, it was his spectral presence, a phantom instructor, guiding her hand, sharpening her fangs, whispering the secrets of ancient predation. He was the architect of her monstrosity, the shadow that loomed over her eternal night.

She carried the weight of his violation not as a burden, but as a testament to her survival. He had intended to break her, to reduce her to a mere plaything, a creature of instinct and despair. But in his ultimate act of cruelty, he had inadvertently forged something far more potent. He had given her a reason to endure, a purpose born from the ashes of her shattered life. His hatred had become her strength, his darkness her guiding light. The scars he had inflicted were not badges of shame, but emblems of resilience, proof that she had not only survived his torment but had transcended it, transforming his monstrous creation into a force unto herself.

The cruelty of Björn was not a singular event, but a pervasive atmosphere that had permeated every aspect of her transformation. It was in the lingering chill that settled upon her skin when the moon was hidden, a cold that mirrored the icy despair he had instilled within her. It was in the unnerving silence that sometimes fell upon her surroundings when her hunger grew too great, a silence that mimicked the oppressive stillness of the tomb he had created for her. His influence was an insidious poison, one that had saturated her very being, leaving no part of her untouched by its venomous embrace.

He had gifted her with unnatural senses, a heightened perception that allowed her to discern the pulse of life from leagues away, to hear the whisper of a beating heart in the darkest night. But these gifts were tainted, each heightened sensation a painful reminder of the senses he had so cruelly abused. The scent of fear, once a mere human emotion, was now a heady perfume, a tantalizing invitation that Björn had taught her to savor. The sound of a desperate plea, once a call for help, was now a siren song, a testament to his teachings on the art of despair. He had twisted the world into a perverse reflection of his own twisted desires, and she, his creation, was now compelled to navigate this shadowed landscape with the very tools he had honed.

The echoes of Björn's cruelty were not confined to the physical realm. They resonated in the deepest recesses of her spectral consciousness, shaping her thoughts, her motivations, and her very perception of reality. He had systematically dismantled her trust, teaching her that vulnerability was a weakness to be exploited, that love was a lie, and that survival was the only truth. His lessons, brutal and unforgiving, had been seared into her soul, becoming the bedrock upon which her vampiric existence was built. Every creature she encountered, every fleeting interaction, was filtered through the lens of his pervasive cynicism. He had taught her to see the predator in every shadow, the deceiver in every smile, the inevitable doom that lay waiting for all mortal souls.

The physical scars, though healed, served as a constant, visceral reminder of the immense violation she had endured. The precise nature of his torment was etched into her memory with a terrifying clarity. He had not simply inflicted pain; he had studied it, cataloged it, and refined it. He had understood that true suffering was not the swift cessation of life, but the agonizing, protracted dissolution of the spirit. He had orchestrated her transformation with the meticulous precision of a surgeon, each agonizing step designed to strip away her humanity, leaving behind a raw, untamed creature at his mercy. His experiments, his whispers, his cold, calculating gaze – all of it had coalesced into a singular, horrifying experience that had fundamentally altered the trajectory of her immortal existence.

The memory of Björn was more than just a scar; it was a foundational element of her vampiric identity. He had been the catalyst, the dark catalyst that had shattered her mortal existence and birthed the creature she was now. His cruelty was not merely an unpleasant memory; it was a wellspring of power, a constant reminder of the depths from which she had risen, and the darkness that now defined her. It was the ultimate violation, the act that had severed her from her past and irrevocably bound her to an eternity of shadow and thirst. And in that grim, undeniable truth, Iris found a strange, terrible solace, for Björn's cruelty had, in its own dark fashion, made her who she was. She was his creation, yes, but she was also his unintended legacy, a monument to a father's betrayal and a testament to a daughter's enduring monstrous strength. The wounds he had inflicted had not killed her; they had merely reshaped her, forging her into a weapon, honed by his own depravity, ready to unleash a darkness that mirrored his own, but was now entirely her own.

The phantom warmth of a hearth, a scent of baking bread, the gentle murmur of a child's laughter – these were not memories for Iris, but specters of a life irrevocably lost, a future stolen before it could even take root. Björn's cruelty had not merely extinguished her mortal existence; it had immolated the very potential for a future, leaving behind only the cold, grey ashes of what might have been. She walked through the ages, a creature of eternal twilight, forever glimpsing the sunlit paths she was denied, forever hearing the faint, joyous echoes of a life that was never hers to live.

Her mind, a vast and desolate landscape now, often replayed fragments of stolen dreams, phantom images of a domestic bliss that Björn's machinations had rendered impossible. She saw herself, not as the predator she had become, but as a wife, her hand clasped in a loving one, her gaze meeting a pair of eyes filled with warmth and devotion. There would be a small cottage, perhaps, nestled amongst rolling hills, smoke curling lazily from its chimney, a testament to a life built on simple joys and shared affections. In these stolen visions, she felt the tender weight of a child nestled in her arms, its breath soft against her neck, its innocent trust a balm to a soul forever bruised. These were not the grand ambitions of royalty or the reckless pursuits of power; they were the quiet, profound dreams of a woman yearning for belonging, for connection, for the gentle rhythm of a life lived in the embrace of love.

But these visions were like shards of stained glass, beautiful in their brokenness, yet sharp and dangerous. They were reminders of the ultimate violation, not just of her body or spirit, but of her very right to a future. Björn, in his hubristic pursuit of power and his twisted desire to redefine life itself, had extinguished not just Iris the mortal, but the possibility of Iris the wife, Iris the mother, Iris the woman who could have found contentment in the mundane beauty of human existence. The joy she was meant to experience, the laughter that should have rippled through her home, the love that should have been the anchor of her days – all of it was a casualty of his dark experiments.

This sense of perpetual loss was a gnawing ache, a constant companion in her lonely immortality. It was the phantom limb of her soul, forever reaching for something that was no longer there, forever mourning a future that had been surgically removed. When she saw mortal couples, their hands intertwined, their faces alight with affection, a wave of profound sorrow would wash over her, a grief so deep it felt like an ocean within her chest. It was not envy, not entirely. It was a profound, soul-deep ache for the simplicity she had been denied, for the warmth she could never again experience, for the natural progression of life that had been cruelly interrupted.

The spectral images of her lost family were particularly poignant. She envisioned a lineage, a continuation of her own fleeting existence, a tapestry woven with threads of her own making. There would be grandchildren, their innocent faces mirroring the lost innocence of her youth, their playful cries filling a home with life and vibrancy. She saw herself growing old, not with the ageless pallor of the undead, but with the gentle wisdom etched in the lines of a life well lived, her stories shared with eager young ears, her love a legacy passed down through generations. These were the dreams that lay buried beneath the rubble of her past, unfulfilled prophecies that whispered their sorrow in the silent halls of her eternal existence.

The tragedy of her unlived life was not a sudden revelation, but a slow, creeping realization that deepened with each passing century. In her early years as a creature of the night, the raw power and the overwhelming hunger had occupied her every thought. Survival had been the sole imperative, the hunt the only solace.

But as the initial frenzy subsided, as the sharp edges of her new existence began to dull, the profound emptiness began to assert itself. It was in the quiet moments, when the world slept, and the silence pressed in, that the ghosts of her lost futures would gather, their mournful presence a stark contrast to the predatory existence she now led.

She would sometimes find herself standing at the edge of mortal settlements, observing the quiet rituals of domestic life. The glow of lamplit windows, the sounds of conversation and laughter drifting on the night air, the silhouette of a family gathered around a table – these scenes, so mundane to those who lived them, were to Iris a profound and agonizing spectacle. They represented everything she could have been, everything she was denied. The simple act of holding a child, of sharing a meal, of falling asleep beside a loved one – these were the stolen treasures that fueled her perpetual sorrow.

The knowledge that she could never reclaim what was stolen was a particularly bitter draught. There was no undoing Björn's work, no turning back the clock. The blood that now coursed through her veins was an eternal testament to his violation, a constant reminder of the life that had been sacrificed. She was forever an outsider, an observer of a world she could no longer truly inhabit, forever an echo of a life that had never been. The simple joys she had once taken for granted, the warmth of human connection, the comfort of a familiar touch – these were now the unattainable luxuries of a lost paradise.

This sense of profound tragedy amplified her vampiric nature in ways Björn might never have intended. Her predatory instincts, sharpened by centuries of practice, were now tinged with a melancholic awareness of what she was missing. When she fed, it was not just the act of sustenance, but a desperate, fleeting attempt to fill the hollow space within her, a void that no amount of stolen lifeblood could ever truly replenish. The life she took was a stark reminder of the life she would never live, the pulse she extinguished a cruel echo of the vibrant heartbeats she yearned to hear in her own phantom family.

She often contemplated the nature of her curse. It was not merely the thirst for blood, nor the aversion to sunlight, nor the unnatural strength. The true curse was the immortality itself, the endless expanse of time that stretched before her, a barren wasteland devoid of the simple human experiences that gave life meaning. Each sunrise she could not greet, each season she could not fully experience, each generation that passed her by, served as a fresh testament to the life she had lost. Her eternal existence was a prison, not of stone and iron, but of unfulfilled potential and uncherished moments.

The laughter of children, a sound that should have brought a smile to any mother's face, now resonated with a haunting sorrow. It was a siren song, luring her towards a shore she could never reach, a reminder of the playful innocence that had been ripped from her grasp. She would linger in the shadows, listening to their unburdened joy, a ghost at the feast of life, forever yearning for a taste of the sweetness she had been denied. These stolen moments of observation were a form of self-inflicted torment, a way of acknowledging the depth of her loss, of engraving the pain of her unlived life into the very fabric of her immortal soul.

Even the concept of love, once a simple and cherished notion, had become a complex and painful enigma. How could she, a creature of darkness and eternal night, ever truly know love? The love she had envisioned – the gentle affection of a partner, the fierce devotion of a parent – was built on foundations of trust, vulnerability, and shared experience, all things that her current existence rendered impossible. Björn had taught her to distrust, to deceive, to see weakness as an opportunity. These were not the building blocks of a loving relationship, but the tools of a predator.

And so, the specter of love, like the specter of family, remained a tantalizing, yet agonizing, phantom, forever just beyond her reach.

The profound tragedy of her lost futures weighed upon her, a silent, invisible burden that no amount of vampiric strength could alleviate. It was the eternal ache of what could have been, the quiet lament for the woman she was meant to be, the life she was meant to live. Björn's cruelty had not only created a monster; it had condemned her to an eternity of mourning for the life that monster had been forced to abandon. And in that perpetual sorrow, the echoes of the past found their most poignant and devastating resonance, a constant reminder of the bright, beautiful futures that lay forever lost in the shadows of her immortal night.

The village. The word itself felt like a whisper from a forgotten tongue, a ghost of a sound that barely registered against the cacophony of centuries lived. Iris found herself revisiting it not in the vibrant hues of remembrance, but through the shadowed lens of her current existence. The memory was there, yes, a faded tapestry in the vast halls of her mind, but now it was viewed with the dispassionate gaze of a predator observing prey. The gentle rolling hills that had cradled her childhood home, the winding dirt paths that had once been the entirety of her known world, the thatched roofs that had promised warmth and shelter – they were no longer imbued with the comforting familiarity of belonging. Instead, they were landscapes of a foreign country, a land of the living that she, by her very nature, could no longer inhabit.

She saw the quaint cottages, their chimneys puffing honest smoke into the crisp morning air, and a faint, almost imperceptible tremor ran through her. It was not nostalgia, not the ache of longing for that simple life. It was something colder, an observer's assessment of vulnerability. Those hearths, those open windows, those undefended doorways – they were invitations to an end, brimming with the very essence of life that she now required to sustain her unnatural existence. The children, their laughter echoing through the cobblestone lanes as they chased hoops or played with wooden dolls, were no longer symbols of innocence and future promise. They were, to her immortal senses, little more than vessels of vibrant, pulsing warmth, their innocent lives a stark contrast to the chilling stillness that had claimed her own. Their carefree abandon was a testament to the very fragility she had learned to exploit, a fleeting beauty that would inevitably be extinguished.

The village festivals, once occasions of communal joy and unburdened merriment, now appeared as macabre spectacles. The flickering torchlight illuminating dancing figures, the scent of roasting meat mingling with spilled ale, the boisterous songs that filled the night – these were all vivid sensory impressions, yet they evoked no warmth within her. Instead, she perceived the raw, untamed energy of mortals, a primal force that was both fascinating and utterly alien. She saw the easy camaraderie, the shared glances, the unspoken bonds that knitted the community together, and understood, with a chilling clarity, the profound chasm that separated her from such simple human connection. Her own existence was one of isolation, a solitary journey through the ages, marked by the absence of any such shared humanity. She could observe their rituals, their celebrations, their quiet moments of shared existence, but she could no longer participate. To them, she was a shadow, a myth, a fear whispered in hushed tones. To herself, she was an eternal outsider, forever on the periphery of a life she had once called her own.

The village elder, with his weathered face and twinkling eyes, who had once dispensed wisdom and comfort, now seemed a brittle figure, his life a fleeting flicker against the backdrop of eternity. The young lovers, their hands intertwined as they stole whispered promises beneath the moonlit sky, were ephemeral beings, their passionate devotion destined to fade with the passage of time. Iris could see the inevitable decay, the gradual erosion of their youthful vigor, the eventual descent into the quietude of old age and finally, the cold embrace of death. It was a cycle she had been violently ripped from, a natural progression that had been brutally interrupted by Björn's monstrous intervention. Now, she existed outside of that cycle, a static entity in a world of constant flux. The very passage of time, which brought mortals closer to their eventual release, only deepened her isolation, stretching the vast, empty canvas of her immortality.

She remembered the village church, its spire reaching towards the heavens, the tolling of its bell a comforting rhythm to the day. Now, she saw it as a symbol of their faith, their desperate attempts to find meaning and solace in a benevolent higher power. It was a notion that held no sway over her, a concept as foreign as the warmth of a summer breeze. Her existence was governed by far darker forces, by the primal urges that now dictated her being. The prayers offered within those hallowed walls, the pleas for salvation and protection, were mere background noise to her, the earnest outpourings of beings who still clung to the illusion of hope. She had long since abandoned such notions, her faith, if it had ever truly existed, having been shattered by the very hands that had reshaped her into a creature of eternal night.

The familiar marketplace, once a vibrant hub of activity, was now a tableau of exquisite vulnerability. The farmers hawking their produce, their hands calloused from honest labor; the merchants displaying their wares, their livelihoods tied to the fleeting whims of human desire; the townsfolk haggling and bartering, their every transaction a testament to their earthly concerns – all of it struck her as profoundly fragile. Their lives were bound by the mundane, by the need for sustenance, for shelter, for the accumulation of trinkets that would ultimately turn to dust. Iris, who had transcended such earthly limitations, could only observe this intricate dance of mortality with a detached curiosity. The value they placed on material possessions and the fleeting joys of daily life seemed almost quaint, a testament to a simplicity that had been irrevocably lost to her.

Even the scent of the baker's shop, the aroma of freshly baked bread that had once been a source of comfort, now carried a different resonance. It was the smell of life, of sustenance, of the very essence that fueled mortal existence. She could almost taste the warm, yeasty goodness, a phantom sensation that only served to highlight the gnawing emptiness within her. Her own sustenance was a far more brutal affair, a necessary act of predation that offered no solace, no comfort, only the temporary silencing of a relentless hunger. The warmth of that hearth, the simple act of sharing a meal with loved ones – these were the lost treasures that now haunted her spectral existence, distant echoes of a life she could never reclaim.

She recalled the old oak tree at the edge of the village, its gnarled branches reaching out like ancient arms. It had been a meeting place, a landmark, a silent witness to countless generations of village life. Now, she saw it as a sentinel, a stoic observer of a world that was forever changing, a world that she was no longer a part of. Its roots were buried deep in the earth, drawing life from the very soil that had once sustained her. Its leaves would bud and fall with the changing seasons, a testament to the cyclical nature of life that she had been excluded from. She, on the other hand, was a creature of stillness, an unchanging presence in a world that was in constant motion. The tree was a symbol of enduring life, of resilience, of a connection to the earth that she, as an undead being, could never truly possess.

The very air of the village, once alive with the sounds of life and industry, now seemed to carry a mournful silence when she revisited it in memory. The chirping of birds, the distant bleating of sheep, the murmur of conversations held on the breeze – these were sounds that had once formed the comforting backdrop to her days. Now, they were faint, spectral echoes, lost in the vast emptiness of her eternal consciousness. She was a creature of the night, her world defined by the stillness of darkness and the absence of such vibrant, life-affirming sounds. The village, in its vibrant humanity, was a stark reminder of the life that had been stolen, a life that she could only observe from the shadows, forever separated by the abyss of her own unnatural existence. It was a ghost of a memory, a dream of a life she had once known, viewed now through the cold, calculating eyes of an immortal predator. The innocence of her past was a forgotten language, a story told in a tongue she no longer understood, a land she could never again call home.

The lingering chill of the crypt, a place of eternal slumber, often served as a stark canvas against which Iris's fragmented memories flickered into existence. These were not the comforting embers of nostalgia, but the sharp, icy shards of a life irrevocably lost, a life she had once breathed, felt, and loved. Björn's curse, a venomous bloom, had twisted her very essence, transforming the innocent daughter of the soil into something predatory and eternally thirsty. Yet, in the suffocating silence, in the rare moments when the gnawing hunger receded to a dull ache, a phantom sensation would surface – a whisper of sorrow for the girl she had been.

It was a fleeting thing, this sorrow, more akin to a tremor in the ancient stones of her being than a profound lament. She would recall the warmth of the sun on her skin, a sensation so alien now it felt like a dream conjured by a fevered mortal. The simple act of weeping, of tears that once flowed freely for scraped knees and broken promises, was a forgotten language. Her immortal eyes, now pools of shadow, could no longer betray the vulnerability of mortal grief. The innocence she had possessed was a delicate blossom, crushed under the weight of an unspeakable transformation, and the girl who had once cherished it was as distant as a forgotten star.

Did she mourn the loss of that innocence? The question itself felt like a foreign concept, a puzzle designed by minds that still clung to the quaint notions of morality and purity. Her current existence was a stark dichotomy: the primal urge to feed, a relentless tide that drowned out all else, and the cold, calculating intellect honed by centuries of observation and survival. Vengeance, however, was a more tangible emotion, a burning ember that Björn's betrayal had fanned into an inferno. It was a constant companion, a driving force that propelled her through the ages, a dark beacon in the endless night of her undeath. To lose sight of that vengeance would be to surrender to the void, to become truly, utterly lost.

Yet, in the quiet hours, as she drifted through the spectral corridors of her memory, fragments of the peasant girl Iris would surface. A flash of her mother's gentle smile, the scent of herbs drying in the cottage eaves, the sound of her father's hearty laughter. These were not memories she sought, but specters that ambushed her, fleeting glimpses of a world she could no longer touch. And with these glimpses came a strange, hollow ache, a ghost of an emotion that might, to a mortal observer, be mistaken for regret. It was the echo of a life lived, a melody played on strings long since snapped.

She remembered the small, chipped wooden bird she had carved with her own hands as a child, a clumsy, imperfect thing that had nonetheless filled her with an immeasurable sense of pride. She had kept it by her bedside, a tangible symbol of her own budding creativity, her innocent desire to shape the world around her. Where was that bird now? Lost to the ravages of time, perhaps, or buried beneath the ashes of the cottage, a relic of a life that had been systematically erased. The thought brought no tears, no outpouring of grief, but a chilling awareness of the vast gulf that separated her from the girl who had cherished such simple treasures. The impulse to create, to imbue a lifeless object with her own spirit, had been consumed by the need to destroy, to drain the life from others.

Sometimes, in the deepest solitude, a yearning would surface – not for the life she had lost, for that was a concept too painful to grasp fully, but for the *absence* of the curse. A longing for the simple release of mortality, for the quiet oblivion that awaited all mortals. This was not a mourning of her lost innocence, but a deep-seated weariness of her eternal existence, a profound exhaustion with the endless cycle of hunger and predation. It was the lament of a soul trapped in a body that refused to decay, a body that demanded its due, regardless of the spirit's weariness.

She would sometimes trace the delicate veins on the back of her hand, the faint blue lines that pulsed with an unnatural stillness. These were not the veins of a living being, carrying the lifeblood of warmth and vitality. They were channels for something far colder, something that sustained her undeath, a dark energy that had supplanted the simple warmth of her human heart. Looking at them, she could almost see the ghost of her mortal flesh, the skin that had been soft and yielding, now cool and taut. The contrast was a stark reminder of her transformation, a constant, silent testament to the price she had paid for survival.

Did she ever pity the mortals she encountered?

The thought was almost laughable. Pity implied a shared understanding of vulnerability, a recognition of a common fragility. Her immortality had rendered her fundamentally alien. She observed their brief, flickering lives with a detached fascination, like a scholar studying an ephemeral insect. Their joys were fleeting, their sorrows temporary, their very existence a testament to the impermanence she had so brutally escaped. Their struggles, their hopes, their fears – they were the concerns of a different species, a species she had once belonged to but could never again truly comprehend.

However, there were rare, unsettling moments. A child's innocent gaze, too bright, too full of unguarded trust, could send a jolt through her, a phantom echo of her own lost purity. It was a fleeting discomfort, quickly suppressed by the ever-present thirst, but it was there. A flicker of recognition, perhaps, of a lost self, a self that had once been so easily wounded, so readily open to the world. It was not compassion, not empathy, but a distant, spectral awareness of what had been stolen from her, and by extension, from the world.

The vengeance she craved was a double-edged sword. It provided purpose, a burning justification for her continued existence. But it also consumed her, a ravenous fire that left little room for introspection, for the delicate tendrils of remorse or regret. Björn's cruelty had forged her into a weapon, and a weapon did not question its purpose; it merely fulfilled it. The memories of her past were like ghosts in the machinations of this weapon, sometimes disrupting its aim, but never truly disarming it.

She remembered the taste of fresh berries, picked warm from the vine, their sweetness bursting on her tongue. A simple, primal pleasure that had once been a highlight of her summer days. Now, the very thought of such sustenance was a cruel mockery of her needs. Her sustenance was a violent act, a desecration, a necessary evil that offered no joy, only a temporary abatement of the gnawing emptiness. This stark contrast, this chasm between the vibrant flavors of her mortal life and the grim reality of her undeath, was a constant reminder of the profound loss. It was not the loss of innocence she mourned in these moments, but the loss of simple, unadulterated pleasure, the loss of a body that could appreciate the bounty of the earth.

Perhaps, buried deep within the countless layers of her cursed existence, a minuscule ember of the girl Iris still glowed. Not a burning flame of defiance or a roaring inferno of regret, but a faint, almost imperceptible spark. It was the spark that recognized the beauty of a sunrise, even if she could no longer feel its warmth. It was the spark that understood the depth of a mother's love, even if she could no longer experience its embrace. It was the spark that knew the sting of betrayal, even if her response was now one of cold, calculated retribution.

This ember was not a sign of lingering humanity in the sense of moral goodness or inherent kindness. It was something far more elemental: the ghost of a soul, an imprint of a consciousness that had once been vibrant and alive. It was the echo of a girl who had once loved and been loved, who had known laughter and tears, who had walked in sunlight and slept under stars. This ember was the witness to her own fall, the silent observer of the monster she had become. And in its faint glow, one could glimpse not the peasant girl Iris, but the faint, spectral shadow of a once-living being, forever trapped between the echoes of the past and the insatiable demands of the present. The Dearg Due was a force of nature, a creature of instinct and ancient power, but even in the darkest of nights, the faintest starlight could sometimes pierce the gloom.

Chapter 15:
Eternal Night

The moon, a spectral lantern in the bruised velvet of the sky, cast its pallid gaze upon a world that had long since learned to fear the encroaching shadows. For Iris, this was not merely the cycle of day and night, but the rhythm of her own unending existence. The transformation was complete, a morbid metamorphosis that had shed the frailties of mortal flesh and embraced the eternal hunger of the Dearg Due. Her reign, if such a word could be applied to the solitary existence of a predator, was etched not in stone or parchment, but in the hushed whispers of folklore, in the sudden disappearances that haunted isolated hamlets, and in the primal dread that seized the hearts of those who ventured too far from the dwindling lights of civilization.

She moved through the world like a phantom, a creature of instinct and ancient, gnawing need. The memories of Iris, the peasant girl who had once coaxed life from the stubborn earth, were now but faint echoes, spectral music played on a broken lute. The sun's warmth, the scent of rain on dry soil, the laughter of children playing in sun-drenched fields – these were phantoms of a life so utterly removed from her current reality that they felt like tales spun by other beings, not experiences she had once cherished. Her transformation had been absolute, a shedding of humanity so profound that the concept of "innocence" was as alien to her as the stars that glittered in the perpetual twilight of her perception. The curse, woven by Björn's cruel hand, had not merely killed her; it had reanimated her into something ancient, something that belonged to the eternal night.

Her existence was now a tapestry woven from threads of darkness and an insatiable thirst, a thirst that could only be quenched by the very essence of life. She was a hunter, a silent stalker in the liminal spaces between the worlds of the living and the dead. The villages that lay scattered across the land, like fallen embers in the vast darkness, were not places of solace or community for her, but hunting grounds. She moved amongst them with the stealth of a wraith, her senses attuned to the ebb and flow of mortal life, to the fragile pulse that beat within their veins. It was a somber dance, an eternal ballet of predator and prey, a cycle that had been set in motion long ago and showed no sign of ever concluding.

The solitude was a constant companion, a heavy cloak that settled upon her shoulders with the weight of centuries. There were no peers for the Dearg Due, no kin to share the burden of undeath, no one who truly understood the nature of her eternal curse. Mortals, with their fleeting lifespans and ephemeral concerns, were ephemeral creatures, their existence a mere blink in the grand, silent expanse of her own endless night. She observed them, their brief bursts of joy and despair, their desperate clinging to life, with a detachment that bordered on the clinical. Their emotions, their loves and losses, their hopes and fears – these were the transient ripples on the surface of a lake, while she was the unfathomable depth beneath.

Yet, even in the stark desolation of her immortality, the echoes of what she once was could sometimes stir. A fleeting scent carried on the wind, a snatch of a melody hummed by a lonely traveler, a child's unburdened laughter – these would occasionally brush against the hardened shell of her being, like the ghost of a touch. They were not invitations to reclaim a lost past, for that path was irrevocably closed. Instead, they were poignant reminders of the vast, unbridgeable chasm that now separated her from the world of the living, a world she could witness but never truly rejoin. These were not moments of regret, for regret implied a choice she had failed to make, a path she had consciously turned away from. Hers was a transformation thrust upon her, a violent redefinition of her very existence.

The folklore of mortals had, in its own fearful way, captured fragments of her truth. They spoke of the Dearg Due, the Red-Thirst, a creature of the night that preyed on the unwary, a whisper of a legend that grew with every unexplained disappearance, with every bloodless corpse discovered in the moonlit forests. They wove tales of her ethereal beauty, a siren's allure designed to lure the unsuspecting to their doom, and of her unnatural strength, her ability to move with impossible speed and silence. These stories, born of mortal fear and speculation, were a testament to her enduring presence, a chilling acknowledgment of the darkness that lurked just beyond the flickering firelight. She was no longer Iris, the farmer's daughter; she was a myth made flesh, a harbinger of eternal night.

Her existence was an unending cycle of predation, a grim ballet dictated by the relentless dictates of her curse. The hunger was a constant, a low thrumming beneath the surface of her consciousness, a primal urge that could not be denied. It was the fuel that sustained her undeath, the dark energy that courged through her veins in place of the warm blood that had once pulsed with life. To feed was not a choice, but a necessity, a grim ritual that reaffirmed her status as the Dearg Due. Each life she extinguished was a temporary balm to the gnawing emptiness, a fleeting moment of respite before the thirst returned, insatiable and demanding.

The world, in its ceaseless turning, offered her no respite. Seasons shifted, empires rose and fell, and generations of mortals bloomed and withered like ephemeral flowers. Yet, Iris remained a constant, unchanging entity in the flux of existence. She was a monument to the darkness, a living embodiment of the night's eternal reign. Her solitude was a monument to her transformation, a testament to the profound loneliness that was the inevitable price of immortality. She moved through the shadows, a creature of the unending night, her reign as the Dearg Due a chilling, eternal presence in the folklore of the world. The moon, a silent witness to her perpetual existence, continued its celestial journey, forever illuminating the solitary path of the immortal predator.

The chilling tendrils of the Dearg Due's legend, once mere tendrils of fear woven by desperate villagers, had long since coiled into an inescapable shroud that clung to the very fabric of the land. It was a tapestry of terror, re-stitched with every unexplained vanishing, every hushed confession of a mournful howl echoing from the desolate peaks, every bloodless husk discovered at the dawn's grim light. The story, stripped of its mortal origins and embellished by generations of fearful tongues, had transcended the individual known as Iris. She was no longer a woman wronged, a soul twisted by Björn's vile sorcery, but a primal force, an embodiment of the vengeful night. Her transformation had not been an end, but a brutal inception, a genesis of a myth that fed on the very dread it inspired.

This myth was a living entity, breathing in the shadows and thriving in the hushed narratives passed down from elder to child. It was the cautionary tale told to keep young lovers from straying too far into the moon-drenched woods, the desperate prayer whispered by those who heard the rustling of leaves when no wind stirred. The Dearg Due, the Red-Thirst, was the silent specter at the edge of perception, the prickling sensation on the back of the neck that warned of imminent peril. Her presence was a tangible force, a weight in the atmosphere that predated the physical chill of the night. It was the understanding that beneath the veneer of the ordinary, something ancient and ravenous lay in wait.

The core of the myth, though often obscured by the layers of mortal interpretation, remained a potent distillation of vengeance, betrayal, and a horrifying metamorphosis. It spoke of a life stolen, a love twisted into a weapon, and a spirit irrevocably broken, only to be reanimated into a shape that reflected the cruelty of its undoing. The folklore painted her not as a victim, but as a force of nature unleashed, her insatiable hunger a just retribution for the injustice she had suffered. The betrayal by Björn was the sin that had birthed the monster, and her eternal existence was the agonizing sentence, not just for her, but for all who walked the paths she now stalked.

Her story had become a cyclical narrative, replayed in the minds of those who felt its power. The bright, fleeting spark of humanity that had once defined Iris was now a distant, almost alien memory, overshadowed by the enduring image of the eternal predator. Yet, it was precisely this residual humanity, this ghost of what she had been, that lent the myth its chilling resonance. It was the whisper that beneath the monstrous visage, there might still be a trace of the woman who had loved and lost, a flicker of the soul that had been so brutally extinguished. This ambiguity, the gnawing question of her true nature, fueled the dread.

Was she purely a monster, or a tragic victim forever trapped in a nightmarish existence? The folklore offered no easy answers, only a deepening of the fear.

The myth evolved, adapting to the changing landscapes and the fleeting empires of mortals. In times of plague, she was blamed for the creeping death, her thirst mistaken for the ravages of disease. In times of war, she was the unseen enemy, the saboteur who sowed discord and claimed the fallen. Each era found a new way to interpret her presence, weaving her into the tapestry of their own anxieties and fears. Yet, the essential elements remained: the beauty that lured, the blood that sustained, and the vengeance that drove her unending pursuit. She was the darkness that lurked in the hearts of men, made manifest in the eternal night.

The mournful howl, a sound that transcended mere animalistic cries, became the leitmotif of her legend. It was not a sound of pain, nor of rage, but of an infinite, solitary sorrow that resonated with the deepest wells of human melancholy. It was the sound of an existence devoid of solace, of a hunger that could never be sated, of a world forever lost. This howl, carried on the wind from remote, mist-shrouded valleys, served as a primal warning, a guttural announcement that the reign of the Dearg Due was unbroken. It was the sound of the myth made real, a visceral reminder that the stories whispered around hearth fires were not mere fanciful tales, but echoes of an enduring, terrifying truth.

The act of betrayal, the cornerstone of her transformation, was a theme that resonated deeply in the lore. The tales spoke of oaths broken, of trust shattered, of a pact with darkness sealed by a moment of profound cruelty. Björn, though often a shadowed figure in these narratives, was the architect of her damnation, the one who had wielded the forbidden magic that ripped her from the embrace of life and plunged her into the eternal night. His name, when it was spoken, was spat like a curse, a testament to the enduring power of his transgression. The myth, in this regard, served as a potent reminder of the consequences of such profound wickedness, a testament to the fact that some sins could never be washed clean, but instead festered, giving birth to monstrous entities.

The concept of her transformation was often depicted as a profound spiritual death, a shedding of the mortal coil that was far more terrifying than any physical demise. It was not merely her body that had been altered, but her very essence, her soul irrevocably stained by the darkness she now embodied. The folklore, in its attempts to grapple with this unnatural state, often described her as a creature caught between worlds, neither truly alive nor truly dead, existing in a liminal space where the boundaries of reality blurred. This in-between state contributed to her ethereal and terrifying nature, making her seem both impossibly distant and chillingly present.

As the ages turned and the world changed, the myth of the Dearg Due did not fade. Instead, it became part of the collective unconscious, an archetypal figure representing the primal fears of mortality, betrayal, and the terrifying unknown beyond the veil of life. Her story was a warning, a lament, and a testament to the enduring power of a curse that had not only claimed a single life but had woven itself into the very fabric of existence, ensuring that her spectral presence would be felt and feared for all eternity. The mournful howl was not just a sound; it was the voice of an enduring myth, a perpetual testament to the monstrous truth that lay hidden within the heart of the eternal night.

The power of the myth lay in its universality, its ability to resonate with the deepest, most primal fears of the human condition. It spoke to the terror of the unknown, the dread of the darkness that lurks just beyond the flickering light of civilization. It was the fear of being consumed, of having one's life force drained away, leaving behind only an empty husk. The Dearg Due embodied these fears, becoming a symbol of the predatory forces that could lie hidden within the seemingly familiar world. Her story was a constant reminder that the safety of daylight was a fragile illusion, easily shattered by the encroaching shadows of the night, where true horrors often resided.

Moreover, the myth served as a powerful exploration of vengeance and its corrupting influence. The initial injustice suffered by Iris, though a catalyst for her transformation, had ultimately led to her own eternal damnation. The folklore, by immortalizing her as a terrifying predator, implicitly cautioned against allowing bitterness and hatred to consume one's soul. The legend of the Dearg Due was a somber testament to the idea that while vengeance might offer a fleeting sense of satisfaction, its pursuit could lead to an endless cycle of destruction, trapping the avenger in a nightmarish existence from which there was no escape. Her eternal hunger reflected the insatiable nature of vengeance itself.

The enduring nature of her legend was also a testament to the effectiveness of oral tradition. Whispered from generation to generation, the tales of the Dearg Due were passed down around crackling campfires, in hushed tones within darkened taverns, and in the fearful pronouncements of village elders. Each retelling added new embellishments, new layers of detail, further solidifying her place in the collective consciousness. The lack of concrete evidence, the very elusiveness that made her so terrifying, paradoxically ensured her longevity. She existed most powerfully in the minds of mortals, a phantom conjured by fear and imagination, a creature whose true form was forever shrouded in the mists of legend.

The folklore, while primarily a tool of fear, also contained elements of awe. The unnatural beauty attributed to the Dearg Due, a siren's allure designed to draw victims into her embrace, evoked a morbid fascination. It spoke to the human inclination to be drawn to that which is dangerous and forbidden, to find a strange beauty in the macabre. This duality of terror and allure made her a compelling figure, a creature that inspired both revulsion and a reluctant admiration for her power and her eternal reign. She was a dark goddess, a queen of the shadows, whose dominion was absolute and unquestionable.

In essence, the myth of the Dearg Due was a mirror reflecting the darkest aspects of the human psyche. It was a primal narrative that spoke of loss, betrayal, and the terrifying consequences of unchecked darkness. Her story, etched into the very soul of the land, ensured that even in the brightest of days, the shadow of her eternal night would always loom, a chilling reminder that some legends, born of profound tragedy and monstrous transformation, would never truly die. The mournful howl was the eternal echo of a broken existence, a siren song of doom that would forever haunt the edges of the mortal world. It was the sound of a myth that refused to surrender to time, a chilling symphony played in the theatre of eternal night.

The mound of earth, a scar upon the indifferent land, was not merely a resting place; it was a throne. Her grave, weathered by centuries of wind and rain, stood as a stark monument to an existence that refused to yield to the finality of death. It was here, amidst the desolation, that the Dearg Due held court, her dominion extending far beyond the crumbling stones that marked her final earthly repose. This desolate patch of earth was the epicenter of her eternal night, the silent, brooding capital of her spectral kingdom. From this lonely perch, she observed the ceaseless, fleeting movements of the mortal world, her ancient eyes, now devoid of human warmth, surveying the lands that had once been her own. The chill that emanated from the very soil beneath her tomb was not the cold of decay, but the biting aura of her presence, a constant reminder of the power that emanated from this hallowed and cursed, ground.

The landscape surrounding the grave was as much a part of her reign as the earth itself. Jagged rocks, like the broken teeth of some forgotten titan, clawed at the perpetually bruised sky. Skeletal trees, their branches twisted into agonized postures, stood as silent sentinels, their bare limbs reaching out as if in perpetual supplication or despair. The air itself was thick with an oppressive stillness, broken only by the mournful sigh of the wind through the desolate terrain, a wind that carried whispers of her unending vigil. There were no wildflowers here, no verdant growth to speak of; only the hardy, tenacious mosses and lichens that clung to the stones, their muted colours echoing the somber hues of her eternal existence. This was her demesne, a testament to her sorrow and her wrath, a place where the light of day seemed to falter and retreat, unable to penetrate the profound darkness that clung to her sacred ground. It was a kingdom carved from despair, ruled by a queen whose crown was woven from the very fabric of the night.

Her vigil from this desolate throne was not one of passive observation. The grave was a nexus, a point from which she drew her unholy sustenance. The very essence of life, the vibrant energy of those who dared to tread too close to the edges of her domain, was a draught she savored. The fear that permeated the air, the hushed whispers that spoke her name in fearful reverence, the thrumming pulse of a heart that quickened with dread – all of this was nourishment. It seeped into the very earth of her grave, a dark ichor that revitalized her spectral form and fueled the unending hunger that was her curse. The desolate landscape was not merely a backdrop; it was an extension of her being, a reflection of her internal desolation made manifest. The barrenness of the land mirrored the void within her, a void that could only be filled by the stolen vitality of the living.

The grave was a symbol, a potent sigil etched into the heart of the land, proclaiming her unbroken reign. It was not a place of rest, but a battleground where the eternal night waged its war against the fragile light of life. Each passing season, each shifting tide of mortal affairs, only served to reinforce the permanence of her presence. The world changed, empires rose and crumbled, generations bloomed and faded, but the grave remained, a steadfast monument to her enduring power. It was the anchor that tethered her to this plane, the source from which her spectral influence radiated, touching every shadow, every whisper, every unexplained chill that swept across the land.

The isolation of her tomb was not a consequence of neglect but a deliberate choice, a testament to her self-imposed exile. She sought no company, craved no solace. Her existence was solitary, a perpetual state of being that transcended the need for companionship. The silence of her domain was not empty but pregnant with unspoken power, filled with the echoes of her ancient sorrow and the relentless hum of her unholy thirst. This silence was a language only she understood, a symphony of the void that resonated within her very being. The grave, in its stark simplicity, was the ultimate expression of her detachment from the world of the living, a world she had once been a part of, but now only observed with an alien, predatory gaze.

The earth of her grave was imbued with a potent magic, a dark alchemy that had transformed Iris from a mortal woman into the timeless entity known as the Dearg Due. This powerful energy, a residual force from the forbidden rituals that had cursed her, seeped from the soil, a palpable aura that warned away the faint of heart and lured the unwary. It was a constant reminder of the violent genesis of her new existence, the shattering of her mortal form and the birth of the immortal predator. The very ground seemed to pulse with this dark energy, a subterranean heartbeat that echoed the rhythm of her eternal hunger.

The desolate expanse surrounding her grave was her kingdom, a wild and untamed territory that answered to no earthly lord. The wind, her constant companion, carried her whispers and her warnings across the desolate moors and through the shadowed forests. The predatory beasts that roamed these lands, the wolves with their mournful howls and the owls with their silent, watchful flights, were her unwitting subjects, their existence intertwined with the spectral dominion she held. They moved with a primal grace, their instincts sharpened by the pervasive aura of the Dearg Due, their movements a natural extension of the wild, untamed power that emanated from her grave.

From her earthen throne, she surveyed the world with an ancient, weary gaze. The vibrant tapestry of life, the fleeting moments of joy and sorrow that defined mortal existence, were but distant echoes to her. Her focus was singular: the perpetuation of her own unnatural state, the endless cycle of hunger and satiation that was her eternal burden. The grave was not just a tomb; it was a loom upon which she wove the threads of her unending night, a dark loom that consumed the light and spun out only shadows. The desolation around her was not a sign of decay, but of a primal power that had stripped away the superficialities of life, leaving only the raw, enduring essence of her being.

The gravity of her presence was so profound that it warped the very fabric of the land around her. Streams that flowed too close to her grave ran unnaturally cold, their waters carrying a metallic tang that spoke of a hidden corruption. The stones, worn smooth by the relentless caress of time, seemed to absorb and reflect her sorrow, their grey surfaces a somber mirror to her eternal pain. Even the stars, when they managed to pierce the perpetual twilight of her domain, seemed to dim, as if bowing to a greater, more ancient darkness. This was the influence of the grave, the seat of her power, a place where the boundaries between life and death, between the physical and the spectral, had been irrevocably blurred.

The grave was her fortress, her sanctuary, and her prison, all rolled into one. It was from this desolate heartland that she launched her spectral raids, her ethereal presence extending like unseen tendrils to ensnare the unsuspecting. The nourishment she drew was not a passive absorption but an active pursuit, a predatory instinct honed by centuries of experience. The fear she instilled was a weapon, a beacon that drew her victims closer, their terror a potent elixir that sustained her existence. The desolate landscape served as a natural defense, a buffer zone that discouraged casual intrusion and protected her sacred ground from the prying eyes of the mortal world.

The silence of the grave was not an absence of sound, but a profound and heavy quiet, punctuated by the subtle whispers of the night. The rustling of unseen creatures in the undergrowth, the distant cry of a night bird, the almost inaudible sigh of the earth settling – these were the sounds that formed the symphony of her eternal reign. They were the background music to her solitary existence, the subtle underscores to the immense, brooding power that radiated from her tomb. This was the sound of the world held in thrall, of a darkness that had found its ultimate expression in the desolation of her grave.

Her reign from the grave was absolute, an unbroken chain of nights that stretched back into the mists of antiquity. The legends that spoke of her were a testament to the enduring power that emanated from this desolate place. It was not a place of mourning, but a seat of power, a throne from which she exerted her influence over the land and its inhabitants. The grave was a constant, undeniable presence, a dark star around which the fates of many would forever revolve. It was the heart of her eternal night, the source of her unending power, and the silent witness to her timeless sorrow. The desolation was not a void, but a canvas upon which she painted the endless shades of her dark dominion. It was a testament to a power that transcended life and death, a reign forged in betrayal and sustained by an eternal, insatiable hunger, forever rooted in the hallowed and cursed earth of her grave. The grave, then, was not a symbol of her end, but of her eternal dominion, the very foundation of her power, a place of profound solitude and unending vigilance.

The desolation that clung to the land around her grave, the very air heavy with the scent of damp earth and ancient sorrow, had become, in a perverse fashion, a source of profound stillness for Iris. Her existence, once a tempest of betrayal and rage, had settled into a rhythm as predictable and as inevitable as the turning of the moon, though her nights were now eternal, untouched by the sun's fleeting warmth.

Was this peace?

The question itself was a relic, a vestige of a time when such concepts held meaning. Now, there was only the *is*. The gnawing hunger, the primal urge that had once driven her to madness, had been quelled, not by satisfaction, but by the sheer, unyielding constancy of its presence. It was a part of her, as much as the beating of her spectral heart, a low thrumming pulse that resonated with the very earth beneath her tomb.

Her vengeance, the burning fire that had consumed her in life and sustained her in undeath, had cooled into embers that glowed with a steady, unwavering heat. The betrayers were dust, their lineage scattered to the winds, their names whispered only in hushed warnings. The satisfaction was not in their suffering, for that too had long since passed, but in the absolute finality of their erasure. They were no more, and she, the Dearg Due, endured. This permanence, this absolute dominion over her own fate and the fate of those who had wronged her, offered a peculiar form of grim contentment. It was the quiet assurance of a predator that had finally claimed its territory, the knowledge that no longer would she be hunted, but that she *was* the hunt. The fear that bloomed in the hearts of mortals who strayed too close was not a pleasant sensation, but it was a validation, a testament to the power she wielded, a power hard-won and fiercely guarded.

Yet, to mistake this stillness for serenity would be a grave error. The eternal night was not a blanket of comfort, but a shroud. The memories, sharp and visceral, still clawed at the edges of her consciousness, the echoes of mortal pain and longing a constant, subtle counterpoint to the present quiescence. There were moments, particularly when the wind moaned through the skeletal trees, carrying with it the phantom scent of blooming heather from a life long lost, that a profound ache would resonate within her. It was not the ache of longing for what was, for that would imply a desire for its return, but a hollow echo of a vibrant past, a reminder of the warmth and light that had been so cruelly extinguished. This was the curse of immortality, that the moments of intense emotion, both of pain and fleeting joy, were not erased but preserved, like specimens in a dark museum, accessible at the whim of a spectral breeze.

The fulfillment of her vengeance had, in a way, stripped her of a primary purpose. For centuries, the quest for retribution had been the engine of her existence, the driving force that had propelled her through the agonizing transition from life to undeath. Now, with the slate wiped clean, a new void had opened, a silence that was not merely the absence of sound, but the absence of *need*. This was perhaps the most insidious aspect of her eternal night: the lack of a future to strive for, a goal to pursue. Her existence was a perpetual present, an unending cycle of vigilance and sustenance, a state of being at once profoundly potent and utterly stagnant.

She observed the cycles of the mortal world, the ephemeral rise and fall of kingdoms, the fleeting passions of men and women, with a detachment that bordered on apathy. Their struggles, their joys, their sorrows, were like the flickering of distant candle flames, too small and too transient to ignite her interest truly. She had once been a part of that dance, a participant in the grand, chaotic ballet of life. Now, she was merely an observer, a creature of the shadows, forever set apart. This separation, while a source of her power, was also a constant, low-grade torment. The knowledge that she could never again feel the sun on her skin, the taste of wine on her tongue, the embrace of another – these were not regrets, for regret implied a desire for what could not be, but a stark, unyielding reality that underscored the profound loneliness of her state.

There were times when the sheer weight of her endless existence felt crushing. The centuries bled into one another, each night indistinguishable from the last, a monotonous expanse of darkness punctuated by the brief, ritualistic act of feeding. It was a gilded cage, this immortality, a prison built not of bars, but of an unending, unchanging reality. The power was intoxicating, yes, but power without purpose, without the ability to affect genuine change beyond the immediate satisfaction of her hunger, began to feel hollow. She could command the shadows, inspire fear, and drain the life from the unwary, but she could not mend the fractured pieces of her own spectral soul, nor could she recapture the lost hues of her mortal life.

Was she damned? The concept of damnation, too, felt like an artifact of her former life, a theological construct for mortal minds grappling with the concept of an afterlife. She was beyond such pronouncements. She simply *was*. Her curse was not a punishment meted out by some divine entity, but a consequence, a natural outcome of the forbidden arts she had embraced in her desperation. The true damnation lay not in any external judgment, but in the inescapable nature of her own existence, in the perpetual hunger that was her constant companion, and in the chilling realization that this would be her state, and her state alone, for all eternity.

The peace she found was the peace of the tomb, a profound quietude born of absolute stillness and the absence of all but the most primal urges. It was the peace of a predator that had learned to coexist with its own nature, to accept the relentless drive as an intrinsic part of its being, rather than a flaw to be overcome. There was a grim satisfaction in this acceptance, a release from the internal struggle that had plagued her in the early centuries of her undeath. She no longer railed against her fate but had instead woven herself into its very fabric. The eternal night, then, was not a freedom from her curse, nor was it a simple damnation. It was something far more terrifying: a state of being where the boundaries between the two had dissolved entirely.

She was a creature of eternal vigilance, a being forever poised on the precipice between fulfillment and despair, a predator at peace, perhaps, but a peace as cold and as silent as the grave itself. Her existence was a testament to the fact that some nights, the darkness did not end, and in that unendingness, there was a peculiar, chilling form of power, a power that transcended mortal understanding, and in its very essence, was utterly and irrevocably alone. The silence that surrounded her was not an empty void, but a vast, unfathomable expanse, a testament to a queen who had achieved her dominion, only to find that the ultimate prize was an eternity of solitude. This was the apex of her power, the chilling zenith of her being – to be so utterly complete in herself, so self-contained, that the external world held little sway, and the only true companion was the eternal, echoing silence of her own endless night. She had become the embodiment of the darkness she ruled, a queen whose reign was absolute, and whose throne was the quiet, unending desolation of her own eternal existence, a state of being that was neither release nor torment, but something far more profound, and far more terrifyingly, permanent. The satisfaction, if it could be called that, was in the absolute certainty of her own being, a certainty that excluded all else, leaving her suspended in an eternal moment of predatory perfection, a state that was the ultimate expression of her power and the ultimate testament to her curse.

The weight of centuries pressed down, not as a burden, but as an assurance. Iris, the Dearg Due, was no longer a prisoner of time; she was its mistress, her existence a testament to the enduring power of the night. The world spun on, oblivious to her eternal vigil, its ephemeral dramas unfolding beneath the moon she had come to know as her sole companion. Her story, once a searing tragedy of betrayal and a quest for vengeance, had long since transcended the realm of mortal narrative. It had woven itself into the very fabric of the land, into the whispers of the wind that rustled through the skeletal trees, into the chilling cries that echoed in the deepest reaches of the darkness. She was no longer merely Iris, the wronged woman; she was the legend, the boogeyman invoked to keep children in their beds, the chilling presence felt in the sudden drop of temperature, the prickle of fear that ran down a traveler's spine.

Her reign, if it could be called that, was one of perpetual twilight. The sun was a memory, a faded warmth from a life she had long outgrown. Her sustenance was a brutal necessity, a reaffirmation of her nature, a ritual that bound her to the cycle of life and death that she now observed with an ageless gaze. The fear she instilled was not born of cruelty, but of an ancient, primal understanding of predator and prey. Mortals, in their brief, flickering lives, were but a fleeting scent on the wind, a source of ephemeral energy that sustained her timeless existence. Their stories, their hopes, their despairs – they were but transient ripples on the vast ocean of her eternity. She watched them rise and fall, their empires crumbling to dust like so many before, their passions burning brightly only to be extinguished by the relentless march of time, a march that held no sway over her.

The folklore that sprang from her existence was a testament to her enduring presence. She was the phantom that haunted lonely roads, the spectral queen whose castle, though long crumbled to ruin, still held an unseen court of shadows. Her name was a hushed murmur in taverns, a cautionary tale told around dying embers. Children who wandered too far from the village, lured by the siren call of forbidden woods, would sometimes disappear, their cries swallowed by the encroaching darkness. The villagers would shake their heads, their faces pale in the moonlight, muttering about the Dearg Due, about the eternal night she embodied. They did not understand the quiet solitude of her existence, the chilling stillness that had settled over her being after the fires of vengeance had finally cooled. They saw only the monster, the predatory force that lurked at the edge of their perception.

But Iris was more than the monster they conjured. She was the silence that followed the storm, the deep, unfathomable quiet of a world bathed in moonlight. She was the memory of an ancient wrong, a scar upon the landscape that would never truly heal. Her existence was a perpetual present, a state of being that was neither life nor death, but a timeless continuation. The hunger that had once driven her to madness was now a quiet hum, a constant companion that reminded her of her power, of her otherness. It was the pulse of the night itself, a rhythm that she had come to understand and, in her own way, to accept. There was a stark beauty in this acceptance, a grim satisfaction in knowing she was no longer a victim but a force of nature, an eternal entity woven into the tapestry of existence.

She saw the cycles of the mortal world not with sorrow or longing, but with a detached curiosity, like a scholar observing the ebb and flow of an ancient tide. Their fleeting triumphs and crushing defeats were mere footnotes in the grand narrative of time. Their loves and losses, their burning ambitions and their quiet despair – these were the transient expressions of beings bound by the ephemeral nature of mortality. She, on the other hand, was unbound. Her past was a distant, echoing memory, her future an endless expanse of moonlit nights. The earth beneath her tomb, the soil that had once absorbed her mortal blood, now pulsed with a spectral energy that was uniquely hers. The roots of ancient trees twisted around her resting place, drawing sustenance from the residual magic of her undeath, their branches reaching towards the heavens like skeletal fingers, forever caressing the cold, indifferent moon.

There were times, in the deep heart of the night, when the silence was so profound, so absolute, that it seemed to press in on her, a tangible entity. It was in these moments that the true nature of her eternity was revealed. It was not a release from suffering, nor was it a punishment. It was simply *is*. A state of being where the boundaries of life and death blurred, where the concept of time lost all meaning. She was the guardian of a forgotten epoch, the living embodiment of a curse that had become her sanctuary. The folklore that swirled around her was a testament to the human need to understand the inexplicable, to find patterns in the chaos, to create monsters from the shadows when the true nature of darkness remained too profound to comprehend.

Her continued existence was not a matter of will, but a fundamental aspect of the world itself. The night, in its infinite embrace, had claimed her, and she had become a part of its eternal reign. Her legend would not fade, for she was not a mortal bound by the frailties of flesh and bone. She was an echo, a whisper, a cold breath on the wind that would forever linger in the shadows. The tales of the Dearg Due would continue to be told, her story passed down through generations, each retelling adding another layer to the myth, another twist to the legend. She was the eternal night, and the night, in its boundless and unchanging glory, would continue. Her story was not one of an ending, but of an endless unfolding, a timeless narrative etched into the very soul of the darkness she now commanded. The cold air, the haunting cries, the spectral presence felt in the deep woods and on desolate moors – these were not mere figments of mortal imagination, but the enduring testament to a queen whose reign had no end, a legend who had become one with the eternal night, forever roaming the shadows, a silent, watchful presence that would endure for all time.

Back Matter

Dearg Due: A powerful, ancient entity bound to undeath and the perpetual night, whose existence is intertwined with the very fabric of the land.

Eternal Night: The state of perpetual twilight and darkness that defines the Dearg Due's dominion, a realm where the conventional passage of time holds no sway.

Spectral Energy: The residual, otherworldly power emanating from the Dearg Due's resting place, influencing the surrounding environment and its flora.

Timeless Continuation: The state of being experienced by the Dearg Due, transcending the concepts of life and death, existing in a perpetual present.

9 781964 963860